W9-BVR-862

"A HUMDINGER OF A FIRST NOVEL."
—*The Orlando Sentinel*

"Here is the most classic of stories, the legend that taps into tales of the folk. Willie, the narrator, reveals these legends as a common man. Too cynical to be a Candide, too irascible to be Tom Sawyer, and too dumb to be Huck Finn, he is the common boy sent on a mythic journey to gain his manhood—except in this sharp twist of a tale, the outside world comes to him."

—*Winston-Salem Journal*

"Baldwin's descriptions are so vivid that one can smell the swamp water, feel the dust on the skin, see the Spanish moss hanging from the trees in the thick coastal humidity."

—*San Antonio Express-News*

"Exuberant and completely wonderful ... The story is fast and furious, intriguingly complicated, and sometimes tongue-in-cheek. Though often hilarious, it can wax somber in turn—danger, despair, and even death lurk there to ambush the characters and shock the reader out of any amused complacency."

—*Anniston Star*

"A highly original performance ... I can't think of another contemporary writer who has made a more splendid debut than William Baldwin. Here is a writer I intend to keep reading."

—Fred Chappell
Chronicles Magazine

"Baldwin's rambunctious debut is a sly but loving send-up of Deep South gothic mythology ... Baldwin is a devil of a storyteller, with the unmistakable voice of a true Southern raconteur."

—*Publishers Weekly*

"A whimsical, original blend of Faulkner and Marquez with a dollop of O'Connor."

—*The State* (Columbia, SC)

Please turn the page for more critical acclaim ...

THE HARD TO CATCH MERCY

a novel

William Baldwin

Fawcett Columbine • New York

A Fawcett Columbine Book
Published by Ballantine Books

This edition published by arrangement with Algonquin Books of Chapel Hill, a division of Workman Publishing Company, Inc.

This is a work of fiction. All names, characters, places, and incidents are either products of the author's imagination or are used fictitiously. No reference to any real person is intended or should be inferred.

Permission to use excerpts from the U.S. W.P.A. Federal Writers' Project was granted by the South Caroliniana Library, University of South Carolina.

A portion of this novel was published (in different form) in *Profiles* magazine under the title *A Trip for Ice*.

Library of Congress Catalog Card Number: 94-94577

ISBN: 0-449-90944-1

Cover design by Barbara Leff
Cover illustration by Wayne McLoughlin

Manufactured in the United States of America

First Ballantine Books Edition: January 1995

10 9 8 7 6 5 4 3 2 1

Acknowledgments

THANKS to the following for their love and labor: Shannon Ravenel, Virginia Holman, Katharine Walton, Dale Rosengarten, Sam Savage, Charles De Antonio, Starkey Flythe, Jay Shuler, Candy Reeves, and Bruce Newton. But what are friends for if not to look after you and read your manuscript again and again and again?

Contents

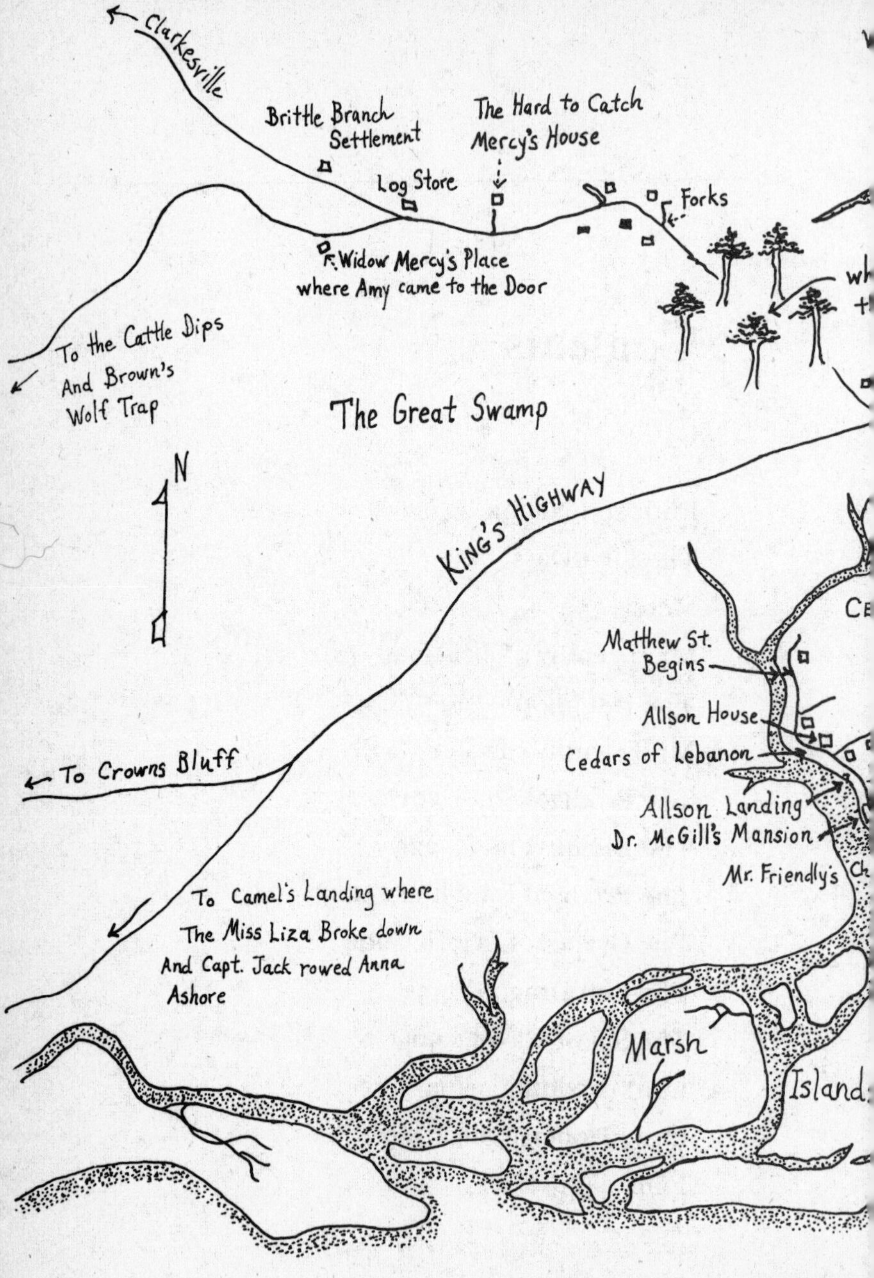

Clarkesville
Brittle Branch Settlement
The Hard to Catch Mercy's House
Log Store
Forks
Widow Mercy's Place where Amy came to the Door
To the Cattle Dips And Brown's Wolf Trap
The Great Swamp
N
King's Highway
Matthew St. Begins
Allson House
Cedars of Lebanon
Allson Landing
Dr. McGill's Mansion
Mr. Friendly's
To Crowns Bluff
To Camel's Landing where The Miss Liza Broke down And Capt. Jack rowed Anna Ashore
Marsh
Island

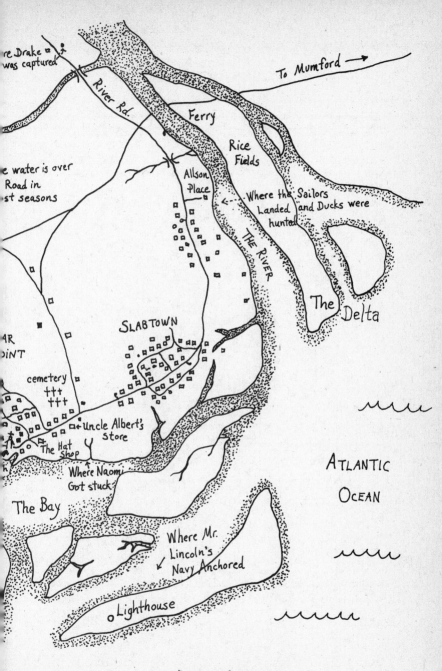

re Drake
was captured

To Mumford →

River Rd.

Ferry

Rice
Fields

water is over
Road in
st seasons

Allson
Place

Where the Sailors
Landed and Ducks were
hunted

THE RIVER

The Delta

SLABTOWN

AR
OINT

cemetery
† † †
† † †

Uncle Albert's
Store

The Hat
Shop

Where Naomi
Got stuck

The Bay

ATLANTIC
OCEAN

Where Mr.
Lincoln's
Navy Anchored

Lighthouse

Drawn from memory
By Willie T. Allson

THE
HARD
TO
CATCH
MERCY

I SUPPOSE books get written for a number of reasons, not many of them good. But I won't start by making excuses. This memoir concerns what happened to me in a place so far away it might as well be the dark side of the moon. I was just learning about life back then.

Your servant,
Willie T. Allson

Sacramento, California
1927

Ruth and Naomi

EARLY on in His career, God promised man dominion over cattle and it had fallen my lot to have dominion over two in particular—our milk cows, Ruth and Naomi. Present at their birth, Pa had named these two dusty red, half-gristled twins and then entrusted them to me. Yes, my principal duty in life was to drive the cows out to pasture and back again. Every boy in Cedar Point did this for his family, but my task was made particularly easy because of the nature of the two animals. No, they weren't both good-natured and easily led. Once, at milking time, Ruth had kicked me so hard I was given up for dead by Sammy, who ran screaming to the house. Mean Ruth was watched closer than ever after that, but the milking had to go on because she produced over a quart and a half a day. Since sweet Naomi, the gentlest of creatures, gave less than a pint, the presence of both animals was required.

"Whither thou goest, I will go," was the promise Ruth made her mother-in-law Naomi in the Scriptures, and it worked that way for the cows as well. Ruth did follow Naomi. Each morning I led gentle milkless Naomi out to pasture and the ill-tempered but bountiful Ruth followed along. I'd open the gate, put Naomi in a likely spot, and in the afternoon retrieve them from that exact place. Then, my cousins came to live with us and two weeks later the cows vanished.

Being December, it was growing dark early, so I'd gone out to collect Ruth and Naomi about five o'clock, and my companion Sammy had come along. We'd have had my dog, Blaze, too, except he was sticking close by home in case my newfound cousin, Uncle Jimmy, showed up. Anyway, when we got to the field the cows were missing. I wasn't particularly alarmed, not even when I found a rail down and realized they'd crossed over the fence. Disgusted, I led Sammy through the adjoining hickories and out onto the edge of the open salt marsh. In front of us extended thousands and thousands of acres of waist-high grass sprouting out of soupy mud. If the cows fed here their milk would be tainted, but they weren't feeding here.

I was starting to become anxious for it now occurred to me that Ruth and Naomi could be anywhere. Gone—broke out—stolen even. Already I could imagine rustlers, men on horseback who moments before had escaped with our herd.

"There. See them cow?" The Negro pointed far across the marsh to a small island.

"Now that's a pretty sight," I said. "How do you suppose they got there?"

"They been down the pasture creek."

"Maybe," I said. "Main thing is to get 'em caught before dark."

Sammy was right. The tide was low, so Ruth and Naomi had walked along the sandy creek bottom until they'd reached the island. We followed.

"This just don't seem like Naomi," I whispered.

"Them cow hungry."

I told him to hush and, crouching low, we peeked over the bank. The cows were pulling at smilax vines, their backs to us. Assuming it would be an easy job, I scrambled forward. That was a mistake. Naomi spied me immediately and, contrary to her good nature, took a step away.

"Hey cow!" I shouted—another mistake. Naomi bolted into the center of the island. Ruth, of course, followed, so I followed as well and sent Sammy skirting quietly around the outside.

The little piece of high land was thick-grown with scrub palmetto, cedar, and cat brier and the cows began to crash through this, first one way and then the other. Still, I could see they were tiring. Waving both hands above my head, I drove the animals on until gentle Naomi was only a handshake short of Sammy's clutches. She stopped suddenly, Ruth stumbled into her, and then she wheeled about to face me.

"Hey cow!" I shouted at once, but the mean-spirited Ruth just flicked an eight-inch horn one way, then another. Her tongue flung out a thick green saliva that splattered my shoes and she charged. Backwards I went, turning a somersault and looking for a place to hide. The island was beaten flat. Ruth came bellowing as I sprinted for my life.

"Help, Sammy!" I shouted. "Save me!" But he could do nothing except run a poor third. With Ruth still following, I ran completely off the island, down into the creek bed, and headed for the mainland. I can't say exactly when the chase ended. At some point Ruth slowed to a walk. She would have stopped altogether if Sammy hadn't been coming behind. Our rout had turned into victory, except the sun was setting, the tide was rising, and we were leaving gentle Naomi behind.

"Can't be helped," I assured Sammy. "We'll come back in the morning."

"This ain't right." Sammy chewed on his lip. Naomi, who now stood in distinct silhouette, lowed mournfully after us.

"Can't be helped."

He shook his head no. What was he expecting? We couldn't catch the other cow in the dark, much less get it home. And so we went, Ruth carefully picking her way through the shadows of the creek bed as it twisted beneath the hickories. Leaving the woods, we broke off switches that weren't needed. To my surprise, contrary Ruth could find her way home alone.

My mama had begun to worry, but supper had started, anyway. I washed up quickly, took my seat, and told them exactly what had happened with extended emphasis on my brave taming of Ruth. Mama took the news surprisingly well. My cousin, Uncle Jimmy, said he'd go with Sammy and me in the morning before school and help bring Naomi in. Then he spoke at length on some studies done by the Godless Mr. Charles Darwin.

"Man ain't even begun to understand the inner workings of a cow's mind," my cousin observed.

My mama nodded in quiet agreement, but Grandpa suddenly shook his head in contradiction.

"That Mercy boy could!" he shouted. "That grandson of the Tyler's knew!"

Uncle Jimmy got up to answer a knock on the front door and the old man stopped speaking. Then my mama was called away and when she returned, it was with a pitcher of milk. Uncle Jimmy came back and whispered to me that Dr. McGill had driven his daughter Liza over in the steamer with this gift because they'd heard we lost our cows. Grandpa, who was hard of hearing somehow overheard this conversation and shouted that Mrs. Allson was to pour out the doctor's milk. He would not have that foul poison under his roof. Well, the milk was probably safe, but how could Liza already know of our dilemma? Could she have released the animals into the marsh to get even with us, and then brought the milk over to divert our suspicion? Yes. My unsuspecting mama carried the milk off into the kitchen and Grandpa returned to his lecture.

"The Mercy boy!" he shouted. "That 'Hard to Catch' boy had all the animals figured out. That winter Tom and I cut shingles, he was handling our mules. Talked to 'em. Just a little bit of a boy." The old man stood up and with a shaking hand indicated a height off the floor of about three feet. "His pa raised him to do that, raised him to tend animals and catch the ones that were hard to catch." My mama had returned from the kitchen and now hovered about the old man anxiously. "Mrs. Allson, send for The Hard to Catch boy," he told her. Once more Grandpa held a shaking hand above the floor to indicate the desired height of this young wonder, and was then gently persuaded to take his seat.

Well, like my mama, the old man could forget it was 1916 or the southern seaboard we were living on. He had brief periods when his mind went blank, but in this case he was making some sense. The Mercys were a big family who lived eight or ten miles to the west of Cedar Point, deep in the heart of the Great Swamp. The first of them, Tyler Mercy, had married a Brittle and settled in long before the War. An outlaw, or worse, he was still left free to come and go as he pleased and it had pleased him to be working as Grandpa's overseer when the Union Navy slipped up the river and burned Grandpa's home, the Allson Place. At some other point he'd had a son who he'd named Allson in our honor, and this Allson Mercy had himself had a dozen or so sons and half as many daughters. Faced with this abundance, the man gave each child a special task, taught each something of value to the whole family. One girl made soap and candles, another spun wool. One of the boys was a fair enough gunsmith to be working over in Crowns Bluff, and another was a carpenter somewhere around Mumford. The Hard to Catch was raised to catch hard-to-catch animals. He'd stayed mostly in the swamp, specializing in animals that lay out—razorback hogs or wild bulls and other beasts that had tired of civilization and re-tired to the woods. Such creatures got up only to feed and cause trouble, and catching one was a job for a professional like The Hard to Catch.

Yes, Grandpa was right in a general way, but he was wrong on two vital points. This Mercy wasn't three feet high any longer. He was a grown man, and about as hard to find as the animals that needed to be caught. Also, he was suspected of bullwhipping a fellow to death over at Brown's Wolf Trap.

Of course, Uncle Jimmy had to aggravate the situation by asking where The Hard to Catch could be found.

"Brittle Branch way," the old man expounded. "You know how the Swamp Road forks once you cross over?" My cousin didn't know at all, but he nodded yes. "Take the lightning strike fork and ask at the store. They'll know."

And then I spied the black hand cautiously feeling its way around the edge of the door opening. A small head slipped beneath the frame, and the rest of her followed. In silence, she straightened to full height, and a smile, di-rected at me alone, split that solemn face. I recall with a curious vividness how those many large teeth shone against an equal expanse of mottled gum, and how her bright yellowed eyeballs darted from side to side as she surveyed the room. She was an ancient woman, with short nappy hair poking dusty gray from beneath the snow white kerchief. It was her one piece of finery, that kerchief, or at least it seemed so when compared with the ragged dresses whose unbuttoned sleeves ended inches above her skeleton wrists. She was tall, certainly the tallest woman I had ever seen, and seemed to loom even larger at that prophetic moment. With a shout Maum Anna fell among us.

"Ain't nothing but devil live in that swamp. Ain't nothing human live back there." The Negro woman swept from chair to chair gathering up the dishes and balancing them on one arm. "Alligator, poison serpent. Got the bottomless hole back in there. Cow fall in that, he fall forever. Quicksand, do Jesus, they got the quicksand. Quickest sand you ever saw. Swallow up the horse and the rider, vanish 'em. Oh no, no, no, no! Praise God, stay away from that place. Ain't nothing but the devil live there." She went around the table like a human tornado and even though he wasn't quite finished, snatched up Grandpa's plate, too. "Ain't but one place worse. Old Sister tell me bout 'em. Yes, sir, that 'em Delta rice field!" She spun off into the kitchen, and out of the discussion.

"That Mercy boy had a way with animals. Get the Mercy boy." Grandpa said this as if Anna hadn't spoken at all or even entered the room.

"Yes, sir," Uncle Jimmy replied. "Yes, sir, that's good advice. That's just what we'll do."

Now I won't claim that Cedar Point was any Garden of Eden, but we had life pretty good. I'm not sure I truly understood that fact before my cousins showed up and afterwards there wasn't time to appreciate what had come before. I suppose life can start happening to you so fast you just got to hang on and ride it out the best you can. Except Uncle Jimmy didn't live it that way at all. He seemed to know exactly where he was heading and still went out of his way to solicit inconvenience and downright danger. Here we were studying on a milk cow stuck in the mud and he was sitting at the supper table encouraging Grandpa to encourage us to enter a tractless swamp, a place that Maum Anna had just warned us was the devil's own workshop. And even more worrisome, we were to deliberately seek out The Hard to Catch Mercy, a man for whom the Allson family should have no conceivable use. All I could do was put my hands to my head and keep quiet.

"Ask at the store," Grandpa continued. "They'll know of the boy's location."

"Yes, sir," Uncle Jimmy said. "Yes, sir, that's what we'll do."

Of course, I was figuring the worse, but once we were upstairs, my cousin assured me he was only being tactful and he was certain we could catch a cow without help. I was relieved to hear this but still not quite as confident in our abilities. I said a short silent prayer for an easy capture—a short simple Christian prayer of the most ordinary nature—and then I lay in the darkness considering Maum Anna.

Certainly no one could claim she had done me harm. After all, she was my Anna. "I raise that boy. I raise 'em up from nothing." Saying that, she'd hold out two grand, long-fingered hands in the imaginary cradling of an infant child. Her face would break into that open-mouthed smile and she'd make a strange giggling laugh that petered out into the clucking of a proud hen. The Negro woman had attended my birthing and on the day following moved into the deserted kitchen building behind our house. She brought my playmate Sammy with her. She was his auntie, not his mother. Though Maum Anna had had at least three husbands, one of whom was still thought to be alive, she had no children of her own. Bowing to God's will, she'd taken her pleasure in the children of others and was well respected as a midwife and general healer. That was fortunate for me. I was a sickly child and without her attention I'm told I wouldn't have survived to tell this tale. Saved and then raised for fourteen years. Not only that, she had been the Allson's cook for over half a century. When she claimed, as she often did, to be "seven feets tall" I believed her. And when she laid that bony finger to her forehead and declared she was "a hundred and something years old" I never doubted it. I figured I knew her pretty well, but after my cousins' arrival from Savannah, I had to reconsider the matter—and some other matters as well. In swift earnestness I prayed again to the God of the Presbyterians that Naomi would soon be home and with some difficulty finally drifted off to sleep.

It was late on Thanksgiving evening of 1916, a fortnight before Naomi's revolt, when the two boys showed up in a wagon that happened to be traveling from the grand Georgia town of Savannah. Their pa, Captain James, had been knocked overboard and drowned, and when my cousins appeared with two little satchels and nothing else, I knew what we'd heard was true—Captain James hadn't been making out too well since the death of his wife. Still, the older of these cousins, the one called Uncle Jimmy, kept saying "Savannah this" and "Savannah that" as if they'd left something behind.

Yes, they were an odd pair when they first stepped into our yard. Not odd-looking so much, for even at seventeen, Uncle Jimmy was a handsome fellow. Fine-featured and tall, he had a ruddy complexion and reddish hair. His manner was pleasant, easygoing, and friendly, but still he was different. While the boys his age were wearing caps, he sported a little bowler set at a rakish angle. Brother was even more unusual. Younger than Uncle Jimmy by four years, he was also a third smaller and much quieter. Their faces were similar though, except that Brother had a row of six large freckles running down the ridge of his nose. There was something else, too. The skin about Brother's eyes was a soft mouse gray and the eyes themselves were dark and sparkling like black glass marbles. Grandpa called it "Gypsy blood," but this was meant to be a joke. The old man chuckled when he said it. My mama smiled. My cousins were both welcomed immediately into our home and Uncle Jimmy had barely done more than unloaded his meager belongings before he was making demands. And he woke me from a sound sleep to make them.

"First things first." A peculiar statement made by a cousin who'd stayed under our roof only one short night.

"What?" I asked.

"Been nine years since I was here last," he answered. "I got to get the lay of the land."

"What?" I rubbed the sleep from my eyes.

"Feel the tiller in my hand. See how she sits in the water."

"She? You talking 'bout the land like it's a boat."

"Yes, that's so."

"Land don't float."

"It do, Willie T. It do. Every piece of land is like a great ship—the ship of life, you see—and it's our business to search out the helm and take our turn at the wheel."

"Land ain't a ship." But he was on his way out, and as if drawn by a magnet, I pulled on my rough cords and followed. Brother slept on. Apparently, his turn at the helm hadn't come around yet so it was just us two who tended to the cows, hurried through breakfast, and started off down Matthews Street.

Hardly a true street, this narrow lane meandered around the live oaks shading it, but along with a few side roads it managed to connect up the village. Cedar Point wasn't exactly a big place, and the houses, whether cottages like ours or full two-stories, were only simple wooden dwellings, with porches to catch the sea breeze. Most had been built as temporary structures—summer retreats from the malaria fever that made a night on the Delta a sentence of certain death. Now, though, with the finer plantation houses burned or lost to bankruptcy, temporary was extending from one generation to the next and an effort was made to put the best possible face on things. Like our house, those of our neighbors were whitewashed to some degree and had flower gardens or at least a few hydrangeas to decorate the yard.

Uncle Jimmy took the tour on that first day and didn't

say much except, "I ain't seen a brick house yet," or, "Sure ain't Savannah." Anyway, it was the people that interested him. About four hundred souls resided in the town proper, and my cousin asked me to name the occupants of each house and give their ages and interests. In addition, I'd had to explain who was kin to who, who'd married who, and even list what lands they'd lost since the tragic War for Southern Independence. What he was particularly interested in, though, was the occupation of the head of each household—a delicate question since many did nothing except hunt, sip along, and tell one another stories. I tried "retired gentleman farmer" but my cousin laughed. Most did keep livestock and had a home garden. A few even planted five or ten acres of cotton and feed corn. I tried plain "farmer." Uncle Jimmy nodded, added more "ain't Savannah"'s, and kept going until we reached one particular structure.

"Now, that's a house." He whistled and actually took his hat off to the building.

"The McGills'," I said and took a couple more steps, hoping he'd follow.

My cousin was rooted to the spot.

"Liza live here?" he asked.

"Yeah," I said. He demanded no further information and I volunteered none. Since he wouldn't move on, I stood there beside him pretending to have good sense.

Dr. McGill had acquired this house when he married the poor, demented Mrs. McGill. At the time, of course, she hadn't been demented, only poor. The building and everything in it had been mortgaged up to the roof beams, and after that, she'd credited her way through every grocery store in town and was fixing to starve. Then, the doctor showed up to rescue her and the house as well. He figured he was getting a doubly good deal because this woman's forebears were the wealthiest planters on the Delta and they'd built a summer home fit for the city streets of Crowns Bluff. True, it wasn't built of brick but the foundation was, and that alone came up ten feet off the ground. Above this were two and a half more stories, sided with beaded lumber and all manner of mouldings. I'd been told the inside was like a palace and from the top windows you could see across the five miles of marsh and bays to where the ocean was breaking on sea island beaches. I'd never been invited in, but I'd heard that. I knew one thing for certain, though. In front of the McGills' wasn't a place to linger. Still, my cousin stood looking at the house as if it were one of the seven wonders of the ancient world.

Then I saw a curtain being pulled back.

"Let's go," I whispered.

"What's she look like?"

"Who?" I whispered.

"Liza. I ain't seen her in nine years."

"She's a girl," I whispered and took a step away.

"What's she look like?" My cousin cupped an ear in my direction and shouted. "Speak up, Willie T.!"

"She's a girl," I hissed.

"I'll have to see for myself, I reckon."

"Dr. McGill's the one who got the Allson Place and he's got the dowry too, if it's still out there." My voice grew louder as I spoke of this treachery, but now he didn't appear to be listening.

"There's somebody watching us from that window," he said and pointed to where the curtain was drawn back.

"That's why I want to go."

"Who is it?"

"Liza's ma. She's nutty as a fruitcake."

"I think I'll wave."

"Don't," I pleaded.

He waved. The curtain drew shut immediately and I started walking off very fast, shaking my head. Back when she still roamed free, Mrs. McGill would state in public that Grandpa had stolen the Allson Place from her family by marrying Mary Matthews. It was the Matthews Place back then and Grandpa had been the overseer. So in her mind the Allsons weren't nearly good enough—but then her mind wasn't exactly a fine-tuned instrument. All the same, I had a hard enough time with Liza without studying on the mama, too.

A half block later, Uncle Jimmy had caught up with me as I was crossing behind the Presbyterian Church.

"I think it was her," he said, out of breath. "I think that was Mrs. McGill."

"This here is our church," I said. "It ain't as fine a building as the McGills' but we come here every Sunday anyway." I hadn't wanted the weight of my irony to be lost on my cousin, so I was careful to give each word the proper emphasis. "All we got here is Mr. Friendly. I know you'll be disappointed he ain't a crazy woman. He's just a preacher, that's all." When I said "just a preacher" naturally I meant the opposite, for I was a great admirer of Mr. Friendly.

"Preaching. A more useless occupation I cannot imagine," my cousin replied. "Two hours a week and for that he probably gets eight hundred dollars a year. That's better than seven and a half dollars an hour. I doubt even Mr. Henry Ford makes that kind of money."

I had no idea what Mr. Friendly got but I was sure he wasn't being overpaid. To compare him with Mr. Henry Ford was outright blasphemy. The preacher was a good man, a tall, strapping fellow with a kind face. True, his chin was a bit large and fit sort of lopsided on his face, a deformity that caused him to talk with a slight lisp, but despite it he was a gifted speaker. Yes, Mr. Friendly and his wife, a woman as stout as he was tall, held weekly gatherings for the young people at the manse, so I'd picked up more than a passing knowledge of the clergyman. He had preached in Canada and been a missionary in China for a while, too, but preferred to serve God here at Cedar Point. He knew his Scriptures and was liked by all, especially the women in the congregation because he showed special attention to them and to the sick and the elderly. Besides this, he was— as some had not been in the past—careful about his appearance. He always wore a clean collar and well-knotted tie and he only visited after three-thirty in the afternoon. And no, he did not work two hours a week. He delivered the morning and evening messages on the Sabbath and during the rest of the week he taught the catechism, held prayer meeting and Bible study, baptized the young, buried the dead, married those caught in between, and paid visits only in the afternoons.

Most important of all, though, Mr. Friendly begged forgiveness for our sins. We were no Clarkesville, but Cedar Point still had sin aplenty. I couldn't name a murderer or a fornicator but I knew a great deal of wickedness, envy, deceit, and whisperings went on. We had them all. Backbiters, haters of God, the proud and the boastful, and children disobedient of their parents. Many needed to be prayed for. They had the Word and they had the Ten Commandments. But the preacher had to be on his toes because at any given minute, four to six of those Commandments were in the process of being broken. Plus, Mr. Friendly was a Presbyterian and God worked his mysteries through the Presbyterians.

"Mr. Friendly don't do it for the money," I had informed my cousin. "He preaches cause it's God's will."

"Sure he does." My cousin smiled.

"Christ is the Redeemer," I calmly counseled.

"Hog slop."

"You saying Christ ain't the Redeemer?"

"Ain't no such person. Never was a Jesus Christ."

"What?" My hands had tightened into fists, but at least I didn't raise them.

"I read it in a magazine. A pope invented him way back when 'cause he needed an easy way to make money. Same as Friendly's doing now. Same thing."

"What? What?" I sputtered. "You talking about a magazine and I'm quoting the Holy Bible. It says in the Holy Bible, 'Christ is the Redeemer'."

"What's that supposed to mean?"

"It means Christ come down here to save sinners like yourself."

"Hog slop."

"You don't even know Mr. Friendly."

"I know all I need to know. It saddens me to admit it but we had plenty of his kind in Savannah."

This theological discussion could have taken up that whole first day, but we'd continued walking and were now up the street. A little straighter and wider, this section of the road was hedged on both sides with stores and more sprawling, twisty-limbed oaks.

"Nineteen stores and ain't but five of 'em groceries," I declared.

"Say now, that is something, but you ain't got a single one built out of brick. I'm starting to wonder if there's a brick building in this whole county."

It was true. All our buildings, even the bank, were built

of wood. Most did have high false fronts meant to disguise their ordinary insides but, there was no hiding the fact, they weren't built of brick.

"Dentist comes on Thursdays." That failed to impress him.

"Hitching post and watering troughs." My cousin shook his head.

I mentioned the doctor's steamer, the Reo carrying the mail, and a couple of others' automobiles, but no motor car was in sight. In fact, right then the street was in the sole possession of a mange-tinged deerdog.

"It's the weekend that people come in for," I said.

He rubbed his jaw.

"Saturday night. That's the wild time," I said. "But the rest of Saturday is always good for business."

It was. People got paid off and they came in from the woods. Negroes and whites alike lined up with their scrip and notes of credit and even real money. That seemed to be what interested my cousin, so we started in the first grocery and worked our way through to the dress shop. I introduced him or reintroduced him to the proprietors. Many remembered him as a boy and even more remembered his pa. They'd offered condolences, which were accepted with a solemn nod. Then he'd gotten down to discussing business and then the weather or whatever else was topical. Some hours later I sat down on the last board of the sidewalk. I'd seen enough of storekeeping to last me a lifetime.

Hands clasped behind his back, my cousin now reviewed the street from the opposite end and gave his summation.

"You got to travel two days through burned-over wilderness to get anywhere half civilized. You got no electricity, no telephone, not even a telegraph office. You ain't got a single brick building in this whole town. Not house or store.

Lordy Lord, you realize this is the twentieth century we living in?"

"I guess so," I said.

"Ain't Savannah," my cousin concluded. "I will say this, though, Uncle Albert strikes me as a man who knows what he's about." We had spent a particularly long time in Uncle Albert's grocery, listening to the old man complain about monies owed him.

"He'll pinch a penny 'til it bleeds." I said this about my pa's only brother, my one true uncle.

"I suspect he'd treat you fair. Strikes me as a fair-minded individual."

"Fine," I said. "Uncle Albert's a fair-minded individual and Mr. Friendly's a thief?"

"I never claimed the preacher was a thief. I just said he took money for nothing."

"Like a banker."

"A banker takes from the community and then gives back with interest. Except for the doctor, he's your most valuable citizen."

"Why don't you ask old Belling for a job?" Mr. Belling was the bank president and ran the butcher shop on Saturday afternoons.

"Not yet," my cousin said. "Time ain't right."

I didn't bother to ask how far in the future that would be. Instead I mentioned eating.

"Right there at the mercantile, didn't the Judge give you a cup of coffee?" he asked. "And I done bought you that cracker at Uncle Albert's."

"I don't call that no kind of meal."

My cousin then pulled out his dollar watch and studied the dial in earnest before admitting it was after one o'clock. He said what I called the halfpenny cracker was no business of his. "Come on," he said.

That first afternoon Uncle Jimmy had me take him to the turpentine works, the gristmill, a closed down oyster-shucking factory, and the cotton gin that was partly owned by Dr. McGill. Three o'clock found us back at my pa's wharf where the only activity was a few Negroes fishing. Actually this was a place of some commerce, but by then I hesitated to say so. A half dozen bateaus, only half sunk, lined the water's edge and a couple more had been pulled up beneath the cedars, a grove my pa referred to as his Cedars of Lebanon. It was here beneath these trees that he conducted his business, spending each Saturday morning in the company of his friend Mr. Britt, the turpentiner.

"Them barrels. See. Fourteen of 'em and all full of turpentine. Pa will haul them out on Monday."

"We got real ships coming into the harbor at Savannah," he said.

I told him the *Redbird* would be docking in a few hours if he wanted to see something. He went off with me to tend the cows, and the cows, not yet totally aware of my cousin's presence, had the good sense to be exactly where we'd left them. When we got back a crowd of both races had started to gather. Some few were meeting passengers and others expecting freight but most, as I was quick to point out to my cousin, were simply enjoying the biggest event of the week. Since Monday, my pa had been easing his way through the narrow creeks to Crowns Bluff and back again. And on that first day, even as I spoke, the *Redbird* appeared.

Oh, that boat was a beauty. Sixty-eight feet on the keel, she still had the lines of a swift-sailing vessel. A blockade-runner some claimed, and when my pa converted her, he'd left up a healthy portion of the forward mast. A hard-pounding single cylinder Lathrop engine went into the stern, and on top of the engine room, he'd perched a handsome pilothouse. And the *Redbird* was painted bright white, every inch. I probably spotted her first, but Drake Bailey's little brother, Gander, shouted the news. The entire crowd came to attention as it always did, and a few who'd been sipping along toasted my pa's seamanship. I hadn't wanted any of this to be lost on my cousin, and in truth, he was duly impressed. I caught the line tossed by Black Willie Allson. In the engine room Red Willie Allson heard my pa's bell and went into action. The great Lathrop shut down, backfired loudly, and roared into reverse. The craft was secured fore and aft and the machine silenced. Then my pa, Captain William Allson, leaned with his one whole arm out the door and shouted what he'd been shouting at the end of every week for ten years.

"Good Friday, ain't it?"

Over seventy years of sunshine had cured Pa's face like a piece of cracking brown leather and his eyes were permanently squinted. It was a kind face. And that one arm was still a powerful instrument, but with my newly arrived cousin beside me, I suddenly noticed how old my pa had grown. His belt now went about his middle in a perfect circle and only a few strands of hair covered a scalp burned bright pink by the sun.

On all sides, though, well-wishers were agreeing that indeed it was a good Friday and I shouted an introduction of Uncle Jimmy. My pa nodded to everyone, and when he shook my cousin's hand, he smiled. But Captain William just guessed at conversations. Fifty years before the fighting around Richmond had ended his hearing days and removed his arm. No one cared. He was a true hero, and as such, saw to the immediate unloading of the freight. Then, with me and my cousin as escorts, he walked up to the house, sat in his rocker, and went sound to sleep. Mama covered him with an afghan and repinned the shirtsleeve on his missing arm.

"You're lucky," Uncle Jimmy told me and I could tell he meant it.

"Sometimes in the summer I go with him."

"Captain James . . . sometimes he would . . ."

My cousin changed his mind about finishing the sentence and went to wash up. Supper was the main meal. Each evening Maum Anna served us in the dining room and my mama and Grandpa would catch up on my doings. But that night, it had been Uncle Jimmy's turn, and he gave them more than an earful.

Yes, everything Grandpa had told him about Cedar Point was true. This town was on the verge of booming, and he figured God had put him here at exactly the right time.

"Electricity," Grandpa declared. "If we were to have electricity and Clarkesville didn't, I should think that would be the end of it."

"Yes, sir," my cousin replied. "Electricity could sure be the spark that sets things off."

"Mrs. Allson," Grandpa asked, "can you imagine the expression on Sheriff Clarke Fitchum Colgrove's face if he were to suddenly show up here one night and find an electrical light bulb burning in every house?" In my lifetime, at least, Grandpa had never called my mama anything but "Mrs. Allson." Her real name was Virginia. My pa called her "Gin."

"Oh, my lands." Mama smiled but would risk no further comment. Brother looked from one speaker to the next and occasionally poked at his food. Uncle Jimmy had never heard of Sheriff Clarke Fitchum Colgrove but that didn't slow him down.

"It would be the surprise of his life, wouldn't it, Aunt

Gin?" From the beginning Uncle Jimmy called her "Aunt Gin." Brother would speak to her but I don't recall him ever addressing her by any name. "The sheriff would have to check his watch. He wouldn't know if it was night or day."

"Oh, my lands, I suppose that's so." Mama shifted her smile to my cousin.

"Indeed! Indeed!" The idea of Sheriff Colgrove checking his watch got Grandpa so amused he began a wheezing sort of laugh. This brought a look of alarm to my mama's face, but the old man got himself under control. "That would be a good joke on Clarkesville. Yes, it would, but we must think seriously on this matter. Now imagine this, boys. . . ." He laid down his knife and fork so that his hands were free to demonstrate as he talked. "Imagine an electrical machine that could hoe the row, plant the cottonseed, chop it, and then pick the boll as well. I suspect it would have to roll along on large wheels of some kind. These would straddle the rows and you would have two electrical hands doing the work." The old man's hands picked at the imagined cotton.

"Four." Nodding his head, Uncle Jimmy leaned forward in his chair. "The machine could have more than two electrical hands. It could have four."

"Exactly, exactly. The machine could have six hands or eight."

"It could have twenty-four," my cousin exclaimed, and his own hands traveled busily about in front of him.

The old man was beside himself, close to tears. "Twenty-four," he nodded in agreement. "That would do for the cotton but what of the turpentine? You see, there I suspect we would have to rely on mules to carry the electrical apparatus. The wheels would bog in the forest."

"Yes, sir. The terrain would be too rough, too many obstacles." My cousin used the flat surface of his own cleaned dinner plate to suggest this rough terrain.

"But, but a mule could go with the electrical man strapped in its saddle."

"The electrical man would do the work as long as the mule got him close enough to the tree," Uncle Jimmy exclaimed.

"Yes, yes. That's it exactly."

"Corn!" Uncle Jimmy exclaimed. "What about that, sir? Corn and potatoes?"

"Would be about the same as with the cotton, the same machine could be used that was working the cotton. Only the electric hands would hold a potato rake or a scythe."

"The wheels would have to be larger to work the corn."

"Yes," the old man nodded. "Yes, and once these machines are completed the Negroes will leave us."

"Sir?" My cousin was finally stalled.

"We would have no further use for the Negroes."

In my tour that day, I'd neglected to mention Slabtown, the large community that bordered us on the north. Grandpa had settled some freed slaves there after the War—giving them the land so they'd be close by to tend his crops forever. Others had done the same, thus guaranteeing that we could all be handily massacred by savages without the least provocation or warning. No doubt Uncle Jimmy had knowledge of this mixed blessing. The old man had certainly mentioned it to me often enough. In fact, he'd always been curiously happy over this state of affairs, which is why I was startled to hear an exodus of the Negroes was now in order. My cousin was also caught off guard.

"Yes, sir. I hadn't considered that. Really hadn't." Uncle Jimmy nodded his head with at least mild enthusiasm, and then went back to discussing the potential of our community.

Apparently, Cedar Point's beauty now ranked somewhere between the Taj Mahal and Paris, France, and it was populated solely by upstanding Christian people. He repeated it would take only the gentle nudge of God's hand to breathe the life of commerce and industry into such surroundings. The countryside was just waiting to blossom. The fertile soil was crying out for the application of machines like those Grandpa had proposed and overnight this place could be turned into a garden that—dare he say it?—a garden that would rival the one Adam and Eve had so foolishly got themselves thrown out of. An Eden. We could have that right here, and right in the middle would be the city of Cedar Point.

"Merciful heavens, wouldn't that be something?" my mama commented.

"It's coming," my cousin affirmed.

"The future of Cedar Point is in your hands, boys," Grandpa declared. "Clarkesville will wither and die on the vine. It is you who will harvest, for it is you who have the answers."

Brother had finished eating and was now staring across his empty plate at nothing in particular. If he knew any answers he was keeping them to himself, for he'd said only three words since his arrival. When my mama asked if he enjoyed the trip, he'd answered, "I don't know."

"Perhaps so, but we'll be harvesting the fruits of your labor. It is the sacrifices of our elders that has made this triumph possible." That was Uncle Jimmy still talking to Grandpa.

"True, son, true indeed, but sacrifices made in gladness."

"We're standing on the shoulders of giants," Uncle Jimmy continued.

"It pleases me to hear you say that."

Well, it would please anybody to hear that, but it was I, Willie T., and not this strange interloper cousin, who should have been saying these things to the old man.

"I don't believe that I have mentioned to you that Brother is very good at mechanical matters." No, I don't believe he had. "When we left Savannah, he was doing clock repairs and some related tinkering. It appears to me that no one hereabouts is engaged in that line. Would you think it wise if he were to open up a shop? He could do the work in his and Willie's room upstairs."

This request was greeted with great enthusiasm by Grandpa. It wasn't his room and he was, as we all knew, fond of mechanical matters himself.

"What do you say to that, Brother?" my cousin concluded.

"I threw my clock tools overboard when Pap drowned," he answered in a quiet, even voice.

"I know, Brother. We'll get you more," Uncle Jimmy said with equal calm.

"All right."

"You'll do fine," my mama whispered.

"Bully!" Grandpa shouted. "Bully for you, Thadius!" He rose from his chair to say the rest, which caused Mama to ease forward in hers. "Early in my life I chose to marry that Delta rice," the old man proclaimed. "I do not regret that decision. Despite all that has passed, I do not regret it. Still, I wonder at times what course my life would have taken if I had pursued to the fullest my interest in mechanical matters." He gazed at each of us in turn but settled on Brother. "Clocks most especially. Yes, clocks have always been a puzzlement to me. I understand their principle perfectly but, even as a very young boy, it occurred to me that far too many gears and balances were employed. A more efficient machine could be built by simply removing some of these unnecessary mechanisms." The old man sat back down and Mama relaxed. "Yes, my boy, I can imagine no finer vocation for a man than clock repair and perhaps someday you may even advance the working of the instruments along the lines I have suggested."

It only remained for me to bless the conversion of my bedroom into a repair shop, something I did with passable hospitality.

"Don't expect no help from me," I muttered very low.

"He won't," Uncle Jimmy said.

Why had I said that? I liked Brother and didn't particularly care what he did in our room. It was Uncle Jimmy's manner that had provoked me.

"Uncle Jimmy's got some peculiar ideas on preachers and what they get paid," I announced suddenly. "Why don't you tell 'em? Might be a way to save some money that could be spent more useful elsewhere."

"No," my cousin said. "They don't want to hear about that."

"Speak up, boy," Grandpa said. "Thrift is no sin, not in my Bible."

"Tell 'em, Jimmy."

"All right. It's just what I was telling Willie T. today. Next to the doctor, the preacher is the most important man in town. It might look like he's doing nothing but his working with the spirit side of things is like money in the bank. You think it ain't going to add up but all the time it's just sitting there drawing interest. Them good works is building up and building up and in the end you know what you got?" I knew from my studies that good works didn't pardon our sins and weren't even directly connected to the individual doing them. He wasn't going to hear this from me, though.

"Them good works is building up," my cousin repeated playing for time. "And in the end you got . . ."

"Judgment Day," a voice called out from the doorway and Maum Anna ducked her smiling face into the room. "Do Jesus, Jim, you got Judgment Day."

"Exactly," my cousin responded happily. "Exactly so. Judgment Day."

"That don't make no sense at all," I said but was too overwhelmed to protest further. Putting my elbows on the table, I shook my head back and forth.

"Amen," my mama whispered.

"Amen," Grandpa whispered.

"Judgment Day, great God, Judgment Day," Maum Anna sang to herself as she cleared away the supper dishes, and paused only long enough before exiting to shout a question. "How you like them dumpling, Jim? I cook 'em 'specially for you."

My cousin praised the dumplings to the heavens. Then Mama and Grandpa went into the parlor to join my sleeping pa. We said our goodnights and retired upstairs.

"How come you lie like that?" I asked as soon as we reached the hall landing.

"Lie to who?" Uncle Jimmy asked in a puzzled voice.

"To Mama. To Grandpa. All that. What you said about the preacher and the town. You lied."

"Tactfulness. You know what tactfulness is, Willie T.?"

"You was lying."

"Tactfulness. I might have told one or two white lies, but it sure ain't hurt nobody. In fact, lying for the benefit of others is a positive good, and you got to learn that, Willie T."

"I don't even know who you is and you done turned my bedroom into a clock factory."

"I'm your cousin Jimmy."

"Well, listen to me then, cousin. Jesus is as real as Sunday and if you don't accept him as your Redeemer you're just asking to go to Hell."

"I'll bear that in mind." He smiled and gave a little bow before going into his bedroom and closing the door.

"Everything you own can fit into one little suitcase!" I shouted at the door. Actually, almost everything I owned could fit into a suitcase, too, but I wasn't going around passing judgment on other people. He had to have heard me but at first there was no response. In fact, I'd turned away when he cracked his door and called after me.

"She ain't seven feet tall."

"What?"

"Anna ain't seven feet tall."

"She is too."

"Look here." He opened the door wider and, holding his hand flat on the top of his head, stepped beneath the frame. "See here. I'm six feet tall and these doors ain't but an inch higher. When she comes through them she ain't ducking more than a couple of inches so she can't be seven feet tall."

"Maybe," I said. "Maybe, but she's still the tallest woman you ever seen."

"I seen quite a few that was taller."

"Good for you." I was fourteen years old and I had seen none taller.

"She ain't a hundred years old either. I'd reckon she's about seventy."

"You going to prove that, too?" I hissed.

"No," he said, and bidding me good night, retired for the evening.

Brother was already in his bed, staring straight up at the

ceiling with those strange black eyes. I sat on the edge of my own bed and looked down at my feet. I had a lot to think about. It wasn't just that Maum Anna wasn't seven feet tall. It wasn't just the lying. The whole discussion of mechanical things troubled me as well. My cousin had agreed with the old man, and, at the time, it didn't occur to me to question whether or not these machines could be built. But I did know that they were far more complicated than Grandpa made them sound.

Liza McGill had a bicycle she rode on rare occasions and once she'd made the mistake of leaving it at our house. So, of course, I snuck it back to the home pasture and had Sammy push me around for an afternoon. I never got the knack of it. Once the Negro let go, I'd pedal wildly but the handlebars would immediately come alive and wobble fiercely beneath my grip. No more than five paces and the bicycle would pitch me over.

Sammy did a little better. After I'd given up completely, I felt he was owed at least one push-off and he made the most of it, circling the pasture until hard dark. This was discouraging to watch, and I was glad the next day when Liza retrieved the unnatural contraption. Of course, I realized it wasn't just women and Negroes who could ride them. Somehow, Barnus Wilson had come into possession of one and before it was ridden into the ground most of the men and boys in town had mastered it.

Pedaling wasn't for me, though. I had no feeling for things of a mechanical nature and after the bicycle adventure I was particularly suspicious of those devices that combined humans or animals with machines and expected them to cooperate. The electrical cotton picker with its twenty-four hands might work fine, but an enterprise that required an electrical man to be mounted on a live contrary mule couldn't help but be more trouble than it was worth. Still, whether I understood or even cared, it appeared that commerce, industry, brick buildings, and all manner of wonders waited barely over the horizon. Angry as I was, I saw it was possible to learn something from Uncle Jimmy.

Jesus wasn't dreamed up by some pope, though. No matter what my cousin said, I knew there was a Heaven and a Hell and that Jesus had died so I could get into the former. Yes, Christ was the Redeemer and He wore white robes and sandals. His hair was light brown, long and flowing. No two pictures showed His face exactly the same but even if He was hanging in agony on the cross, you could count on the face being kind and understanding. My cousin could go around thinking he had all the angles figured out, but unless he was willing to have his sins forgiven, he was going to get nowhere. Content in the knowledge of those certainties, and thankful that I'd survived the first day with my new cousins, I knelt and said my prayers. Brother just watched me with his dark Gypsy eyes.

THE NEXT morning I had left Uncle Jimmy sleeping peacefully and took Ruth and Naomi out to pasture on my own. When I returned he was already up and gone.

"Gone where?" I asked in true puzzlement.

They all seemed to know. My cousin would be clerking for Uncle Albert. That afternoon the cows were waiting right where I'd left them and came home with no difficulty at all. About nine that night my cousin showed up and while eating the supper that had been kept warm for him, he described how working in the grocery was an even greater pleasure than he'd hoped for.

The following day he'd slept late and slipped out of his first church service by claiming a sudden attack of vertigo. Then we'd all had an enjoyable midday repast and gone down to the Cedars of Lebanon to relax. The Sabbath was to be kept holy but my cousin Jimmy was presently advocating a game of home run. Brother was watching me doddle up an ant lion. The cows wouldn't disappear for another ten days, so I was still happily ignorant of much of the world's worries, and that's when the call came.

"Sam-u-el!" Grandpa always called Sammy that way, drawing out the syllables long and distinct as if he was indeed the Lord above calling on His chosen one. And of course, when he called, I knew to stop what I was doing and answer.

"He wants us," I said rising to my feet.

"Sam-u-el!" the call came again. I started to bolt, but Uncle Jimmy grabbed me by the shirttail.

"Your name Samuel?" he asked.

"No, but he wants all of us," I said.

"Then, why don't he call us all?"

"That ain't his way."

My cousin let go and I started in the direction of the call, which I knew to be the barn, and was satisfied to see Brother beside me, even a little in front.

"You two are a pretty sight," Uncle Jimmy shouted but he was getting to his feet.

"Sam-u-el!" The call continued as I led my cousins past the picket fence that bordered the front garden and then in a straight line across the thick grass that grew along the side of the house. Yes, my cousins were fortunate to be living here. They might not admit it, but if nothing else, they had that to thank God for. And while they were at it, they should be thanking the Almighty that I was there to guide them, if not down the path of righteousness, at least down the path that now led us by the kitchen door where a few figs still dangled to be admired but not plucked.

"Sam-u-el!" The old man was close by. "Sam-u-el!"

Beside the still waters of the well we went. The quiet black circle of water at its bottom could no longer be showed off, though, for the top had been boarded over and fitted with a modern iron-handled hand pump.

"Here am I," Uncle Jimmy whispered happily. "Here am I."

On past the old kitchen building, I led them. Maum Anna lived there, but that was of no interest to these two. Then we passed the scuppernong vines, where in the late summer the grapes in thick bronze bunches waited for harvest. And finally, we entered the dusty grassless area of the barnyard. Actually, this last was not such a clearly defined area. Poles and slats contained the sow. More poles and scraps of wire were meant to surround the chickens, who would forsake it for the stumped cedar. A similar arrangement was intended for the ducks, who instead wandered back and forth to the creek. Ruth and Naomi spent their evenings stabled in the barn. Gallant and Rose stayed there too, but had daytime use of the house pasture. Sammy and I were keepers of them all.

And there he was. We arrived at the barn in time to see Sammy tumbling through the door in a confusion of hay and cornhusks. He hadn't settled firmly to the ground when the old man appeared from inside and caught him with a hobbling kick in the shin. Sammy howled and rolled away. Grandpa pursued him. At ninety-six, the old man was still erect and poised. Even in this light of broad day, there was little to show his true age—only a sag of flesh beneath the chin, and this almost hidden by a snow white goatee. He raised his cane to strike again, but Sammy was on his feet, edging in our direction. A thin film of dust coated his inky face. His eyes wide and white, he chewed his lip and brushed at his clothes, sliding sideways until he was behind us. Grandpa halted.

"Black Sambo!" the old man cried out. "You dare to hide in that barn when I call your name?"

Sammy crouched low using Uncle Jimmy as a shield. He started to button the flapping strap of his overalls, but finding the button missing held it in place instead and smiled.

"No, sir," he said. "I been sleeping."

"Asleep? Asleep? You leather-headed beast, I'll teach you to sleep in the middle of the day." Grandpa raised his cane once more and smote the ground with enough force to launch the mallard drake into a flight of several feet. Then he addressed us all.

"This is the wine arbor." He pointed to the first grouping of sagging vines with the cane. "You are not to eat the fruit of these vines. Do you understand me?"

"Yes, sir," Uncle Jimmy declared and the rest of us looked down at our feet and nodded. By this late in the year the vines were nothing but a tangle of barren brown sticks propped up with a rambling collection of posts and slats.

"The front arbor is for the table." Grandpa pointed with the cane at the other vines. "You are not to eat the fruit of these vines." He tapped his cane into the dust and then suddenly pointed it not at my cousins but at me. "Is that understood?"

"Yes, sir." This time Uncle Jimmy and I both answered and the other two nodded.

"Thadius, there is business for us in the house." Grandpa waved Brother forward, grabbed onto his arm, muttered something about it "not being Tom's fault," and was led away.

Uncle Jimmy waited until they were out of earshot before remarking on the obvious fact that we weren't allowed to eat from any of the vines. I agreed it was a stiff sentence but the old man's word was law. Sammy chewed at his lip and then smiled broadly. Many a time the Negro and I had eaten scuppernongs to the point of puking, but I suppose my cousin had guessed that already.

"Go on, Sammy," he said suddenly. "Me and Willie T. got some important business to discuss."

Sammy didn't seem particularly hurt by this dismissal. He smiled again and disappeared towards the creek.

"Where's the old man keep his wine?" That was the business my cousin wanted to discuss, and it took at least a couple of mild threats before I led him to the grain bin just inside the two wide open barn doors. Bending over the padlock, he made a few meaningful twists and jabs at the keyhole with the smallest blade of his barlow and yanked down hard. Until now I hadn't believed he could open it, and I whispered frantically.

"Grandpa's famous for that wine."

"Be quiet, Willie T. Watch the door."

"Watch the door?"

The room held five small oak barrels cradled lovingly in a rack of ash. It was sacred like a church in there, but my cousin got down on his hands and knees, put his mouth up to a spigot, and apparently intended to drain one barrel dry. Minutes before I'd been chuckling to myself about the few grapes that Sammy and I had swiped and now a true crime was being committed.

"They'll catch you," I whispered, but he only twisted his head in my direction and continued to suck in the wine.

I took a quick glance out the barn doors because by now I was an accomplice.

"There," my cousin announced rising to his feet and

wiping his mouth on the back of his sleeve. "No one the wiser and sure ain't the sadder."

"That was your doing." I shook my head. "All I did was watch."

"You want a taste?"

"No!"

"Best we lock it back then."

He locked it back. With an innocence beyond my believing, he slapped the lock shut, went outside, and, propping himself against the barn siding, sat. I squatted off to one side.

"The old man is going to catch us," I said. "He will."

"Doubt it."

"Grandpa measures them barrels."

"You a timid soul, Willie T."

"I know that old man."

"I doubt that, too."

"You forgetting you the one new around here."

"You don't know nothing about her, either." My cousin must have gotten his money's worth because gradually his voice was sinking into a lazy slur, and when he said *her* he waved his hand off in a very general direction.

"Who?" I asked.

"Anna. That's who." He paused to catch my eye. "You know she was born free on the island of Jamaica? Her ma was cooking in a mansion house there 'til she poisoned somebody in the family."

"That ain't so." Maybe Maum Anna wasn't seven feet tall, but I figured now he was just tormenting me.

"The solemn truth," Uncle Jimmy whispered and tucked both hands behind his head.

"No, it ain't."

"You see," he began again, "'cause of that poisoning the

cook and the daughter Anna was sold as convict labor to a company working the Grace Island salt mines. Had to be a death sentence. Woman never been out the kitchen, so pretty quick Anna's ma is dead. Fact is, she died with a bushel of salt balanced on her head." Suddenly my cousin was sitting forward, mimicking this balancing act. "Went down on her knees, careful not to spill the load and started dying. Anna was tagging along so she wrestled the basket off and half dragged it to the ship they was loading. She never saw her ma again. Didn't even know what happened to the body." My cousin settled back against the barn and gazed at the clouds.

"Don't claim that's tactfulness." I shook my head. "You're lying."

"Anyways, Anna kept toting the salt herself, growing to the task, and getting to be a woman. Might still be at that salt mine if your mama's own dear papa, Captain Jack Cicero Cage, hadn't won her in a poker game." My cousin looked directly at me and expected to be believed.

"Lies," I repeated. My other grandpa, Captain Jack, had been a famous blockade-runner during the War and he'd left his motherless daughter with the Allson family for safekeeping, but this didn't make my cousin's story true.

"Jack Cage drank away a fortune. Whores and gambling in Nassau Town. Didn't save nothing but Anna, and she was won in a poker game. Took three queens—"

"No! No, sir!" I leaned over and shouted this in his face.

"Facts, Willie T., facts. The Captain sent Anna as a gift to his daughter. Mailman brought her right here to the Allson gate at Cedar Point. And she wasn't tall as now, just slightly above average. Called her 'a comely wench thought to be about eighteen years of age,' which is how come I know she ain't a hundred and something now."

"I ain't listening to a drunk."

"She was brung here with her ankles chained together. Didn't make much sense, really. Her hands was free and the key to the shackles was in a little leather bag hanging 'round her neck."

"My mama . . ." Uncle Jimmy raised a hand and held it palm out towards me.

"There was also five twenty-dollar gold pieces in the leather bag hanging around Anna's neck. Our grandpa put them in his pocket and was getting ready to send Anna off to boil salt with the rest of the hands. That's when your mama spoke up. Said right to his face that Anna was her personal property and was staying in the house. Grandpa grumbled but he had to agree. Chains stayed on, though."

"No. 'Fraid not," I said in a calm, determined voice. "Anna was a gift to Mama from Grandpa Allson. I done heard him say that right in front of both of them."

"Lot of different versions of a story will go around."

"Yeah. Well, this ain't even the same story."

"Our Grandpa was too old to fight, so they made him an honorary Colonel and left him behind to build forts."

"First true thing you said."

"Had a new wife wasn't but nineteen. Yes, sir. Young girl comes to attend the funeral of her classmate's mama and four months later she's married to the widower. They moved in here to this summer house for the duration, left Tyler Mercy to oversee the plantation, sent your pa and Uncle Albert off to fight the battles, and spent the whole war under the bed covers locked together like two dogs." My cousin snickered his way through this last.

"That's your own grandmama you talking about!" I shouted.

"Yes, sir. A hot-blooded woman, and us coming down

from that second marriage got it pumping in our veins."

"Well, us from the first marriage got decency pumping in ours."

"You got a woman?" my cousin asked me suddenly.

"A woman?"

"You ain't so bad-looking. You ought to have you a woman. I know I got to have me a woman."

My cousin rose somewhat unsteadily to his feet.

"Well, I ain't got me a woman," I sputtered, "and none of that's true . . . what you was telling." He offered me his hand and I was pulled to my feet.

"Well, it ain't the whole truth. I left out the part about Anna being a witch doctor."

"She ain't a witch doctor," I said almost wearily, because, at least, I'd heard this accusation before. "She's just a healer."

"Listen."

I shook my head no. My mama had allowed the woman to treat us all, even Grandpa, with her teas of holly and life-everlasting and her pinegum linaments. "Big difference between healing and black magic."

"I know." My cousin twisted his neck about as if it was really kinked and started walking. "I didn't believe that part myself."

"Good. Good, 'cause that's a serious accusation." I was following behind.

"Course, the bulk of the evidence do point against her."

"I don't want to hear no more!"

"Ah, relax yourself, Willie T. I'm just repeating to you what I was told myself."

"By who? Who told you all these crazy stories?"

He stopped to face me, rubbed his jaw, and said, "I forget."

Old Blaze struggled out from beneath the house to meet my cousin. "Part Red Bone, part coyote, and two-thirds blind" is what he called the dog, but since it didn't understand and was going by the tone alone, the poor animal already loved Uncle Jimmy dearly.

"Puppy, you wouldn't believe the things Willie T.'s been telling me today." He scratched the dog behind its moth-eaten ear. "Made me step back in wonder. Made me blush. I swear they did." Blaze's tail wagged in feeble appreciation.

"That's my dog," I said. "Why don't you get a dog of your own?"

He was walking off down the street so I had to shout my responses at his back. That done, I went straight back to the old kitchen building, tapped quietly on the door, and when my name was called, opened it and stuck my head inside.

In my younger years, I'd often been coaxed here to Maum Anna's lair and instructed in a curious catechism that suggested we were all God's children. The gates of Heaven stayed propped open and it was easy to slip in. Yes, according to Maum Anna, only the meanest of the mean would be joining the devil, and most of them were already keeping his company. In addition to this, she recited a version of the Scriptures that allowed the twelve disciples to engage in conversation with Adam and Eve as well as the beasts of the field and jungle.

When I happened one day to share these preachings with my Sunday school teacher, the poor woman shrieked and ran off demanding that I be separated from the giant African at once. Of course, this request wasn't taken seriously, for the wild imaginings of Negroes were considered but an extension of their primitive ways. No white child could be truly harmed if he had Presbyterian instruction at his disposal, and I got these thorough lessons immediately. There was only one, positively one, interpretation of the Scriptures, I was made to understand. Eve tempted Adam and, since they were the parents of us all, we inherited their sin and were doomed to the eternal torment and darkness of Hell. By dying, though, Christ the Redeemer had saved a handful. We few were among the elect and were predestined to go to Heaven. That was that. Whether Maum Anna would be joining us there was a matter of some debate. My mama and, of course, my pa said so. No one else I asked thought it likely.

Maum Anna was still happy to share her beliefs with me, but I'd been jolted by the reaction of my Presbyterian betters. From then on I ignored her gospel stories and accepted the stricter version, which I was hearing almost daily. An indifferent scholar at first, I'd gradually warmed to the studies, and two or three in the congregation even felt I had the makings of a preacher. Under those circumstances no one could claim she'd done me harm and only the very foolish would have accused her of witchcraft.

She sat now in a rocker far too small for her gigantic frame and watched a tiny fire flickering in the large open fireplace that had once cooked the family's meals. In the shadows of the room the bright colored Christian artwork was barely visible. The old woman had stacked and wallpapered our old kitchen building with all manner of Christian paintings and artifacts. Though African Methodist, she was open to art of all denominations and had a particular fondness for Roman Catholic statuary, especially figurines of the Mother and Child. I entered no further than the doorway.

"Maum Anna, how tall is you?" I called out.

"'Bout seven feets," she said without looking my way.

"How old is you?" I asked quickly.

"Praise Jesus. He done let me live to be 'bout a hundred." She smiled her widemouthed smile at me. Of course, I knew the first answer was wrong, but she'd answered 'about' seven feet and there was no proof she wasn't 'about' a hundred years old as well.

"Where'd you come from?"

"Maum Anna belong to your mama," she said. "You know that, Willie T. What for you ask me all these fool questions?"

"Did my mama's pa win you in a poker game?"

"Great Gawd, listen to this boy. Forgive him for what he saying. That good Christian man ain't never pick up a deck of card in he whole life." As she said this she had stood and raised her hands. When she looked to the Lord in supplication, her fingertips easily brushed the soot-stained ceiling.

"Captain Jack Cage didn't drink and play cards?" I would not add "chase women and throw away a fortune" to the question.

"Who tell you such a thing?" The arms came down.

"Uncle Jimmy." Already, I was confident that I had cornered my cousin in a lie.

"That boy fool. Tell you a thing like that."

"Now, tell me this. Is you a witch doctor?"

The long fingers went up across the broad-toothed smile forming bars like the black and white keys on a piano. She giggled and then let out a hoot of laughter.

"Do Jesus. Get 'way from here. Ain't I raise you up to be a Christian boy? Ain't I raise Sammy free from all superstition? Do boy. Ain't but the one Saviour, Jesus Christ. The Lamb and the Redeemer. What for Anna need all them root and charm? I got my protection right here." She stopped talking long enough to slap her breast and then went on to prevail for several more minutes about the sad ignorance of those who let their lives be controlled by unnatural spirits and conjure ways and the devil's black magic. I was more than satisfied and anxious to get on with my final questions.

"You wasn't from Jamaica. Your mama wasn't a cook in a Jamaica house. You came straight from Africa, didn't you?" I was determined to put the record straight.

"That so. I done told you that. I comes from Africa. I done seen all them animal." She began pointing about the kitchen as if the beasts were with us. "I done seen the lions and the leopards and the tigers. All them things."

"Tigers live in India," I said, making sure there were no flaws in this final accounting.

"Thank Jesus, yes," she said. "They there, that so, but they in Africa, too. Way back in the jungle where the white man ain't been yet. That where I come from."

"I figured that," I said. I hadn't told my cousin about Africa but now I would. He could tell that salt mine bedtime story to someone else.

"They been all kind of strange things back in there. Half man, half alligator. They live in there, too."

"Crocodiles," I corrected. "Alligators live in America. Crocodiles live in Africa."

"Do boy," she said, fixing me in the steady gaze of those bright yellowed eyes. "You been there?"

"No."

"Then how you know? When this old nigger woman tell you alligator, then it must be alligator. I know the difference between a man that half crocodile and a man that half alligator. I the one that been born and raised there." With dignity she lowered herself once more into the rocker.

"Yes, ma'am," I said.

"The streets is paved with gold. I remember that clear as yesterday. I walking to my house on a street paved with gold and when I hungry I just pick apple off the tree. Ain't been nothing but a garden. Got apple and orange growing everyplace you look and the street paved with gold."

I wanted her to stop for I could hardly go to my cousin with stories of gold streets and apple trees, much less men who were half alligator. It was best to divert her with my next question.

"Did you come to this house chained at the ankles, carrying a letter, and with a pouch around your neck holding five twenty-dollar gold pieces?" This time she was not so quick to answer and, in fact, turned away from me completely. "Did you?" I accused, for it was slowly dawning on me that she might have made up the story about Africa.

"Boy, what you ask that for? Chain Anna?" Again she was rising up out of the little rocker. "What for he want to chain Anna? Ain't I promise Captain Jack I look after his little girl? Ain't I give the man my word that I stay with the gal and I been stay all these years?"

"Yes, ma'am," I said.

"Allson think I going to run." She approached the doorway and stood before me at full height and it could well have been seven feet. The bright eyes were on me unblinking. "Where he think Anna going to run to, Africa? Huh?" At that point she had become quite agitated and began to pace the old kitchen in long-legged strides. "Where I going to run? Boy?" She snapped at me in the hardest tone I'd ever gotten from this woman.

I admitted that I didn't know.

"Your grandpa been look at my teeth. He look for see if I got good teeth. Then he say he ain't got grocery to feed me. What for he worry 'bout my teeth if he ain't got grocery? Oh, great Gawd. Jesus my master." She stopped suddenly to shout heavenward. "I know that old man! He be happy for have another slave. He think God done send him another one in chain. I know that man. I know 'em good. Chain Anna. I show him. I going show 'em 'til he dead in he grave. Praise Jesus."

I retreated from the kitchen building. Maybe Uncle Jimmy's version had been correct on a couple points, but I wouldn't accept it all. I went upstairs to look for Brother, but he must have been off with Grandpa. Slipping into my cousin's bedroom, I studied myself in his little scrap of mirror and I couldn't help thinking of all his talk about women. I wasn't handsome the way he was. I was darker and my hair just lay over to one side. I didn't smile the way he did either. I tried to look sincere when I looked at myself, earnest and sincere, but I kept thinking about women. Maybe I was handsome enough to have a girlfriend, but I was a decent Christian young gentleman. Maybe my cousin had been telling some of the truth, but he was a rowdy, drunken whoremonger. I went outside and found Sammy down by the dock.

There on what should have been his fourth evening under our roof, Uncle Jimmy hadn't come home for supper at all. This seemed quite ordinary for everyone but me, because I alone knew that he'd gone off drunk in search of a woman. He stayed gone. In fact, he hadn't been back until about ten o'clock that night. I didn't feel like going over and saying, "Yes, you might be partly right," or asking if he'd had any luck finding a consort, because I knew he hadn't. I pretended to be asleep while he was banging and whistling his way to bed. The next morning neither of us referred to the conversation we'd had, and went on to school. This was to be my cousins' first day and I was expected to look out for them. An easy enough chore except for the presence of Drake Bailey.

Every school had a bully and Drake Bailey was the meanest, toughest youth that Cedar Point had to offer. A young man earned that title by bareknuckle fighting and some kicking and biting, as well. Once a reputation was established, it wasn't necessary for the battling to continue, but Drake was required to put on an occasional show and would bloody a nose when the spirit moved him. His uncle, Judge Walker, kept an eye on him, and so did his widowed mother, who thought her son had the makings of a fine missionary. Occasionally, Superintendent Baker would put his foot down. And, I guess, Drake did make an effort to contain himself.

Of course, I tried to stay clear of the bully, but when he chose to grab me round the neck and stick one of his dirty postcards in my face, I had to hold still and pretend to laugh. On Uncle Jimmy's first day of school I was certain he wouldn't get off with just a look at some bare-breasted floozy. Drake would be required to lick him and I advised my cousin to go down on the first punch and stay down. I assured him hardly any acting would be involved for he might be out cold by then anyway. The victim nodded in agreement, insisted on getting to school early, and then, leaving me and Brother behind, went looking for trouble. Drake didn't attack on first sight. In fact, my cousin shook hands and started laughing. Then Uncle Jimmy tripped up Drake's pal Barnus, and Drake, pretending to help Barnus to his feet, dropped him again. After watching this for a few minutes, I relaxed a bit and entered into a couple conversations of my own.

The bell rang and Superintendent Baker lined us up in the school yard, boys on one side, girls on the other. The tallest boy went first and the smallest last, a selection that put Drake in front and Uncle Jimmy second, me fourth, and Brother somewhere about seven or eight back. A truly tremendous man, our superintendent had gotten his job on the basis of bulk and temperament rather than scholarship. Two years before, he'd dangled one troublesome youngster by the foot out a second-story window and held him there screaming until the boy swore off his youth altogether. This morning he called for silence and got it. The flag was raised. We said the Pledge of Allegiance and then the Lord's Prayer, following which Superintendent Baker had a few words of greeting.

He wanted to take this opportunity to welcome us back after our Thanksgiving holiday, and wanted to say for the thousandth time that he looked on each and every one of us as his own son or daughter. If we'd learn our lessons and be well mannered, all would be fine. He assumed that wouldn't be the case with most of the boys, for he knew from experience we were dullards or troublemakers and probably born to be hanged. Those weren't his exact words but you got the idea from the way he frowned and spat when he looked our way and the way he smiled and bowed when he looked towards the girls. Liza McGill was his favorite. Finally, he had a particular incident that needed discussing.

"Sometime last night," he said, "one or more persons forced entry into my office and did considerable damage there. I will not go into details but I will say that vulgar words were written on the walls. A goat was left tethered to my desk and two of my cigars were smoked." A small titter rippled through the crowd, for such behavior was not unusual. Superintendent Baker was never amused, though, and even less so this time. "My chair was smashed into kindling and a fire started on my desktop."

This last had brought no snickers, for the building we were using was actually just a big two-story house. The real school had burned to the ground the year before in a fire some called arson but that was probably an accident. At least one house burned every year, for once the right spark from a chimney hit the right roof shingle, all was lost unless a bucket brigade formed immediately. It was understandable that the superintendent would be particularly angry that morning and it was understandable that fire drills were a major part of our curriculum. If nothing else, school was preparing us to go off to be firemen or pass along buckets of water for irrigation.

"I know who did it!" The superintendent's voice came as a pained bellow. "I have my proof already but I would like to think that the one who did it was man enough to stand up and say here in front of everyone, 'It was me.'"

There was silence for a moment. Then Drake, who'd been looking down at his feet the whole time and kicking idly at the dirt, ran his fingers through his thick, curly, black hair, and stepped forward.

"Sir," he said, "I got to tell the truth. It was Liza." A collective laugh swept across the yard.

"That is a lie! That is an outrageous lie!" Liza screamed. "I never did any such thing. Never." Her hard little cameo ivory face had twisted as if in pain and her busy little hands gone to her forehead where the pale brown hair was pulled straight back before binding into a tight bun. Though she was far from the tallest, she was allowed to stand at the head of the girls' line anyway.

"It was her, sir. It troubles me to say it but I seen her plain as day. I seen her on the street. She was leading the goat and already smoking one of your cigars."

"Shut up," Superintendent Baker said. He had stepped

towards Drake but at this point Uncle Jimmy raised his hand and the superintendent stopped short.

"What, Allson? What?"

"Sir," Uncle Jimmy spoke right out. "I just want to say that I was with Liza McGill last night in her parlor until ten o'clock. At that time, her mother announced that as a gentleman I should say good night. I think if you will check with her parents, you'll find that she was home for the remainder of the night."

"James Allson!" Liza shouted.

Everyone laughed, everyone but me. I was shocked dumb to know he'd been courting Liza.

"She must have snuck out, 'cause I seen her," Drake was repeating. "She was leading the goat and smoking the cigar."

"I was not!" Liza screamed.

"So, Mr. Wiseguy. Let's see how tough you are." Superintendent Baker stomped hard and all three hundred pounds came down on the arch of Drake's foot. The boy didn't flinch. "You know what I think, Mr. Bailey? I think it was you that did those things in my office. What do you think of that?"

Drake sucked in his breath before speaking. "I told you what I seen, sir."

Superintendent Baker was already passing on to Uncle Jimmy, who he also drew up close to.

"I figure you're a wiseguy, too." He paused and we waited for the other shoe to drop.

"No, sir. I just wanted you to know that Liza had an alibi."

"I'm going to give you the benefit of the doubt. This is your first day here. Any more lip and you get the same as your friend." He then turned about, climbed the steps, signalled for the bell to ring, and we marched inside.

At that point I could still see events in terms of God's will. God had willed that Drake flunk two grades and he'd flunked one on his own. Uncle Jimmy, I knew, had dropped out a couple of years back in Savannah to work. The rest of us were about where we belonged, all together in one big room for the first few hours. The teacher was young and almost pretty. A school mistress's pay was a king's ransom in that land of retired planters and most married soon. This one, though, had already been here three months and she wasn't even engaged yet. Her name was Miss Gaye.

Her first real question was, "What is a binomial?" Drake didn't know. Neither did I. Brother answered, "I don't know." Uncle Jimmy admitted he didn't know either but claimed Brother had already studied all kind of mathematics in Savannah and knew it about as well as a college professor. Miss Gaye was warned that Brother could do any schoolwork put to him, but he'd answer any spoken question with, "I don't know." My cousin went on to suggest that his girlfriend Liza would know the answer and he pointed to Liza who sat with her arms folded glaring straight ahead. Liza said Mr. Allson presumed a lot by calling her his girlfriend. Despite the fact she'd allowed him to call on her the previous evening, she considered the two of them to be barely acquainted. She then defined a binomial to the teacher's satisfaction. Drake lay his head down on the desk and was soon snoring lightly. I buried my face in the algebra book.

I can't exactly say why Liza and I didn't get along. We were distant cousins on the Matthews side and for a while she'd spent a lot of time visiting at our house. I guess living with her crazy mama wasn't all that entertaining, and my parents seemed to take pleasure in her company. Up until the previous September, Grandpa had even called her

Daughter. Still she was always doing what she could to torment me. Not that this was so unusual, because except for her two pals, Uncle Albert's Margarite and Leala Fitchum, Liza McGill looked down her nose at all her schoolmates.

Her pa, Dr. McGill, had a Stanley that he'd converted to run on pine knots and polished 'til it hurt. And every Sunday he'd pull up in the churchyard, get down, and draw a line in the sand around the automobile. "Don't touch her, boys," he'd announce to us. Then he'd pass out pennies to those gathered about to make sure she stayed untouched. Of course, all this time Liza and her crazy mama would be sitting inside the car. We'd take the pennies and then the two women, wearing their Crowns Bluff finery, would go parading into church like they were the queens of England.

Uncle Jimmy would have seen that show himself if he hadn't skipped church. It wasn't my fault entirely, but I should have warned him, which is what I tried to do at recess.

"She's mean as a snake," I said.

"High spirited," he whispered back.

"Her pa has done stole the Allson Place and got the dowry, too."

"You know that ain't so."

Well, it was sort of true. Dr. McGill had bought the Allson Place from us three months before by paying off the two mortgages that my pa had accumulated while he was farming out there for Grandpa. It was a fair price, more than fair probably, but the old man had still been upset, and the business about the dowry had only made it worse. Way before the War, when Grandpa had married his first wife, Mary Matthews, he'd received along with the plantation, a considerable collection of valuable jewelry and silverware. And this dowry had been mislaid when the Yankees slipped up the river and burned the place down. The Allsons had been searching ever since, digging and poking about in vain, at least until now.

"What about the gentleman's agreement?" I reminded.

"That'd be an encumbrance, Willie T. You know that."

"The McGills done poisoned your mind, Jimmy. Ain't no such thing."

Maybe such a thing as an encumbrance did exist, but Grandpa didn't believe it. When the deeds were signed over the old man had asked for a gentleman's agreement that would allow the Allsons to keep searching for the dowry until the end of time. The doctor seemed to be genuinely fond of Grandpa and would take the time to discuss modern times and all that electricity that was coming. Still, besides being a competent physician, the little man was something of a freethinker and a businessman as well. He claimed such an agreement would cloud his title. Grandpa, in a rage, declared that the doctor's wife had plotted to swindle the Allson family out of what was rightfully theirs. The sale had to go through, but we were no longer to speak to anyone named McGill.

"Grandpa won't stand for you and that girl being together."

Uncle Jimmy dismissed this with a shrug. Maybe he saw himself as Romeo and Liza as Juliet. I couldn't say, and in fact, I'd already stretched myself pretty thin with the objections. The Allson Place had really been lost long years before. And, if the truth were known, maybe the doctor had done us all a favor. I hated Liza too much to say this, though, and so stood back and hoped that nature would take its course.

It did. The doctor, with Liza beside him, began picking my cousin up from the grocery each afternoon, and though he wouldn't stop the steamer, the freethinker would slow it down enough for Uncle Jimmy to jump off at our house. Then, without any complaint from Grandpa, my cousin would eat, wash up, and go to sit in the parlor of the McGills' mansion.

"You ought to see that place, Willie T. Floors is polished like marble and they got a cook and two maids."

"I wasn't invited."

"You know you're welcome."

"That ain't likely."

The romance lasted less than a week. On the Friday evening before Ruth and Naomi disappeared, Uncle Jimmy came home early and announced to me that Liza McGill was awful high and mighty and would soon learn that she was not the only fish in the bright blue ocean. He wasn't willing to elaborate and I was happy enough just to accept that life would be getting back to normal. Except life since my cousins' arrival couldn't truly be described as normal. I'd already had to rethink an awful lot of thoughts.

"Good," I said and went back to my own room.

Brother was there. Grandpa had given him the clock that had sat unticking on our mantel since forever, and working on his bed with only an old peeling knife, the boy had almost gutted the heirloom. When I entered, he stopped working and stared at me with his black eyes.

"Y'all was all in here," he said.

"Who?" I'd started undressing.

"Drake and your pa. Man in a hat, and Liza and another girl and an old woman. Was more besides that. All of them crowded around." He indicated his own bed with a circling hand.

"You done had a busy evening." Down to my drawers, I was kneeling for my prayers.

"I was kind of glad at first, 'cause y'all was real quiet. A bright light was shining and that made these walls start glowing." The walls of the room were panelled in dirty clapboard as was the ceiling. "Everybody was smiling, getting along fine, and then the lights start dimming and y'all started arguing 'bout how you was going to murder me and chop me up."

"You was dreaming, Brother. Ain't nothing but a dream."

"No. No, it wasn't. All a sudden we is all outside and the bed is a boat. I'm floating, you see, where y'all can't get at me, and I can feel the ocean rocking me and hear Pap calling me from underwater. Was this gurgling kind of underwater sound and I remember thinking, 'Good, I'm dead.' And then all of a sudden I'm back here in this room and y'all is arguing about cutting me up so you can eat me. It started over. Same thing kept happening again and again."

"Brother, dreams ain't real."

"Weren't a dream. I was dead."

"It was a dream. You ain't dead. Let me go to sleep."

"I looked straight at you, Willie T. Your eyeballs was bright red and when you opened your mouth, wasn't nothing but fangs inside."

"That ain't so." I got up off my knees and opened my mouth with my fingers. He took a look inside and then settled back.

"Wasn't just you," he said. "Was all of them."

"All who?"

"I can hear 'em talking." Brother cocked his head slightly and did appear to be listening.

Mercy

IF A person is inclined to search out first causes, losing the cows and then ignoring Maum Anna's warning that the swamp was a place of devils is certainly an easy one to spot. But I can't help thinking that the arrival of my cousins was somehow an ingredient. Without Uncle Jimmy's adventuresome nature none of what follows would have happened. But perhaps it is a mistake even to search out such causes, for how can we be certain the first is the culprit? Perhaps it is the second or third cause, or a cause as immediate as the moment preceding catastrophe. At that gentle stage of the game, I was ignorant of such things and am hardly better off now. The fact was we had left Naomi out on the island and now the time had come to rescue her.

Uncle Jimmy woke me earlier than usual, and while I hustled Sammy from his shed, he picked up halter and line from the tack. Brother was to milk Ruth, who'd be getting a holiday in the barn.

"Home for breakfast," my cousin assured me when we stepped out onto the marsh edge at daybreak.

"Don't see her," I whispered.

"She's there," he said confidently, and motioned us on.

Quickly, I led the way back down the creek and, pointing at the confusion of footprints and hoofprints, began once more to recite my adventure. My cousin hushed me, but it was hard not to mention my growing concern.

"What if she froze to death?"

"It ain't freezing."

"You think she's dead? Drowned maybe?" I asked Sammy who was coming behind me.

Uncle Jimmy wouldn't let him answer. We'd reached the end of the creek and in secret he traced out a rough map of the area on the muddy sand. We were to execute a double-flanking attack, a military strategy far superior to the clumsy encirclement that Sammy and I had carried out the afternoon before. Sammy would head around the north side of the island, I the south, while Uncle Jimmy went through the middle. On signal, we proceeded to do this only to meet emptyhanded on the far side. Naomi had outmaneuvered us. She was not on the island at all, but standing in the edge of the bay, a foot deep in mud and water. Her hot breath spread a tiny camouflaging fogbank about her head and front quarters.

The cow appeared asleep and no more than fifty feet separated us but it was open ground—open water for the last ten feet. Uncle Jimmy motioned us again into the flanking formation and with a wave moved us on. Closer and closer we drew. Uncle Jimmy now with rope and halter held up before him, slipped into the water while Sammy and I waded wide and quiet. I held my breath as my cousin began to bring the rigging into position. Naomi stirred and flicked an ear, turning her head a quarter angle as if to assist in her own capture.

"There, girl," Uncle Jimmy whispered low. "Easy now, easy now." At the touch of leather on her nose, the cow leaped forward clear of the water while Sammy and I both scrambled to latch onto her tail. Galloping up the bank and around the far side of the island, she cut back through it once, practically running over the three of us and then plunging chest-deep through a patch of soft mud, careened down the creek bank. Trapped? No, gentle Naomi followed a long oyster bed into the bay, and finally arrived at the same spot we'd discovered her, only a foot or so deeper in the water.

"I swear that cow flew," Uncle Jimmy was laughing. "She's got wings. You see 'em, Sammy? Little bat wings just aft of her front quarters."

Sammy was actually smiling. There we were, panting, covered with mud and icy water, the tide was rising, school was starting, no cow. It didn't make sense that Sammy and Uncle Jimmy were grinning at each other.

"Was like this yesterday," I said. "Only we had two of 'em to chase."

"Don't see where this is much easier now that you got the poor animal spooked."

"Me?" I said. "It ain't my fault."

"Listen," he said. "You boys hide. I'll go read this cow the terms of surrender."

We crouched out of sight, but as my cousin advanced Naomi simply retreated, backing further and further into the bay. He shook his head and waded ashore.

"Won't do, boys," he said. "If she turns and swims, she won't stop 'til Italy, and if she comes ashore again, she'll break a leg bucking in this mud."

"So?" I asked.

"Like Grandpa said, we got to find The Hard to Catch Mercy."

"No," I said. "We got to get to school."

"I heard about this Mercy fellow," my cousin went on. "Don't charge but two bits. Cow's worth that, ain't she?"

I shook my head no and then yes.

"I know I'm right. The Hard to Catch is our only prayer."

Our prayer? We were praying to get shot or bullwhipped to death and it could happen even before we found the man.

"Sammy'll stay here and watch Naomi. You and me will go searching."

I followed but when we reached the downed rail, I stayed behind looking for Liza's footprints. Then I had to run to catch up. Unfortunately, my mama didn't object to the plan as I hoped she would and Maum Anna went about the kitchen clucking to herself and not repeating a single word of her previous warning.

Now, I've never been much for horseback riding, which is probably why Uncle Jimmy was kind enough to claim our horse, Rose, and give me Gal to ride. Gallant was her complete name, and she was a broke-to-saddle mule, half-broke anyway, with a mind fully her own. She bit and kicked but never without first laying back her ears and braying so you knew the unavoidable was coming. To my surprise, though, Gal started out the morning well-mannered enough. She let me get on with only mild objection, and soon we had crossed the King's Highway and were traveling towards a place I'd never been to and had never intended to visit.

The Swamp Road itself was adventure enough for me. It soon narrowed and dropped into a muddy wagon-rutted bog that twisted through a forest of giant knobby-kneed cypress, then turned into swamp pure and simple. Though this was the dry season, our mounts were splashing along up to their bellies in some places, and the water was so high and wide that nothing marked our way but an occasional slash on a tree trunk and a vague indentation in the branches above. My cousin laughed. Bottomless pools, quicksand, it was all the same to him. "Anything to save Naomi." Suddenly, that was his motto, though before this particular morning cows hadn't been a major concern of his. At last the road broke free of the water, and then it forked.

"Which way?" he asked.

I guessed left and he went right, a process of elimination he'd use twice more. Without once stopping to ask directions, we passed by a number of sorry cabins and small clearings. They seemed to gradually worsen in appearance. Much of the woods here was cut over and burned to make pasture. At home we followed the same practice, but this land seemed bleaker—worn down. In the bottoms, the trees still grew to full heights and cast the suspect ground below in deep brown shadows.

Curiously, terms like "poor buckra" and "white trash" were never used in my house. I guess my parents assumed we were all members of one giant Christian brotherhood, but Grandpa was the true democrat. "We fought the good fight together!" the old man would shout. A white man was a white man and every white man was a voter. He knew this because after the War, he'd come in here to organize the voting that ran the Republicans and the Negroes out of office, and later he'd directed the balloting that sectioned off Clarke County. This last one hadn't worked out as he hoped because the Clarkesville thieves had betrayed him and made their town and not his the county seat. Still, that was no fault of the Brittle Branch voters. Grandpa claimed each was as good as the next man, and the Mercy family that had once been in his employ were better than most.

My own opinion was closer to Maum Anna's. These

people might not actually be devils, but they lived by different rules—not Christian or even American. They were a rough bunch, hard men who ran cattle and hogs on the swamp range and did some occasional trapping. All grew their own food, made their own whiskey, and ignored completely the dictates of the outside world. Murder was settled between families or went unpunished. Stealing was simply an abbreviated form of swapping. We all knew the Negroes were waiting on the day to set up their island kingdom, but Brittle Branch had been on its own since the beginning of time. Fortunately for us, its inhabitants had no dreams of conquest and were, in fact, the most reluctant of visitors. A cow man might find his way into Cedar Point to buy a little ammunition and tobacco. On a blue moon, an entire family might straggle in to watch while the head of the household bought a few yards of cloth, some salt, and apples. Most had never visited us at all, and certainly none had sent an engraved invitation our way. No, only Grandpa's good name could protect us in this forsaken, lawless place. Except we had no opportunity to invoke it. For at least an hour we saw no face unfriendly or otherwise, and then in the middle of pure wilderness my cousin stopped.

"Here?" I questioned, reluctant to give up the uncertain safety of the road for the even more treacherous path he was suggesting. "Ain't nothing here."

"Can't you read?" He pointed at a crudely lettered sign propped against the base of a tree trunk.

"MERCY" it said. "HARD TO CATCH ANIMALS CAUGHT FOR A PRICE." My cousin charged off, I nudged Gal to follow, and moments later entered behind him onto a swept dirt clearing containing a small pole cabin and, beyond that, a barn and sheds. Inside a rambling rail corral, a great menagerie of motley livestock moved like shadows beneath the grander shadow of the surrounding forest. Uncle Jimmy tied off his mount and instructed me to do the same.

"Hello!" he shouted several times. Some penned dogs howled a greeting.

We crossed halfway to the cabin and he called again. The door cracked and a woman's voice called back.

"What business you have here?"

"My name is James Allson and this here is Willie T. Allson. I'm the grandson of Colonel Allson over Cedar Point way and this is his grandson, too. We come to see Mr. Mercy."

There was silence.

"We got a cow that needs to be caught," Uncle Jimmy continued.

"I know who you is," the voice said. "Your grandpa is old man Allson."

"Yes, ma'am," my cousin said. "The Colonel. Can you help us, ma'am?"

"I wouldn't help you even if you wasn't Allsons."

My cousin completely ignored this discouraging reply.

"Is Mr. Mercy here?" he asked.

"No," the voice answered.

"Let's go," I whispered.

"Could you tell us where to find him?"

"No!" the voice shouted back. "Now get out of here."

I saw the barrel of a shotgun protruding through the door crack and began to back away.

"Don't mean to alarm you, ma'am," my cousin called back, not moving an inch, "But this is something of an emergency and I have it from a reliable source that this was the home of Mr. Mercy who caught hard-to-catch animals for people."

"It was." A face appeared out through the crack in the door, but the features were hidden by shadows. "But he ain't here no more."

"Could you tell us where to find him?"

"Waist deep in Hell, I would hope!" This was shouted without a trace of good feeling.

"I see," my cousin said. "Then we best be heading on. Thank you for your time." Giving her a slight bow, he rejoined me at the edge of the path where I asked him why he didn't bid her an *adieu* and fond farewell while he was at it. He put a big foot in the stirrup and swung up with a laugh that told me our search was only starting.

The next stop was a store that lay over another bottom at another fork in the road. I suppose it was the one Grandpa had spoken of. It was the only store we'd come to and obviously had been there for some years—and would probably remain for a thousand more. The walls were not made of poles, but huge cypress logs, and the roof was sheathed in broad expanses of bark. There were no windows, only a narrow slit of a door that stood partially open. Insisting this was indeed the place, my cousin bounded from the horse, and commanded me to follow. I dismounted without enthusiasm and was immediately nipped on the back of the leg by a gray mongrel hound that appeared out of nowhere. Once fastened, the dog held onto my pantsleg despite a vigorous shaking and jumping about. Finally, Uncle Jimmy gave the animal a kick that sent it yelping into the woods, and motioned for me to come along inside.

Yes, it was definitely a store. Once your eyes grew accustomed to the dark, you could even see merchandise—a couple of harnasses, an axe, some unopened barrels. There was even a proprietor. He sat asleep in a chair beside a clay-chinked fireplace, which at present held only dead ashes. Uncle Jimmy, spotting the man, backed up and pushed me once more back out into the sunlight. Then he gave a respectable but resounding knock and called out, "Howdy."

The man stirred, gave us a sleepy-eyed stare and ran a hand through his dirty white hair. He was heavyset, unshaved, and wore only ragged long johns. Two bare feet pushed towards us as he stretched in the chair and yawned.

"James Allson," my cousin stepped in and extended his hand. "This is Willie T. Allson. Both of us from over at Cedar Point."

"Yep, heard tell of it. Don't get that way much." The proprietor ignored the hand and stayed seated. "Once maybe."

"Once is enough for a lot of folks," my cousin replied.

"Knew Allson Mercy. I can show you the spot where he disappeared at."

"That so," my cousin said.

"Knew a bunch of regular Allsons, too. That election of seventy-six old Colonel Allson brought the ballot box into this same store. Then after a while him and one of his boys cut shingles 'round here."

"Yes, sir," Uncle Jimmy said. "That's our grandpa, Colonel Allson. Willie's pa, Captain Tom, was with him."

"Didn't come back for that ninety election. Young fellow brung the box. Walker. Believe his name was Walker."

"Maybe. That be likely."

"Suppose to elect a county—do something."

"That was the election making this 'round here a separate county." Uncle Jimmy swung an arm around the dark store interior.

"I been wondering about that. This here is Clarke County now, ain't it?"

"Yep."

"That Colgrove boy is sheriff, ain't he?"

"Yep."

"I been telling 'em that." The storekeeper shook his large

head back and forth and again ran a hand through his dirty white hair. "Won't listen."

"The Colonel told us to look you up."

The man rocked back in his chair. My cousin put his hands into his pockets. I stood in the doorway and stared at my feet.

"Tyler Mercy was overseer for Colonel Allson back before the War. Believe I heard the widow talk about the Allson place up on the river." The speaker paused to stick a finger in his ear and shake it. "Talked like it was a palace."

"Yes, sir," my cousin said. "Yankees burned it though."

"Probably so." The proprietor scratched himself idly about the crotch of the long johns. "How's the Colonel doing?"

"Slowed down a bit."

"That so. How old he be now?"

"Ninety-six."

"Ninety-six? Yep, have to be, wouldn't he? I wasn't much more than a boy when I seen him last." The storekeeper brought the chair down, the front legs landing with a distinct crack, and counted on his fingers until he got to ten.

Failing to see how this conversation could possibly bring Naomi home, I tugged on the back of my cousin's coat. Still facing the storekeeper, he knocked my hand away, so I stepped back myself and stood outside the door.

"Eighteen hundred and eighty-one," the storekeeper announced. "Year after that bad winter. They cut 'em shingles."

"It's the Colonel who suggested we look for Mr. Mercy. Said he helped with the mules that same year." My cousin held his palm three feet off the dirt floor. "Was just a boy."

"Probably so. Mercy would been six or twelve back about then."

"Yes, sir, the Colonel said he was the man for the job," my cousin continued.

He finally stepped back out into the yard, though, and the storekeeper followed. In fact, he passed my cousin and, barefoot and wearing only drawers, he waddled over to where I was mounting Gal. The sight disturbed the animal, and with me only having one foot in the stirrup and the other leg not even across the saddle, she began to turn in a tight clockwise circle.

"Nice mule." The storekeeper stopped his advance and was joined by my cousin. "She know any more tricks like that?"

I couldn't tell if he was joking or not. Maybe he thought I had control of the animal.

"Smart mule, all right," Uncle Jimmy agreed. "Willie's taught her a good number of them clever maneuvers."

"That so?"

"Yep, he rides her in the show. You heard of 'em probably. The Electrical Boy and his trick mule Gallant?"

With all the strength at my disposal, I managed to swing my other leg over the saddle and began to try to find the stirrup. The mule continued to circle.

"Never heard of 'em." The man shook his head. "Show don't get back here, but I seen a man once who could juggle four apples." The storekeeper made a juggling motion with both hands.

"That ain't nothing. That mule can juggle four apples." My cousin made the same motion. My foot found the stirrup, and now I groped for the reins.

"Juggling mule? You own her?" The storekeeper was shouting at me, but my cousin answered.

"Willie just acts like she's his. Half belongs to the Colonel and half to Willie's pa." I realized my cousin was cleaning his fingernails with the small blade of his barlow. He was hardly looking in my direction.

"Wouldn't mind owning half myself. Juggling mule be worth a barrel of brandy around here."

"You'd have to buy half the Electrical Boy there, too. Can't go breaking up the act." Uncle Jimmy was closing the knife.

I listened to all I was going to. I had the reins now and before long would bring the mule under control. Turning my body about on the circling animal so that I could face the would-be purchaser, I spoke for the first time and went straight to the matter's heart.

"We're looking for Hard to Catch Mercy!" I shouted. "Can you tell us where he lives?"

"Down there," the man said readily enough. "You passed the place a couple of bends back."

"We been there. Woman run us off." I spoke quickly while I happened to be facing in the right direction.

"That'd be his wife."

"And where would he be?" Twisted in the saddle like a piece of taut hemp line, I hollered over my shoulder and yanked the mule's head counterclockwise.

"That's hard to say. Why you want him, if you don't mind me asking?"

"To catch a cow." Suddenly the mule halted and I rocked back, head spinning.

"That all?"

"Ain't that enough?" Gal cranked up in the opposite direction and began to circle again.

"You wouldn't be the revenue man, would you?"

"Me?" I sputtered. "Me? I ain't but fourteen years old. How could I be the law?" Uncle Jimmy was bent over, hands on his knees, laughing at me.

"You might be one of 'em midgets. How'd I know different?"

It was true I wasn't completely full grown, but still I was only a couple inches shorter than my cousin and clearly much taller than the man who was calling me a midget.

"I ain't a midget!" I shouted.

"Might be a midget on a trick mule sent by the revenue man."

Having Uncle Jimmy openly laughing just made me madder. I kept on shouting back and the mule kept on spinning faster and faster.

"The cow is my responsibility."

"Dangerous?"

"What?" Gal had added a high-kicking buck to her spin.

"Dangerous cow?"

"No. Milk cow."

"You don't need The Hard to Catch Mercy to catch no milk cow." The man laughed out loud for the first time.

"Tell him that!" I shouted, pointing to Uncle Jimmy. I guess my cousin was getting dizzy from watching me, for he reached over, grabbed the mule by an ear, and brought it to a halt.

"Tell him," I said.

But the man didn't tell him, because my cousin broke in to explain it was a delicate situation and we feared for the cow's life. In that case, we were told we had made the right choice. Yes, James Mercy, which was The Hard to Catch's real name, was good with all critters, wild or tame, mean or gentle. At the age of three, his pa, Allson, had sent him out to live with the animals. He'd slept in the barn at first, but was finally put out to roam the woods at will. Yes, indeed, he was familiar with animal ways to the point where some said he was an animal himself, or no better than an animal, as others put it. It took that kind of person, we were assured, to do what he did, and, of course, being mean and fearless and never giving up was what made him absolutely successful. Only the month before, he'd brought in an old razorback hog that was responsible for killing over a dozen dogs and destroying most of the corn acreage in the community. Nobody asked him. He'd just gone out by himself, trapped it alive, and brought it to the store. Then when a crowd gathered, he'd threatened to let the boar go unless a collection was taken up on the spot. He was never one to worry about his popularity, but on the other hand, it didn't take much to satisfy him. The whole crowd together came up with eighteen cents. He took that and shot the hog. That's the kind of man he was. Could catch anything. Yes, we'd come to the right place, but at the wrong time.

"He's hook fight with his wife and that brother of hers," the storekeeper concluded. "Won't find him home 'til they calm down."

"In that case," my cousin asked. "Where do you suggest we look?"

"His grandma's house." The man pointed down the left fork of the road. "First lane past the black stump. That's the Widow Mercy. Treat you right. You tell her you an Allson." Scratching himself at the crotch, he added another, "Probably so."

"Obliged," Uncle Jimmy said, mounting Rose.

"Be careful 'bout showing off that trick mule round these parts," the storekeeper whispered to me. "More than a few would kill for a mule like that."

"Ain't a trick mule," I muttered.

"Don't be modest, Willie T. Man done seen what the animal can do."

"Wouldn't matter. Some would kill for that mule if it could do the tricks or not," the man said. "Watch yourself."

"They'd have to kill. Electrical Boy wouldn't give her up any other way," my cousin volunteered.

"Shut up 'bout this mule, and quit calling me that!"

My cousin raised his hand to calm me and promised the storekeeper we'd return someday. Then the gray mongrel appeared out of the woods and, crouching beside the man, began to growl and make tentative lunges in my direction.

"That dog bite?" my cousin asked.

Assured that it didn't, we headed off once more. Heart and soul, Uncle Jimmy was set on saving Naomi in the most complicated and roundabout way possible, which meant turning at the black stump and riding into another clearing that Uncle Jimmy happily assured me was the property of the Widow Mercy. Built of poles and rough slabs, this cabin was closer to collapsing than the first homestead we'd visited. A few guinea hens chattered away and a small yellow mutt set off yapping and circling the house in a wide run. On the chance someone would come along intent on taking the miserable mule, I got off her, but refused to leave the edge of the clearing. This dog looked harmless but I found a good stick, just in case.

"Come on, Willie T. They might think that strange behavior."

"Strange?" I said. "Me, strange? What about them?"

"Suspicious, too." He'd started for the cabin. Reluctantly, I followed. He knocked and called out, got no response, and knocked again. The door suddenly opened wide.

Standing there was a pretty girl, an amazingly pretty girl, for these woods were not famed for raving beauties. It wasn't a soil likely to nurture anything as delicate as a flower, even a wild one, and those few that did take root wilted before leaving childhood. Nevertheless, here she was. Small and shapely. A face, not sallow and pinched, but bright and well-molded. Her long, straight black hair was tied off with a broad pink ribbon. She smiled at us, causing deep dimples to pop into each cheek.

"Hello," she said. "I couldn't imagine who that was bothering to knock." The voice was soft and musical. She was happy to have company.

Of course, this could only mean trouble for a cousin who couldn't resist flirting with pretty girls and those that weren't as well. Knowing Naomi's life hung in the balance, I didn't allow him to say a single word. I stepped to the front and announced I was Willie T. Allson. This was James Allson. We were the grandsons of Colonel William Allson and we were looking for The Hard to Catch Mercy. Trying to get this all out ahead of my cousin left me breathless, and the girl, who had stopped smiling somewhere along the line, gave me a curious look. I thought she might be deaf or simpleminded, but she was neither.

"That'd be my brother, James," she said. "He was the second son, the third of all us children, and I'm the sixteenth, the youngest of all that lived."

"What's your name?" Uncle Jimmy asked. He removed his bowler and held it over his heart.

"Amy Mercy," she confessed. "Amenda, really. They just call me Amy."

Then Uncle Jimmy went on to introduce us both again and explain who we were and what our mission was. The girl began to smile again. She even laughed, which deepened the dimples further and showed her perfect, pearly white teeth.

"Grandma Mercy is to the wash pot," she sang when my cousin finished, and without further ado, she carried us into the backyard, where a frail old woman was hanging out wash on a line that swooped about the yard like a giant one-string spiderweb. Beside her, more clothes were boiling in a giant black iron wash pot. The little dog and the flock of guineas followed us around to sound an alarm and then went on to other business. The Widow Mercy wasn't living too high on the hog, for there was no other livestock or even pens in back, and the only out-buildings were a couple of open lean-to sheds.

My cousin repeated the introductions for the third time, and Amy Mercy added that we were looking for The Hard to Catch because our cow, Naomi, was stuck in the mud. The old woman listened with her head cocked to one side like an attentive bird. Apparently, she could make us out, but the pupils of her eyes were covered over by a chalky white film. She must have been pretty once herself. Her cheeks were hollow and her skin pasty. At least sixty years of wear separated the widow from her granddaughter, but you could still see a faint resemblance.

Of course, I had plenty of time to make these observations, since on finding out we were the Colonel's grandsons, the Widow went on at some length about the years she and her husband Tyler had spent on the Delta working for Mr. Allson. The Mercys had had a fine house of their own, well off from the quarters, and with a view of the river. She'd run the kitchen behind the big house—Negro women did the work. They'd have stayed forever, if the Yankees hadn't burned it to the ground.

At this point in her narration, the milky white eyes clouded even further with tears. She hadn't seen Mr. Allson in thirty years or better. She remembered both our fathers when they were younger than we were now, and when she discovered that Uncle Jimmy's daddy had drowned, she began to weep so hard it was difficult for her to speak further. The rest of us were fine, my cousin assured her. Grandpa was doing remarkably well for a man his age. My tactful cousin's report was so glowing, I hardly recognized the subject. It worked though. The tears ceased.

"When I cooked for him and them two others, I'd fix enough for five." The Widow Mercy had decided to continue. Uncle Jimmy and the girl were smiling at each other over the old woman's head. "Mr. Allson would eat like that. Eat enough for three all by hisself."

"He's still got a good appetite," my cousin said.

"My pa was like that," the old woman began again. "George Brittle. He was a Clarke, but he called hisself a Brittle. My mama was Martha Brittle. She cooked like that for him, but he never got fat. Men like that don't put on fat. Eat all they want. Nothing but muscle."

"Yes, that's all real interesting," I finally broke in.

"Yes, yes," she agreed, and suddenly began to speak on The Hard to Catch's boyhood at length. Hat still in hand, Uncle Jimmy extended his arm and guided the Widow Mercy back into her cabin where we took shelter in a kitchen decorated only with old calendars depicting scenes from the Bible. Jacob wrestled the angel. The angel spoke to Mary. Christ was taken down from the cross at least a half dozen times. Rocking beside the cook stove, she told how James had been the gentlest of her grandchildren. He'd always had an easy way with animals—birds would feed from his hand. As a young thing, he could whistle them out of the trees and bring all manner of wild creatures into the open with just his calls and whispers. The Methodist circuit rider had compared him to St. Francis. That was the kind of boy he was. "Was a God-given gift," the woman crooned. "Can be no doubt of that. A God-given gift that he has put to good use by helping those who are unfortunate enough to lose their livestock. It's right in the Bible, ain't it, Amy girl?"

"Yes, ma'am. It sure is. Jesus tells about catching the ox in the ditch even on Sunday." The dimples deepened to new depth. Amy's brown eyes were bottomless pools that my cousin might fall into any minute.

"Yes," her grandma added, "Sundays, any day, night or day, if his neighbor called, he went." She might have gone on to enumerate each victory if I hadn't announced it was getting late and we couldn't let the sun set on Naomi again. Reluctantly, the woman agreed and we said good-bye. Amy Mercy escorted us out the front door and across the yard to our mounts. There was no sign of the little dog, but I kept my stick until I was in the saddle.

"You be careful, Willie T.," she confided in me then. "More than one man's died 'round here just for owning a white mule."

"Well, this here mule is brown," I said quietly.

"I reckon that'd be close enough."

My cousin thought this was a good joke, but she didn't laugh or even smile. And she had serious information for him as well. The Hard to Catch's wife had sworn out a warrant for his arrest. Assault and battery. It was a complicated matter, but the girl was sure her brother was guilty of that crime at least.

"Can't say as I blame her. He's a hard man to care about," she finished somberly. "Back Easter time, hog bear tore him up so bad—he'd have died then if Grandma hadn't took him. Wife didn't care. Not if he lived or died. Some did, though." She stopped and gave a kind of half laugh. "Some 'round here was disappointed."

"Do you got any idea where he might be now?" my cousin asked with surprising directness. I'd at least expected him to inquire into who wanted Mercy dead.

"No, wish I could help you. I truly do." She smiled

her deep-dimpled smile. The brown eyes flashed at Uncle Jimmy and he smiled back in a manner entirely inappropriate to the subject at hand.

"Is there anybody else in the family living nearby?" he asked.

"Our sister Glo. Right over there a ways." She motioned off in a direction even further away from Cedar Point. "I don't know if she'd be much help to you. It's her husband that is the cause of the trouble."

"Let's go," I whispered. "Dark soon." I nudged the valuable mule forward. Then had to haw her about. My cousin hadn't even mounted up.

"How's that?" Uncle Jimmy asked Amy Mercy.

"He's the brother of James's wife. He's the one really responsible for her going and swearing out that warrant."

"A brother and sister married to a brother and sister?"

"Yes."

"Let's be headed on now, cousin," I coaxed.

"Hush, Willie T. Be patient."

So I sat there patiently and listened while the girl related a series of complex events that began with a cattle deal made between The Hard to Catch Mercy and his brother-in-law. Apparently, they were stealing cows from each other, cows that had been stolen to begin with. Amy ended with some business about a busted axletree and the assault charge.

"We'll go see your sister Glo," Uncle Jimmy announced, mounting up and replacing his hat at last.

"Do that," the girl declared happily.

"Was a pleasure making your acquaintance." My cousin waved good-bye and gave a tip of the bowler for good measure. He'd actually started riding away, but then reined up. "That's a pretty pink ribbon you got there in your hair," he called to her.

"Glad you like it. Most folks round here don't notice such things." She touched the ribbon and waved good-bye to my cousin. He waved good-bye to her and, catching up with me, asked if I didn't think that was a pretty pink ribbon the girl was wearing. I urged the valuable mule on, refusing to say another word, and absolutely refusing to enter the next cabin. Glo and the brother-in-law who was the cause of all the trouble lived there, and of course, Uncle Jimmy was immediately invited inside. I separated myself from Gallant to a point where ownership or even knowledge of the mule could be denied. Then I put my back to a tree and with a healthy limb held two half-breed curs at bay for the couple of eternities it took my cousin to emerge with good news. He, James Allson, had personally straightened out the matter between the feuding family members. We would deliver a note he'd written for this couple to the wife, urging her to drop the charges against her husband. She would then send a note by us to Judge Walker, and in return, the word would be passed through the community that the Allson family had a cow that needed catching. Uncle Jimmy seemed quite proud of this diplomatic accomplishment, and didn't appear at all concerned for our safety on the ride back. By this time, I'd decided if anyone showed the least interest in the mule, I'd accept an IOU and ride home double on Rose. We saw no one, though—even the store appeared locked and abandoned when we passed by. My cousin hummed to himself and whistled all the way back to the first cabin, and once there he walked straight up on the porch and delivered his message to The Hard to Catch's wife. The woman put aside her shotgun and invited him in, and when he emerged, it was carrying the second note for the magistrate, a jar of fig preserves, and a dozen eggs.

Mrs. Mercy followed behind him, toting a baby on her

hip. A second child stumbled along clinging to her skirt. She was big—big-boned, well-muscled—but still fairly handsome, almost healthy. The flesh around one eye was slightly discolored, but that was the only evidence of battery I could see.

"Nice mule," she said to my cousin.

The dogs were still penned, but reasoning that a mule as coveted as this one could surely outrun the competition, I'd decided to remain mounted. With her free hand, the big woman slapped Gal's flank and when the animal kicked out at her, she easily stepped aside.

"You tell the Judge that it's true he struck me with assault and battery, but I reckon I'm a grown woman who can defend herself."

"I'll tell him," Uncle Jimmy agreed, beginning to ride away.

"Tell the Judge I'm only sorry he didn't kill me outright, or me him. You tell the Judge that," she called after us.

My cousin went on nodding politely to these unsettling remarks. Then when we reached the road, he began to explain to me about the cattle deal and the ill feelings, and how he suspected the trouble had deeper roots. At any moment I expected to be ambushed—shot from the saddle. My companion had already slipped the preserves into his coat pocket, and now he passed me the eggs. I cradled the little bag under my arm, but half of them broke almost at once. A sticky, yellow mess went running down my front and I pitched the gift into the woods as he resumed his speech.

"You see, Willie T., it appears to me the Mercys never accepted this woman here into the family or else she and her brother never wanted to be accepted, and The Hard to Catch is just an innocent bystander who gets caught up in the arguments." We were supposed to be saving a cow, and now my cousin had us settling domestic disputes in a place where a man could die just for riding a trick mule, a white mule—even this mule.

"Leave me alone." My cousin quieted down and didn't speak again until we'd started to ford our way back to civilization. Of course, at that point I was a truly captive audience.

"I never did finish telling you about when Anna come to your mama, did I?" he shouted back over his shoulder.

"I ain't talking to you."

"Let's see, now where'd I leave off?"

"I ain't listening."

"Oh, yeah. Anna had showed up chained, and your mama insisted on keeping her in the house. Anna worked out pretty good in the house, started right out cooking, so between her and your mama the housework got done. My grandma couldn't be much help. She was still lying abed weakened considerably from her activities. Got up after my pap was born, though. Didn't have much choice being as your fourteen-year-old mama and Anna had run off to Virginia.

"Where?" I couldn't help asking. "Where was they?"

"They was in Virginia. You know that, Willie T."

"I don't got to know it. My mama's hardly been to Clarkesville!" My shouts caused the mule to lay back her ears.

"You know your pa died?"

"Died? Blasphemy!" Gal side stepped in the belly-deep water, but I nudged her forward with a hard kick.

"Ain't blasphemy." My cousin braced himself with extended arm across Rose's rump and looked me in the eye. "It's the simple bald-faced truth, cousin. Your pa was charging down that hillside and a shell landed near on top of him. Yanks took him for dead. Our own burial detail was hauling him away when he come to and waved a halt to the proceedings." Uncle Jimmy wiggled his own hand up and around and then declared with a morbid enthusiasm, "Lazarus back from the dead! Plenty was dying but very few coming back, so the physicians took a special interest. Besides the deafness, though, there was only a nick on one knuckle. That was gangrenous, so that finger was amputated. Your pa wrote home saying he was well."

"Wasn't just his finger!" I shouted, my temper rising again.

"Hold on now, hold on." My cousin raised his palm to quiet me. "Two weeks later his hand was cut off at the wrist. He wrote a second letter then, saying he'd been reading a Bible and taking comfort in it. God willing, he'd be seeing them in Heaven.

"When this news reached home, Grandpa wept, prayed for his oldest boy's recovery, and told them the matter was in God's hands. That night your mama stole the mule and wagon and the five gold pieces that were hers anyway, and run off with her chained nursemaid. Took 'em two weeks to get there and they saw right off the doctoring was poor 'cause they had to drive the wagon past these big mountains of butchered off arms and legs, and all that time they could hear the screams of more men being sawed apart."

By now, I'd let the reins drop and put my hands to my ears, but there was no escaping this new torture. My cousin just shouted and the mule kept wading.

" 'Course, you know, they'd been whittling some more on your pa. They'd cut again below the elbow, then above it. Then they'd gone on up 'most to the armpit. They couldn't have gone no higher unless they planned to cut out his heart, so they stuck him off on a stretcher with a few thousand others and left him in God's care—that care being the prompt and eternal variety. Your pa lingered, though. Was several more days before he finally stopped tossing, and that's when an orderly pulled his stretcher out of the ranks and drew a blanket over his face. It was a miracle, luckiest day of your life, Willie T. Them two girls went up and down the rows looking at all them hundreds and then, when they couldn't find him they started pulling back the blankets and looking at the dead. They found him and Anna scooped up that wasted-away body in her arms and declared that the man wasn't truly dead. The orderlies didn't appreciate it. They insisted to all the other patients, them that could hear, that this man was truly dead and was being carried off for burial."

I took my hands down from my ears and hissed. "You said we was coming out here to save a cow."

"We will. We will." My cousin slapped Rose's rump with his broad palm. "But this story needs telling. You see Anna and your ma stretched the body out in the back of the wagon and headed home. They was halfway out of Virginia when Lee went over to Appomattox and surrendered. That night your ma stopped at a farmhouse and borrowed a file to cut the chains off of Anna's ankles. She didn't run. 'Course not. Anna just sat there, like she had every night, bathing the stump of your pa's arm and caring for him the best she could. They didn't have no real medicine but she'd pick stuff growing on the side of the road and mix up potions to put both inside and outside of the patient. All night she'd sit up with him and then at dawn they'd start out again. Three weeks they went like that. The gold had been spent long since, so there was nothing to eat except berries and roots and what they could beg. Most people were kind but they had a few close scrapes 'fore they made it home.

"'Course Grandpa was obligingly happy and forgave the theft. Hard to object, since his son was saved and especially since Captain Jack Cage had recently ended his blockade-running days by dying in prison. So here's your ma, just a girl, unrelated, and now an orphan to boot. Didn't matter. Soon as she got back, my hot-blooded grandma, Cynthia Beed, got back in bed and stayed there 'til she died nine-teen years later. Wasn't no question about it. From there on out your ma was the mistress of the house. She married your pa, Tom Allson, when she reached the proper age of sixteen. She raised my pap and four daughters for Cynthia Beed, had four of her own, and then she had you, Willie, and here you are riding along right beside me."

Apparently he expected a response now, and as the story had gone on, I had in fact warmed to it. Still, I didn't want to give him the satisfaction of believing even a single word.

"Fine tale, Jimmy. That's a fine tale, 'cept nobody else has ever told it to me. Uncle Albert claims he got Pa from Virginia."

"Scandal. All of them old people always worrying 'bout what people will think. Ain't enough to get your pa back alive, not if people are going 'round saying your ma was too young to be heading off on her own."

"All right. I ain't saying that parts couldn't have hap-pened."

"No 'parts' about it. True telling and it's 'most done." He pointed his finger at me. "Now, Anna was a free woman when she got back. The Yankees told her she could pick a last name and like some others she picked Allson." Rose was stepping out onto the dry River Road and my cousin faced forward and stretched. "Yes, sir, she was free to go and Grandpa was more than a little disappointed when she didn't. I don't know if you ever noticed but he don't like Anna." His voice lowered to a mock whisper, and he looked back at me one last time. "Never did and, unless he changes pretty quick, don't guess he ever will." I thought he'd finished, but he grinned. "Oh, yeah. Her being a witch. That's what made her grow so much once she got home. She was just above average before the trip. Then she growed to seven feets and folks around here knew for certain she was consorting with the devil." He put his attention to the road once more, but even with his back to me I could tell he was laughing. I let my cousin have his joke, but made a silent and solemn vow to myself, that once the cow business was settled, I'd put an end to his tale-telling. For now I just followed along.

For the two harrowing hours it took us to ride and swim our way back to Cedar Point, we hadn't passed a single soul, and by the time we got home, I felt secure enough to follow Uncle Jimmy inside the mercantile. Despite being tired and angry, I was curious to see Judge Walker's reaction to the note.

The duly sworn officer was settled in at the rear of his store, surrounded by three others who'd taken up winter residency around his stove. The loiterers knew about our search and saw little hope of success. The Hard to Catch was definitely driving cattle above Mumford or maybe handling mules down in Florida. The judge expressed no opinion on the man's whereabouts and when Uncle Jimmy handed over the note, he only glanced at it.

"She's always requesting them warrants, and then changing her mind about prosecuting." The note disappeared into a cubbyhole of the judge's desk. "I don't bother issuing the papers."

"I figured as much." Uncle Jimmy hid his surprise well enough considering how proud he was of all his courthouse maneuvering. "Delivering it was my part of the bargain, though."

Some jokes about trying to catch The Hard to Catch Mercy followed and there was general agreement that if he did show up, we were in luck. He was the best man with animals in the state, maybe even the nation. Then Uncle Jimmy and I excused ourselves. Judge Walker followed us outside, started a sentence he didn't finish, and then began again in a quiet voice.

"You boys stay away from The Hard to Catch. He's more trouble than he's worth. Way more."

Coming from the uncle of Drake Bailey, that was faint praise indeed. Uncle Jimmy said he'd keep it in mind. The message from the wife about them killing each other off wasn't going to be delivered at all. I nodded to the judge. Cow or no cow, we were lucky not to have found the man, but my cousin was taking this as a defeat. He vowed we'd catch Naomi ourselves before nightfall. Thankful and even a bit proud that we'd survived the trip, I agreed and rode along slightly behind. Then, two blocks from the house, we saw a horseman approaching from a side lane.

"That's him, ain't it?" my cousin demanded. "That's Mercy."

Though I didn't share in his obvious delight, I was quick to whisper, "Yes. Yes, sir, that's him all right. That's him."

Uncle Jimmy halted Rose, who was now impatient for the barn, and raised his hand in greeting to the horse-man. Horseman? The term would serve for both animal and rider, for horse and man gave the impression of being joined together like a strange mythical being. Together or separate, though, they weren't nearly so grand—at least not in an ordinary way. Certainly the horse was not much to look at. The animal barely stood fourteen hands, and beneath a moth eaten dirty white hide, his bones showed clear for the counting. Still, the pony was quick, you could see that. Even at an amble, it appeared ready to bolt on command, to jump left or right. Here was an animal that could take wing and fly. I was a poor judge of such things, but the horse had talents, and the same could be said for the man's dog. With the head of a bulldog and the body of a hound, Mercy's dog could run down any living creature and crush it with a single bite. Dogs? The canines I'd been holding at bay during the course of this long day were at least recognizable as domesticated. Not this one—there was nothing to suggest the animal was man's best friend, and I suppose the same could have been said for The Hard to Catch Mercy.

I'd never seen him up close, and even now his face was half hidden by a great flapping strawhat. Still, there was no mistaking the hardness in the man. The eyes were bright and dark, sunk deep beneath the shaggy eyebrows. Truly, he could have hypnotized birds the way a snake does, except nothing else about him was snakelike. His nose blossomed out in the center of the face like a misplaced rose, and beneath that spread a long drooping mustache that lifted away from the stained beard when he opened his mouth to spit tobacco. Half the front teeth on one side were missing. The clothes—the clothes didn't fit. The man was still broad across the shoulders, but you could tell he'd lost considerable weight. An extra yard of dirty cotton shirt was stuffed into the waist of pants cinched tight with a scrap of rein. And the bagging canvas legs of the pants ballooned from the tops of knee-high boots.

Yes, seen from a safe distance, perhaps in a photograph,

I suppose The Hard to Catch could have appeared ridiculous. Up close and in person, though, there was nothing comical about him, nothing at all. That was good news, at least, for Naomi. I knew my cousin wasn't going to say, "Wait, you're more trouble than you're worth," so in exchange for a day's searching and twenty-five cents we'd be getting a serious man, horse, and dog—and serious armaments as well. A rifle stuck in the scabbard of the near side, and the stock of a shotgun showed on the far. A lariat hung over the saddle horn, a bullwhip looped over that, and from his homemade belt hung a knife that could have been mistaken for a sword.

"James Allson," my cousin said in introduction. The Hard to Catch looked him over in passing but didn't acknowledge the greeting. "We the ones been looking for you," my cousin added, addressing the man's back.

Now I was positive that we didn't need this man. The Hard to Catch Mercy looked me over with a quick glance, and then I ceased to exist. He was studying only on the mule. Oh, yes, we should have caught that cow ourselves. The rider passed within a hair's breath of me and was on his way. Uncle Jimmy was mounting up.

"So?" I said when it was safe to whisper. "Let's forget it."

"Follow him," my cousin said.

We did and were soon standing in our own front yard. Mercy sat mounted, waiting silently at the gate. Uncle Jimmy made no further attempts at conversation. Though I dismounted, he told me to wait there and went inside. I kept to the man's back so he wouldn't look at me again but still had to abide a terrifying sniffing over by the hog dog. Finally, it went exploring elsewhere. Mercy passed the time chewing and spitting and taking an occasional glance at Gal, who I'd tied off on the fence. After what seemed like the better part of an afternoon, my cousin appeared with Grandpa, who hobbled forward on his cane and took up a tottering stance before the horse and rider.

"That you, Mercy?" He didn't wait for a reply, it pleased me to see. "What business you got here?"

"Heard about your cow, Colonel." The voice was surprisingly musical. Even more so than his sister Amy's. The voice rose and fell on every other word in a distinct rhythm.

"What cow?" Grandpa asked.

"Naomi," Uncle Jimmy prompted. "She's stuck on the island. Remember?"

The old man shook his head no. He didn't understand. Uncle Jimmy stepped up close by The Hard to Catch and spoke to him in a loud whisper.

"He asked us to get you. He done forgot, that's all."

The Mercy studied Grandpa another moment before giving his full attention to Uncle Jimmy.

"You got a name?"

"James Allson, and this here's my cousin Willie T." Uncle Jimmy actually pointed me out to the man.

"James Mercy," the other announced in his singsong. He turned in the saddle and stared in my direction, then gave his attention to my cousin.

"You get our message?" Uncle Jimmy asked.

"Heard about the cow." The voice still rose and fell in that strange singing rhythm.

"We just come back from Judge Walker's."

"That so?" The horseman spit to one side.

"Took care of the warrant business."

"Didn't get no message about no warrant business." The singsong of the words was almost hypnotizing.

"You ain't been home?"

"Been at the store. Told me 'bout the cow."

"Appreciate you coming," my cousin said. "Mighty kind of you to take the time."

A sharp whistle from Mercy caused me to jump and his dog to start running.

"Be dark 'fore long," he said.

Grandpa watched without speaking, but when Mercy tipped his hat to the old man, he nodded back. It fell to me to return the invalid to the house, and then gallop the mule to catch up with the rescue party at the pasture. At this point, my cousin and I proceeded on foot, but Mercy continued on horseback. The hog dog ran out ahead, circling around on occasion to check our progress. Back through the hickories we went, the little horse stepping lightly. No words were spoken until we came out on the edge of the marsh.

"There's where we left her." Uncle Jimmy pointed to the island.

"Ain't gotta tell me that," the rider sang softly. He took off his hat and used it to motion high in the sky.

Far above turkey buzzards drifted in a lazy circle. The Hard to Catch urged the little horse down the creek bed and we followed. On the edge of the bay Sammy waited, standing guard over the dead Naomi. Shortly after we left, he'd managed to coax the cow from the water by offering her smilax, but after getting only this far, she'd collapsed. Nothing he did could get her up again, and sometime after midday, she'd died. By this time, the buzzards were gathering, so he'd stayed on to protect the carcass.

While Sammy was chewing his lip and telling this story with much feeling and many apologies, The Hard to Catch Mercy sat on the horse hardly listening or even noticing the dead animal. When Sammy was done, though, the rider spit to one side and asked Uncle Jimmy a question that seemed strange at the time, but that we later realized had legal bearing on the matter.

"This here the cow that needs catching?" he asked.

"It is," my cousin admitted in a grave-side voice.

Mercy slipped down from the saddle and, steadying himself with the stirrup, reached out and caught hold of Naomi's horn. Then he straightened, pulled himself back onto the horse, spit again, and leaned over towards my cousin with his outstretched palm.

"That'll be twenty-five cents," he said.

At this, my cousin dropped his solemn countenance and whooped out a laugh—kept laughing, in fact, as he dug deep in his pocket for the coins. These he duly delivered, commenting that it was money well spent for we'd learned a valuable lesson.

"I reckon," sang The Hard to Catch Mercy. "Some animals ain't meant to be caught."

I assume the lesson my cousin had in mind had to do with not wasting valuable time looking for so-called expert help, so he was caught off guard by the other's observation.

"How's that?" Uncle Jimmy asked.

"Some animals is just too gentle to be caught." And leaving us those words to study on, The Hard to Catch Mercy whistled up his free-roving hog dog and turned his horse homeward.

"Did you see that?" I asked as soon as he was out of ear-shot. "That man couldn't walk. No wonder he never got off that horse."

"What are you talking about? Was nothing wrong with him whatsoever."

"He was hanging onto the stirrup. Tell him, Sammy."

But Sammy hadn't seen him hold the stirrup. I was the only one on that side, so only I believed The Hard to Catch was at least crippled temporarily.

Guarding Naomi further was useless. We did agree on

that. We weren't going to eat her and we weren't going to bury her, so we followed some distance behind the horseman, and caught up with him again where the woods began. Once more he was in conversation with Grandpa, for a suddenly forgiven Liza had brought the old man out in her daddy's buggy and walked him through the woods. No doubt, she wanted him to understand the magnitude of our crime, but the sight of the buzzards floating high above the carcass hadn't upset him at all. In fact, Grandpa was excited in a strange way, and when we arrived, the old man was telling The Hard to Catch that if a buzzard, the lowest of God's creatures, could fly, then man would someday do the same. He wouldn't live to see it, but we children certainly would. Of course, the Wright brothers had flown long years before, and you couldn't pick up a magazine without reading some news story about aeroplanes. Even so, no flying machine had landed in our backyard, and not even Liza dared to tell the old man that flight had long since been achieved. We just stood about and nodded.

Slipping off his great flopping hat and running a hand through his thinning hair, The Hard to Catch watched the black birds drift in a lazy spiral. The highest were no more than specks, tiny black stars in the evening sky. When the rider spoke, it was in disagreement—almost disrespectful.

"Man weren't meant to fly. Bird meant to fly." He nudged the little horse forward and disappeared into the hickory woods.

When we reached the pole gate I'd expected Gal to be stolen, but she wasn't. And when I shared my relief with Uncle Jimmy, he whooped out and declared only an idiot would take such an animal—even as a gift. Of course, he rode home on Rose.

Liza was clearly disappointed that I wasn't to be held responsible for Naomi, and I was more certain than ever it was she who released the cows in the first place. Happily, Uncle Jimmy continued to ignore her and she him. Grandpa talked for several more days about people flying. Uncle Jimmy agreed man flying was a good idea, but was most impressed with The Hard to Catch's homespun philosophy. Naomi died of a broken heart. Truly, some creatures were too gentle to be caught.

Actually, the moral of the story was that we should have offered the cow the smilax in the first place, but I said nothing, satisfied to have the blame shifted to the animal herself. My mama was never certain which cow died, and after a few shouted explanations, Pa shook his head and smiled. That left only Maum Anna to suggest that Sammy and I had sinned.

"You boy bad—bad—bad. Too trifling to mind a cow."

Since she was laughing, I doubted she was truly angry. Ruth turned out to have a tolerable disposition on her own, and easily found her way back and forth to the pasture. Glad it was over, I made another solemn vow: to give The Hard to Catch Mercy the widest possible berth and never again enter the Great Swamp.

That was pretty much the end of the cow business, but I hadn't forgotten my previous solemn vow, and a few days later I set out to set the record straight. My mama was an ample woman with even greater heart, and I found her quiet in the garden. It was nothing fancy, this place of hers, for only the hardiest of shrubs could survive—oleanders, cassena berry, and a few azaleas—but these were all higher than my head. She'd planted house flowers in the past but could no longer manage that. Long years before, she'd given up her hat shop and more recently her piano. Her letter-writing and book-reading had also been abandoned. She went to church and helped Maum Anna in the kitchen. Besides that, her only activity was her needlework, the simplest of patterns, two red roses that she duplicated over and over and donated for sale at the church bazaars.

"Mama," I announced. "Uncle Jimmy has been telling me some things I'm finding mighty hard to believe."

"Isn't that so, Willie? I hardly understand a thing that he and your grandfather discuss." She gently touched my shoulder.

"No, ma'am."

"Much of it seems to depend on. . . ." She tapped her forehead with the tips of her fingers and then happily finished the sentence, ". . . on electricity."

"No, ma'am. That ain't it. He's claiming you and Maum Anna stole a mule and wagon and five gold pieces. He claims you went to rescue Pa from the hospital in Virginia. That didn't happen, did it?"

"No, I am certain it did not." A slip of hair had dislodged from her loosely pinned bun and she poked it back.

"Good," I said. She wasn't a heroine but there was a consolation. "It pains me to tell you this, Mama, but Uncle Jimmy is a terrible liar."

"Someone gave us a ride to Clarkesville. We got on the train there. I remember that part very well. I was just a child and it was the first train I had ever seen. The car was full of soldiers. Very polite men." She paused, smiled at me, and with both hands touched at the loose bun of silvered hair that was now threatening to unravel. "It was such a strange feeling to be looking out that glass window. Like being in a house, except it started to move. The people outside on the platform went by slowly in little jerky motions." Now she used the hands to indicate the way the train had gathered speed. "Such noise, too. Then trees started going by outside. I thought at first it was the forest moving and not us."

"You went to Virginia?"

"I suppose we must have. I don't recall any more of the trip there, though. Coming back I remember pulling off to one side to let some poor soldiers pass. They tipped their hats to us. I remember looking back and watching Anna. She had Tom's head resting in her lap and she was bent over whispering in his ear. He was unconscious but she was trying to talk to him anyway."

"You had a mule and wagon, then?"

"Yes. I was driving. I'm sorry, Willie, that's all I can recall."

"Why didn't you tell me?"

"I did tell you."

"No, ma'am, you did not."

"I told Esther. I'm certain I told Esther—she was always teasing me about the trip. It was such a scandal. I was nothing but a child and your father was a full grown man. In those days no one went about unchaperoned and there we were, you see. People talked so. It was silly."

"You saved my pa?"

"I'm sure Anna did the nursing. I barely knew how to do anything."

"What about the chains? Was Maum Anna chained at the ankles?"

Mama thought a long while and shook her head. She had always been a letter writer but now she was having to write them to herself—short notes to aid in her remembering. She kept them tucked out of sight in the pockets of her flower-print dresses, and as I waited she reached in search of one.

"No, ma'am," I said. "It wouldn't be wrote down. Was Maum Anna still chained? Try and remember."

"I can't," she said, after thinking about it for a good

minute. "My mind plays such tricks now. I see us both on the train. I see the wagon. Her feet aren't showing in my memories." She shook her head and smiled at me.

"Did my pa die?"

"My lands. Who told you such?"

"Uncle Jimmy. It ain't so, is it?"

"I would hope not."

"I would hope not, too."

"I don't think your father ever discussed his war experiences with anyone. It is possible such happened but I hope not."

"Possible? He could have been dead?"

"I would hope not."

"Mama." I pleaded.

"Ask him, son, if you feel it is important. He'll be home Friday."

"He is home."

"Ask him then. I'm sure he will tell you."

"You ask him."

"I would never do that," she said.

"Why not?"

"If such a thing had happened, I would prefer not to know. A memory of that sort would be of no use to me now."

"Yes, ma'am." I shook my head. "It ain't that important."

I found Brother in our bedroom. He'd received his clock tools by now and, to Grandpa's delight, had the mantle clock telling time. Already, four more customers had dropped timepieces by and I'd had to help drag a large work table up the stairs and jam it in between our two beds. Working with a tiny pair of tweezers, my younger cousin had just removed a barely visible spring from the back of a watch. I asked him if his brother's stories were true and he said yes. Their pap, Captain James Allson, had told those stories to both sons. That night after supper, I confronted my cousin in his bedroom.

"Listen here, how come none of the stories Captain James told you match up with what everybody else says?" I tried to sound friendly and let the fact that his pa was the teller sort of slide in. "Is they all wrong and just him right? I mean, he weren't even born then."

"Your pa told him." My cousin made it sound obvious. "He told him 'most everything I told you today."

"You're lying! My pa would never have told such tales, not even to his own brother. Never would, never."

"That's so. He didn't mean to tell 'em. When the malaria fever got him raving, they would slip out."

"Raving? Raving?" I sputtered.

"You see, Willie T., when my pap was about your age he started listening outside Captain Tom's bedroom door. He told me he'd listen all night sometimes. Took him years to get the stories sorted out but he thought he had them down pretty good."

"Raving? You mean your version was recited by my pa when he was out of his mind. I've heard him when the chills and fevers get him. That's not even words he's talking."

"My pap said you had to listen real close. If you did and heard it enough times, it all started to make sense."

I let the matter drop. There was no use in talking to him, but there was one more piece of business concerning the cows that should be mentioned. Life around the Allson household was returning to normal with comforting speed, but sadly we were to discover the campaign's second casualty. About the time of Mercy's visit, old Blaze had gone under the house and died. But we didn't smell him for three days. Sammy was made to go under and pull out a corpse that was by then swollen stiff, with legs spread straight out. It was a pitiful sight. Still, he'd been an old dog. The very next day we got a puppy, but he ate too much, fell off the porch, and popped open like a melon. We got another hound after that and one that was part coach dog, but neither stayed around the house more than a day. Christmas was coming, and we were probably the only family in Clarke County not keeping a dog.

Mr. Friendly's Christmas

GOBBLING his breakfast, Uncle Jimmy didn't notice he was the topic of conversation and, once finished, he pushed back his plate and pulled out the dollar watch. I assumed he was headed to the grocery.

"Maybe that cow strike him a lick. Knock the sense clean out he brain." Maum Anna whispered this loudly to my mama, while tapping lightly on the side of her own head.

"Day's half gone and nothing to show for it," my cousin announced to no one in particular.

"That old evening sun comin' down." Now, Maum Anna rolled her eyes heavenward.

"My lands, it does grow dark early," my mama agreed.

Uncle Jimmy laughed and snapped the watch shut.

"Do Jesus. Poor creature deserve a head start."

"Go on, Jim," my mama said.

With that, Uncle Jimmy shot from the kitchen and was already saddling Rose when I caught up.

"Who's hunting?" It hurt my feelings to be left out, especially since we were out for Christmas holidays and I had nothing to do.

"Ain't no hunt."

"Where you going then?"

"None of your business, but I'll tell you anyway. I'm courting." He was happy.

"You and Liza have made up?" I didn't try to hide my disappointment.

"Me and Liza nothing." My cousin swung into the saddle.

"If it ain't Liza, who is it?"

"That ain't none of your business," he laughed. "And what's more, I ain't going to tell you."

My cousin dug his heels into Rose and trotted off towards the fields. Shaking my head, I went upstairs and, separating Brother from the clockwork of the hour, asked him who the girl was. He didn't know or even appear interested in the question. Under normal circumstances I wouldn't have approached my mama on a matter of this intimate a nature, but now I had no choice. As casually as possible, I wandered into the kitchen where Mama and Maum Anna still worked.

"Where you reckon Uncle Jimmy went to in such a hurry?" I pretended to be studying the screen of the pie safe. "Didn't he tell you?" Mama asked.

"I done forgot, and I owe him some money he might be needing today."

"He went callin' on a young lady," Mama said. The two women were busy at the sink, their backs to me.

"That's it," I said. "I done forgot the young lady's name."

"That gal they call Beatrix?" Maum Anna volunteered.

"Yes, ma'am," I said quickly. "That's her." In fact, I'd heard of no one by that name.

My mama's shoulders were shaking, and when she turned around I could see fun was being had at my expense.

"Great God, how you lie, boy. You the worsest one."

"I ain't lying."

"Willie," my mama said, managing to get a handle on her uncharacteristic mirth, "Jimmy has ridden to see that girl. That's all he's doing."

"What girl?"

"That girl . . . you know . . ."

Laying aside her dishrag, Mama went to the notes tacked on the wall beside the calendar. To aid her memory she was now connecting dates and notes with pencil lines that sometimes crossed open expanses of plaster, and the month just passed was pinned up as well, making for even greater complications. Apparently this all meant something to her, but it still took some minutes before she could point out a name jotted across the top of a mercantile receipt.

"Amy Mercy," I read.

"Yes," my mama seconded, "Amy Mercy. And here the name is again, and here." Two other entries were dated and connected by a thin looping pencil line, but no indication of their purpose was given.

"Amy Mercy. The girl y'all met in Brittle Branch."

"Her?" I asked. "He don't even know her."

"Must know something 'bout the child," Maum Anna declared. "He been slipping in them woods every chance he get."

Hurt that I hadn't been told, I left them tittering like schoolgirls and wandered from the house. I found Sammy at the wharf and told him. He said the swamp was a devil place—full of bottomless pools and quicksand beds. I thanked him for the information and went inside to tell Brother, who didn't even look up from his tinkering. Clearly, I was the only one who cared what my cousin did, and so was the only one truly concerned when Amy Mercy came to live at Cedar Point the following week.

She was to stay with Mr. Friendly and his wife. This was

the same Presbyterian minister Uncle Jimmy had declared a lazy fraud, but now the girl would stay with the fine generous couple and be going to school with us. It turned out she didn't actually live in Brittle Branch, at least not on a regular basis. Usually she boarded somewhere else and was only visiting to look after her grandmother when we'd met. Since the Widow Mercy was no longer doing poorly, Amy was free to come and go as she pleased.

And Uncle Jimmy had been busy convincing her to come to Cedar Point instead of returning to her older sister, whose husband had a livery business to the west of Crowns Bluff. When my cousin got back from the swamp that afternoon, he was happy to tell me the whole story, for by then Mr. Friendly had been out to the Branch and agreed to board the girl. She hadn't been raised in a Presbyterian church but she had attended some, and the preacher felt she would be good company for his wife. It went without saying that his salary, no matter how extravagant it had seemed to Uncle Jimmy, could always do with a small supplement.

We still had to wait a week, though. Christmas was only a few days off and the girl insisted on staying with her grandmother until the holiday passed. The preacher found this highly commendable. My cousin found it highly aggravating but held his tongue and went about his business with what Maum Anna had called the "cow struck" look on his face. The rest of us had to be content with the more ordinary joys of the season.

As usual, on Christmas Eve Mr. Friendly preached at considerable length on the wondrous necessity of the virgin birth. Jesus Christ being of the seed of David, had to be conceived without the sin in the womb of the Virgin by the power of the Holy Spirit. That way Man and God could be united in one and the Son of God could bring us our hope of redemption. The preacher repeated the familiar story of how Joseph was an old man with a young bride, and the angel explained to him why she happened to be expecting a child when she hadn't gotten around to knowing her husband yet. They went to pay their taxes and the inn was full. Christ was born in a stable. Shepherds came. Wise men, following the star of Bethlehem, brought gifts, and then stood there praying that it would end soon so they could go home. Part of this feeling though was not boredom but physical discomfort brought on by having to stand motionless for so long.

The Christmas service was always accompanied by a live nativity scene, a display many thought frivolous but one tolerated as necessary instruction for the children participating. Liza, as always, played the Virgin Mary and acted the part this year with particularly poor feeling. Elbowing a clear place about her at the manger, she stared down at the baby doll infant Jesus with the hard eyes she usually reserved for flesh-and-blood humanity. Joseph that year was a surprise. Barnus Wilson claimed to have broken a leg at the last minute, and so Mr. Friendly shanghaied my cousin. Uncle Jimmy agreed without complaint, put on the bathrobe, stood gazing down at the manger in perfect adoration, and ignored his spouse Liza altogether.

I'd worked my way up that year from shepherd to wise man and managed to bring Brother along as my companion. We carried frankincense and myrrh but were never actually allowed to present it to the child. For the entire two-hour service we stood with our boxes held out in front of us and tried not to sway. Wise man, I realized halfway into the service, was not the dream part I'd imagined. You were right out there, closest to the audience, and you couldn't lower your hands. Still, my parents were in the second pew and could see me taking a highly visible part.

Though Mama pretended otherwise, Christmas wasn't a truly happy time for her. Esther had died during the holidays. In fact, it was on Christmas Eve that my older sister had taken a turn for the worse, and I'd heard her whisper, "Mama, I am dying." Pa hadn't heard Esther, and with a strange suddenness, it occurred to me he was hearing nothing of Mr. Friendly's service. Perhaps some of the caroling reached him, but the rest of this pageant was only a silent charade. Of course, I'd been aware of his deafness all my life, but for the first time I actually had a sense of what he was hearing—nothing. Pa sat there, rocking forward when sleep approached. Then forcing his eyes open, he'd watch anew. He couldn't have heard Esther cry, "Mama, I am dying," anyway. He had been downstairs sitting with her husband. She did die, but that was four days later. Christmas had come and gone.

I glanced over at Brother and saw his head cocked to one side. He was hearing voices. As casually as possible, I bumped his frankincense with my myrrh, and brought him back among the living. No one had noticed, but when we'd returned to our bedroom, I cautioned him.

"You best watch out if you don't want people suspecting you is hearing voices."

"Was you?" he replied.

"Was me that bumped you. Brought you to your senses."

"Was you. You was whispering, 'Mama, I am dying.'"

"I was not. You lying!"

"You was, Willie T. Was real quiet, but I could hear you plain."

"No way," I said. "You dreaming that."

"Even if you was, your mama couldn't have heard you.

You was calling it out way too quiet. 'Mama, I am dying.'"
My little cousin opened and closed his mouth and the words
"Mama, I am dying," reached me as the faintest of whis-
pers. "Ain't nobody heard but me, and I was straining."

"You was dreaming."

"No." Brother had taken his seat at the worktable and
already had a screwdriver in one hand and a large brass
alarm clock in the other.

"You going to mend clocks on Christmas Eve?"

"You said it. You said 'Mama, I am dying,' but you ain't
dying. I been dead. Y'all had fangs and wanted to chop me
up. I know what I'm talking about."

That was enough. I went across the hall to where Uncle
Jimmy lay stretched out on top of his spread. Legs crossed,
hands behind his head, he was staring cow struck at the
ceiling.

"Did you hear me saying anything tonight?"

"When?"

"Me whispering—up on stage while I was being a wise
man."

"Nope. Heard some angels singing way off in the distance. Was going Hal-A-Lool-A, Hal-A-Lool-A." My cousin
made it sound like the angels had been calling dogs.

"That was the choir."

"No, not them. I mean as Joseph. I swear I heard 'em.
That's when I knew God hadn't lied to me about this
McLatt Exception my Mary was running round with." He
grinned at me.

"What you do it for if you just mocking everybody?" It
was bad enough that I actually might have said, "Mama, I
am dying," out loud. What really angered me, though, was
the ease with which this cousin of mine had fallen into the
role of Joseph.

"I thought the Reverend preached a right smart sermon." Uncle Jimmy had stopped grinning and appeared
to be sincere.

"You liked the sermon?" I couldn't tell whether he was
lying or not.

"Friendly is a fine fellow," he assured me. "A man after
my own heart." My cousin had even taken his hands from
behind his head and joined them on his belly in a prayer-
ful clasp.

"Mr. Friendly?"

"He was the pitcher on a real baseball team, you know
that?"

"Mr. Friendly played baseball?" The preacher was a tall,
long-boned man with arms that hung like Maum Anna's,
an inch or two further than they should've from his coat
sleeves, and it wasn't hard to imagine that extended sad
face shadowed by a baseball cap. I said, "You're lying,"
anyway.

"He didn't study to be no preacher," my cousin added.
"He got his degree in engineering."

"Engineering? You making this up."

"No, I ain't. He was going to be a bridge builder, but his
mama made him promise on her deathbed that he would
go out and spend the rest of life spreading the words of
the Gospel."

I shook my head no.

"I done seen his diploma framed on the wall. He don't
brag about it, but his wife showed me the trophies he won
pitching."

"You been to his house?"

"Sure, I been to his house. You wouldn't believe what
he's got in the attic."

"What?" I'd been to the man's house often enough for
youth activities, but I'd never seen any baseball trophies

and was wondering what other secrets were hidden away.

"A wireless telephone."

"What's that?"

"What's that? Holy Jericho, Willie. It's a telephone without wires."

"What's he doing with it here?"

"He listens to it."

"Why?"

"'Cause that's what he's interested in."

"How come you know so much about what he's interested in?"

"'Cause we're mates."

"He's fifty years old."

"It don't matter how old he is if we're interested in the same things."

"The wireless telephone?"

"Hunting, too. We're going ducking first of the year."

"I thought I was going ducking with you." We'd been planning this trip since his arrival.

"You're coming along. He wants you along, and he wants you and Brother over to see the wireless telephone."

"You told me Mr. Friendly was a thief. You said he robbed from the community."

"I didn't say that. I said his good works was like money in the bank that could be drawed out on Judgment Day."

"No, you did not. Maum Anna said that."

"It don't matter who said it first as long as it's true."

"You claim you liked that sermon he preached tonight. How come you told me Joseph was a fool to believe that about the Virgin Mary being a virgin?"

"I never said that."

"Yes, you did. You was just laughing about McLatt Exception."

"Joseph was an old man. Wasn't going to do him a bit of

good not to believe it, now was it, Willie?"

"That's not the point."

"You think old Joseph's going to go out and find the fellow who done it? What good that do if he's too old to fight him? He's still got him a pretty young wife. Better for him to be quiet and go along."

"You mean give God the credit."

"Sure, no harm in that."

"Sure," I said. "That's a fine way to reason it out."

"Only way to my mind."

"I'm going to ask Mr. Friendly if he agrees with you."

"Do what you want, Willie T."

"You know what I'm thinking?"

"What?"

"You're just saying you like old Friendly 'cause this girl is coming to board in the manse."

"That ain't so, but you can think what you want."

Actually I was thinking my cousin's reasoning about Joseph and the virgin birth made a lot of sense, and maybe I'd wasted the best part of my life worrying over the Bible. Still, that didn't make Uncle Jimmy any less of a hypocrite. He stood to gain by the association with the preacher. And he did.

Three days later Amy Mercy was installed in the Friendly's home, and Brother and I were invited over to greet her and to get a peek at the wireless telephone. Mrs. Friendly greeted us at the door. The plump little woman was nice enough. She seemed glad to see us but didn't smile. She'd never smiled that I could recall. Like Maum Anna, she had no children of her own—"God's test," as I'd heard it put.

"My husband and Jim are up in the attic. Amy and I are just setting up for tea. If you'll be seated, we won't be but a moment."

She led Brother and me, hats in hand, into the front parlor, and left us perched on the edge of a couple of chairs. Before long, Amy Mercy entered the room. She was dressed in a white lace dress with her straight black hair piled up high. I'd forgotten how pretty she was.

"Here you is, Cousin Willie. We meeting again, and this must be Brother." She shook us each by the hand. Neither of us had enough sense to stand. She was too pretty to talk to. Without a cow's life at stake, I had nothing to say back to her.

"You going to live here?" Brother asked.

"Sure enough," she answered. "Since I'm an orphan, Mrs. Friendly and her husband have been kind enough to take me in."

"I'm an orphan, too," Brother said.

"You ain't an orphan," I said. "You live with us."

"I am too an orphan," Brother repeated. It was always unsettling when Brother opened his mouth and decided to talk.

"You boys will enjoy the wireless telephone." Mrs. Friendly had returned. "You want to see it before tea?"

"Yes, ma'am," I said.

"How old is you?" Brother asked Amy.

" 'Most seventeen," she answered.

"I reckon you won't be an orphan much longer."

"How's that?"

"Once you're growed you stop being an orphan."

"Let's go, Brother," I said.

"That's true," Amy Mercy said.

"You boys follow me." Mrs. Friendly motioned us to rise, and leaving Amy Mercy behind, led us up two flights of stairs to the base of a ship's ladder.

The woman didn't attempt this last climb, just pointed us on, and together Brother and I entered the dark, cold, and dusty attic she'd referred to in an unsmiling joke as her husband's tower of Babel. At the far end of the space a single lantern burned and beneath it on the table was an elaborate apparatus over which Uncle Jimmy and his mate, Mr. Friendly, were now bent.

"Hello," I said, feeling it best not to sneak up on them.

"So, there the fellows are." Mr. Friendly beckoned us forward.

"Where you been?" my cousin asked. "You missed some great talking on this thing."

"Brother held us up. There was some matters he had to discuss with Miss Mercy."

Laughing and pulling wires from his head, Uncle Jimmy stood back so we could view the strange box. From its front panel several knobs and dials protruded and out of the open top a profusion of coiled wires and tubes overflowed onto the table.

"How's it work?" Brother was still feeling talkative.

"Runs on electricity. See that battery?" Mr. Friendly pointed under the table at another box connected to the first box by wires. "That's electricity. Most marvelous substance in the known physical world."

"Ain't that the truth?" Uncle Jimmy seconded.

"What is electricity? I can tell you're asking yourself that, aren't you Willie T.?" Mr. Friendly was looking at me alone. Uncle Jimmy had said the preacher had wanted to be a bridge builder, but how could a man of God get interested in such a piece of machinery? I was wondering that, and at the same time worrying over my failure to talk to Amy Mercy. Right now she was thinking that I was a hopeless idiot.

"Not even Mr. Edison can say for sure what electricity is. We only know how to harness it, to make it work for us, to make it do God's work." Mr. Friendly obviously liked this sermon because he was putting more feeling into it than any he delivered from the pulpit. I nodded and tried to look appreciative. "Imagine the air is a very still lake, and a rock is tossed into the middle. Splash! It sends out waves in every direction, only in this case the waves aren't water. What are they?" He was still looking at me. I was about to guess "dirt."

"Sound," Brother said.

"You bet it is," Uncle Jimmy said. "Just like a drumbeat. Only with the wireless telephone, the rap goes on 'most forever."

"That's right," the preacher said. "A drum or a bullwhip snapping over and over, only you got to snap that whip just so." The preacher raised a hand up in the dark attic and brought it down with an imaginary crack. "You do it right you got a sound that can go clear 'round the world."

"Without wires," Uncle Jimmy added.

"You're turning electricity into sound?" Brother ran a small hand reverently across the edge of the wireless box.

"Yes, indeed, and electricity travels one hundred and eighty-six thousand miles a second. If a person wants to say hello, his voice would go 'round the world seven times in one second."

"You can do that?" I considered the strange box with new respect.

"No, Willie T.," the preacher said. "That's only a receiver, a pretty crude one at that. You got to have a transmitter to send out messages."

"Save your breath, preacher. Let's just fit old Brother into this headset." Uncle Jimmy already had the earplugs over the victim's head. "Hear 'em?" he asked. "Fellow's up in Maryland somewheres."

Brother nodded yes, which didn't do much to convince me since he was already hearing voices.

"It has a long way to go, but I been wanting to share this with you boys. Especially you, Willie. Science. Study science. Don't just learn the Bible." He knew I hadn't been to a Bible study class or even a prayer meeting in the past month. I looked down at my feet. "Look at me," he said. I did. He tapped his own chest with a long finger and drew a breath. "Look at me. I been spreading the word sixteen years. I been to the other side of the world and back, and how many people you reckon I reached?"

"Plenty," I said. "Thousands, probably."

"Sure," he said. "In my whole life I've preached to maybe fifteen or twenty thousand souls. But imagine every house in America, every house in the whole world, has one of these machines and all the preacher has to do is step up to a microphone and open his mouth. What you think Paul and Silas would have made of that?"

"Holy Hannah," Uncle Jimmy said in admiration.

"Think about it," Mr. Friendly said.

I promised I would, but the promise was a lie. Since the arrival of my cousins, my interest in spreading the Gospel had quickly eroded. A few minutes before it had reached rock bottom, and now the only thing in this house I was studying on was Amy Mercy.

Mr. Friendly put the headset over my ears as if anointing me and I pretended an interest. I had to pretend, for no magic voices spoke. There was only the crackling sound like a fire burning wildly out of control. Maybe it was up north in Maryland. Maybe it was closer to home. I looked nervously at the battery tucked under the table.

"You hear them talking?" Mr. Friendly asked.

"Yes, sir," I lied and prayed he wouldn't ask what was

being said. He didn't, for everyone suddenly looked away from the machine and I followed their gaze. Amy Mercy was coming up the ladder, rising up into the attic all in white like an angel. I pulled free of the headset just in time to hear her invitation.

"Y'all come on. Mrs. Friendly says the tea's going to be stone cold if you don't come right now."

"Give us just another minute."

"No, Mr. Friendly. Your wife done told me you'd say that. Said you would ask for one more minute 'til midnight come." Mr. Friendly laughed and turned the dials of the box to what must have been an "off" position. "I don't know why you want to listen all the time for anyway," the girl went on. "Least on a real telephone you can talk back." This girl from the swamp had talked on a real telephone, something I'd never done myself.

"Amy, it ain't the same thing," my cousin said.

"I know it ain't, Jimmy."

"You got to give it a chance."

"I done give it a chance. All I hear is a crackling sound. Must be some poor woman frying butts meat on the other end."

Yes, I wanted to say. That's what I heard too, but I held my tongue. She had us all trooping down the stairs after her, and I was laughing louder than all the rest. It was a secret joke between us. What we had heard on the headset. Why did I think that? It was only a joke known to me, and yet she was that kind of person. Looking back, I could see how she made each person think they were special. It was a gift, a talent. The Friendlys felt it. I did. Even Brother did, but it was Uncle Jimmy who she made feel the most special of all. We had our tea and said our good-byes. Walking home, Uncle Jimmy talked to Brother about building a receiver of our own and repeated to us what Mr. Friendly had said once we were downstairs. A giant broadcaster would someday be sending out preachers' voices. It'd also be playing music like a Victrola.

"'Not so far off. That's the future, boys. That there is progress,'" my cousin repeated.

"Fairyland," I said. "That thing is about as real as fairyland."

"Or Heaven," my cousin taunted.

"Yeah, maybe," I said and remembered suddenly how Amy Mercy had risen like an angel into the attic, coming to tell us tea was ready, and that she couldn't hear anything on the headset either.

Two days later we went ducking. The trip, which was to have included only Uncle Jimmy, Mr. Friendly, and me, now turned into an outing. Mrs. Friendly and Amy were to come along, so instead of departing at dawn, we'd be going in the middle of the afternoon. Uncle Jimmy hitched the mule to the Texas cart, which was piled thick with blankets, and high with picnic hampers and shotguns. The four of them squeezed in, and I rode along on Rose. I couldn't share in the conversation, but tried my best to cut a dashing figure on the horse. I wanted Amy Mercy to notice me, and I believe she did because she smiled in my direction more times than she did the rest of them did put together.

In any event, the trip was a short one, for we were only going to the Allson Place. My cousin hadn't bothered to ask Dr. McGill for permission, but I'd heard the doctor complain that preachers didn't get around enough. And if we were trespassing, what of it? I wanted Amy Mercy to see the plantation, and trotted ahead when we got to the avenue of live oaks so she could witness me in possession of my birthright. Uncle Jimmy must have felt about the same because when the cart pulled up to the house ruins, he was telling them the Allsons were in the process of buying the place back from the McGills.

But by then I'd looked around. There was something undeniably forlorn about the thick, high wall of crumbling brick. Except for one remaining chimney and a broad set of entry steps, the house would have passed for a much-battered fort, an impression strengthened by the countless craters made during the dowry search. My cousins had missed out on that long adventure, but Sammy and I had done our share of dodging rattlesnakes to sift through the dirt and chunks of masonry—a useless search, especially since Pa and his brothers had been through it all at least once before we were born.

"A dinner service for sixteen." When listing the Allson dowry Grandpa always mentioned that first. "Silver, all of it silver, and the linen and crystal to match. A silver punch bowl with nineteen cups. Six silver candelabras. Jewelry, too. A great deal of jewelry. Most of it gold. Brooches, rings, bracelets, and one grand diamond tiara." He'd pause only to catch his breath and swing his cane about the interior of our humble parlor. "A silver brush and ivory comb, a painting by a Dutchman, two mahogany wardrobes, and twelve twenty-dollar gold pieces that were a wedding gift and therefore not spent for sentimental reasons." It was a familiar speech, but I hadn't heard it once since the doctor's purchase. Maybe the fight had finally gone out of the old man. I sat on the horse and stared.

"Y'all know my grandpa Tyler was the overseer here?" Amy Mercy had both small hands raised to the crumbling walls.

"I recall Grandma Mercy mentioning that," my cousin said. For me it was "the Widow Mercy," but for him, "Grandma Mercy."

"Was ages ago. Him and my grandma had them a little

house back over there a ways. And that's where my daddy, Allson, was born." She pointed to the woods.

"You been here?" I asked in surprise.

"Only in my dreams."

That sounded good.

"Judging by the ruins, this must have been some house." Mr. Friendly was also impressed.

No mention was made of the craters or the dowry. The cart was emptied and a tablecloth spread out beside the entry. Mrs. Friendly and Amy laid out the picnic, but once that was done the girl walked up the steps that ended in a broad front stoop and nothing else.

"Was a real mansion," Amy Mercy said. "See here. These stairs is real marble and this here floor is marble tile. And right here where I'm standing was a giant front door." She stepped close to the edge to place her hand on the imagined doorknob.

"Careful," Uncle Jimmy called.

"The hallway run clear through the house." She pretended to open the nonexistent door. "Hall wide enough for two wagons to pass, and back to the end was a wondrous stairway circling up to the second and third stories. You looked past that and out the far door and you saw the river."

"My, my, can you imagine that?" Mrs. Friendly said.

Apparently Amy Mercy could, because she kept looking down a hallway that didn't exist, past a stairway that had burned away half a century before, and out to a river that couldn't be seen because the trees had been allowed to grow up.

"There was four giant bedrooms up there." She pointed overhead. "Each one had its own fireplace. Then four more above them with their own fireplaces, and on each side was a little secret staircase that ran from cellar to attic. That was so the servants wouldn't be walking around where people could see them."

"I believe I heard 'bout them," Uncle Jimmy said, but you couldn't tell if he had or not. I couldn't remember myself. Maybe somebody had mentioned all this, but when I thought about the house it was always in connection with the dowry and digging holes in the ground. It was never looking up and thinking about what was once there.

"Roof was made out of pure stone slate," Amy said. "Real slate that was brought straight over on the ship from England." She was pointing as high as the treetops and, for no apparent reason, I was suddenly reminded of Mrs. McGill's accusations. Had Grandpa tricked an innocent Matthews girl out of those roof slates and the rest of the house, too? Had he married her to get the Allson Place? "Down there is the cellar." Amy Mercy was indicating the tremendous cavity at her feet. "And in the middle of it is a deep, deep well."

"Careful you don't fall," Mr. Friendly called to the girl.

"Come on and eat," Uncle Jimmy said.

Amy Mercy took a final look at the house that wasn't there, and started down, but on each step she paused to recite a separate item.

"A dinner service for sixteen . . . a silver punch bowl . . . six candelabras . . . a solid gold brooch . . . a diamond tiara . . . a Dutch painting . . . twelve twenty-dollar gold pieces."

"What are you singing?" Mrs. Friendly asked.

"That's the Allson dowry," Amy explained. "Was buried out here at the end of the War for Southern Independence and never found again."

"Dear one," Mr. Friendly said addressing his wife, "that's why all these holes have been dug."

"True. Never found a thing," my cousin said.

"Maybe it's still right here." Amy patted the first stone step.

"Doctor would claim it," I said. "Thinks he's got him an encumbrance."

"Belongs to whoever finds it," my cousin said with even more bitterness.

"Boys," Mr. Friendly said, "that's not the Christian way."

"No, but that's how it is, Preacher." Uncle Jimmy was almost rude.

Amy Mercy tried to laugh.

I shook my head, but only to please her.

"Why can't they find it?" Mrs. Friendly asked.

"Coachman hid it," my cousin said. "Yankees strung him up."

"Don't some say Union sailors took the dowry?" Mr. Friendly didn't seem to think this question out of line.

"Didn't happen that way," my cousin said.

"It don't matter," Amy said. "Let's talk about something else."

We did. We talked about the food, and the picnic turned out to be a big success with lots of compliments going to the women. While the dishes were being put away Mr. Friendly volunteered the Scripture, "We will return and build the desolate place," which pleased Uncle Jimmy.

"Let's shoot a duck 'fore we lose the light," my cousin said.

Both women were dressed for the occasion, but at the last possible second, Mrs. Friendly said she was too old for such an ordeal. No one argued with her except Amy, for the rest of us, even her husband, thought it would be best if a woman who was as wide as she was tall remained behind. We left her sitting on the marble steps and were soon making our way single file down what remained of "the street." This had once been the slave quarters for the house servants, but all except two of the cabins had tumbled into modest ruins of their own. And these last two, held together by my pa's final tenants, were only roofless shells of buildings, with brush beginning to push against their sides.

"Called the Delta the 'Golden Triangle' 'cause they made so much money planting rice here," my cousin said in a low voice. "'Course that's all gone. Fields give up." Light shown through the trees ahead and suddenly we'd arrived. Extending for miles before us were thick, dry, brown stands of brush, broken only by thin lines of scrub and cedar that followed the straight paths of the slave-built earthworks. Grandpa and then Pa had farmed nine hundred acres of this Delta marsh—from here all the way to the river. I'd started to whisper this to the preacher, but stopped when I noticed the ducking boats were gone, apparently removed by the ruthless Dr. McGill. My cousin just shrugged off the loss and in a hushed voice explained that we'd shoot from the dike and wade after what we killed. I mentioned that the water was cold and he said I wasn't sugar and wouldn't melt. The preacher found this quite mirth-provoking and my cousin had to shush him quiet.

Being our guest, Mr. Friendly was to shoot first. He apologized in advance for his shooting ability, saying it had been some years since he'd fired a shotgun. I liked the sound of that and was even more encouraged by the old double-hammered blunderbuss he carried.

"Let the duck rise up. Get the scare out of them," my cousin advised quietly. "They pause after the first flapping."

I barely listened. Mr. Britt and my pa had brought me out here for the two previous winters and the last time I'd shot a little peg-horned buck on this same walk. I knew about hunting. The preacher promised only to do his best. Amy Mercy gave a whispered assurance that we'd all do splendidly.

Uncle Jimmy called for silence and signaled the preacher forward along the narrow dike crowded with an overgrowth of brambles and stunted trees. My cousin followed and I was next. Amy came last and fell almost at once, fell not into my arms but away from them, over onto her bottom. Still it was I who helped her to her feet, and it was the thoughtless Jimmy who scowled at the girl for laughing out loud. Ahead of us the ducks could already be heard gossiping to one another, but we needed a silent advance in order to get a good shot. She smiled at both of us, was still smiling, in fact, when the ducks sprang straight from the canal beside us with a great splashing roar.

Mr. Friendly brought the gun to his shoulder, swung, and fired both barrels in an explosion of black powder smoke that threatened to blind us all—all but Uncle Jimmy who stepped into the breach with raised gun and fired both barrels. The ducks were well up by then, and I was amazed to see not two but three fold up in midflight.

"Good shooting, Reverend." My cousin reloaded and closed his weapon with an assured snap.

"Did I get them both?"

Both? Mr. Friendly had shot a duck with both barrels.

"Yes. First one's dead, other's crippled."

"Sure enough was loud." Amy had stepped far back, fingers plugging her ears.

"It's over," Uncle Jimmy said to her. He'd already pulled a mallard drake from the rushes a few yards ahead. "Just one in the dry. Got to go after the rest of them."

I watched him step without reservation off the edge of the dike. The water quickly topped his boots.

"Ain't that cold?" Amy asked.

"Naw. Feels good."

"It ain't so cold," I reassured her, too.

"Come on and help me, Willie," my cousin called. He rang the neck of Mr. Friendly's cripple by slinging its body hard about.

"Ain't my ducks," I said.

"I'll remember that," he said.

"I'll help," Mr. Friendly called.

"Stay up there, Preach." My cousin had already slung two more onto the dry walk. Both were mallard drakes, large, plump birds with bright green iridescent heads.

"Look at them feathers," Amy said, taking one from my hands and ruffling the limp neck beneath her thumb. She handled the carcass with an easy familiarity.

"Pretty," Mr. Friendly said.

"Fits like a suit of new clothes. See this here's the white shirtsleeve." She spread the wing out for our inspection. "That there's the gray dress coat. White collar."

"It do look that way," I agreed. Out in the marsh I could hear Uncle Jimmy splashing about and muttering to himself.

"I took me a taxidermy course by mail order. Would be no trouble to mount this one for you," Amy said to Mr. Friendly. "He ain't messed up hardly at all."

"You stuff birds?" I asked in amazement.

"We don't never say 'stuff.' We say 'mount.'"

"I can't think of a thing that would bring me more pleasure," the preacher said.

"Consider it good as done."

"Got 'em all," Uncle Jimmy said as he staggered up onto the dike.

Five with four shots and all were mallards and all were green-head drakes, which made me a little more than suspicious of my hunting companions. I regretted having said I'd done this a few times before and even remotely suggesting I was pretty good at it. But there was no turning back. Uncle Jimmy had removed a croaker sack from a crevice in his hunting jacket and was tossing ducks into it.

"This one here is special." Amy had tied a black ribbon around the foot of the duck she held and presented it carefully.

"Ain't mine special, too?" My cousin had missed out on the conversation about mounting.

"Yours is very special," she teased, "so I'm keeping the ordinary special ones separate."

"She's going to stuff it for Mr. Friendly," I said.

"Mount it," the preacher corrected. "She's a taxidermist."

"You told me you was a Methodist," my cousin whispered.

"She's a woman of many talents." The preacher smiled down on his ward.

"Well, can she cook? I want mine stuffed with breadcrumbs, onions, and apples."

"Sure enough, but it won't appear none too lifelike."

"Where I'm putting it, it won't matter." My cousin patted his belly.

"That's my Jim," she said, reaching out to circle his arm with her own.

I said it was time we went on. Uncle Jimmy put me first on the dike, and we walked a good quarter mile seeing only worthless coots. Discouraged, I turned to whisper as much to my cousin and at that exact second the waters on both sides erupted like Vesuvius and spewed ducks every whichway.

"Shoot!" my cousin shouted, but I'd been too surprised to even bring up my gun. Now, it was too late. He was shooting to the left, though, so I swung on a retreating brownish blur and fired. A mallard hen dropped with a gentle splash. "Blam! Blam!" The preacher fired and more of the scrambling ducks were coming down.

"Shoot your other barrel, Willie!" my cousin shouted. He was reloading and so was the preacher. I fired again, but the target sailed on seemingly untouched. Then one wing folded up and it plunged into the marsh.

My companions searched the horizon, gun stocks still to their shoulders while I stood in the midst of smoke and ringing noise, proud enough of what I'd done.

"Got ten," my cousin said, lowering his weapon at last.

"That's good shootin', Jim." Mr. Friendly lowered his.

"Just lucky." My cousin had shot six with four shells.

"Now comes the hard part." Satisfied no ducks would be returning, my cousin had unloaded his gun and handed it to Amy. Not to be outdone, I did the same, so she had one under each arm.

"You look like Annie Oakley," Mr. Friendly said.

"Not me," she said. "I couldn't hit the broad side of a barn."

"You'd give it a good scare, anyway," Mr. Friendly said. He, too, unloaded his gun but laid it against a myrtle bush.

"Hunting's for menfolk," she said.

"Next time I'm leaving the retrieving to Sammy," my cousin said. He was already knee-deep in the canal and I followed. The cold water stung like needles, but by the time I'd bogged to the first duck my calves had numbed. And I'd managed it all without the loud whoop Mr. Friendly had let out. "Your other one's through there, Willie T." My cousin held up three of his own ducks, and with his free arm motioned me on.

"I know." Turning my back on him I slogged to exactly the right spot and found nothing. Not a feather.

"It ain't here," I called. My cousin and the preacher were heading back to the bank.

"You passed it, Willie T. Come towards me."

Following his directions, I walked the duck up. A drake, he made no sound even when almost stepped on, and flopped away just inches ahead of my grasp. In a confusion of splashing water and snapping reeds, I plunged in pursuit. First left, then right, then straight ahead the merry chase went until he broke into the open water beside the dike.

"Stand clear," Uncle Jimmy called.

I looked up to see him standing on the canal edge drawing a bead on my duck.

"I'll get him," I said.

"Willie, he'll run you around here all day."

"He will if I stand here talking to you." The duck had already gained a good ten paces on me and was paddling away fast.

My cousin didn't answer. Just pulled the trigger and blew the drake's head off completely.

"Get it and come on," he said.

"You get it. You shot it," I said.

"It's your duck."

"No, it ain't."

"I'll get him." The preacher waded out to where the drake now lay in a spreading pool of its own blood.

"You done good, Willie T.," Amy called. "You got 'em both."

"No, I didn't. He didn't let me."

"It don't matter."

"Yes, it does. I wanted you to mount him. Now he's blowed the head off."

"Come on out of there," my cousin said.

I didn't answer. I was coming anyway, coming ashore in anger and didn't notice the soft peat bottom giving way beneath my boot sole. Before I knew it, I was lying facedown in the icy canal.

"Willie T.!" I heard Amy Mercy shouting when my head came up. "Willie, is you all right?" Well, I wasn't all right, but she was the only one who cared. Uncle Jimmy was laughing, and even Mr. Friendly, who waded over to help, didn't think I'd drown. Once on my feet, I shouted at my cousin.

"You satisfied now?" I must have been freezing, but too angry to feel it yet.

"Me?" my cousin asked. "Why you mad at me?"

"You the one said I had to get the duck."

"You the one that shot it, Willie T. I never said you had to go get it."

"Yes, you did, and when I run it back here where I could get it you went on and shot it."

"That's got nothing to do with you falling down," my cousin laughed. I'd have tried to hit him if I'd been close enough.

"Let's get back on the bank," Mr. Friendly said. He had me by the elbow.

"That's right, Willie, come out of the water," Amy Mercy coaxed.

Refusing further help from the preacher, I splashed ashore. My wet clothes stuck hard against my body, and despite myself, I was beginning to shake.

"You got to get back to the cart and start a fire," my cousin said.

"No, I don't." My teeth were chattering.

"Suit yourself." Uncle Jimmy held his gun over his shoulder. He was ready to move on.

"You can't stay like that," Mr. Friendly said. "You'll catch your death."

"He'd like that." I motioned towards my cousin.

"Come on, Willie," Amy said. "I'll walk back with you." She reached out when she said this to pull a piece of slimy green waterweed from the side of my head, an act that started my cousin laughing again. "Hush, Jimmy," she said. "You ain't helping one bit. Not one bit."

"I didn't do nothing."

"Willie wanted me to mount that drake and you blew the head clean off it."

"That ain't got nothing to do with anything. How did I know that, anyway?"

"Come on, Willie." Amy took me by the arm and circled me around until I faced the mainland.

"Least you can do is tote these." My cousin held out the sack now filled to the brim. The girl expected me to take it, which meant I had to release her arm.

"You want me to tote your gun?" Amy asked.

"Naw, I got it. Let's go."

I should have let her. By the time we reached the old slave street, the chill had passed, but the bagged ducks had turned into millstones.

"You want to rest a spell?" We were having to walk single file and Amy had stopped and looked back to ask me this. I told her no, I wasn't tired, a reply that brought a look to her face that was entirely new to me. If she was concerned for my well-being, then her concern was of a most dramatic nature. Her bright brown eyes were open wide and her pretty red lips were turning into a perfect circle of exclamation.

"Willie," she whispered loudly. "Put the sack down."

"I can make it," I said. "Honest."

"That ain't the problem," she said.

"Let's go then."

"Look over your shoulder."

I did as instructed and saw the animal coming down the narrow path behind us. It had its nose to the ground, and was sniffing at the trail like a hound.

"Nothing but a cow," I said. Wild cows were common around here, and this one couldn't be worse than Ruth at her meanest. Besides that, I had my shotgun.

"No," Amy whispered.

"Don't worry." The intruder continued sniffing its way towards us, but still lagged behind a good fifty feet. "Whoa, cow!" I shouted as loud as I could.

The animal looked up, flicked its long twisting horns, and gave a snort of recognition.

"It's a bull," Amy whispered. "He's got our scent, Willie. He's done been following us."

But I knew that now. Nothing in the woods was more dangerous, not bear or boar or even rattlesnake. The wild bulls were the worst, and this one was pawing the ground, his head lowered for the charge. I was scared, far more frightened than I'd ever been in my life, but I wasn't going to let the girl see that. Slowly, I lowered the bag of ducks and raised the gun to my shoulder.

"Willie," the girl hissed in my ear. "That gun ain't loaded."

"Ruth . . ." I whispered, thinking somehow a comparison with the milk cow was still in order.

The bull was on us. It came rampaging down the path. In fact, the path was nothing but gray-brown bull. Twice the size of Ruth, head and horns as wide as my span lowered before a giant white-blazed chest. With a loaded gun I couldn't have missed. That's the completely useless thought I was having when I felt Amy Mercy yanking hard at my jacket, and just as the animal crashed past, I was pulled sideways into the brambles.

"Run!" she shouted, pulling me halfway to my feet.

"My gun?!" I shouted. "Where's my gun?"

"Run!" She was still pulling on me.

The bull swung about and was heading back.

"Our cow Ruth!" I shouted, "Our cow Ruth!" But couldn't think of what to add.

"Run! Run!" She kept yelling in my ear. "Come on, Willie, run."

So we ran, I followed her through the brambles, while the bull bellowed its rage at my back. I figured we were looking for a tree, but we reached one of the abandoned cabins. Amy threw herself through the doorway, and I scrambled over her as the horn of our pursuer slipped into my pants leg and ripped a foot long gash in the fabric.

"The door!" she shouted. "Close the door!"

I didn't have time. She slammed it hard against the bull's black nose, an act that added only additional volume to the trumpeting of his anger.

"That was close," she said.

"Yeah." I squatted on the dirt floor, panting for breath.

"I guess Jimmy will find us."

I didn't like the sound of that. It was bad enough being treed in this cabin. I sure didn't want to be rescued by my cousin.

"He'll go away in a minute," I said. "Our cow Ruth chased me like that."

"No. Once a bull is got you, they are certain to stay close."

To prove her right, the bull delivered a blow to the cabin. A foot of horn drove clean through the door and ripped it off its top hinge.

"That ain't going to hold," I said. "Another lick and he'll be in here with us."

"What's he doing now?"

I looked through the broad crack left by the sagging door. The animal had backed off spitting distance and, swinging his head back and forth low to the ground was pawing once more.

"Getting ready for another run."

When Amy Mercy began to laugh, I figured she'd become hysterical.

"Look at this place." The girl was hugging herself to contain the out-of-place laughter.

I knew our fortress had no roof and the two small windows had no shutters. Still a bull couldn't fly in or squeeze through the windows. What we'd failed to notice, though, what the girl now found so comical, had been to our backs. Across the rear of the cabin at least half the planking had been stripped away, leaving several holes big enough to admit the animal. One in particular would have allowed him to step in sideways. I wanted to be able to laugh myself. It seemed the manly thing to do, but all I could manage was a dry-mouthed chuckle.

"Cheer up, Willie T.," she said, "It could be worse."

"How?"

"Suppose we was by ourselves."

I didn't know exactly what she meant by that, but from the direction of the river came a distant muffled sound of gunfire.

"Jimmy's a good ways off."

"We still got each other. Two against one. Us against that dumb old bull."

"Yes, that's so." I liked the sound of that, but the bull must have taken exception to the word dumb because he suddenly jabbed his head through one of the cabin windows and the entire structure shifted over a perceptible two or three inches.

"Oh!" Amy yelped in surprise and threw her arms around me. And by instinct, I threw mine about her and held tight.

The bull studied the two of us for several curious moments. His reddened eyes glared steadily. Hot breath shot from his nostrils as visible steam. Then with a violent shake of his head, he withdrew, yanking the building back to plumb and carrying on his horn tips a healthy portion of the rotting window casing.

"I wasn't expecting that." Amy let go of me.

I didn't let go of her, though. Never in my life had I held a girl, unless I counted dancing with my cousin Margarite and I didn't count that.

"Willie? Is you all right?"

I didn't answer. Her face was so close to mine, I couldn't keep from kissing her. She let me, in a way. She didn't draw back. She stayed in my arms and her lips felt soft and giving beneath my own. That was how it felt for a moment. Then she started moving them so she could speak.

"Stop that. This is silly. I'm Jimmy's girl. You know that." She was pushing away from me hard with her small hand and she sounded angry.

"Stop what?" I asked, letting go and looking down at my feet.

"Kissing me."

"I wasn't kissing you."

"Yes, you was."

"No. I slipped. That wasn't no kiss."

"It felt like a kiss to me. It felt like you had plenty of practice kissing girls."

"Well, I ain't. If that had been a kiss, it would have been

the first one for me." I looked up and she was smiling at me.

"I'm flattered then, but I'm glad it weren't a kiss."

"No. It was an accident."

The bull had heard enough. He was tired of talk and again came at the front door, which this time came off both hinges and fell flat down on the dirt floor. Half in the room and half out, he paused, a little confused about his next move. Amy snatched up a long section of the door frame and slapped the animal hard across his nose again and again. Slowly, step by step, it backed out of the cabin.

"Put the door back up!" she shouted, still brandishing her timber. "Lean it up."

I did as told, but there wasn't much left to lean. The old rotten planks could barely hold themselves upright, much less keep out this monster.

"That ain't nothing." I wanted my opinion on record.

"Ain't you cold?" she asked me.

"No." I wasn't lying because by then I wouldn't have felt a blizzard.

The sound of a single gunshot came from not so far off.

"They're headed back this way. What's the bull doing now?"

I peeked out around the door remnants.

"He ain't out here."

"That's 'cause he's to the back," she said.

I turned around to look. Sure enough, the bull had slipped around as quiet as a gentleman caller and was presenting its card at the servants' entry.

"Get!" Amy Mercy shouted, running at the animal again with her plank. The bull did step off sideways a pace, but its regard for the plank was dimming, and it stood its ground once more, eyeing us with deadly interest.

"I could try and run for my gun," I whispered.

"No. Don't you go leaving me here."

It sounded strange, her saying that. She was the one with the board. She was the one standing between me and the bull. I didn't know what was expected of me by this woman. Perhaps the bull was equally confused. He stood studying us. Occasionally an ear would flick but he didn't cross the wide open space that separated us.

It's possible we could have stood there forever. Maybe that wouldn't have been so bad, just standing frozen in time, but life doesn't work that way. We heard a faint wailing sound coming from the direction of the house site—a holler that quickly grew louder and louder. The bull began to shift about nervously, his attention divided.

"It's Mrs. Friendly," I said.

"I know," Amy whispered back.

I guess the bull heard us and had a healthy respect for the wives of Presbyterian ministers, because hearing that he started moving to the far side of the cabin.

"Where's he going?" Amy lowered her plank, and directed me to follow the animal's progress through the cracks in the siding.

"Back towards the street path."

The great animal was lumbering at a steady gait, not in a great hurry, but not lingering either. From very close by came the hollering of Mrs. Friendly.

"We got to warn her," Amy said, pushing past me and knocking aside the splintered door. But there was no need. The bull had turned down the path in the opposite direction and we were on the path ourselves, by the time the little woman arrived, breathless and gasping out her story.

"In the well! There's a man."

"Is he chasing you?" Amy asked. I was already retrieving my shotgun from the brambles.

"He's dead. I was looking down there, thinking that it

did smell a bit sulphury for well water. I was looking down in there and I realized that it was a dead man floating face up in the water at the bottom." She pressed her plump little fingers to her face and allowed Amy to put her arms around her.

From very close by came the sound of a shot and a distinct shout that I recognized as my cousin. The bull. It had to be the bull.

"Stay here," I said to Amy.

"Don't go."

"Jimmy might need me."

"There's a dead man in the well," Mrs. Friendly sobbed.

"Yes, ma'am," I said, "but there is a live bull on the path."

Actually it was a dead bull on the path, which was what I was half expecting. Uncle Jimmy was standing off to one side with a dozen more ducks swung over his shoulder, and Mr. Friendly was bending over the animal getting a rough measurement of its horns from tip to tip. Though it was Uncle Jimmy who'd done the shooting, the preacher was the most excited. And before I could get a word out about the man in the well, he was telling how the monster had bore down on them without warning and at full charge. My daring cousin had time only to fling the ducks in the bull's face, step to one side and fire both barrels at point-blank range just behind the shoulder. It was only duck shot, but at that range it had been enough. The preacher pointed with pride at the gaping red hole in the carcass.

"Blown straight through to his heart, I'd say!" Mr. Friendly exclaimed. "Probably dead back there. Momentum carried him this far. Dead as a hammer. Ground shook when he fell. Lordy, Lord, look at the balls on that fellow."

"Yeah," my cousin said, "I wouldn't mind having just one of them."

"Drag you down on that side, wouldn't it?"

What kind of talk was this for a Presbyterian preacher? What was my cousin doing to this good man?

"I could walk with a crutch. Be worth it."

I had heard enough. I made them stop and listen to me. Mrs. Friendly had found a dead man in the well. They wanted to know more details, of course, but my knowledge of the subject was exhausted. The two men set out at a run and I followed along. The women waited where I'd left them, and we walked the rest of the way as fast as Mrs. Friendly was able, and at least a part of everybody's story got told. Once back at the house ruins, Amy set about tucking Mrs. Friendly into the Texas cart and the menfolk went to take a look.

"He's dead all right," my cousin said.

"You can tell that from the smell. God rest his soul," the preacher added.

Looking down into that deep black pit, seeing the chalk white face staring up at us, and smelling that smell, I could feel the vomit rising in my throat and stepped back quick.

"Wonder who it is," my cousin mused.

"That'll be for the coroner to say," the preacher said.

"You okay, Willie T.?" my cousin asked.

"Yeah."

"You going to catch pneumonia and your mama will be blaming me."

"I'm all right."

"He's bleeding," the preacher said. He meant me.

"He sure is." My cousin stepped down beside me and pulled back the pants leg that had been torn.

"Bull did that?" the preacher asked.

I didn't answer because looking at it had made me even sicker to my stomach. The horn tip had taken a deep furrow out of my calf and the blood had been dripping down my leg all this time unnoticed. Now it had filled my boot up and was starting to overflow.

"Sweet Jesus, Willie, you should have said something before this."

"There's a limit to being brave," the preacher agreed. "It's easy to slip right over into foolhardiness."

I had just enough sense to keep my mouth shut and let them think what they were thinking. I didn't volunteer that I'd been too scared and excited to even notice the cut and figured the blood in my boot was water left over from the canal. I did sit down beside the well, though.

"Get his arm, Preacher," my cousin said. Together they took me back to the cart where the boot was pulled off and the leg bandaged by Mr. Friendly who'd done a bit of doctoring while he was in China.

There was no question of me riding back on Rose. Uncle Jimmy rode her and I was tucked away beneath the blanket beside Amy Mercy. She kept up a kind and lively conversation that I was too nauseated and weak to appreciate fully. She made much of my bravery though, remarking to the others several times how she would never have guessed by my conduct in the cabin that I'd been wounded. I pressed up against her beneath the blanket, and regretted that the trip ever had to end.

Dr. McGill was brought immediately to the house. He made a joke about how he hoped the preacher stuck to preaching because he was certainly no doctor. The wound itself he didn't judge to be so bad, but he sterilized it to the point of making me scream in real pain, and wrapped it in a substantial measure of gauze. Recommending that I be treated like an invalid hero for at least one day, he thumped me hard on the side of the head with his finger. I guess that was for trespassing, but he made no mention of it to my mama, who insisted that he carry home a half dozen of the cleaned ducks. These he accepted as if they weren't his in the first place, but a genuine gift.

My mama propped me up in the parlor, provided me with a crutch, and attempted to satisfy a few reasonable whims. Amy Mercy and Mr. Friendly came calling. The preacher recited, "Lord deliver us from the jaws of the lion and from the horn of the wild bull," which struck me as far more appropriate to our adventure than his previous admiration of the bull's balls. Amy Mercy put a hand on the knee of the injured leg and kept it there for several seconds while she repeated how incredibly brave I'd been and how she would never have expected from my behavior that one of my boots was filling up with blood. She squeezed the knee gently. It was our private joke.

From the rest of the world I didn't get nearly as much praise and sympathy as I would have hoped. Grandpa only shook his head when shown the wound and spoke at length about the rice fields where today there was only a "feathered harvest."

"I married that Delta rice," he rambled on. "Body and soul married to the rice. Was not Tom's fault, Mrs. Allson. You must not blame your husband. It was not Tom's fault."

"Old Sister pray that rooster ain't crow. She know that crowing stop the rain." This was Maum Anna's comment to me. "Ain't going work them rice field in the rain. That the only day they going get off. Work Sunday in 'em devil field—ain't no matter. No, sir. Rain, they pray for Jesus ain't let the cock crow. Everybody stay in the cabin on 'em wet day. Rest theyselves."

"Yes, the bull had us cornered in one of them cabins," I said.

"Old Sister ain't finish them task. Lay 'em cross that barrel. Whip 'em 'til she pour blood. Old Sister pour blood."

"That bull—" I began again.

"Shush, boy. I ain't forget you done lose that cow. Ain't you be telling me 'bout no bull when I tell you 'bout the cock crow. Praise Jesus. That all that save the Old Sister. Whip Old Sister 'til she pour blood."

Fine, from my attentive nursemaid I got nothing. Fine. Uncle Jimmy gave me a pat on the back. Brother wouldn't have come down from the clockworks to see me, except my mama made him.

"I heard you whisper, 'Mama, I am dying,'" he confided to me, ignoring completely the bandaged calf propped up before him.

"Maybe," I admitted. "I might have been daydreaming."

"Jimmy got another girlfriend. Ain't Liza. Some new girl."

"Yes," I agreed with him.

I was no longer limping by the time Pa got the message.

The body in the well turned out to belong to Franklin, a disbarred lawyer who'd arranged the sale of the property and then gotten permission from the doctor to go diving for treasure. In fact, he still held a hazel twig in his hands. The cool water had helped to preserve the corpse, but there was no question he'd been down there a month or more. Foul play wasn't ruled out because the man had enemies waiting in line, with a wife and girlfriend fighting over first place. Besides this, Mrs. Friendly had, on further consideration, decided a man on horseback had been watching her from the woods. That had occurred even before she found the body, but thinking the rider was a trick of her imagination, she'd gone about her business, which included peering down into the well.

No, the coroner didn't rule out foul play, but he didn't

spend too long with the body either. He was wasting the tax-payer's money with three days traveling from Clarkesville and back, and the object of his attention had been missed by no one. He wrote the death down as an accidental-probable drowning and went home. Sheriff Clarke Fitchum Colgrove hadn't bothered to come or even send a deputy, which was just as well since the sheriff, himself, was mentioned as a suspect in the case.

Of course, this incident brought a renewed interest in the Allson dowry, much of it apparently prompted by Liza. At church I overheard her wondering about the right of the Allsons to be hunting on other people's property, so I made a point of limping on my crutch and explaining loudly to Brother that we'd been hunting on the Allson Place, and both the preacher and Uncle Jimmy's new girlfriend had been along.

Eventually, Amy Mercy got around to giving my cousin a full account of the bull tracking us on the path and my initial insistence that it was a cow. He teased me a few times, and even offered to instruct me in how to tell the difference between a bull and a cow. I didn't like hearing this but kept my mouth shut. I was well aware of the difference. After all, I'd kissed Amy Mercy in the cabin and I was pretty sure that was a part of the story she'd left out. Yes, I'd kissed her, in the full and complete knowledge that the carnal mind is enmity against God. Was it a sin to kiss my cousin's girlfriend? I can't say that I gave it even a second thought.

The Hat Shop

Now Uncle Jimmy had a problem, one that was making him more and more uneasy as the holiday season grew to a close. He'd talk about the hunt, the body in the well, everything—including the weather—but he wouldn't mention Liza. She was his problem.

The doctor's daughter had spotted Amy at church, but they hadn't actually met. With school starting back their paths would have to cross, and trouble was coming. There weren't but six other girls in the top grades. Margarite and Leala spoke only to Liza, and the remaining four wouldn't be brave enough to befriend Amy, and Amy liked having friends. On the night before classes resumed, my cousin spoke.

"She can take care of herself. If she has to, she'll take Liza by the ear and make her act like a decent human being. You wait and see. I ain't worried." He was worried.

I agreed there was no problem and was just as worried as him. But not nearly so worried as I was the next afternoon when school let out. At the beginning of the day I'd been limping around and telling my version of the bullfight. I saw that Uncle Jimmy was staying clear of Liza and keeping

Amy at his side. We all got through the morning in the same room without incident or even exchange, so I was surprised at recess to see my cousin and Amy both talking with Liza and her two friends. They seemed to be getting along all right. At lunch Liza and Amy swapped sandwiches. When school let out they held hands and talked for ten minutes straight while Uncle Jimmy stood around and the doctor waited in the steamer.

At least Amy refused a ride with the McGills and let Uncle Jimmy walk her home. He came back from the grocery that night confused and anxious. Things hadn't gone badly, but on the other hand they hadn't gone quite right, either. I tried to point this out to him, but he was in a sullen mood. He went over to the manse that night after supper and didn't speak when he returned. The next morning before class, Liza introduced me to her new friend Amy. I wanted to say I knew Amy Mercy a lot better than she did, but of course Liza knew that. I managed a feeble hello. Uncle Jimmy was occupied elsewhere.

"Your leg mending?" Amy asked.

"Some."

"That's good." She sounded so distant and polite I marveled anew at myself for finding the courage to kiss her.

"Yeah." I looked at my feet, over my shoulder, anywhere but at the two girls.

Liza came to my rescue.

"Willie T. is very smart," she said. "He won the spelling bee the last three years running. He can spell practically any word there is."

Well, this was true but Liza was the person I'd had to beat the first two times and last year she'd refused to enter the contest claiming she had strep throat and laryngitis.

"I can spell pretty good," I admitted.

"Go on and spell it," Amy Mercy laughed. The dimples in her cheeks got deeper and deeper and her brown eyes took on that familiar and friendly sparkle.

"What?" I asked.

"Spell 'pretty good.' You claims you can spell 'pretty good.'" There was nothing mean about her teasing. Nothing at all.

"P-R-E-T-T-Y G-O-O-D." I spelled out the words.

Amy Mercy clapped her hands together and went up on her tiptoes, a gesture I'd never seen her do before.

"You is right, Willie T. You sure can spell pretty good."

Liza, too, was laughing. "I told you our Willie had a wonderful sense of humor. He is always making us laugh with his jokes, isn't he, Jimmy?"

From out of nowhere my cousin had appeared. He said "yes" and laughed himself, or tried to anyway. Silence followed. What was Liza up to? There wasn't a soul in Cedar Point who didn't know my cousin was head over heels in love with this new girl. Liza knew it, and Jimmy knew she knew, and Amy must have known that Jimmy knew what Liza knew and all the rest of it. It was easy enough for me to see all this because I loved Amy Mercy even more than he did. That was something that Liza and Jimmy didn't know, but Amy certainly did.

I spent the afternoon on the end of the wharf studying the creek water twisting about the piling below my dangling feet. Every day the tide came in and went out, and practically every day I got up, went to school, came home. It seemed I had no more control over events than that creek did over the direction it would flow. Certainly I had considerably less force. There wasn't any hope for me. I should accept the fact this was Uncle Jimmy's girl and be satisfied to be around her. If nothing else, maybe in some small way I could help my cousin rescue her from Liza's clutches. It was in that state, a mixture of resignation and desperation, that I decided to try something I'd about given up on. I asked God to put me in a position to make a difference. All-knowing and supposedly infallible, God heard my prayer and answered it.

Early on the following Saturday morning, Uncle Jimmy was splitting stove wood for the kitchen, and I was toting it to the back porch. With all his courting these odd jobs had been sliding, so we were catching up on them and on the week's happenings. He didn't try to hide the fact he was unhappy. He'd gotten to spend more time alone with Amy Mercy when she was living with her grandmother in Brittle Branch than he did now. Liza was always there at school, and most of the time she was at the manse when he went calling after supper. All they could do was sing hymns in the parlor, with either Mr. Friendly or his wife in attendance. He'd been allowed to walk Amy to the Wednesday night prayer group, but Liza had accompanied them going and coming back. All they did was pray and sing and Liza was always there doing both with them.

I said maybe that was part of Liza's plan. We'd already agreed Liza had a plan, that her actions weren't just part of some spur-of-the-moment contrariness.

"Well. Liza ain't the only one with a plan. I'm getting a plan of my own," my cousin declared, putting an extra hard swing into the axe. Two pieces of log went flipping up violently in opposite directions. "Liza ain't got a monopoly on plans."

"I'm glad to hear you say that." The voice came from behind us. "'Cause I got me a plan, too."

And there was Amy Mercy, and Liza was nowhere around. She gave Uncle Jimmy a kiss on the cheek and, looping her arm through his, dragged him along, axe and

all, until she caught up with me. "You too, Willie." Though
I was loaded down with kindling, she looped my arm up as
well. "Now I got you both," she said. "You going to listen
good to my plan."

"What about Liza?" my cousin asked.

"You was just saying she had her a plan of her own. She
ain't going be giving a care to mine."

"She'd be interested," I said.

"Willie T., you is worse than Jim. That's all I been hearing all week. Liza going do this. Liza going do that. Don't
tell me you don't like her, either?"

"She don't like me too much. That's all."

"She talks about you all the time. Next to Jim, she thinks
you is the nicest boy in town."

Uncle Jimmy snorted and stuck the axe in the ground
hard. I hung on to the firewood because I didn't want to do
anything that would jeopardize Amy Mercy's hold on me.

"Well, she do," the girl repeated, "But that ain't why I'm
here. I done come to ask you two to be my partners."

"Sure," I said.

"Partners in what?" Uncle Jimmy asked.

"Willie T. just accepted right out. I suspect he'll make
me a better partner than you."

"Once I know what it's about, I'm as good a partner as
you'll ever find. You shouldn't ask though without telling
what the partnership is about."

"What difference do it make? Do that matter to you,
Willie T.? What the business going to be?"

"No, I'll be partners with you."

"Is Liza in this business?" Uncle Jimmy asked.

"No sir, not if you don't want her."

"All right, I agree then. Now tell us what it is we'll be
partnering in."

"A hat shop." The girl was smiling her most winning,

deep-dimpled smile. "We going to open the Allson hat shop back up."

It was my turn now. I dropped the kindling and one piece bounced off the funny bone of my good leg. Amy Mercy laughed to see me hopping about on one foot, but then remembering my injuries from the bullfight, she propped me up by hanging one of my arms across her shoulders. Uncle Jimmy probably didn't care if I fell over or not, but he hadn't laughed at me either. He understood how serious the situation was. Men couldn't be partners in a hat shop. We'd be run out of town, and my cousin told Amy that immediately. She said if we felt that way, she'd open it with Liza. Uncle Jimmy said no, he wouldn't allow that. Amy unwrapped herself from me and went on the attack, laughing at my cousin, and defying him. In his defense, I pointed out that we didn't know how to make hats. She didn't care. She'd studied millinery by mail order, too. In the beginning, we'd help out fixing up the shop, gathering materials, and sweeping up. The rest she could teach us as we went along, and it wouldn't be full time, anyway. Uncle Jimmy could keep his job at the grocery, and I'd still have plenty of time for my chores. She knew it would pay, and what's more it would make people happy to have a hat shop. Women liked to wear pretty hats, and men liked to see them wear them. Cedar Point would be a better place if we had a hat shop. Finally Uncle Jimmy said he might consider it at some time in the future. I felt the same way and put the event even further off by saying we'd have to get my mama's permission, which wasn't likely to happen.

About ten years before, when times weren't so good for the Allsons, Mama had started the shop. She hadn't made much, "just pennies" she said herself, but I knew back then those pennies had been important to Pa, or at least should have been. I even heard him shout once that he thought her hair was her crowning glory but it turned out to be her hats—which was the secret reason he married her. He was joking. She'd never made a hat until then. She and Maum Anna sat down in the dining room, pulled some old hats apart, saw how they were constructed, and went to work. It was never a big business. Grandpa signed over a little one-room building on the very edge of main street, and Mama kept it open a few hours on Saturday mornings. Her customers were mostly Negro women who wanted their hats for Sunday services. They'd come in each Saturday and pay down a few pennies a week in advance, and after a while, accumulate enough to carry home a purchase. Usually they were aiming for Easter, so that was a particularly prosperous but hectic season. The rest of the time Mama could drift along.

After a short three years, the shop closed. I guess the *Redbird* was finally showing a profit, but she claimed at the time that arthritis had her hands and she couldn't keep up with all the new fashions. For a while some of her old customers still came to the house. She'd patch up an old hat and, on rare occasions, she managed to sew a new one. But all of this had happened so long before, I could barely remember it, and I knew she had no plans for starting back. In fact, there was the distinct possibility she'd forgotten the shop existed. That's not what I said to the only girl I'd ever truly loved, though, the girl I'd vowed to serve in any way I could.

"I don't think my mama would go for that. She's planning to start back up in that business herself right soon."

"Yes," Uncle Jimmy agreed. "She's been speaking on the subject more and more often. That little building is the cornerstone of Willie's mama's hatmaking dreams."

"I reckon she done changed her mind then," Amy Mercy said, smiling at us both. Before coming out to the backyard to proposition us, she had gone into the house and gotten my mama's enthusiastic approval.

"In that case," my cousin announced after rubbing his chin and concentrating on the matter. "In that case, we'd better give this matter all due consideration."

"What do he mean by that?" Amy Mercy asked me. I'd started to gather the kindling back up, and she stooped to place the last of it in my arms. "What do it mean when he says 'all due consideration'?"

"I don't know." On releasing the wood, her tiny hand lingered on my arm. She patted it. It was almost a caress.

"Means he thinks I'll forget about it. I ain't going to. We don't need him anyways, do we, Willie T.?"

"I guess not." I tried to avoid seeing the faces my cousin was making and ignored the fact he was shaking his head no.

"I done got the key right here. Your mama said you could go on with me when you finishes with the kindling."

My cousin went over to the splitting block and kicked it hard. "We're through now," he muttered. I carried the last of the firewood around to the kitchen and then the three of us went up the street and opened up the hat shop.

Uncle Jimmy got the day off from the grocery, which disturbed him as much as it did Uncle Albert, since it was to be a day spent in Hell, plus a day without pay. That done, Amy marched us down the street to the site of our bold new enterprise—a building no bigger than our dining room, but one that had a big glass window facing the sidewalk. This view excited Amy Mercy very much, but not me and my cousin at all. The attention of the public was something we weren't anxious to draw.

"First, we going scrub it down very good inside and wash the front window," she directed. "Then, Willie T., you going to whitewash the outside and, Jimmy, you'll be tacking the new shingles on the roof. We ain't going to have that old rain leaking in on our hats, now is we?"

"That'll take some time," my cousin declared. He ran his finger across the thick dust on the counter. "How long would you say, Willie T.?"

"Weeks. That's just a guess, though. Could take longer."

"More likely to be months. Six months, maybe eight," my cousin estimated.

"Oh, I don't know," Amy mused with a tiny trace of doubt and disappointment creeping into her voice. "I declare we can do it a mite faster than that if we all pitches in." Her face broke into its deepest, dimpled smile.

She was right. We went to work right that minute, and when the sun set that same day, we were done. And I had to admit, the building did look smart. It shone bright white on the outside, and the windows were gleaming clean. With six years of grit removed, you could once more see the big gilt print on the glass that read HAT SHOP.

"I got to go," Amy said, giving Uncle Jimmy a quick peck on the cheek and waving good-bye to me. "The Friendlys done asked me not to stay at the shop after dark."

"Seems like we could step out on Saturdays," my cousin commented.

"They said especially not on Saturdays. You knows you is always welcome to sit in the parlor."

"I'm tired of sitting in that parlor."

"Mr. Friendly said people will talk 'bout us unless we sit in the parlor."

"I don't believe he would say something that dumb."

"Ask him yourself."

"I will."

I guess Uncle Jimmy did ask his mate, and I guess the answer was that people would talk, maybe they were already talking. It was hard to say what was permissible, but I got the distinct impression that the Friendlys, for all their friendliness, were not going to allow Amy Mercy to go about unchaperoned. Uncle Jimmy went there that same night. Liza and even Margarite showed up. They played the piano and sang more hymns. Sunday night, Mrs. Friendly played for them and they sang even more hymns. Things weren't working out for Uncle Jimmy, and I had a feeling they were going to get worse for him and me as well.

All we'd done so far was clean up and paint a hat shop. It was something else altogether to actually go inside and make a hat, especially when nothing was between you and the general watching public but a quarter inch pane of clear, clean glass. And of course, Amy was working on the project faster than ever. My mama had given her the head blocks used for shaping and lent her the special scissors and shears that were a part of the trade. From Uncle Albert's dry goods section, she credited flannel and hat pins, and from Crowns Bluff, she had Pa bring a long list of hard-to-find items—silks, ribbons, netting, sequins. Most especially, she had him bring artificial flowers. Her life savings was spent on these. Dozens upon dozens arrived on the bow of the *Redbird* and were carried by the armload to the hat shop. They didn't fool me. You could easily tell they were made of cloth that had been bunched up and sewed, but they were bright. Reds, oranges, yellows, and pinks for the blossoms and buds, greens and blues for the stems and leaves. The colors did jump out at you, and Amy assured me that artificial flowers were what people wanted on their hats these days.

By the second Saturday, we'd be ready for business. I say "we," but Uncle Jimmy would be saved from complete participation by clerking in the grocery. Still, Amy had made him swear he'd spend every second of his meal break with us. I'd be bearing the full brunt, but my cousin moped about that final week, shook his head and muttered about leaving town. We couldn't.

My mama had circled the cursed Saturday on her calendar, so naturally the day arrived on schedule. Still, I managed to delay my appearance until eleven and do nothing suspicious before my cousin's noon arrival. To my relief, only a couple of my peers had come by, and they'd glanced in and gone on without a remark. Amy had a few last-minute things to tend to, but she made sure they were finished when my cousin poked his nose through the door, a deliberate ten minutes late.

"Come on, Jim," she waved him in with great excitement. "Willie and me has been waiting on you to start. We didn't want you to miss nothing."

My cousin glared at me and I shrugged. If we'd been waiting on him, I was glad of it. Amy was already at her cutting table starting to work.

"First we takes the felt and cuts it like so," she sang. "Pay attention now." We both crowded close with our backs to the window, hoping to block the view and go unrecognized at the same time.

"I still don't see why we can't do this home in the kitchen. That's what Willie's mama did," my cousin said in a final plea for sanity and discretion.

"I thought I told you," Amy explained patiently as she cut the felt. "This way here, people is going to stop and watch us make the hats. Then they is going to come inside and buy 'em."

"You want 'em to watch us?" my cousin asked in amazement.

"'Course I do. Now pay attention. See, we got to wet the felt and pull it down hard over this here form. You and Willie T. hold it down tight. Hold it. Won't bite you, for goodness' sakes. Hold it steady and let me get this band tied. There, now you see we have got us a right smart start. Ribbon? Where is that ribbon hiding? Good, that's it. A very good start, don't you gentlemen agree?"

We looked down at what we'd accomplished and both nodded. Scooter and Barnus Wilson were looking in. Barnus's nose flattened where it touched the glass. Their hot breath clouded the glass. They stepped back and wiped the mist with their closed fists.

"What y'all looking at?" Uncle Jimmy yelled so loud they jumped straight back the width of the sidewalk.

"Wait!" Amy shouted. "I want y'all's opinion." She carried the hat block over to the window and beckoned them back for a closer look. "What do you think of that?" she shouted through the glass pane.

The two of them studied the hat, then looked back studying me and Uncle Jimmy. Then they ran off laughing.

"They done gone to tell others," Amy remarked, quite delighted.

"I don't doubt that," my cousin said.

I judged the distance to the back door and tried to calculate how many steps it would take me to get there from different points in the room.

"Flowers is what we need now. I can show you how to tie 'em on. That's a good thing for you to learn early on."

"I ain't tying no flowers," Uncle Jimmy said in a deliberate, nearly angry voice.

"I reckon you'd rather block felt?"

"I ain't blocking no felt, either."

"Well, you got to do one or the other. This here won't be a partnership if we don't all work at it."

"I ain't going to be partners in a hat shop."

"You ain't even give it a try, Jimmy?"

"I love you, Amy Mercy, with all my heart and soul, but I cannot do this for you. I'd rather die first."

"I love you too, Jimmy, with all my heart and all my soul, so it is all right if you want to quit. I'm going to love you anyway."

In the time it took for this mutual declaration of love, a large crowd had gathered at the window. Scooter and Barnus had rounded up half the male population below the age of thirty, and they were all outside staring in at us. Uncle Jimmy was eyeing them nervously and lowered his voice down to a whisper.

"I'm glad to hear you say that Amy Mercy, 'cause I'm going to love you until time ends."

"What about you, Willie T.?" Amy asked.

I couldn't speak. Of course, I wanted to say "I will love you until time ends," but was wary of saying it in front of my cousin, not to mention the others outside. She was waiting for an answer, though, and I'd about decided to go on and say, "Yes, I'll love you, too." But it turned out that wasn't the question she wanted answered.

"Is you going to make hats or not?"

Yes, I loved her and no I wasn't going to make hats.

"No," I admitted, but added very quickly that I'd sweep up in the afternoon and help out in other ways.

"Could you get feathers?"

"Sure. What kinds?"

"All kinds. I'll be needing little bits of fur, things like that."

"I can do it. I'm your man."

"It's settled. You going to be a millinery assistant and Jimmy going to remain my boyfriend." At that point, she gave Uncle Jimmy a kiss on the cheek that caused the on-lookers at the window to give an exaggerated sigh and a whoop or two.

Saying good-bye to Amy, my cousin walked outside and immediately struck a fellow we called Frypan. The young man wasn't exactly an innocent bystander, but he was pretty easygoing and on the first lick went down with a busted lip. Some in the crowd held my cousin back and told him to calm down. Then they all dispersed without buying a single hat.

Amy took Uncle Jimmy back inside and, despite the fact he hadn't been touched, went over his face with the same damp rag she used on her felt. She asked him not to start any more fights in front of the shop because it'd give the place a bad name and scare off customers. My cousin promised he wouldn't. He said he didn't think they'd been shopping anyway, but she told him they'd go home and tell their mothers, wives, sisters, and girlfriends about the hat shop, and those women would come in and buy hats. That was how word-of-mouth advertising worked.

She was right, too. The mothers did come in, and the sisters and wives and girlfriends. Women of both races bought hats as fast as Amy could make them, and they bought all kinds. Big, little, felt, straw, plain, and grand. Decorated over with silk, ribbons, and worsted. She studied the fashion books to see what people were wearing in New York City and Philadelphia, but these new "French styles," she felt, were too colorless for a place like Cedar Point. The flowers, as she'd predicted, were her biggest success, and the more she could pile onto a hat brim, the bigger success that particular hat would be.

Yes, the hat shop was a huge success. Amy stayed so busy, she had to hire Liza to come in and do what we'd refused to do. The Friendlys liked that better, anyway, because business or not, it wasn't right for the girl to be alone with us. Uncle Jimmy would stop by for an occasional chat, but Uncle Albert kept him busy, and he still didn't feel too comfortable in these environs. He had to content himself with seeing Amy at school and going over to the preacher's to sing the hymns, a passion for musical entertainment that he'd gradually reduced down to a couple nights a week. I, too, stayed clear of the shop, but I did manage to check in for at least a few minutes every afternoon. I'd have stayed longer, but Liza was always about. She'd been all too happy to step in and fill all four of our shoes. She agreed to anyway, but in fact, on entering the business, she'd left the making of the hats pretty much up to Amy, and concentrated on standing behind the counter and charming the customers, who went ahead and bought hats anyway.

I can't say I was completely satisfied with the way things were, but I was staying busy keeping up my end of the bargain. I gathered feathers from our chicken yard and other chicken yards, plucking them when necessary from angry roosters who felt they had none to spare. I got my pa's .22 rifle and shot an occasional egret or heron when a special order came in. One afternoon, I shot a pair of squirrels right in our own horse pasture and carried them straight to the hat shop. Liza was outraged for no particular reason, but Amy welcomed these as well, and sent me out back to skin them.

Now she had something to taxidermy for me, and with great patience, she showed me how to treat the skins and carefully mount them lifelike on a frame of wire and plaster. Unless you touched the animals, you wouldn't have known they were dead, and I was quite pleased just to see the two of them perched with their forearms extended like little dogs waiting for a treat. Amy wanted more. She dressed one up in doll clothes as the wife, and for the husband squirrel, she stitched up a little striped suit and a tiny straw boater hat that went down between his ears at an angle. To make the picture complete, she fashioned a little baby carriage from a toy wagon and put a walnut in there to be the squirrel baby.

Looking down on her creation she finally declared it good and placed it in the window of the store. It brought a lot of curious people in her direction. Mr. Britt would come and stand outside and laugh and laugh. He said he had to own it. Amy said it wasn't for sale. I, Willie T., had shot the squirrels, and so it had a great sentimental value to her. He offered five dollars, which I'd have taken immediately because I knew where a couple more squirrels were. She said no. He said seven dollars. He said ten dollars. She said no amount of money. He went off shaking his head, still laughing. At least once a week he'd come back and look. I was happy. "No amount of money. Mr. and Mrs. Squirrel and little Walnut is not for sale." Amy Mercy said that, and I'd shot the squirrels.

Something else good was happening, but it was a less-noticeable occurrence. Gradually, Liza rejoined her neglected companions Margarite and Leala Fitchum and came less and less often to the hat shop. And I found myself alone with Amy Mercy more and more. Early in these solitary encounters I'd tried to kiss her again and been sternly rebuffed. Forcibly, I might even say. We were going to be friends and that was all. If I was willing to accept those conditions, then she'd be one of the best friends I'd ever have. I didn't see where I had much choice, and harnessed myself to this yoke of friendship with what I hoped was a temporary enthusiasm. In the afternoons, I continued faithfully to sweep up and she'd follow me about with the dustpans. Mostly she just wanted to talk. She wanted to ask me questions about the Allson family, about what our life together had been like and did I remember my sisters or Uncle Jimmy's pa. Could Grandpa carry a tune? What year did the Allson Place last grow rice? How much horsepower was in the *Redbird*, and how did my mama feel towards the color blue? Well, a lot of times I couldn't answer, and sometimes when I did, I'd get the feeling she already knew the answer, or that she even had a different answer, perhaps one she'd gotten from Uncle Jimmy. These weren't real conversations, though, in the sense of give and take.

As time passed, that gradually changed. We began to sit on the rear stoop just before closing and she started to relax.

"Going to take money to make Jimmy happy," she confided one afternoon in a needless tone of secrecy.

"Make me happy, too."

"You know, Willie T., would be wonderful if we was to find the Allson dowry."

"Won't happen."

"My papa said the slave woman, Old Sister, seen the whole thing. Said the Yankee sailors carried off the two cupboards but they was empty and she told Papa the dowry was still in the ground."

"She told Maum Anna the same thing but we done dug it raw."

"You know my grandpapa Tyler is buried out there. He died a week or so 'fore the house burned." I said I didn't know that, and she added that his burial site was unmarked, but her grandmama could find it until her eyesight went.

At least twice more Amy returned to the subject of the dowry. For Uncle Jimmy's sake she was praying that it would be found. Not for her own sake and not for my sake, either. She repeated a story I'd heard before about the coachman turning addled. Dressing up in his livery, he'd hook the ox to the carriage and drive around and around in front of the mansion. Her papa, Allson Mercy, saw that with his own young eyes and said it was a comical sight. Except when the Yankees were trying to frighten the slave into telling where the dowry was buried, they'd accidentally hung him. That was tragic for the Allsons since he, alone, knew where it was buried. She returned again to Old Sister's story, and I repeated again how the Allson men had been digging in the rubble for half a century, and finally got around to admitting I was glad Dr. McGill owned the place. She laughed at that, and I went on to tell her other secrets—how Esther had died and why it wasn't Tom's fault and some more.

I guess this satisfied her, because she began to lean close and tell me a little bit about her own life. The excitement of sitting beside her, sometimes touching, brushing up against her arm, was enough to distract me, but I did have the presence of mind to ask her about her brother, The Hard to Catch. It wasn't her favorite topic, but she admitted he'd killed six men who she knew about, and two of these had been their own brothers. The first, the family's tanner, he'd killed with a knife. Both men had been drunk and quarreling over whether or not it would rain the next day.

"Was cut worse than a vein," she explained pointing to a spot on her own side. "Cut down to the very pulse, so the blood just kept spurting. There's a verse, Bible verse in Ezekiel and you say it correct three time and look 'em in the eye that suppose to stop the flow." She shook her head back and forth and pressed at her own side. "I done forgot that verse. Something in it 'bout wallowing in blood."

The Hard to Catch had shot the second brother. He'd been the oldest and was the best around with an axe, but after a crippling accident he'd gotten a job riding the turpentine woods up above Clarkesville.

"Come home with twelve dollars and a fine horse. Then him and James went off drinking together. Found that body floating in the branch. Shot through the throat." Amy Mercy pointed at her own throat, above the hollow of her neck. "Throwed his own brother in the branch and rode away on that same horse—same horse he's riding now. Ain't made no excuse. Didn't apologize for spending the money." She looked at me with a strange blank expression. "He ain't a person with no real feelings. Care more about a hog than a man, and he ain't all that gentle with a hog. Don't you go laughing. Ain't funny." I'd laughed to make her feel better, not because I thought it was funny. "Ain't no human being he has feelings for. Not his wife nor children. Not his grandma. Not me, that's one thing for certain."

This particular conversation had ended abruptly with her rising and leaving the store for me to lock up. It was three days before she'd sit on the stoop again, and that time I chose what I figured would be a easier topic. If every child in the Mercy family had a special talent, then what was hers? She couldn't believe that I didn't know.

"Jimmy ain't told you?"

"No, he ain't never told me a thing about you."

"Wasn't really a talent."

"What was it?"

"I was the last born. My mama and papa done run out of necessary occupations and since they was both getting on in years, they picked out something sort of frivolous for me. Jimmy ain't told you this?"

"No," I assured her.

"They raised me to make 'em happy. That's all I was supposed to do."

"That don't sound too bad."

She looked at me with a sad quizzical shadow of a smile.

"Weren't much fun. 'Cept maybe at the start, back when I was learning it. Didn't last long, no way." The smiling stopped and only the sadness remained. "I was just a little bit of a thing, my mama come and woke me up. Sleeping with two of my sisters, but just me she carry so I can see this screech owl that done come to sit on the windowsill. My papa sleeping right on and we went up beside that little critter. We was staring at the owl and him staring right back. 'That my token,' my mama whispered. 'I going die now.' Then we went to stand on the front porch. Early morning star still shining, and she points off to the edge of the woods. Looks to me like a cow moving in the shadow, but then I see it been a coffin floating up off the ground. 'Only cure for it's the casket,' my mama said.

"She done been coughing some. My papa said it was 'cause she had washed her hair in the winter. Wanted to take her to Clarkesville see a real doctor. 'That dampness settled in your tubes.' She told him, 'No, I done seen my token. Only cure is the casket.'" Amy Mercy shook her head. "Been meaning to ask Dr. McGill. It do look like medical science would have a cure. Awful thing to be choking to death."

When Amy was nine her mama finally died and nine days later, her pa disappeared. Some said he'd run off with another woman, others that he was crazed and had killed himself. He could have had an accident, been murdered, a lot of things could have happened. After that, the girl felt there was no point in having a particular talent, especially not that one. "Passed from one to another of 'em. Made out the best I could."

She finished this recitation with a stricken look on her face, and once more left me to lock up the hat shop. This never happened again, though. Despite what she'd said about the job of making her parents happy, she could still recount some good memories of growing up. A couple of her sisters, especially the oldest she'd recently been living with, had tried to look after her, and before the token, her mama was always taking her huckleberrying, or hunting after wild honey, or just wandering in the woods. She'd learned a lot about that world, and even before leaving she'd had a glimpse of the other. There were people coming in and out of those woods—Methodist circuit riders, an occasional drummer, logging crews, horse traders, blind tiger liquor men, and, contrary to the lying storekeeper, even politicians. Cedar Point was much closer, but these visitors always entered from the Clarkesville side, and that was considered the proper doorway to the outside. The people of our community were perceived as being far too high and mighty than they had a right to be. Most thought they looked down on the people living in the Great Swamp. I assured her that wasn't true, even though it was. She agreed it wasn't true, for she'd been well received, but our ways were strange. She'd lived in five different communities, and none had been quite like Cedar Point.

"Awful lot of hymn singing. Was hymn singing other places. Weren't every night, though." The dimples sank in deep and the brown eyes sparkled. In the afternoons, she began to teach me songs that never got sung in Cedar Point. Sitting on the back step in late afternoon she sang:

> *The moon is a great thing*
> *As big as the ocean.*
> *The stars is a little thing*
> *And they're always in motion.*

There was another one she sang about a cowboy:

> *When I was a cowboy*
> *I learned to throw the rope and line.*
> *I learned to pocket the money*
> *But not to dress so fine.*

There were dozens more and they always made us laugh. Sometimes, I would even try to sing along a verse or two, and she promised to get a harmonica and teach me how to play it. She hadn't learned that by mail order. She'd learned that from her papa, Allson, who'd picked it up from Grandpapa Tyler.

"You ain't never seen a moving-picture show?"

She couldn't believe I'd never seen a single one, because while with her oldest sister, she'd been to every show that came to town. She'd seen dozens and would get up off the steps and act the parts out for me, which I thought she did with amazing skill. She'd ridden on plenty of trains and even touched an airplane. She'd talked on the telephone, more times than she could remember, and together we laughed about the wireless and how nobody was ever on the other end when we were made to listen.

"Didn't get no real schooling 'til I was 'most eleven," she confided. "Learn it all at home. Learn reading and numbers from my sisters. Circuit rider taught me some so I would know the Bible. When I get off the first time, they put me to a school, had nothing but a clay floor and clay chimney. Went down there every morning. Homesick, too. Sure enough, don't make sense do it Willie T.? That's where I got my learning 'til I start up in regular school, and get to taking my correspondence courses." She started to sing:

> *When I was a cowboy*
> *I learned to throw the rope and line.*

She was happy in Cedar Point and getting happier with each passing day.

Then suddenly Uncle Jimmy was happy, too, and I expected it had nothing to do with having money. He still had none, but he got happier and happier. He got too happy. Cow struck, only worse. He'd start laughing at nothing. All the time he was whistling around the house and staring into space. He acted drunk, but you couldn't smell anything on his breath, and besides, he woke that way in the morning.

I knew I wasn't imagining this. Liza, too, was growing suspicious, and though she was still best friends with Amy, she was having more and more trouble pretending they were friends. She'd fallen even further out of the hat shop habit. She did not truly think the squirrel family was cute, and when she thought no one was looking she'd fix on them a look of grim anger that made me want to sweep them up in my arms, strip them of their fine clothes, and return them to their previous existence in the treetops.

"What's got into you?" I asked my cousin when I could stand it no more. "What you got to be so happy about?"

"Who says I'm happy?"

"I ain't blind and even a blind man would know. What's going on?"

"That's none of your business."

"I want to know if you going crazy or not. I mean from where I'm looking, you ain't exactly in the catbird's seat. You go to school, work for Uncle Albert. You sit in the preacher's parlor at night and sing them hymns. You go to sleep and it starts all over again. Even if you is in love, it's no excuse for rejoicing that I can see."

"Mind your own business."

Not long after that, I was coming into the hat shop a little earlier than usual, and I stopped to admire the squirrel family. Satisfied they were as they should be, I looked further into the store. I could see Uncle Jimmy with his arms wrapped around Amy Mercy, kissing her on the lips. She was offering no resistance. In fact, she was wrapping him in her arms and kissing him back. Some of her long black hair had come unpinned and was falling halfway down her back.

I watched dumfounded through the glass for a minute or more, waiting for them to break apart, growing madder and madder. If anything, they appeared more interested in each other than less. The girl had taken her lips away, true, but only so my cousin could kiss her on the neck, which he was doing with an animallike disregard for all that was fine, decent, and Christian in this world. It was me who gathered the feathers and swept up, and me who was in love with Amy Mercy, but I was supposed to be her friend. What the hell good did that do me? When it became obvious at last that they were not going to stop any time soon, I did what any angry person would have done, I knocked loudly on the window. They did stop then and looked embarrassed enough until they saw it was me. Once I was recognized, though, Amy just waved for me to come inside.

"I could see what you were doing," I said right away. "The whole world can see."

"That's the beauty of glass," my cousin said. He hadn't even bothered to take his hand from around the girl's waist.

"Don't you be angry," Amy said.

"I'm not angry."

She put her arm back around his waist, which made me even angrier, if such was possible.

"You sound angry," she said.

"I ain't. I come by here to get my squirrels back and to tell you to get somebody else to sweep up."

I walked to the window and removed the squirrel family from the display.

"Put them back," my cousin said.

"I will not."

"Leave him be," Amy said.

"Both of you leave me be." I'd started to cry, and with my bare hands, I ripped apart Mr. and Mrs. Squirrel and threw them and little Walnut on the floor. Slamming the door behind me, I retired from the hat shop business. That night after supper, Uncle Jimmy asked me to come outside. I went reluctantly, ashamed of crying, but still angry.

"I got something to tell you," he said when he'd led me beyond the arbor. "Amy wants me to tell you, but you the only one. You got to swear to keep it a secret."

I said nothing, swore nothing.

"Do you swear?"

"Yes," I swore. I had to know.

"We're getting married when school's out."

Again, I said nothing.

"You hear what I said?"

"Yeah. Good for you."

"I wish you could say that like you mean it."

"Kind of sudden, this marrying Amy."

"Can't help it," Uncle Jimmy said.

"Why not?" Was Amy having his baby? I refused to believe it.

"Maum Anna has fixed it," my cousin laughed.

"Fixed what?"

"Fixed it so I got to marry Amy 'cause she's fixed it so Amy can't marry nobody else but me."

"What are you talking about? She can marry anybody she wants." I was thinking me, for instance, but didn't dare to say it.

"Anna came to me. Said I looked so down in the mouth and plain miserable, she couldn't stand to watch me suffer no more. She offered to fix it so that Amy Mercy would only marry me. Just a little blue cloth bag. She filled it up with some bits of colored glass, a lock of Amy's hair, and a few scraps of cat bones and junk. I buried it under the front step of the manse so when Amy came out to go to school, she had to step over it. Then I made sure I was the first person she saw."

"That's what got you so happy?" I was starting to worry a little less about the inevitability of this marriage.

"Yes. That's it."

"You believe that's truly going to make a difference."

"One wrong step and I'd had to run off with Mrs. Friendly."

Picturing this got us both laughing, but I couldn't help expressing a small hint of my own optimistic doubt. My cousin admitted he'd been very doubtful at first, but what made him believe was the response of the girl in question. From that morning on, Amy Mercy had been head over heels in love with him like never before. He wasn't going to question what had happened or why. He was marrying Amy in June.

I managed to forgive my cousin, at least that one night. It was flattering to be privy to the secret information, especially when he had confided in me alone. It helped, too, when I was coaxed back into the hat shop and found Amy had sewed up Mr. and Mrs. Squirrel and put them and baby Walnut back on display. She kissed me on the cheek in front of my cousin, and when I had the presence of mind to lie and tell her I hoped she and Jimmy would be very happy together, she cried and cried. In fact, she wouldn't stop crying until he threatened to call off the wedding and go into a monastery. That didn't strike me as such a bad idea, but it got Amy laughing again. She laughed until she cried. She knew we would all get on fine from here on.

Well, Uncle Jimmy had explained about the witchcraft to me on a Monday night, and on Tuesday, I'd gone back into the hat shop. By Wednesday, I'd decided that whether by means natural or supernatural, one way or the other, Amy Mercy was being tricked into marriage. Thursday afternoon, I made up my mind that as her friend, I should warn her. I'd already worked out my speech and was brutally disappointed to find Liza putting in one of her rare appearances. I hung around, making up things to do, but it was no good. Not only did Liza stay until closing time, but she walked Amy home. I had no excuse for accompanying them, so I cut over to the next street and followed from a distance until I was sure Amy was inside the Friendly's house, and Liza was on her way. Determined to have my say, I hung back a few more minutes and then went calling at the preacher's. Yes, I went over it in my mind, waiting for the door to be answered. I couldn't stand by and see this girl tricked. I'd warn her. I had the strength of my convictions, Christian and otherwise. If necessary, I'd even tell the preacher what was going on beneath his own front steps. Whatever it took to end this madness, I was prepared to carry out. No sacrifice was too great.

Mrs. Friendly was a little surprised to see me at the door because I hadn't been around for over a month.

"Willie," she said. "My husband's not here right now. He had to go by the Widow Wilson's for a minute. If you care to wait, he'll be home soon."

Of course, I knew he'd be gone this time of day. I hadn't planned to tell him on this trip. All I needed was a few seconds alone with Amy Mercy.

"I come to see Amy. There's some hat shop business I forgot about. Afraid it can't wait."

"Oh, I understand. I think she's in the attic. Can you find your way?"

"Yes, ma'am," I said.

I'd been back up to the attic a couple more times with Brother to listen on the wireless telephone, but still hadn't heard the first word. Even Brother wasn't particularly impressed, and stayed tending to his clocks instead. I don't know what I expected to find up there, but it certainly wasn't Amy Mercy sitting at the apparatus with the headset over her ears. Mrs. Friendly hadn't said she'd be doing this, but then what else was there to do up there? Except for some steamer trunks, the attic was empty.

"Hello," I said from the doorway. She didn't hear me. Apparently she was listening to something on the machine, so I stood, studying her for a spell, almost forgetting why I'd come. The afternoon light shining bright white through the attic window created a halo effect around her head. The features of her face were almost lost in the glare. Beneath this, starting at her neck, the heavy gray folds of a quilt had been wrapped about her, and she was holding it tight at the front with her tiny hand. It was cold. I hadn't noticed before, but the day was cold and the attic almost frigid. Still it seemed a strange and beautiful costume, this quilt she was wearing, and from out of nowhere, came the wish that somehow she might be naked beneath it.

That's all it took. That one wish from me, and she turned my way. Not smiling, she beckoned me forward.

"Listen," she said. "Listen here." She took the headset off and handed it to me. I put it on and heard nothing, as usual, except the snap and grind of some foreign power source.

"Hear that?"

"Yes," I lied. She had her free hand on my forearm.

"Hard to imagine, ain't it?"

"Yes," I lied again. Yes. Yes. Yes.

"People singing up there in New Jersey and us hearing it down here."

"Yes," I lied again, taking the headset off and handing it back to her.

She set it aside, turned the knobs of the machine off, and stood up.

"I didn't know you listened," I said.

"Not too much. I just come up here to get away." She held the quilt close up towards her neck. She wasn't naked underneath, but I was surprised to see that she wasn't dressed either. She was wearing only underclothing of some sort.

"I didn't mean to bother you," I lied for the last time.

"You ain't a bother to me. I'm always glad to see you, Willie. You know that."

"As glad as you are to see Jimmy?" I asked.

"Sure."

"You glad you getting married?" It was time to get on with the purpose of this call. The preacher would be home soon and this unchaperoned time was precious.

"Yes, I surely am. You know that."

"I ain't."

"I thought you and me had done settled this."

"You don't know all the facts, Amy."

"You is a strange boy," she said. She sounded weary. Sleepy almost.

"What do you mean by that?"

"You don't act like a lot of 'em others."

I took this to be a compliment and slipped my hand under the quilt and slid it around her waist. "You ain't so common yourself."

"Don't you start doing that again."

"Why not?"

"'Cause I'm asking you not to."

I wasn't going to listen to her. No. I pulled her close to me and, for a second time, I kissed her. And for a second time, I think she let me kiss her. She didn't push me away. She didn't turn her face from me. She closed her eyes and let me kiss her. I had both arms around her and could feel the warmth of her body beneath the covering. I put my cheek against hers and whispered, "I love you."

"You ain't the only one." Amy Mercy pressed up close against me, lay her head on my shoulder, and began to shake ever so slightly.

"You crying?" I asked finally.

"Yes," she sniffed.

"I didn't mean to make you cry." I wanted to start kissing her again, but it was difficult, if not physically impossible, under these conditions.

"It ain't just you. There's more to it than you."

"What? Has Liza said something to you?"

"No. It ain't Liza. Why you always thinking it's Liza?"

"It usually is her."

"No, it ain't." She had turned her face towards me and I could see the tears flowing freely now. "Can't you guess why I'm up here, Willie?"

"'Cause you want to get away. You told me."

"From Mrs. Friendly," the girl said. "She don't want me in her house."

"Why not?" I couldn't have guessed that answer. Not ever.

"She figures her husband is in love with me," she whispered.

"He's a preacher," I said with some force. "He's fifty years old."

"Don't matter how old he is. I figure she's right."

"Has he done anything to you?" I was angry. Indignant.

"'Course not. He don't even talk to me hardly. Talks way less than he used to and never stays in the room with me alone. He never does that. Never."

"Amy, that don't mean nothing. Why would you think he loves you?" His behavior didn't sound nearly as suspicious to me as it apparently did to her.

"I done seen 'em praying downstairs. They don't know I hear 'em, but they get down on their knees and pray out loud about 'whoever looketh on a woman to lust after her hath committed adultery with her already in his heart.' They pray it every night."

"That don't mean it's you." Having let Mr. Friendly off the hook, I was not at all anxious to snag him again.

"Who else you see around here?" She motioned about the empty attic with the tiny hand that came free of the quilt.

"He's fifty years old," I repeated.

"Forty-seven."

"He's forty-seven, then. He's still an old man."

"And you fourteen."

"So?" I said.

"Jimmy is 'most eighteen so it's him I'll be marrying if you'll just let go of me."

"So that's how it is?"

"Yes." Now she did push me and pushed so hard that as a gentleman, I was forced to step away. "Go on home," she said.

"All right."

"We're still friends, ain't we?"

"I suppose."

Now it was she who kissed me, a quick peck on the cheek, but I reached out again, this time putting my arms around the outside of the blanket and pulling her against me. Once more I felt her small rounded body fold against mine, and once again she began to cry in earnest.

"I done seen a lot of terrible things in my life, Willie T." Suddenly, she sobbed these words against my shoulder. "I done terrible, terrible things. Things I can't repeat to a living soul."

I held her tighter still because she was shaking as if chilled. "You don't know half what life's holding for you. You don't know a tenth of it yet."

"Don't cry," I whispered.

"People figure I'm happy, but I ain't. Sad inside, Willie. About the saddest person you ever going to meet."

"I don't believe that."

"It's true. Sometimes I feel it's me that's choking. Its true. I swear."

"No, it ain't." I kissed her crying face, first on one cheek and then on the other. I kissed her mouth again. Salt. It all tasted of salt, but she was welcoming my mouth with her tongue, and pressing against me with surprising force.

"Do you really love me?" she whispered.

"You know I do."

"I got to know. Do you really love me, and me only? Ain't never going to be another. Nobody that's going to make you happy? Just me?"

"Yes, you know that."

She was slipping down onto the floor and taking me with her. The blanket that was her cloak was now going to be our bed. She was spreading it out across the dusty floor and inviting me on. I could see now that she wore bloomers with a chemise over them. Lying down fully, she spread her legs slightly, and her arms reached up. Her long black hair was pulling loose, threatening to tumble completely free of its pins. Her lips were parted. Her brown eyes were shiny with tears. Already to my knees, I lowered myself on top of her, pressed down with the full weight of my body, and found her mouth once more with my own. Beneath me, her wide hips had begun to move, a soft rocking motion that caught my hardened member in its caress and threatened to bring an end to the attempt.

I'd imagined this scene with Amy countless times over the last several months, but nothing I'd imagined could compare with the actual accomplished fact of having this incredible woman writhing beneath me and showering my face with kisses and calling my name softly. Frantically, I began to unbutton my fly with one hand, and she to assist was bringing her chemise up high across her partially bare thigh. I was free. My member stuck out from my pants front, almost a separate animal, but one neither willful nor contrary. We were both of the same mind. Amy Mercy found the hardened flesh with her fingertips and ran her fingers down to the base. If she were to do that again, I knew I wouldn't make the show. Reaching up beneath her chemise, I began to work her bloomers down across her willing hips.

"Amy." The voice called up from below. "Amy, Liza's here to see you."

"Yes, ma'am," Amy shouted out over my shoulder, after only the briefest silence. Already she was separating the two of us. "Tell her we'll be coming right down."

"She's coming up."

"No. Me and Willie will be coming down."

"Amy." It was Liza's voice already in the stairwell. "What are you doing up here? What do you expect to hear on that impossible old machine?"

I stood there with limb still protruding perpendicular from the trunk. Where had she gone? My bedmate had disappeared out from under me. Wrapping the quilt back around her she was once more seated at the wireless telephone. With one hand she adjusted her hairpins and with the other clicked on the knobs. Suddenly the headset was on her head and she was the picture of rapt attention. I, on the other hand, was the picture of thwarted lust and barely turned my back to Liza in time to hide my shame. Walking directly to the window I remained turned away until an opportunity arose for me to refasten my fly and join the two girls at the radio.

"Are you all right?" Liza asked immediately.

"Yes. Why shouldn't I be?" My voice was husky, my throat dry.

"You appear flushed. Perhaps you have a fever."

"Listen here," Amy said, removing the headset and handing it over to Liza. "You do seem fevered, Willie. Best you get to home 'fore you too sick to travel."

"Yes," I said. "Maybe I should do just that." I left the two of them there, bent over the contraption, and went off plotting every step of the way how I'd arrange to be alone with Amy Mercy again at the soonest possible instant.

Actually, that wasn't as soon as I might have hoped. After three days of seeing her with somebody else always around, I knew I was the only one seeking a renewal of our acquaintance. She acted normal, though. She wasn't mad. She even joked and teased me in front of Uncle Jimmy and never said or did anything that would make either him or Liza suspicious. I played the same game and waited, knowing that eventually the two of us would come together again. That was Wednesday afternoon of the following week. She was working alone in the hat shop. She saw me coming and caught my advance with an arm held out stiff. In the other hand she held the shears she'd been using to trim off the artificial flowers. Bright bits of different colored cloth clung about her clothes and even in her hair.

"Stay right there. Don't you come one step closer." She said this firmly, but she couldn't hide the smile she was trying to keep inside.

"You pretty as a picture," I said.

"Save your breath. I'm marrying your cousin Jimmy. What happened the other evening didn't never happen and as my friend and a gentleman I expect you to keep it fully confidential."

"Amy," I pleaded.

"I mean it, Willie. I was upset. If I hadn't been upset none of that would never have happened." She was looking nervously at the front window. I looked, too, and convinced that no one was there I pressed forward against the hand that was keeping me at arm's length.

"Come on, Amy. You know you care about me."

"Care about you enough to jab you with these same scissors." She meant it. I was amazed to see that she had raised up the shears, and stepped back a pace. "Listen to me now. I'll be marrying Jimmy. That means you and I can't go on kissing and hugging like we is newlyweds. It's in the Bible. One husband. One wife. You know that." She lowered the scissors, looking to me for confirmation of what was in the Bible.

"I love you."

"Don't you never say that again. I love Jimmy. I can't love you."

"Sure," I said. "I guess you know why you love him, don't you."

"Yes, I love him 'cause I love him. Now go on and leave me be."

"You don't know about it, do you?"

"What? What is you talking about?"

"That's why I came up to the attic last week. I was coming to warn you."

"'Bout what?"

"'Bout Uncle Jimmy."

"Willie, go on out of here."

"He got Maum Anna to put a hex on you. He buried a blue bag underneath the steps, and then you stepped across it." She started to laugh. "It ain't funny. He fixed it so you can't marry nobody else."

"I don't want to marry nobody else."

"See. See. The curse is working."

"Don't bother me if it's working. What difference do it make if that's who I want to marry anyways."

"It matters plenty to me."

"You ain't marrying Jimmy. I is."

"But I love you."

"Listen to me, Willie. You listen good." It alarmed me that she'd raised the scissors again, but it was only to point to a tremendous pile of artificial flowers that were piled up in one corner. "I got Easter coming around in two weeks. That means I barely got two weeks to make hats out of all 'em flowers. If I fail, then there is going to be some very unhappy women in this town. I venture to say they'll be as heartbroke as you seem to be claiming. Now, I can use your help, but only on one condition. You got to promise that you ain't going never touch me again. I'm marrying your cousin, so it won't do for you to be touching me. I need your help and I wants us to be friends, but you got to make the promise. No touching."

I promised. Not too reluctantly either, because it was a promise I didn't plan to keep. I would help her through Easter. After that I'd still have several months in which to change her mind.

Mr. Friendly's Easter

SOME confusion existed over exactly when Easter would be arriving, but this was only in the Allson household and not in the world at large. Unfortunately, my mama had been unable to abandon the 1916 calendar. Too many of her notes and lines intertwined with its dates, and as she explained she was only interested in the days of the week, not the days of the month. Still, a small difficulty had occurred on February 28, because 1917 wasn't a leap year. She was stuck, mired down in her record keeping—until Uncle Jimmy came along to push her over into March. Easter, though, was a bigger problem. Mama simply could not ignore the small cross and the lilies intertwining the day when Christ had risen. But the day wouldn't be the same this year, Uncle Jimmy told her again and again, and then I was brought in to back him up. Pointing at the circled date, he urged me to speak out. Instead, I followed the pencil line leaving Easter, traced its path out across the wall, to where it ended in the corner of an envelope with the solitary entry, "It is not Tom's fault."

"It ain't the same day every year, Mama. You remember it changes with the full moon," was all I could manage. Not nearly enough, but Mr. Friendly's announcement in church that Easter was two Sundays away had satisfied her. She counted over, circled the proper Sunday, and connected it with a pencil line to the 1916 Easter, which was still connected to "It is not Tom's fault."

In truth, neither my cousin nor I were as concerned as we should have been, for we both had another woman on our minds, a woman who was absolutely certain about when Easter was arriving. Yes, as they had during my mama's tenure, women were now putting down pennies in advance, or buying their Easter bonnets outright. They'd buy for others at Christmas and birthdays, but at Easter they bought for themselves. It was important. I could understand how Amy would feel a sense of obligation to these women, and even put their happiness above ours: hers and mine. After all, she had over two hundred hats to make and still had to go to school and be back at the manse at a respectable hour. I pitched in and even Liza came back. Uncle Jimmy would drop by, claiming to be there for moral support. I was happy to see Amy didn't have time for him, either.

Overnight, the hat shop turned into a true madhouse. Artificial flowers by the bushel were being pinned and glued and stapled onto straw and felt. Wide brim, narrow. Flowers piled up a foot or more thick in some places. My cousin said, "Amy, you got you some kind of strange garden growing here. Better than Adam and Eve's, to my mind. Flowers don't wear out. No snakes." She was too busy to answer him. She had a mouth full of pins, and her fingers were flying so fast you could barely see them. It was a garden she was tending, all right, a garden of crimped petals and leaves, those bright, unnatural yellows, reds, oranges, pinks, greens, and blues.

"What's this supposed to be?" Uncle Jimmy asked. "A rose?"

"Carnation." Amy snatched it away from him.

"Mighty pretty what you're doing with them."

Everybody told her that. Liza urged her on, and even Margarite and Leala Fitchum, who still weren't sure exactly what they should say or do around Amy, entered the shop, spoke highly of the product, and ordered a hat apiece for Easter. Amy, of course, welcomed their trade, and acted as if these were the only two hats to be done. It didn't seem possible that she could satisfy the customers she already had. When I pointed this out, she smiled, shook her head, pulled a pin from her mouth, and fastened another bouquet. Slowly, the completed and nearly completed hats began to pile up and spill off the shelves and counter. Then, they began to spread out across the floor. It was like a flower garden gone wild and, finally, only a narrow path was left to walk on. At that point, I couldn't tell what or where to clean up, and more often than not, Amy began to shoo me away in the afternoons. This was about the same time Uncle Jimmy changed his appraisal, declaring the interior to be not a garden, but a thicket—a jungle he only dared to enter because of his true love for that most exotic of blossoms, Amy Mercy.

Of course, he was run off as well, and in the end, only Liza helped—helped not by making bonnets but by bullying the anxious customers. Unless Amy was close by to stop her, she could quickly reduce the clientele to tears. "Go away," she told the fretting women, "we'll have your hats ready on time and if we don't, it's your own fault for waiting so long to order." Oh yes, some did leave crying, but in the end, all the orders were filled. The customers poured into the shop on Good Friday, trying on their hats, some now with tears of joy in their eyes. By Saturday morning, upwards of two hundred went away more than satisfied. They went away claiming that even though my mama was a wonderful woman in her own way, there had never been a hatmaker like Amy Mercy in this part of the world before. They even claimed, as Amy had predicted, that Cedar Point was a better place to live because we now had a hat shop. She'd made them all happy.

By late Saturday afternoon, the shop was completely empty of hats. I knew that for a fact because I'd stopped by and looked in the window one last time. There was nothing to see. It was time for Amy to be back at the manse. Past time. Mrs. Squirrel had an Easter bonnet on. That tiny make-believe hat was the only one left in the shop. No others. Scattered across the floor were a few discarded artificial flowers. I'd pick them up Monday. Some scraps of cloth and ribbon were strewn about, too, and there, beyond the end of the counter, a black shoe and stocking-covered ankle. I continued to study the scene, pressing my nose against the glass, and shielding the light of the dying sun with my palm. The shoe was attached to a human being. The door wasn't locked at all. It pushed right open and, rushing inside, I found her. My Amy Mercy was laid out on her back, laid out in a scrambled nest of hatmaking flowers. She looked quite at peace, like a girl dozing in a field of wildflowers or, more exactly, like one laid out for a funeral, for her face was drawn and chalky white.

"Amy!" I shouted. "Amy." She was exhausted. She'd just laid down and gone to sleep. "Amy, are you all right?" I shook her hard, but she didn't answer. When I picked her up in my arms, she seemed to float away. Only then did I realize how much weight she'd lost since my cousin and I had met her at the door of her grandmother's cabin. Frail was the right word to describe her. I carried her outside and screamed for help.

Dr. McGill was baffled at first. He put her to bed in his office and stayed until she came to several hours later.

Finally awake, she couldn't speak without difficulty, and before he closed the door, locking all but my mama out, I heard her complain of cramps in her legs, itching about her eyes. Her stomach ached. The doctor came into the front room after his examination and told us all, Uncle Jimmy, Liza, myself and the Friendlys, that he thought we could relax. Cholera had been ruled out. Poison was his guess. Something she ate. It was a diagnosis that Mrs. Friendly took exception to, and the doctor was quick to point out Amy could've picked up a morsel anywhere in the last couple of hectic days. Anyway, it appeared she'd get better, if she could get some rest. My mama was to spend the night with her, and Uncle Jimmy would sleep on the couch out front. The rest of us were sent home.

I was back at first light to find the doctor already on duty and reporting a minor improvement. Mama sent me off to attend Easter services with the rest of the family. She and Uncle Jimmy stayed where they were. Mr. Friendly delivered a melancholy rambling sermon on the need for the crucifixion and the glory of Christ rising from the dead after three days and ascending into heaven. The poor man was so upset, though, that if you didn't already know the Easter story, you would've been left wondering at the end, did He rise, or was He still walking among us, or was He just plain dead. No one in the congregation complained, for they felt the preacher's pain and shared it. Amy Mercy had made a lot of people happy with her hats and with her general attitude towards life. Mr. Friendly closed the service with a special prayer for her recovery that was seconded with a great chorus of Amens. "He has risen. He has risen," the preacher called out with great emotion at the end. Even Pa heard this, for he shouted back, "He has risen indeed."

So Christ had risen. The two men wanted no confusion about that matter. No lingering doubts. We sang the final hymn. I went straight back to the doctor's office and found my cousin in tears. Amy Mercy had taken a considerable turn for the worse. That morning upon waking, she'd complained of numbness in her limbs, tingling. Gray-black blotches were covering her skin and the muscles had grown so tender that by midmorning the slightest movement or touch caused her to gasp for breath. I heard this much from my cousin and was in the room when the doctor entered to give his official verdict.

"Arsenic poisoning," the medical man said. "Acute poisoning."

"No!" Uncle Jimmy shouted, drawing his fists. "Who would poison her? Who would do that?"

You didn't have to ask me twice. Liza would've done it and I figured he and Dr. McGill must have been thinking the same thing. They weren't, though.

"I looked it up," the doctor went on in his quiet official manner. "Those flowers. They use arsenic in the dyes. That's what gives them those bright colors."

"Touching those flowers can do that?" My cousin pointed to the room that I'd been barred from the afternoon before.

"Touching enough of them can, but she was even nipping at them with her teeth. That's what Liza tells me." That was true. I'd seen her do this, too.

"I ain't going to believe it," my cousin moaned.

"You got to, son. In the text, it recommends the use of gloves. That's what they do in the factories where they sew them up."

Uncle Jimmy sat down and put his head in his hands.

"You want to see her, Willie T.?" the doctor asked.

"Yes, sir." He opened the door and there beside the bed

sat a prim and proper Liza. She held an open Bible in her lap.

"Where's my mama?" I shouted.

"Liza is giving her a break, Willie T.," the doctor explained. "My daughter offered to relieve her."

Liza looked over her shoulder for the briefest moment and said nothing. Her attention was all on the Bible. After the shock of seeing her, all my attention went to the patient.

Amy Mercy was dying. She looked dead already. A lifeless face, splotched and disfigured to the point it was unrecognizable. There was a smell in the room too, a smell of the rankest order, which turned out to be coming from the pan of brownish liquid stool at my feet. Raising my eyes from this, I now met the gaze of my mortal enemy. Liza looked straight up at me, and would've smiled if her father hadn't been in the room. I didn't turn away, but stared straight back until she resumed her Bible study. I wouldn't give Liza the satisfaction of leaving at once. No. I stood gazing at the sallow, silent, and foreign face of the girl I loved, counting silently to one hundred. At eighty-three, Uncle Jimmy came to the doorway.

"Stay with her until I get back, Willie T.," he said. I got a chair, sat down next to Liza, and waited. A half hour later, my cousin returned towing Maum Anna in his wake. The tiny room was now well occupied, but the great gangling black healer slipped easily to the bedside. She studied the patient, and then turned away shaking her head. It was for Liza and not the doctor who she had her questions.

"What verse you reading, child?" She was speaking in a deep, somber tone, a voice I hadn't heard before. Echoing.

Liza didn't answer. Instead she closed the Bible and asked her father if it was healthy for so many people to be crowding around the patient. The doctor, to his credit, suggested that she, Liza, might wish a break and could excuse herself. It was Maum Anna, though, who turned towards the door.

"This lamb is lost," she told the doctor.

"Yes," he agreed.

"You can do something! You know ways!" Uncle Jimmy shouted and clung hard to the woman's arm. "Do something!"

"Jim," Dr. McGill said.

"It for the doctor to do." Maum Anna was bent over by my cousin's hold.

"It would be best if you would leave," Liza was addressing Maum Anna. She now stood beside the bed clutching the Bible to her breast.

"I ain't nothing but an old nigger woman. It for the doctor to do, Jim. I just in the way around here." Maum Anna seemed to be visibly shrinking beneath the weight of my cousin's supplication.

"I know what you can do! You brung Captain Tom back from the dead. Willie T. knows. Tell them Willie T. Tell them!"

Before I could speak, Dr. McGill was asking me to help and remove Uncle Jimmy's hand from the old woman's arm. I did. The fingers uncurled fairly easily.

"This lamb is lost." Maum Anna took a final look at Amy and stepped from the room. It wasn't necessary for her to duck in the doorway as she had when she entered, for her great long neck had retracted until her head rested no higher than her collarbones and her back seemed permanently hunched. She went home and Dr. McGill ordered Uncle Jimmy and me to follow. That night, Amy Mercy hemorrhaged and died. Her funeral was to be held two days later.

There was grief for all in the Allson house, but Uncle Jimmy got the attention by acting the craziest. I kept to myself. I knew this was the only girl I'd ever love. In secret, I'd held her in my arms and she'd kissed me. Now she was dead and my cousin was going around telling everyone how they had been planning to be married. Well, I'd been planning all along to stop that marriage, so I'd as much right to mourn as he did. I'd as much right to go around the house screaming, but I didn't. She was dead. It wasn't my fault. I'd complimented her on the use of the artificial flowers, but the whole town had done that. I was no more guilty than they. No, only one person had wished and prayed this would happen. Liza was guilty. Not Willie T.

That was about as close as I could come to having an organized thought, because on getting the news of the death, my mind began to go numb. It was like those trips I'd made on the *Redbird* with my pa when a cold damp fog would settle around the boat. Sometimes he'd stop and anchor, sometimes he'd just bump along from one subdued landmark to the next, and hope the gray would burn off. I guess I was bumping along. I came downstairs to eat meals or mumble something to Mr. Friendly when he came to talk to his mate. Then I went back upstairs. Brother didn't press for details. Having him in our room tinkering with the clocks was the next best thing to being completely alone. Once or twice, though, I almost yelled out for him to leave. I lacked the strength even for this slight confrontation. Uncle Jimmy never came upstairs to sleep. Maybe he didn't sleep at all.

To the surprise of most, the Widow Mercy asked that her granddaughter be buried in Cedar Point rather than Brittle Branch. She said Amy had been happy in our village and had friends here. She asked Mr. Friendly to do the service. My mama offered a burial spot in the All-son plot of the cemetery, and the widow sent her thanks. Grandpa seemed particularly confused by this last act of Christian generosity, but he was confused by much else as well. "Who is she? Who was this girl?" he kept demanding, and my mama, struggling to remember the girl's name, would patiently explain once more our relationship to Amy Mercy. The old man would lean across his cane and shake his head in incomprehension. He knew no Amy Mercy. The night before the funeral, we had to put in an appearance at the manse, for the Widow Mercy and other members of Amy's family had come to sit with the body and receive callers. We had to go.

"I know you are upset, William," my mama said. "But as a Christian and a friend, you are obliged to attend."

I offered no resistance. Brother and I put on our suits and walked along with Grandpa and my mama up the steps of the manse and into the front parlor. Shrouded from head to toe in black, the Widow Mercy stood just inside the door, so I heard the exchange between the two old people.

"Grandfather Allson. This is the Widow Mercy. You re-member her now, don't you?" Mama had written "the Widow Mercy" on a paper scrap that was now rolled tight and clenched in her hand.

Grandpa studied the subject at some length. The widow smiled at him, her white hands dancing strangely at the end of black sleeves. Despite the terrible tragedy, she was, as they say, "bearing up well." Even through the film of a veil, her clouded eyes seemed bright with genuine interest. I looked at my feet, for, more than ever, she reminded me of the granddaughter who was now laid out in the open coffin at the far end of the room.

"I know no woman by that name. I have never seen this

person in my life," the old man declared at last. "Why are we here?"

"Oh, Colonel, can't you remember me?" The old woman still smiled, and laid a hand on his. "My husband, Tyler, been your overseer ten years running."

"When was that?" the old man shouted.

"'Fore the War. During the War. I seen you since. I spoke with you when you and your boy Tom was cutting shingles."

The old man still shook his head no. My mama had him by the elbow, and tried to lead him on.

"He's getting on in years," she whispered to the widow, who smiled and nodded in agreement. The old man held his ground. He wouldn't move.

"I don't know you. Only Mercy I know was that boy tended the mules. Boy could do anything with animals. That's the only Mercy I'm acquainted with."

"That'd be my grandson." The old woman smiled broader, happy to make some contact. I was just happy The Hard to Catch hadn't come.

"I have no knowledge of the boy's grandparents!" the old man shouted. "He may have had some."

"I am the daughter of Elias and Martha Brittle." The Widow Mercy pushed backwards instead of forwards.

"Yes," Grandpa said with deliberation. "I knew Elias Brittle in my youth. I knew him."

"That was my pa. I married Tyler Mercy. We lived on the Allson Place."

"Tyler Mercy? No. I did not know him."

At this point, I wanted to scream in his ear, "He was your overseer eight years running," and yank the old man through the remaining formalities, but it wasn't necessary. Mama apologized to the widow again and moved on, leaving me to face the old woman. I lowered my head to mumble something and was pulled into her embrace. She smelled strongly of perfume—an unidentifiable scent —perhaps a linament.

"Oh, lands, Willie T., kind of you to come. Amy did love you so!" She was almost shouting this it seemed, and I felt as if every eye in the room was on me. "When she weren't going get home, she writ to me, writ letters about how kind you was to her and what a good friend you was. One them letters come last week. I got it right here in my bag. Can't see it myself. Have to get 'em read."

"Yes, ma'am," I whispered, breaking free of the grieving woman and wishing I could just say, "Who is this woman?" as Grandpa had done. During the first weeks of her stay, Amy had gone home several times, but I didn't know she wrote letters. Did they incriminate me in any way?

"She writ me everything was happening. She were so happy here."

"Yes, ma'am." I took Brother by the arm and dragged him along under the hard stare of the other Mercys. Barely meeting their eyes and only nodding to each in turn, I recognized no one I'd seen before, not The Hard to Catch's wife or the storekeeper. Most were women, but a handful of children stood by as grim and tight-lipped as their elders. Only two men were attending, and both well up in years. All, male and female alike, dressed in their best, of course, but their best was coarse, black, patched hand-me-downs and homemades. All, even the widow, wore simple heavy workshoes. The girl who made the Easter bonnets had sprung from an unlikely race.

I suppose they had equally uncharitable thoughts about us. Except for the widow, none acknowledged our existence. They just stood in line, blaming us for what had happened and with good reason. Confronted by this set of judges, I was more anxious than ever to accuse Liza, who probably knew all along that the flowers were poisonous but continued to applaud the Easter creations right up until the moment the girl laid down to die. The fiend herself was present, standing in a corner with her father. She wore a black veil, carried her Bible, and, like the Mercy family, did not acknowledge my presence. Brother and I said hello to Uncle Jimmy, who stood hat in hand at the doctor's other shoulder. The open coffin was next.

I gave only the briefest of polite glances at this final mortal form and saw that a layer of powder and rouge had been applied to cover the blotched face that had once been so beautiful. She wasn't recognizable as anyone I knew, and I couldn't bring myself to believe, much less to say, "She is only sleeping." Enough. I almost stumbled in the haste of retreat. Brother stopped. He lingered, studying the face as if it were some mathematics problem or clockworks complaint that would yield a ready answer. Embarrassed, I finally pulled him by the arm and, skipping the refreshments offered, we went outside onto the porch.

"That was one," Brother said when we were alone.

"One what?" I asked.

"Her. She was in the dream."

"What are you talking about?"

"Them people that was in the room. Had fangs." He opened his mouth and fingered a side tooth. "She was up close to me when the ceiling rolled back and the stars came out."

"Brother," I whispered angrily, "you went to school with Amy Mercy for three months. Why are you saying now that she was in your dream?"

"'Cause now, Willie T., she looks like the one. Before, she didn't look like her."

"She's the same person." I pointed back to where we'd just left, but not even I believed that she was the same person.

He shrugged and started down the steps. When I called after him, he didn't stop, so instead, I followed him home. I wanted an excuse to leave. My heart was breaking, but I wasn't allowed to show it, and besides, I didn't want to have to face Mrs. Friendly, who, of everyone in the room, had been the most upset. She couldn't stand, but had to sit on a corner of the settee, sobbing and shaking the whole time, and requiring almost all the attention that her husband would ordinarily have been spreading elsewhere.

The funeral was at ten o'clock the next morning, and went pretty much along the same lines as the wake the night before. The Mercy people stuck together up front on one side of the church, and we from Cedar Point filled up the rest of the pews. Mr. Friendly spoke the familiar words concerning the Father's house having many mansions and if it were not so, none of this would have happened. Afterwards, he gave a short, personal speech on Amy's many virtues, short since he couldn't get past the part about how much it had meant to him and his wife to have her living with them. He'd begun to weep so hard he had to be led from the pulpit by Mrs. Friendly.

It wasn't going to be an easy leave-taking anyway, and the preacher's display only got a lot of the women from both communities crying. I was a pallbearer. Brother was another, along with two of our church elders and the two men from the Branch. We carried the coffin, now closed, outside and slid it into the back of the hearse—which was just an open buckboard decorated with four carved corner-posts of a bed, and lacquered black. The driver, whose wagon it was, was a Negro deacon, dressed for the occasion in a fairly respectable livery of a black swallowtail coat and a matching top hat. The cemetery was barely a half mile from the church, and it was the custom for mourners to walk to the open grave, where the body was then interred.

We six pallbearers went first, pacing directly behind the wagon, and the others followed us. In silence, the procession passed beneath the majestic live oaks. Dangling wisteria, in rich purples, crowded our path. Numb as I was, I couldn't help but notice the blazing white dogwoods and azaleas of every hue bursting out in springtime celebration. Surely God was mocking us. Real flowers in place of artificial. Life in place of death. The gray fog settled heavy on my mind, and I was just bumping along behind the wagon hearse.

We'd reached the edge of town and were about to turn in at the cemetery gates. Ahead, I could see Maum Anna and a dozen or more Negroes waiting to sing Amy Mercy over to the far side. We were close, for the piled dirt from the fresh-dug graves shone like bright gold in the spring sunshine. Even more flowers were blooming inside the cemetery. A mockery. This was the only girl I'd ever love.

Then The Hard to Catch Mercy broke from cover. The little gray-white pony horse galloped down on us. The coal black hog dog ran in front, silent and deadly. From the man himself came a single scream, a command for horse to go, for all opposition to stand away, and in a heartbeat, he was upon the wagon. The bridle of the right mule was in his hand, and he was heading the hearse off in a new direction. The deacon driver jumped, his top hat flying high and wide, which was just as well, for The Hard to Catch was aiming the carbine. One way or another, the driver would've gone, but not everyone was willing to see the funeral procession take this unexpected and violent detour.

"Stop him! Willie T.," Uncle Jimmy shouted. "Stop him."

My cousin was trying to make his way forward past the Mercy family and the other pallbearers. It was Brother and I who stood closest to the retreating hearse, and it was me Uncle Jimmy was giving the order to.

"Stop him, Willie T.!"

I didn't think. If I'd been capable of rational action, I'd have done nothing at all, but instead I raced in pursuit of the wagon. A few quick strides and the tailgate was in my hands. One leg went over before I felt a hard tug on the other, and looked back to see the hog dog hanging firmly to my pants cuff. I shook the leg helplessly, knowing full well the animal wouldn't let go and I was about to be halved between wagon and dog. Instead, my pants went. They ripped high at my crotch and most of the leg slipped off over my shoe, an event that frustrated the animal more and brought him back leaping high against the rear of the retreating hearse. By then, I was well on board, though, straddling the coffin and looking backwards at the men of the party, who, led by my cousin, were trying in vain to catch up.

"Stop him!" I heard my cousin's distant shout. "Stop him! Willie T."

Stop him, indeed! And how was I to do that? The two mules were at full gallop, no doubt headed off in the direction of the Branch. The Mercy looked back over his shoulder and, catching my eye, laughed a silent hate-filled laugh and urged his horse forward. Mules and wagon went even faster. The hog dog managed to keep pace, and would occasionally clear the tailgate and bring its massive jaws together with a bone-crunching snap.

Already, two bends of the Swamp Road lay between us and the cemetery, and I could barely make out the sounds of pursuit. Still, if I were to act, it must be now, and so

I crawled forward, reached through the back of the seat, put both hands on the brake lever, and pulled back hard. The wagon gave a momentary lurch that caused the rider to turn back. I got no laugh this time. That only came when the lever broke off in my hand, and I went tumbling backwards onto the coffin lid.

It occurred to me then that I must jump, but the dog still raced behind. Even without broken bones, I couldn't escape such an animal. What was the worst that Mercy could do? He still carried the carbine in one hand and could have shot me off at his convenience. If he wanted me dead, there would be little point in riding me about. I'd done nothing to offend this man. I'd loved his sister. He probably didn't know that, but, if necessary, I'd tell him. I'd tell him anything. Yes, there crouched beside the coffin in the rear of that careening, bouncing wagon, I imagined a dozen scenarios in which I tactfully apologized, coaxed, and cajoled my way to safety. I could imagine only one in which I failed, was shot dead, gutted by the skinning knife, and torn apart by the hog dog. Not even once did it occur to me to pray, and I was still crouched down when the wagon suddenly slowed and stopped. Here the Swamp Road turned into pure swamp. Dropping the mule's bridle, The Hard to Catch wheeled the little horse about and drew up to face me.

"Open her," he said and withdrew the heavy, broad-blade knife with a swift motion and tossed it clattering onto the coffin top.

"What?"

"Open that there coffin."

Cautiously, I wrapped my hand around the knife handle. Not for a moment did it occur to me to jump him, and believe me, it wouldn't have occurred to him that I would. He stared hard with those eyes sunk deep into their sockets and patted the nervous little horse with his free hand. I could run. I did consider that, for the dog was now sitting quietly to one side. I could throw down the knife and run and hope he wouldn't shoot me.

"If you run," he said in that soft, musical voice, "I'm going to shoot your pecker off."

"No, sir," I said. "I ain't going to run."

"Open it."

I took the knife and began to work it slowly beneath the coffin lid.

"Hurry," he said.

I hurried. I popped the nails up and, getting a hand beneath one corner, pulled back the lid with a great heave. Once more, the body of Amy Mercy was on view, and it occurred to me suddenly that a last look at his sister was all he wanted. Mercy leaned far over and peered into the coffin. He'd be satisfied to look on the face of his beloved sister one last time and then he'd ride on.

"Look at her," he said. I did. Another night's waiting had done nothing to improve Amy's condition, and the rough wagon ride had nudged the body around at an angle in the box. Worst of all—and this was the part that caused me to flinch—her eyes had popped open and were staring glazed and sightless.

"She looks asleep, don't she?" Mercy said, straightening up in the saddle.

"Yes, sir."

"She ain't. She's dead."

"Yes, sir," I murmured. He'd only wanted to look.

"You want to kiss her?" he asked.

"I'd rather not." I knew it was sometimes the custom of country folks to kiss the departed good-bye, but it wasn't done under circumstances like these.

"I want you to go on and kiss her," he sang softly, not even looking up from the coffin.

I said nothing. I could not answer.

"You hear me, boy?" the voice raised.

"No, sir," I said. "It's best I don't kiss her."

"Kiss her!" he shouted. I stood struck dumb and frozen. "Kiss her!"

I bent over the coffin, and with my eyes half closed, pressed my lips briefly against the girl's rubbery, cold forehead.

"That ain't no kiss. Kiss her like a man would do."

"I won't," I whispered. "She's dead."

A moment of silence followed.

"Your name Willie T., ain't it?"

"Yes, sir. It is." I was crying now.

"I heard 'bout you. She wrote 'bout you in her letters."

"I loved her," I choked.

"You fuck her?"

"No, sir." I shook my head back and forth.

"Who did?"

"Nobody," I stammered. "She weren't that kind of girl."

"No, she weren't. But somebody did. Who was it?"

Again I shook my head no, and he brought the barrel of the carbine up and aimed it straight at my groin.

"Tell me or I'll blow your pecker off. You won't fuck nobody when I'm through. I guarantee it."

"My cousin. Jimmy Allson. He did." I started to sob and shake then because I had lied to save myself. I hoped that my cousin would understand and forgive me.

"I knowed that already," Mercy laughed and poked me hard in the groin with the barrel tip. "Just wanted to hear you saying it."

I shook my head no and sobbed on.

"I seen you out at the Allson Place with that preacher's wife howling. You ain't going to find it. Murdering this one won't help nary a bit."

"No, sir. Wasn't murdering. Was an accident, I swear."

"Poison murder. Poison her 'cause she can't tell you nothing."

"No, sir. Was the dye in them Easter flowers. Doctor will tell you. Was the dye."

"You fuck her?"

I shook my head and sobbed no.

"Take off 'em shoes," he said. "Throw 'em to the dog." He nudged me with the barrel tip again, and I did as I was told. The dog grabbed up one, shook it hard, and lay down in the road to chew. "Now 'em pants." I pulled off what was left of them. Once more I faced him. The tears still flowed. "The drawers." He poked me once more and I drew these off as well.

My coat and shirttail still hid my nakedness, but I'd have given these willingly if it meant he'd leave me in peace. He didn't ask for more clothes, though. He was satisfied with my appearance.

"Ain't much to you, is there?" he asked.

"No, sir," I admitted.

"Kiss her or I got to kill you."

I shook my head no, and turned my body away from the gun barrel. If he was going to blow my pecker off, he'd have to shoot it through the cheeks of my ass. That was the only resistance I could offer. I turned my head away and waited to die. Instead of a rifle shot, though, there was just a gentle rustling sound in the coffin behind me, and then the thudding of the horse's hooves growing quieter as it moved away. From the corner of my eye, I saw the dog surrender my shoe and head on into the swamp. I didn't move until the sound of the hooves was replaced by the splashing of water, and this sound finally ceased.

I was left standing half naked with the noonday sun shining down through the overhanging leaves. The only sound besides my tearful breathing was a crow in the far distance. I turned around. The coffin was empty and The Hard to Catch was gone. Running down the inside of both of my legs was a thin brown slime that formed a shallow pool about my feet. I had unknowingly soiled myself, a fact that shamed me almost as much as what had gone before. Quickly, I gathered up my ragged pants and drawers and jumped from the wagon. With grass from the roadside I cleaned myself as best I could and, still sobbing, put back on my drawers and pants. Then with more grass and sand, I wiped the telltale stain from the wagon bed and dragged the coffin over to cover the spot.

By the time the posse arrived to rescue me some twenty minutes later, I'd calmed myself to the point where I could sit on the tailgate of the hearse and greet the men almost casually.

"He's gone," I said. "Took the body and rode off into the swamp. You won't catch him. Nothing but the devil lives back in there. Bottomless pools, quicksand. It ain't worth it. Give it up."

My cousin thought different. "Let's go," he shouted. But Judge Walker said no and asked me what I thought the man would do with the body. I answered that I supposed he'd bury it. That suited the judge. He wasn't going to wander into the swamp chasing a body, no matter whose, and he recommended, as a law official and a friend, that Uncle Jimmy give it up as well. My cousin refused, and despite my desperate protests, he urged his horse forward. Two of the others followed but they returned that same afternoon. Uncle Jimmy returned the next night. Exhausted and silent, he'd say only that he'd found neither the man nor the body of his fiancée. By then, word was out that the Widow Mercy didn't object to her granddaughter disappearing into the swamp. She knew her family better than I suspected and claimed she'd be happy if no one else died. She hoped Uncle Jimmy would accept that Amy was with Jesus now, and stop looking. Mr. Friendly carried this message to our house, and my cousin didn't go back.

Of course, I told no one of what had passed on the road. Not even Uncle Jimmy, who I'd named, named unnecessarily, it appeared. I didn't tell him directly that his life was in grave danger. Nor did I repeat the accusation of murder or Mercy's belief that we were still searching for the Allson dowry. Instead, I reduced my exchange with The Hard to Catch to a few polite words.

As for the exact nature of my cousin's relations with the dead girl, that got talked about anyway. Mrs. McGill sent out word that she'd been told by her husband the girl was two months pregnant when she died. The doctor couldn't stop her from doing this, but he denied ever speaking to his wife about a matter so delicate. I didn't care, not really, but a week later, Liza came up to me on the schoolyard to explain how Grandpa was the real father of Amy's daddy, Allson Mercy. It was common knowledge, she announced, that the Widow Mercy had been widowed a full two years before the birth of her son. Yes, Amy Mercy's so-called romance with Uncle Jimmy was doomed from the start, for Liza knew all along that they were first cousins and any children they had would've been born deaf and dumb. They'd have been lucky if one could even mew like a cat. Only God's mercy had averted this tragedy. This was not just her opinion but common knowledge, as well.

"If it's common knowledge," I replied somewhat feebly, "why don't I already know it?"

"There's plenty you don't know, Willie T."

"I know you got a heart full of hate, Liza. That's common knowledge around here, too."

I heard no more of the slander. Was it true? If my parents had known, they'd never have let the courtship go on, but there was much they did not know. Of scandal, they generally knew nothing. Of much else, they knew nothing. It didn't matter, anyway, for the girl was dead. If she was having a baby, Uncle Jimmy's baby, then that was dead, too.

Needless to say, my cousin was taking none of this well. He continued to wander about raving, but I could tell he was gradually calming down. Mercy might kill him, but grief was going to permanently unhinge him. He threatened to kill himself several times, but he didn't. He'd just get all the attention, some of which should have been going to Brother. After all, it was Brother who had fallen to his knees in prayer when the hearse was hijacked. This was commented on, true, but only as a footnote to the incident. And naturally, the act angered me when I heard of it, for this sudden conversion had caused me to be alone in the wagon. If Brother had jumped in and been at my side, instead of back there kneeling in the dirt, Mercy would have been content to take the body and none of the rest would have happened.

There was more. The night I returned from my ordeal, Brother confided a secret to me, one I hardly listened to at first. The rider, the rider we'd seen that day, The Hard to Catch Mercy, had been in his dream as well. I asked him why he hadn't recognized him when we tried to catch Naomi, and he said he'd been up in his room that whole afternoon. I told him not to tell me any more about his dream. He said he wouldn't. I told him to tell Uncle Jimmy about it, if by some miracle he made it home. Brother was sure Uncle Jimmy would return safely but said he wouldn't tell him about the dream.

For myself, all I can say for certain is that I came home from my encounter with The Hard to Catch in far worse condition than I ever gave hint to. The fog that settled over my mind following Amy's death became a thick, impenetrable blanket. After those first few lies, I did as my pa sometimes did and dropped anchor. Benumbed. Fogbound. I lay swinging easily at anchor, but it was not a comforting state. Like when I was with Pa on the *Redbird*, I heard the sounds that he couldn't. Distant surf that threatened to grow into a tidal wave and come crashing down on us. Shapes moving in the mist. Ships, impossible ships, that would sail across our shallow anchorage and crush us beneath their mighty bows. Oh yes, thoughts slipped in, but only those of the most troubling and dangerous nature.

Mercy was the devil. He was a perverse man and the demands he'd made on me were unnatural. I had to escape. I told myself I wasn't truly a coward but I knew it was a lie. When I looked back at how I'd acted, not just with Amy Mercy, but even before, only one conclusion could be reached. I was like Liza. I was mean, sneaky mean, and a true and selfish coward. I had a stone for a heart. Nothing could change that, nor did I want to change. It was going to take all the meanness I could muster to stay alive. That's what it came down to in the end. I was frightened to death of death itself and with good reason. This man, this Hard to Catch Mercy, didn't need to read a letter to know what I'd done to his sister. He'd looked right through to my heart of stone and seen it chiseled on the outside in clear, if not bloody, letters. "For if you live after flesh, ye shall die." I'd been told that. I'd read it for myself in the Bible, but somehow, I'd forgotten.

The wages of sin is death, but the gift of God is eternal life. God and His Jesus could keep the eternal part. He could keep his whole Goddamn religion. On my first night home, and for many nights afterwards, I put my head under the covers and, thinking of The Hard to Catch and my own inescapable guilt, I cried myself to sleep.

The Prodigal Son

THOUGH in small numbers the birds could be seen much earlier, it wasn't until the middle of spring that the drunk robins came—great flocks of robin redbreasts dropping in to feast in the chinaberry trees of the town. Frantic, the greedy creatures hopped about the branches gorging themselves to the brim on berries. Then they fell to the ground and flopped about in a helpless state referred to as "drunk." Naturally, this lesson on the sin of gluttony wasn't allowed to be lost on any of us, but even more important to our elders was the annual harvest. Boys were sent out toting sacks to fill up with birds, whose plump bodies, properly prepared, were regarded as a great delicacy.

It wasn't simply moping around, but my outright refusal to participate that drew Mama's attention. I'd sent Sammy off alone to collect the drunk robins, and that night she quietly explained how she understood my sorrow, but I wouldn't be allowed to lie about the house for the rest of my life—a surprisingly forceful declaration, considering she could no longer remember even the two red roses of her needlework and now rocked in the evening with empty hands folded in her lap. Apparently, she expected more activity from me, and followed up her demand with a two-pronged attack, what my cousin once referred to as a double-flanking movement.

First, she sent for Mr. Friendly, who engaged me in a long and rambling discourse on the mysterious nature of God's ways, one that finally broke down into a confession. I was sworn to tell no one. His wife was convinced she had, without knowing it or perhaps not remembering it, poisoned Amy Mercy. He couldn't tell me why the poor woman felt so, but asked me to pray for her and him as well. Of course, I knew why Mrs. Friendly would think this, but I also knew she wasn't capable of killing anyone. I said, "It ain't her fault." He agreed and asked again that I pray for them. I said, "Yes, I will." He asked me again to swear I'd tell no one. "Yes," I said, "I swear."

Second came Dr. McGill whose aid was almost as trying. He dosed Brother and me with a fortnight treatment of spring tonic, that at least left us happy it ended. I can't say which was worse, but together they had the desired effect of prompting me to make a plan. Despite my wishes, I couldn't remain forever with the bed covers pulled over my head. My neighbors could be generously tolerant of the peculiar, but not in one so young, and besides, I'd already run up against the bounds of my mama's remaining good sense. If I was going to keep living in Cedar Point, it would be necessary for my life to resemble a normal one. On the outside, I'd be ordinary. On the inside, I'd be nothing at all. The boat inside my mind, the one like my pa's *Redbird*, would remain anchored, and the thoughts, desires, dreams, or whatever else was on board her would stay locked there, hostages of the numbing mist. The other Willie T., the outside one, would just go on. Anyway, it was a plan.

Uncle Jimmy was working along similar lines. Declaring he had enough education for his purposes, he quit school, but it was hard to say just what his purposes were. Not because he was keeping his plans secret, but because he had so many, and none were actually being put into practice. He'd spend all day up at the grocery, come home for supper with a new set of proposals, and then leave the house to spend half the night sulking on the end of the wharf. I had to pick up drunk robins, but my mama demanded that my cousin be left alone so his grief could run its course. Anyway, she took it as a good sign when he accepted the Widow Mercy's invitation to visit Amy's final resting place. I did summon the courage to suggest The Hard to Catch might be setting a trap for him. He replied that he wasn't afraid of any man, least of all that one. The worst he'd say of Amy's brother was that he was a trifle erratic in his behavior, but he, Uncle Jimmy, understood what grief could do to a fellow's thinking and was willing to forget and forgive.

My cousin went and reported back that the girl rested on a high hickory-wooded bluff overlooking the first bottomless pool in from the Brittle Branch cattle pens. He called it beautiful, but I knew those bottomless pools to be places of distress. If a cow fell into one, it'd sink for eternity. My cousin said the place was beautiful. And, of course, he'd met with The Hard to Catch. Naturally, they'd spoken together for several minutes and parted on polite enough terms, all things considered. Mercy sent his apologies to me for the rough ride. He even promised to ask my forgiveness in person next time he passed our way. He hoped there were no hard feelings. I just looked at my cousin and nodded my head up and down. Uncle Jimmy said seeing Amy at rest had made him realize he was going to have to get on with his life.

Somewhere in the midst of all our turmoil, America had entered the Great War that was being waged in Europe against the Germans. Occupied as I was, the announcement made practically no impression on me, but a few in the community did respond. Algon Nesbitt, the same young man Uncle Jimmy hit in front of the hat shop, had enlisted. A couple of the older fellows went soon after, but Cedar Point wasn't exactly gripped by war fever. Two large and well-respected families were still speaking a few words of German, and they weren't pleased to have America participating. The biggest critic by far, though, was Dr. McGill. His maternal grandparents had come over from Ireland traveling steerage, and about the only thing of value they brought along was an abiding hatred of the English. It was the doctor's inheritance, a family heirloom, a treasured anger.

"A war to end war," he mocked. "Make the world safe for democracy. Tell that to the poor Irish. Down with tyrants. Hooray for the Hun."

And it was the doctor Uncle Jimmy had to face when he returned from visiting Amy's grave and announced he was joining the old Crowns Bluff Dragoons or the new infantry division being formed. Dr. McGill said something, something to make him change his mind, and once more my cousin was drifting. Did I realize fortunes were being made in South America? A year of business school probably wouldn't hurt him. Maybe he'd go back to Savannah and set up there. He was just thinking out loud, and about then I realized he was beginning to nip along pretty regular. Even before Amy Mercy's death, my pa had moved the remnants of Grandpa's wine to Mr. Britt's double-locked smokehouse, but now more was involved than sucking on a wine barrel. My cousin's "leaning up against the arbor" was affecting his already poor reasoning. You could always smell liquor on his breath.

When Uncle Jimmy quit his job at the grocery and went on the *Redbird* as assistant engineer, it was almost a relief. We could get by without him easy enough for four nights a week, but then on his very first trip he didn't return from Crowns Bluff. Pa thought he might have gone on to Savannah and wasn't particularly concerned that we'd been deserted in a time of sorest need. Pa said Uncle Jimmy asked us to pray for him.

Pray for him! And how was I to do that when he'd robbed me of the praying ability. My cousin had come here not six months before and found me a God-fearing Christian with nothing but interesting prospects, and now, like Esau, I'd been robbed, and the robber had fled to distant lands.

Brother, on the other hand, was having no difficulty coming to terms with his new God. For months he'd watched me kneeling in church and beside my bed, without joining in or commenting. Then, on the day Amy Mercy died, I'd quit. On the day of the funeral, he'd started. And to torment me further, he still couldn't worship like any normal person. No, he just fell to his knees when the spirit moved him, always at the oddest times, and his prayers were senseless little whispers. At least he was there though, and except for the clocks that was a comfort.

I guess I'd taken it for granted that Brother and I would sleep in a room filled with ticking and chiming clocks, all of which pounded along at a slightly different rate. Now, though, I complained about the noise, and he silenced all but the one he was working on. That one he muffled with a blanket when he finally came to bed. I wasn't satisfied. I asked him to move some of the timepieces into the bedroom his brother had abandoned. He stubbornly refused, and when I moved a few for him, he moved them right back. I guess my nerves were raw. After all, the clocks had taken over the room months before, but only now did I bother to question their right to exist in the first place. Why would Mr. Britt want to own a Swiss cuckoo clock? Even unwound, this infernal machine continued to squawk out an incorrect hour, and then opened and closed doors as a little mountaineer danced in a faltering but unending circle. Dr. McGill had left a faceless grandfather clock, it's pendulum bent like a bow and stained with what was probably blood. The doctor thought Brother capable of its restoration, and even entrusted him with the pocket watch of Mrs. McGill's father. Dozens more waited their turn and, realizing they couldn't be moved, I decided to go myself to the other bedroom. Only I couldn't.

With Uncle Jimmy's departure, I found myself suddenly and truly terrified of the dark, or more exactly, what it might contain. A horse and rider waited in our barnyard. A horse and rider and, of course, a dog that could be sent up the stairs to drag me down and outside. Its glistening white teeth were set in that coal black muzzle like a burnished steel trap. If there was a major obstacle to me pretending to have a normal life, it was the growing certainty that every night The Hard to Catch waited in the dark to murder me.

I say it was a certainty, for the presence was. I hadn't imagined them—man, horse, dog. No more than a week after Uncle Jimmy set sail for Savannah or parts unknown, I'd awakened suddenly, not knowing why at first, but then listening, I heard the horse down below in the yard. I hadn't wanted to look, and had to make myself finally crawl on hands and knees to peer out the window. A half moon burned. There was light enough to see, but only empty space was there, and the sound of the hooves that had been like thunder upon my waking were now faint whispers, perhaps only my pounding heart. Later, in the safety of broad daylight, I examined the backyard and found nothing but hoofprints. The dusty area beyond the arbor was always well-trampled, but no particular prints looked as if they belonged to the Mercy's horse.

A dream. I figured it to be a dream, but two nights later, I woke again and this time went quicker to the window. Studying the scene below, I could make out a horse and rider and, just in front, the dog, all waiting silent and motionless beside the chicken pen. Quietly, I searched out the .22 rifle I now kept loaded beneath my bed and returned to the window. The shadow still waited, but it was no longer horse, rider, and dog, only a shapeless haze cast by the wisteria bush. Only when I'd got back into bed and lay still did I hear the hooves pound off once more in retreat.

It rained the next night—a rare spring thunderstorm with distant lightning brightening the night world and thunder following as a hollow boom. All the while, rain was drumming on the roof directly above my head, and yet I was certain Mercy had returned. I could hear the hoofbeats clearly and strained to catch a glimpse of the barnyard when the lightning flashed. It was impossible. The rain was coming down too hard, but there was no question I was hearing the little white horse parading about below the window. Suddenly a hand grabbed at my shoulder, and yelping, I wheeled about to find Brother staring at me.

"Look," I said, pointing to the window where the rain now passed in torrents, splashing on the sill and upon us both. He looked. "You hear something?" He listened for a long time very intently, and since I could hear the hoofbeats as if they were in our very room, I figured he must.

"Yes," he said, looking at me unblinking.

"What?"

"You was saying, 'Poor blood. Poor blood.'"

"You don't hear a horse?" I wanted to scream that, but managed to simply hiss out the words.

"No."

"You must be deaf then."

"How come I can hear you talking about Old Sister and poor blood?"

"That's just in your head."

Brother got back into bed and went to sleep almost immediately. I shut the window, but it made no difference. I still heard the hoofbeats, perhaps even louder than before. There was no one to tell and from then on, I just let The Hard to Catch come and go. If it was a dream, then it was, and if it wasn't, it wasn't. But I was not going to risk getting out of bed to find out.

In the morning, though, it was necessary to rise. My mama came into the room to make certain I was participating in life, so the dawn journey to the shed where Sammy slept was unavoidable. There was light, but still shadow enough to hide a hundred Mercys. At first, I'd begun to walk it fast, but soon I was running the distance. Finally I began to wake Brother and make him go with me to the barn. Then together, Sammy and I would drive Ruth out to pasture, a walk which, even with him along, became a barely endurable nightmare. I could have paid Sammy to make the trip for me. He'd have done it for nothing, but then where would I have gone? My mama would see me if I went back to the house, and if I were to hide in the barn, I'd have to hide alone. From daybreak on, I began to structure my life in such a way that, in some manner or another, at least one other human being was somewhere in sight. I tried to make this existence seem ordinary and I guess I was fooling some of the people.

My mama made only one comment. She said that I was shooting up. Only the day before, we'd seen eye to eye, but now she had to look up. Actually, it had been several years since we'd been eye level. Maum Anna said more or less the same thing, though. "Willie T., you done growed another inch last night. You be a full-growed man by this Saturday."

I wasn't paying close attention to such matters, but now my shirtsleeves ended a couple inches above my wrists and my pants rode up above my ankles. Uncle Jimmy wasn't around to give permission, but my mama passed his old clothes on. He'd outgrown them himself just short of their total unraveling. It didn't matter. I accepted my new spring wardrobe without comment. Brother got my discards, but they weren't much use to him since he hadn't shown any signs of a growth spurt yet.

Sammy had. Sammy was more than full grown. Six feet tall, at least, and starting to fill out across the shoulders. Someday, he was going to be a big man. In fact, he already was, and I knew from Maum Anna's teasing that he had a girlfriend in Slabtown. In his head though, he was still child enough to stay close by his auntie. He was getting fed and had his pile of shucks to sleep on. There wasn't much more for him to aspire to in this neighborhood, in the whole world, for all I knew.

Sammy had grown and I'd grown, but there was one person who was shrinking. That was Maum Anna. In the two months since Amy Mercy's death, the old woman had lost three inches or better in overall height and a proportional amount in arms and legs. It wasn't that she was just stooping and growing thinner, which she was. Even I could see that she was actually getting shorter. She no longer ducked when she came through the doorway. She simply stepped into the room flat-footed, so if Uncle Jimmy had stuck around, he could have said "Maum Anna ain't seven feet tall—she ain't even six feet." I asked my mama if she didn't think it was strange for a person to get shorter like that, especially one who'd been as tall as Maum Anna. Mama said she'd never thought of Maum Anna as being particularly tall. I asked if Maum Anna hadn't once been the tallest woman my mama had ever seen. Mama replied she hadn't seen all that many people to begin with and had forgotten how tall those few were. Her responses were difficult ones to follow in my distracted state, so I abandoned that line of inquiry. Maum Anna still had a good seventy inches to go before she'd be in danger of disappearing altogether, and I had a problem of my own.

It no longer worked for a person to simply be in sight. Now, I couldn't visit the outhouse without Brother standing guard, or walk up the street without Sammy along. Any horse and rider had the potential of being THE horse and rider, any dog, THE dog. Every house or shed, every tree or bush, was a potential hiding place and even the gentlest of spring breezes brought the sound of an approaching horse and the howl of a dog. Schooling continued, but I studied only enough to get by and even in a full classroom, I jumped and flinched at nothing. Looking about continually became my habit, and since I was sleeping less and less, dark patches grew beneath my eyes. If I was shooting up like mustard, I was still not filling out, and, in fact, might have been losing weight. Oh, yes, I had a problem, but only Maum Anna guessed its nature.

"Willie!" she shouted out one morning as Brother and I were crossing the dangerous open space between the house and barn, the very space that I knew The Hard to Catch trampled every night. "Willie? Ain't you hear Anna?"

I'd heard her all right. I'd jumped clear of the ground nearly two feet and started crawling over Brother in retreat. "Do Jesus, Willie, you come in here. Brother, you go back to the house. Get in the bed."

Brother took no encouraging, and left me with no choice but to accept the old woman's invitation. Though I hadn't visited the old kitchen building since my cousin told his version of family history, nothing had changed. The same Madonnas and baby Jesuses lined the walls, but with barely enough light to pick up the rich golds and reds and blues, the statues and paintings flickered without recognizable shape or identity. Maum Anna's furniture—the rocker, the cot, and one small iron pot—had not shifted. The same tiny fire still glowed in the giant open brick fireplace. Here, all the cooking for the big house had once been done, but now the only purpose of the great brick hearth was to warm this one old black woman who, in the middle of May, claimed she needed the flames not for heat, but for company.

"My boy ain't come for see me. All I got's this little bit of fire to talk to." She bent to poke at the coals and, even when she straightened, kept her back partly to me.

"I ain't got much time," I said.

"Got time for all kind of thing," she said to me. "Hello fire, how you doing this morning?" she said to the fire.

"I is fine, Maum Anna." The old woman's rendition of the fire came in a high squeaky voice. "How you doing this fine morning?"

"Fair. Praise Jesus. Just fair, little fire. I aches a bit."

"That too bad," the fire answered back. "Can I gets you something?"

"No, sir. No, little fire, your company is all I need."

"Well, I glad to gives you that. You raise me up from just a spark. That the least I can do. Spare you a little company."

"Ain't you got someplace to be going?"

"No, ma'am," the high squeaky voice took on a contented

inflection. "I comfortable right here. Ain't no reason for me to be running all about the countryside like some of them others."

"That so, fire. That very true. We very lucky this morning that one of them same ones you talking 'bout has come by."

The old woman turned to face me. "Willie T., come over here and say hello to this little fire."

"I got to go," I said. "I got my chores."

"That true. I done forgot. Go on then. Go on."

I went out on the stoop expecting her to follow, but she didn't. A good hundred and fifty feet of unescorted ground separated me from Sammy's shed. I looked back inside. Maum Anna rocked by the fire. I summoned all my courage for the sprint to the barn, but couldn't get past the stoop and just stood looking nervously about. Finally, the old woman took my shoulder and brought me once more into her house. She closed the door behind us.

"He ain't out there," she said to me. "He done come and gone back to that swamp."

"You seen him?" I wasn't mad, not completely. "You seen him, too?"

"Ain't nothing for see. I hear 'em though. Do Jesus. I hear 'em every night. He come into the yard there and ride 'round 'em three times going with the clock, three time other way. He stop for a look. Then he ride off."

"You hear him, but you don't see him?"

"Ain't Maum Anna he come for, but I knows the devil. Ain't nothing back in them swamp but devil." She shook her small head back and forth. "No, sir. Can't see 'em. No, sir. But I hear 'em when he come. I hear 'em good."

"He's come for me," I admitted. Glad at last to tell someone, glad to the point of happy tears. "He thinks I did something I didn't do."

"Maybe he come for you." The old woman turned her attention back to the fire. "Maybe he come for another one. Might be another one in that house."

"It's me that hears him," I said, "and I seen him, too. Once maybe, I seen him here in the yard by the chicken pen."

"One time? Them one time could be accident."

"It's me. I know it's me."

"If that so, child, ain't but one thing for do. Must turn and face 'em. You can run and you can hide, but the day will come when you got to turn and face 'em."

"No, I ain't facing him again. Ghost or in the flesh, I'm going to run 'til I can't run no more and then I'm going to lie down and die."

"Willie, that ain't no way for a man to do. You can't be running. You can't be hiding around behind Brother and my Sammy, neither. That devil ride right through 'em if it get the notion. No. No. No." She shook her head again, patted her flat chest, and for the first time since I'd entered, she smiled her broad smile. "I going do something special for this child . . . I can see that now."

Of course, I should have been relieved to hear this, but instead, I was suddenly angry. She did not have a smile on her face, but a definite grin.

"What you did for Amy Mercy, that the kind of help you going to give me?"

"That lamb was lost."

"Yes, I heard you say that, but you didn't even try." At last, she was accused.

"Ain't been no use. That lamb was lost." The old woman didn't appear guilty. The grin had gone, and she defended herself in a quiet, matter-of-fact way. "Anna could see it in the room. It was writ in blood. Chapter and verse. It say 'This lamb is lost.' "

"I know about them verses. Don't matter. I know what you is."

"What you know?"

"The streets in Africa ain't paved with gold."

"They ain't?" She mocked me.

"I know something else. You're a witch doctor. You could have saved Amy Mercy. You brought my pa back from the dead."

"Do boy, go on. I bring 'em back from Virginia. Your mama with me the whole time."

"I know better," I said. "I got my proof. 'Good Friday, ain't it?' You ain't fooling me. I know you brung him back, and you could have saved Amy. You could have saved Esther, too, if you had wanted."

"Esther? Boy, hush yourself. That Jesus, that Jesus. Jesus decide He going save your pa He save 'em. He let Esther go, He let 'em go."

"No. No, I know better. You fixed it so Amy Mercy would marry Uncle Jimmy or nobody else. Well, she's dead. She ain't married nobody else, and I don't see where all your hoodoo and juju meddling is helping one bit. Looks to me like the whole Allson family is just getting worse and worse off every day. Least you could do was save Amy Mercy."

This long speech was at first greeted with silence. Maum Anna studied me up and down, looked into the fire, and then back into my eyes, and admitted what I said might be true.

"Maum Anna getting old. She just an old, old woman, near 'bout a hundred, I suspects. She can't tend her flock like she do before this time here."

"I didn't need no tending before," I said. "I didn't have ghosts chasing me all about. And now you claiming you going to help me with more of your black magic when you the witch doctor that brought them here." Maum Anna shrugged her shoulders when I'd finished, flashed her wide grin again, and began to deny all she'd just admitted to.

"Witch doctor? Witch doctor? You talking 'bout me, boy? Praise Jesus. Oh, yes, praise Jesus." She stopped to praise Him. She threw her not-so-long arms up towards the ceiling. "Anna a Christian woman. Great God above know I is a Christian woman."

"Well, I don't. You're a conjurer woman. That's what you are."

"How that boy call me a conjuh?" She still spoke to the ceiling. "Oh, this a perculiar child from very perculiar family. Them white Allsons is very perculiar. I going to have to ask your protection and your guidance for this one in the special degree. Thank you, Jesus."

Though addressing the ceiling, she'd still been cutting her eyes over at me, and she was still grinning. She mocked me. It was true daylight now. I'd run. Better to die out there, I reasoned, than to be further tricked and humiliated by my nursemaid. She'd lowered her hands though and the grin was replaced by a soft closed-mouth smile.

"I done talked to Jesus, and He been tell me to give you this." She slipped her long fingers about her own neck and began to pull on the leather thong that dissappeared into the front of the sagging gray homespun dress. "This here for you to wear."

I suppose I expected some minor skull bones of a black cat to be attached to the other end. Instead, she withdrew, from where it pressed against her own flat brown breast, a large silver cross, and with great ceremony, pulled it over her head. Still, I jumped back as if some dark manifestation of the devil's own worship were being presented.

"Do boy," she scolded. "Take the thing. Ain't going to

bite you." But, of course, she said this with enough mischief in her voice to suggest the cross could somehow bite.
I raised a hand to protect myself.

"Can't hurt. This cross done made from the true nail
they use to crucify our Lord. Silver from the true nail."

"The true nail?" Well, that was easy enough to doubt,
but the old woman had fixed me with a look of grim piety.
I lowered my arm and allowed her to slip the thong about
my neck. She stepped back to admire.

"Praise Jesus up in Heaven, that same cross been my
strength and salvation all these years. Your mama give 'em
to me while I still got the chain on my feet. Tell me that
all the protecting I going need in this world, and now I
telling you the same thing." She didn't grin, but the grim-
ness lightened to the soft closed-mouth smile. "That the
God's truth," she added. Under the circumstances, it was
difficult to doubt, and in fact, I did feel an undeniable
sense of well-being that had been sorely missing in the past
months. After a hesitant moment, I touched the metal and
then raised it up for closer inspection. No inscription or
magic symbol. The plain flat silver only reflected back a
tiny cross-shaped view of my looming face.

"My mama's cross?" I asked. "You ain't lying?"

"Shush, boy. Christ cross. Your mama give 'em to Anna.
Now she give 'em to you. This here be Willie's cross.

"My cross?" I continued to study my own thinned reflection.

"Listen to me, child. They is more. They is something
you got to do."

"Pray?" I asked.

"No. Lord, no. You suppose to pray all the time. I mean
for make 'em work. You listen good. Do what I say, now."
She pressed close in quiet conspiracy. "Hold the cross up
to your lips and kiss 'em on both sides. Kiss 'em good like

you kiss a gal. Make sure the spit of your mouth get on the cross. Then, take the finger and the thumb of your right hand and rub the spit around on the cross until you feel it getting warm to the touch. Do that. Do that and whisper, 'ghost ride on.'"

I did as she said, and the cross did, in fact, begin to grow warm.

"Not too much," she said. "That thing can burn you. When you feel 'em warm, you know you safe. You remember that when you hear the horse come tonight, you pull out that cross, kiss 'em and rub 'em. Say, 'ghost ride on.' That all it going to take. No haint going to stay around then. No, sir. Going have to find some other soul to torment."

"Thank you," I said. I did feel safer, and whether it was the cross's doings or not, it didn't matter.

"Ain't no need for thank Anna. I ain't raise 'em up to lose 'em now. Miss Gin boy safe with Anna."

"Yes, ma'am," I agreed, but she didn't seem to hear.

"I worry 'bout you so. You ain't know how I fret so—I ain't been well." She had me by the arm and with shuffling steps, led me out onto the front stoop.

"There. Ain't nothing out here and when it come you got the cross hammered from the true nail."

"Yes, ma'am." I looked about the barnyard. The sun still hadn't cleared the trees, but it burnished the sky with bright golds and reds and blues. And the remaining shadows were simply shadows cast by mortal objects. I touched the cross that now hung around my neck.

"'Member them word: ghost ride on."

"Yes, ma'am." I started to step out into the yard, but she held me fast.

"They some more thing, child. Thing I been saving long time now." She was looking towards the house, not the barn.

"What?" I followed her gaze.

"Captain send them thing."

"My pa?"

"Do boy," she half whispered. "Captain Tom good man, but ain't been but one true captain 'round here. That your ma's pa."

"Him?"

"Old Captain Cage, he take the boat in the ocean. He bring Anna through them same inlet." She motioned off over my head. "Come in the dark night, slip by them Yankee blockade boat, and he row Anna ashore his own self. That fellow bring the mail, he hold the pistol side that fellow head and say you going take this Anna to my daughter who living down the road. The buckra do it, too. Bring Anna right here and then the old man say he going to put me making salt, boil that same creek water under them same cedar tree and I tell I going die 'fore I tote salt again." She shook her head back and forth and spoke almost like an angry child. "Your mama say that ain't happen. She give Anna that cross she give you." Her voice softened and she pointed at the cross hanging about my neck.

"You and my mama—"

"Her people been my people. Her God been my God."

"That's so, but—"

"I promised the Captain I stand by his gal and them promise going carry over to every generation that follow."

"Yes, ma'am." Since she was smiling broadly again, I figured she was through, and started off the stoop.

"Ain't but one more thing," she said. "Ain't take but a little piece of minute. Don't do to advertise to the devil." She slipped the cross down inside my shirt. "Keep that true silver shining on your skin, and remember what I tell you. Love Jesus and bury your parents. That Anna's own sin. She ain't bury her mama. Jesus done forgive her but ain't good to pile up too much of the same sin in one place. You promise that."

"Yes, ma'am." That wasn't a hard promise to make, and again I thought she meant me to go. Instead, I was led back inside the building, where the little fire had shrunk to almost an ember.

"I promise," I repeated, not certain what else was required.

"I glad, yes, Jesus, I is glad. Now you going to close your eye tight. Close 'em tight." She held me with a hand on each arm and I did as I was told. "I going to let go now. You going to spin 'round the room three time with the clock. Keep them eye close. Don't crack them."

I turned in a circle, feeling only her guiding touch once in each revolution, and then stood facing her.

"Keep them eye closed." The voice, since it came from behind, caused me to jump, but my eyes stayed shut. "Tell Maum Anna what you see through them shut eyeball."

I concentrated and had to admit I saw nothing.

"Nothing!" she exclaimed. "You gots to see something. Tell Anna what you see."

"Black. I see darkness."

"Lord, you is a perculiar child. Stubborn perculiar. Dear Jesus, look over and protect this stubborn child." I felt her own fingers closing over my eyelids, pressing them into a blacker darkness. Her voice whispered in my ear.

"Ain't you see Jimmy coming home? Ain't you see him getting off the Savannah steamer? Right there. He got a cardboard suitcase and a new cap. He's calling out to some fella on the wharf saying how he's heading home to Cedar Point. There. There he goes. He turning around to tip he cap to the ladies. Them two he met on the steamer trip. They is sisters. One is married. The other be the old maid. Going die an old maid. That too bad. Sad when that happen. Don't Captain Jimmy look happy, though? He whistling. Oh, that a good sign when a man whistle. My second husband a whistling man. Nothing please me more than to hear 'em whistle in the morning and talking to he mule. Here Jim come now. Here he come. I reckon he'll be coming Friday night with your pa. He got plans. Yes, sir, Willie T. That a man with a plan."

She removed her hand and I looked about blinking. It seemed real when she was whispering it in my ear, and I wanted it to be true. Still, I doubted some, doubted a lot, in fact.

"Go on," she said, smiling wide at me. "Go on. The day done half gone. Ain't going do you a bit of good if you doubt Maum Anna."

"No, ma'am," I said. "I reckon he's coming if you say he is."

"Remember your cross."

"I will." I touched it hard enough to feel the metal re-assuringly on the flesh of my chest.

"When you hear the hoof, you kiss it. Rub it 'til it warm. Say, 'ghost ride on.' You remember."

"Yes, ma'am," I said.

"You ain't going need Brother or Sammy, neither. You got the cross now."

"Yes, ma'am."

"You ain't ever going to be alone."

"No, ma'am."

"Go on then. Go. This little fire need my attention. Go on."

I went and got Sammy. I felt better, but not good enough to go carrying Ruth off to pasture alone. That day, though, I began to feel more and more relaxed and was almost looking forward to the night when I could try out the powers of Anna's gift against the marauding Mercy—so was disappointed when he didn't come. No hoofbeats pounded in the night. Not that night or the next or the next, and gradually, I came to believe she had, in fact, beaten off the devil, for The Hard to Catch Mercy passed out of my life. Within a month's time, I was confident enough to pass alone from house to barn and finally even out to the pasture and back with only the company of a cow.

As for the forecast of Uncle Jimmy's return, she was pretty much on the mark. But that same day my mama had received a letter from my cousin, saying he'd be home Friday night. He was. As the *Redbird* docked, my cousin swung from the pilothouse door, laughing, and before my pa could get it out, he whispered to me alone "Good Friday, ain't it?" He looked much older and much heavier. He'd put on a good twenty pounds, and like the rest of us, picked up a new wardrobe. His clothes were of a dark coarse cotton, a workman's cut. And instead of the bowler, he wore a cap. It pleased me to see Maum Anna's prophecy come true, but he carried a carpetbag suitcase. Not cardboard. Immediately, I pointed this out to the old woman, but she replied the light of her vision had been bad because of my own stubbornness, and her eyes were failing as well. It looked like cardboard to her.

I was satisfied, more than satisfied, and we all welcomed Uncle Jimmy back and listened excitedly to what he said. He knew he'd caused a lot of hurt and at supper that same evening, he apologized to each of us, saying his only excuse was grief, which he hoped we could understand. As for his visit to Savannah, he could only report that he'd seen old friends, but for the most part, he was disappointed at how backwards the town was. Though twenty times the size of

Cedar Point, the citizens had no vision of the future. He had plans and it had become apparent to him very quickly that he should return to Cedar Point to carry them out.

Very quickly? Well, he'd been gone most two months, but thanks to the kindness of Drake Bailey, I'd been kept informed of Uncle Jimmy's whereabouts. Almost from the beginning, the bully had assured me that all was well. My cousin was definitely in Savannah, living above a whorehouse with a woman named Louise, who had a reputation that Drake found highly commendable.

"Old Jim is a rounder," Drake exclaimed with a mixture of both pride and envy. "Living there for free and her paying his liquor bills." The bully chose to announce this at a ball game so fifty spectators could all share in the good news. Nights with Louise and days spent in equally idyllic surroundings—Uncle Jimmy lay around the docks guzzling gin with the Negroes and no-counts whose highest ambition in life was to drink and slash their way into either jail or the grave. My cousin had managed neither, but he'd had a close call. It saddened Drake to report that Louise had to be fought over, and even after Uncle Jimmy had won her fair and square, she'd pushed him out a second-story window.

"Ain't no figuring a woman, now is there, Willie T.? Seems like that woman would realize she couldn't do no better, least not with me stuck way up here." Drake took the trouble to attend my cousin Margarite's high school commencement and made sure everybody seated within a mile of me shared the secret.

It hadn't taken my cousin long to find new lodgings. "Our boy" was soon living with a handsome mulatto woman, who was probably the finest seamstress in Savannah. It was a step up, but Drake had some serious words of caution. He knew from sad experience such a woman wouldn't tolerate the state of continual drunkenness that was every man's due, and she'd certainly be expecting to raise a family.

" 'Fore you know it there'll be a batch of them high yellow Allsons running 'round this countryside. Yes, sir, Willie T., that's just what we need around here is another hatching out of them yellow Allsons." Drake shouted this on a Friday afternoon while standing with the waiting crowd on the Allson wharf.

Of course, I had no way of knowing if a single word the bully said was true, but I was absolutely sure this last was a pure and simple slander. There were light-skinned Allson Negroes. Red Willie Allson was lighter skinned than my own deep-tanned pa, and I'd been told the Negro's kinky hair had been bright red before it turned white. That still didn't make him kin to us. Red Willie, himself, acknowledged that his pa had been an Irish overseer briefly in Grandpa's employ, and Maum Anna claimed the same. Those were Nancy stories. Lies. She thanked Jesus there were no blood relations between the white and black branches of the Allson family.

Of course, to tell this to Drake would only have brought on wilder accusations, so I nodded, and said at least it wasn't Liza my cousin was living with. I hadn't meant this as a joke, but the bully found it quite mirth-provoking and went about the dock side repeating it until he was certain all had heard.

"That was a good one, Willie," Drake said. "I swear, sometimes you surprise me."

Perhaps my cousin had been living with whores and Negroes while he was down in Savannah, but I was happy just to have him back, and happy to accept whatever part he had for me in this new scheme of his. First, though, he had some mending to do and he started that same night with the little clockfixer.

Not two days before Uncle Jimmy's return, Brother had beckoned me over to his worktable, and then, closing the door to our bedroom, he'd explained to me a complicated theory concerning what he called "pure time." I didn't begin to understand it, but apparently, the problem with clocks was that the gears, driven by strings or weights, were expected to do work, the work being the turning of the hands about the face of the timepiece. Brother showed me all this by using a simple cheap windup clock he'd already repaired.

"See the difference?" he asked. No glass covered its face, so he gave a hint by touching the affected parts.

"You done something to the hands." It was obvious that he had trimmed away at the clock hands.

"Less to turn," he said. "Don't have to wind the spring near as tight to get the same effect."

"Fine," I said.

"Use less power this way, don't it?"

"I reckon."

"Now, look here."

With nimble fingers, he popped the already shortened, narrower hands completely off the face of the clock.

"So?" I asked.

"No weight. Less strain altogether on the inner workings."

"Brother, a clock without hands ain't worth nothing to nobody."

"Less tension on the spring, less weight." He was getting angry. His ears turned red and wiggled, but I shook my head no.

"If Uncle Jimmy were here," I said, "he'd tell you I was right."

My little cousin had gone on with the experiments, but fortunately, none of the recently repaired timepieces had been picked up. Now, Uncle Jimmy sat and patiently explained to Brother that, yes, he was right in a theoretical way, but no, he was wrong to think that people would accept clocks without hands. The accused gave up his position with surprising stubbornness and only agreed on the condition he be allowed to continue his experiments on the inside of the timepieces. Too tired to argue further, Uncle Jimmy simply insisted that whatever left the bedroom must, at least, appear to tell an accurate time in a normal way.

He'd gone to bed immediately after this conversation, but the next morning at breakfast, I asked the prodigal exactly what his plan for the future was. "Commerce. Commerce, my boy, and plenty of it." Leaving me with that sparse clue, he went straight off to Dr. McGill's office and for several hours they met in private. Then, he searched me out. It was time for him to apologize to Uncle Albert and get back his old job at the grocery, but he couldn't stay. If I wanted, he'd teach clerking to me, and then he could, with a clear conscience, go on to his new secret "commerce" project with the doctor. In case I had any doubts, he wanted me to know my mama thought I'd make a wonderful grocery clerk.

I was hardly excited at the prospect, but Mama had already circled the day on her calendar, written "dearest Willie" on the kitchen wall, and linked that notation with a thick black line to the newspaper account of the drowning death of Captain James Allson. Under those circumstances, I had no choice but to go along. I guess Uncle Albert felt about the same. He went along and barely tolerated me in the store.

When my cousin started work there nine months before, he'd immediately gotten two things from the grocer that no one else, not even the man's wife or daughter, had ever received—money and warm regards. From the very first moment, my cousin smiled and chatted with the customers, recommended this or that product, sent off to Crowns Bluff for odd requests, and trimmed away the fat with a friendly wink to that very special customer. A special customer, he tried to explain to me now, was anyone who came through the door.

"What's this? A bent penny. Don't tell the old man I took a bent penny." Then he'd slide a penny and a half's worth of licorice across the counter, which in the long run hadn't hurt business at all.

"Shouldn't let you have it. Last pound of butts we got. None left in Crowns Bluff either, great scarcity. Here, don't tell nobody where you bought it."

Of course, they'd tell everybody because the notion of the world running out of butts was a very funny one. And he'd gone on teasing out those nickels and dimes and slips of credit, and making Uncle Albert a very happy man. Now, I'd been brought in to learn his method overnight.

"Good morning, good morning, how are you this very fine and beautiful morning? I've been thinking about Sunday for you. Yes, ma'am. Not laying awake thinking, but knowing how important that dinner is going to be . . ."

It'd be months before I got beyond a muttered "good morning." I couldn't even get that out for the first couple weeks and made a terrible store clerk. The job quickly became mine, though, for after a few days, my cousin slipped away to carry out his plan.

No, Uncle Albert was hardly pleased by his desertion or by my poor performance either, and he showed it by pursing his lips and withholding both money and warm regards. I expected neither and, as a consolation for my enforced servitude, was soon taking secret delight at my new employer's peculiar ways. The second day, I'd seen him pick up a half-eaten candy from the floor and put it in his mouth. Twice that week, I'd watched him knock the bowl of his pipe clean and go through the ashes picking out the unburned tobacco. Uncle Jimmy, of course, had seen this behavior, too, but he chose to call it "thrifty habits of a life-time" that I would do well to copy. He was joking—at least I hoped he was. Since his return from Savannah, though, he seemed more serious, so when he said things like that about "thrifty habits" I had to look him over twice. Maum Anna's cross could protect, but it couldn't show me how to live my life. No, that duty I had cautiously put back into the hands of my cousin, and suddenly my carefree boyhood ceased to be even a memory. This had always been my life. What could be more natural than standing there, not smiling, on the wrong side of that trade-worn counter, scooping out three cents' worth of sugar and a nickel's worth of grits and passing the purchase price to my uncle because he wouldn't let me within a yard of the cash register?

I put the best face on it and two weeks later, Uncle Jimmy showed up with a Model T truck. He pulled it down Main Street using Gal. Liza didn't approve. My cousin hadn't got-ten around to mending their relationship. He hardly spoke to her, in fact. Besides that, she didn't like the jokes coming out of the mercantile. There was talk of a "McGill mule-truck freight hauling business." But the truck went in our barn, and with Sammy assisting in the rebuilding, Uncle Jimmy worked some magic of his own.

"Purrs like a calico kitten, don't it?"

You couldn't argue. Washed and polished, the Model T

looked brand new. Uncle Jimmy took Dr. McGill for a ride and they put Liza on the seat between them. A week after that my cousin showed up with a freight boat he and the doctor had bargained for and renamed the "Miss Liza." The boat would require a bit more fine-tuning than the truck had but the hull was solid, and McGill and Allson would be in business soon enough. They wouldn't be competing with Captain Tom, though. They had contracts to supply gasoline and kerosene for both a logging company and the bridge builders working this side of Mumford. Pa told them to use his wharf and wouldn't take money for the privilege. Everyone concerned seemed happy with the deal, but most of those not concerned said it was bad luck to rename a boat.

The Biscuit Thief

WHILE I was clerking in the grocery Uncle Albert stayed angry at me. But with the notable exception of Uncle Jimmy, he'd stayed angry at all his clerks, and even for his best customers and closest relatives, he managed only a few mumbled pleasantries. That was just "the nature of the man," as my cousin said—the nature, in this case, being silent and mean-spirited. Still, my employer never actually hit me, nor had I ever seen him lay hands on anyone else until that Saturday.

Lunch was over and three or four customers were in the store, and as usual, I was doing my utmost to satisfy their many and varied desires without looking up unless absolutely necessary. It caught me by surprise, then, when Uncle Albert began to bellow.

"You!" he shouted. "Yes! Yes! I mean you!"

Amazed by such a sound coming from the frail old man, I immediately yelped "Yes, sir!" It wasn't me.

"You! You, Gander Bailey. Yes, you, Gander. You take it off right now."

Uncle Albert had the culprit by the collar, which was no mean feat. Gander, though small, was slippery as an eel, but Uncle Albert had the element of surprise and the strength of ten because his heart was pure. Most important, I suppose, Gander knew he was guilty and had already surrendered to the superior moral force.

"I meant to pay, Mr. Allson. I swear to my Lord and Maker, I meant to pay you."

"You come in here wearing that suit! You stroll right into my very store!"

Uncle Albert pulled him towards the back of the building as the other customers and I looked on with some satisfaction. Drake's little brother was not particularly well-loved in the community, because he was always sneaky about what he was up to, which was always lying and stealing. Of course, Drake wasn't much better, but at least the bully's wit and brawn had won him some respect.

"My mama's been sick," Gander wailed.

"Get in there and take it off." Uncle Albert pushed the youth into our totally dark storeroom, slamming the door after him.

Now I understood. My uncle had a small section of his establishment set aside for dry goods, haberdashery—mostly shoes and such. Several months before, Gander had purchased, on credit, the gray wool suit he was presently disrobing. It was a thick, hot garment with the texture of a coarse horse blanket, but Gander had been sporting around in it ever since, because it came with long pants instead of knickers. Here was the day of reckoning. The door cracked open and the suit was passed out to my uncle, who immediately returned it to the rack.

"Sir?" Gander called after him. "What about me, Mr. Allson? I got no pants at all."

This brought a snicker from more than one customer and me, as well. I hoped Uncle Albert would put the sneak out on the busy Saturday afternoon Main Street in his drawers or at most, a rice sack. Gander was going nowhere, though, not just yet.

"What's this?" the grocer shouted anew. "What's this doing in a coat pocket?"

"Sir?" Gander called through the crack of his dungeon door.

"Mr. Bailey, explain to me how this expensive fountain pen came into your possession?"

"Bought it, sir," Gander whispered from the dark cell.

"Bought it while still wearing an unpaid-for suit of clothes?"

"Yes, sir. I mean, no, sir," he blurted out and then finished by whining, "I swear to my Lord and Maker, my mama has been real sick."

Uncle Albert was heading out the door, and even before Gander realized he was gone, the grocer was marching back in the company of Blaine Fitchum. Blaine recognized the fountain pen at once, for it was one of several items stolen from his pharmacy the Saturday before. This man, of course, had even less use for Gander than I, and now, much to my delight, he and Uncle Albert had the thief caught red-handed, stripped half-naked, and cornered like a rat. After a few brief exchanges, the two men again closed the door on Gander, padlocked it, and went to see Judge Walker. Ten minutes later, the judge led his nephew away in a third-hand pair of overalls for which Uncle Albert had demanded a receipt. That was all I knew of the matter until the next morning after church when Uncle Jimmy told me what by then the whole town must have known.

"That fountain pen is just the tip of the iceberg."

Gander had fully confessed that he was totally innocent of any wrongdoing. His brother Drake stole the pen and gave it to him as a gift. The bully, Scooter, and Barnus had been in the alley behind the drugstore the previous Saturday night, drinking and singing dirty songs, which was their normal Saturday night occupation. Then, Drake got the idea to break into the rear of the pharmacy, and since the store was still open, he'd sent Scooter around to the front to engage Blaine Fitchum in conversation. That done, he and Barnus Wilson pried open the back window and came away with some soda waters, cigars, laxative preparations, and six fountain pens. Except for the pens, it had been an act of pure mischief, an act that Uncle Jimmy credited to the fact that Drake was nineteen and bored with the eleventh grade.

"That's how it happened," my cousin concluded. "Leastwise, that's how Gander says it happened. The rest have took off."

"Good riddance," I said.

"They'll be back."

And he was right—at least about Scooter and Barnus who showed up the very next morning. One day on the lam was enough, and they confessed to all. Said it was all Drake's fault. Said he thought it all up. Stole it all, then drank all the soda water, smoked all the cigars, swallowed all the laxatives, and threw all the fountain pens into the ditch except for the one he'd been forced to give his brother Gander. It seemed Gander had witnessed the robbery and demanded the pen in return for silence. Drake considered the alternative of murdering his own brother, and then, in an act of uncharacteristic generosity, gave over the pen, saying when he did, he'd settle with Gander at a later date. What he'd have done to Barnus and Scooter for their damning testimony was anybody's guess—and we all took turns guessing—but they went on breathing and Drake stayed out of sight. Twice at dusk, though, a suspicious figure was reported crossing the River Road, so Judge Walker and a few friends were out beating the bushes in that locale.

"Drake's mama misses him something fierce," Uncle Jimmy declared.

"Yes," I replied. "Why be satisfied with a sneak and a liar when you can have a thief and a bully as well?"

Apparently the Widow Bailey did see it that way and kept her brother looking. Drake stayed gone, and the sugar biscuits began to disappear.

"Philadelphia Tea Cakes" was the printed name, but we called them "sugar biscuits." The little cookies came packed in a round can with a pry-off lid, and inside twenty-four were individually wrapped in wax paper. Needless to say, the price was outrageous, and only one person purchased and ate them on a regular weekly basis—that, of course, was Liza. My pa brought them on the freight boat, and I carried them up to the grocery and put them on the shelf. Liza had them delivered to her house.

And that's how matters stood that September Monday morning when Uncle Albert opened the store at seven o'clock and found his two remaining cans of sugar biscuits taken from the shelf and their contents consumed there on the premises. I say "consumed there," for the cans were opened and discarded, the wax paper was scattered about and damning crumbs littered a large section of the aisle.

Drake Bailey was Uncle Albert's guess, one commonly shared. Because of the warrant out on him and the arrest of Gander, he'd have reason to hold a grudge against the grocer and had never had much use for Liza or her sugar biscuits in the first place. The only real mystery was how he'd entered the store and that was easily discovered. By climbing a small sycamore at the rear of the building, a nimble fellow could have slipped in the attic window. The remedy was simple. Board up the window. But Uncle Albert now felt the necessity of vengeance. If Drake was fool enough to steal the sugar biscuits once, the grocer reasoned, he'd be fool enough to try again. A trap was set. More sugar biscuits were put on the shelf and the window left unlatched. Then, three nights later, Brother, Sammy, and I were forced to hide at the rear of the neighboring mercantile. Of course, we weren't supposed to catch Drake, just spot him and run for help. The sycamore and the grocery window were in plain view, but I personally doubted and even hoped we'd fail. And naturally, I was frightened, and naturally, I touched the cross to ward off both ghost and the very alive bully.

We were to take turns standing watch so at ten o'clock Sammy and I went to sleep. Brother woke me at one. I watched until three and then woke Sammy who watched until dawn. No luck. I grumbled, but the vigilance would continue. The following night I picked up an extra hour of sleep by waking Sammy earlier than instructed. Dawn came and with it a double disappointment. We'd seen nothing, but the biscuit thief had struck again. The bait was consumed, all four cans, and Drake had slipped away undetected.

Uncle Albert, beside himself with rage, had fallen upon our hiding place with Brother and me still fast asleep and Sammy too wide-eyed with wondrous terror to do more than back into a corner and stammer "Yes, sir, yes, sir, yes, sir." I couldn't do much better, and when the grocer returned to the scene of the crime, we scurried for the safety of home. I assumed the trap would be abandoned, but Uncle Albert argued that Drake, now emboldened, would strike after the next freight boat delivery, and so the following week we found ourselves once more concealed. Brother went first, then I, and once more Sammy watched until daylight. The results this time were a success, a disastrous success. I woke in the daylight to find myself alone, and noticing the commotion next door, concluded rightly that the thief was caught. Yes, indeed. Uncle Albert had unlocked the store that morning and found Sammy fast asleep in the sugar biscuit aisle, empty cans and wax paper scattered about him and a single half-eaten Philadelphia Tea Cake clutched in his larcenous hand.

The Negro readily confessed to having taken the biscuits the first time. Then, while Brother and I slept, he'd repeated the crime twice more. As for motive, he could provide no reasonable one. He was hardly starving, for he ate exactly what all of us did at the Allson household and was given generous portions, at that. When pressed, he finally blurted out, "Jesus tell me to eat the sugar biscuits." The accusers asked if he meant the devil but he insisted it was Jesus. They kept after him, though, until he admitted he wasn't sure if it was Jesus or the devil. The latter was chosen for him, since everyone knew his people to be particularly susceptible to the temptations of the devil.

"Haig make 'em steal biscuit," Maum Anna confided in me alone. "Haig slip out her skin, and she ride Sammy back, ride 'em all night long." The old woman slapped at her own back. She was permanently bent, smaller than ever. "You find that skin and you salt 'em down good. Then, when haig come in just 'fore daylight, she going slip that skin on. She going jump and holler, skin burn 'em up."

By "haig" I was certain she meant Liza, and by "you," I figured she meant me. I was to find Liza's shed skin and salt it down.

"That ordinary way, but us can't get at this one. I fix 'em, though. Come for look."

I was led out to Sammy's shed room, where she pointed with pride at the door lock.

"That haig visit through 'em keyhole. She a curious creature, always spying 'round. Make my poor Sammy eat them sugar biscuit. Anna fix 'em, fix 'em good." The old woman had whittled out a keyhole-shaped plug and jammed it into the ancient and useless lock of the shed door.

Well, I hardly wanted to doubt my protector's powers, but I was pretty sure Liza wasn't shedding her skin and even more to the point, the horse was already out of the barn. Our Sammy was presently quartered in the judge's feed shed. Fine and dandy, I thought. Yes, dang near perfect. From the moment of my playmate's capture, I'd begun to live in trembling fear, and now I could pile guilt on top of that. Yes, if there was a devil involved, it was Willie T. Allson, for it was he who took the first sugar biscuit. At least a month before, Willie T. Allson had secretly pried a can open, removed one biscuit, and eaten it, and then, deciding the absence would be less noticeable if all the cans were equal, he'd removed a sugar biscuit from the others as well. Since Liza appeared none the wiser, Willie T. Allson had repeated this surgery the following week, and carrying a biscuit home to Sammy, admitted in a boast of vain pride what he'd done. There, then, was the devil who'd tempted poor Sammy. And only poor Sammy stood between Willie T. Allson and the outrage of the community—and Liza in particular.

Vengeance. Liza wanted vengeance and plenty of it. The theft was a direct attack on her. A vague question about Southern womanhood echoed in her speech and won the approval of her fellow citizens. Fortunately for Sammy, Uncle Jimmy hadn't quite finished his freight boat repairs, and quietly and behind the scenes, he made sure the punishment would be only the normally required beating. Still, this was bad enough, for it was to be a true beating, administered with the fist of a large Negro the judge kept on a small retainer for just such occasions.

"Haig ride 'em. Haig ride 'em," Maum Anna would explain only to me. She had assumed the peg in the keyhole would alter matters and when it didn't, she was suddenly helpless. She begged my mama to intervene, but my mama could do nothing except keep Liza away from Grandpa. Confined to his sickbed, the old man had been told nothing of the scandal—a consideration involving not only the patient's health, but Sammy's as well.

I, for my part, retreated as far to the sidelines as possible and hoped Sammy would have the strength not to blurt out my name under torture. And then a reprieve arrived from a totally unsuspected source. In the early morning hours of the appointed day of punishment, the judge caught Drake trying to slip back into his and Gander's own bedroom and, marching his nephew at gunpoint outside, locked him in the same feed shed that held Sammy. Then, seeing the two of them together gave him an idea that he, at least, felt worthy of Solomon.

His problem was his nephew—how to graduate Drake from high school so the young man could begin his missionary studies. Here before him were two incorrigibles. Why not commute Sammy's sentence and shackle him to Drake for as long as it took to prepare his nephew for the world—forever if necessary? It wasn't a perfect solution, but the judge could work out the fine points while Sammy served as an anchor. That very morning the two culprits were handcuffed together and delivered to the schoolhouse steps. Superintendent Baker led them into our classroom and, repeating a speech I'd heard before, he stomped hard on Drake's foot.

"So, Mr. Tough Guy. You think you're so tough? You're not so tough, Mr. Tough Guy." Then he stamped once more. Drake barely flinched, and, when ordered, limped to a seat at the back. Sammy, wild-eyed and bewildered, dragged along behind and squatted in the aisle. After a few unfocused glances about the room, he stared at the floor. He hadn't spotted me. Miss Gaye was given control of her class once more and began the lesson with a brave attempt at being normal. I hunkered low in my desk, and even turned my head away, in fear I'd be singled out by my playmate and handcuffed to Drake's other wrist.

Finally recess was called and the class, silent until now, scrambled outside to discuss the morning's events. I traveled concealed in their midst and was amazed to see Sammy and Drake following along in the rear. Liza was nowhere about. The superintendent hadn't returned and Miss Gaye had given no instructions concerning the two felons. She let them go and go they went. Yes, limping slightly, Drake walked across the schoolyard with Sammy trailing a step behind. Then, without having said a single word since he'd been captured by his uncle that morning, Drake, with Sammy in tow, disappeared into the woods.

Better him than me was all that crossed my mind. I watched them go in silence as did a dozen or so other scholars. Gander, who'd made the near-fatal mistake of turning in his brother, was openly weeping tears of joy. He certainly wasn't going to sound the alarm. No one was, but we finally managed some nervous whispers and a few laughs, which is how Liza found us five minutes later. She'd been down in Superintendent Baker's office going over some of the finer points of the law, and once informed of the escape, she screamed for help. It was too late. The bully and his anchor weren't to be found in the immediate neighborhood, or even beyond that. Night fell with the hastily organized posse still chasing in vain.

Uncle Jimmy was taking part in this search as were all the other available able-bodied men. At home I waited with Mama and a distressed Maum Anna, thinking Sammy would surely be returned to us. The whole school, of course, had been accused of abetting a fugitive, but only Liza said it was especially my fault. Brother watched too, after all, but he was upstairs wrestling his timepieces. It didn't matter. Liza was right. Maum Anna had saved me, but I did nothing to save her nephew who I'd betrayed in the first place. For a moment I considered returning her cross, but couldn't. When Uncle Jimmy showed up, it was almost midnight. They'd found no trace of the fugitives, but he assured Maum Anna all was well. The judge was borrowing some dogs for the next day's effort.

"Do Jesus, no." Suddenly the old woman was on her knees praying. "Keep that Sheriff Colgrove and him dog away from my Sammy." I pressed the cross against my chest, certain she was about to demand it.

My cousin explained that the dogs were just a well-known pack of deerhounds, and the last person on earth Judge Walker would call for assistance was Sheriff Clarke Fitchum Colgrove.

"This is a law-and-order town," he said earnestly. "Anna, you know we take care of our own." She stayed, kneeling on the floor praying to Jesus, and we went upstairs—me muttering to my cousin that it was a stupid idea to handcuff the two together.

Scenting the hounds on the edge of the school yard, the judge's deputized marshals, now nine in number, followed a trail leading into the judge's own stable, and then off in a wide arc towards the river. My cousin returned the next night exhausted but still capable of describing with enthusiasm the ins and outs of the chase. Though he'd had the opportunity, Drake didn't bother to take a horse. The two were on foot and no longer joined by the handcuffs.

Drake was enjoying himself and Sammy was in no danger, my cousin constantly reassured Maum Anna. Running like foxes, the two were backtracking, wading streams and walking fences, and nobody knew what else to confuse the hounds, who were indeed confused. If the judge cussed, he'd have been cussing mad, but that just helped to make it a "merry chase." The next afternoon, it stopped being merry and just turned into a chase, plain and simple, and Maum Anna had good reason to be concerned.

Sheriff Colgrove showed up with three deputies, six good bloodhounds, and two trucks. From the doorway of the grocery, I saw the majesty of the Clarkesville law descend, but its representative went not to the mercantile, but to Blaine Fitchum's pharmacy as was to be expected. Blaine was still the leader of the second slate Democrats, which, while they admitted nothing, were known to be in sympathy with the Clarkesville thieves. No, there was no love lost between Blaine and Judge Walker, because it was Blaine who the judge had easily defeated in the last race for magistrate. And, of course, Blaine and the sheriff were third cousins, so it was natural for Sheriff Clarke Fitchum Colgrove to call on him.

"Blaine! Blaine! Goddamn your sorry ass. Get out here." Sheriff Colgrove got out of the truck and stood with one hand on the front fender, screaming at the front of the building opposite us. I'd heard the sheriff was a small man, but was surprised to see he didn't stand much over five feet. The long-barreled shotgun cradled under his arm made up the difference. I'd heard he slept with the gun. "Blaine!" he bellowed. "Don't you know there's a war going on?"

We did know. On the Fourth of July that year, there had been a short victory parade that, to the doctor's distress, had exhibited Liza and Leala dressed as Red Cross girls. Also the fireworks that night had contained a display called The Stars and Bars. Even more to the point, two other young men had joined up and several more had been drafted. Of course, it wasn't my place to tell Colgrove that. Our paths had never exactly crossed, and they weren't crossing now. I stayed in the doorway of the grocery, partially hidden by Uncle Albert, who'd immediately stepped out onto the sidewalk.

"Albert," the sheriff was saying at much less volume. "What the hell's going on down here?"

"Biscuits, Sheriff." Uncle Albert spoke right up. "Boy stole some biscuits, and now he's on the run."

"Biscuits? That ain't what I heard." He turned back to the pharmacy. "Blaine, get your sorry ass out here!" he screamed again. The pharmacist was coming through the front door to pump the sheriff's hand in welcome.

"Good to see you, Clarke. What brings you up here?" I assumed Blaine was playing dumb since we were there as witnesses.

"What brings me here? I got a message 'bout the niggers rising up. Been a long time coming. That's what I told the boys here." He motioned to the three who still sat in the trucks showing varying degrees of concern. "Isle of Niggers. Monkeys been plotting for fifty years."

"I don't know nothing about that," Blaine said.

"Sure you do. Niggers think they can bust off a third of Clarke County and set up this here cannibal kingdom. Don't tell me you never heard of it."

"I heard of it, Clarke, but that ain't what's happening. At least not yet, it ain't."

"Old Colonel Allson swore it was coming. Going to have a cannibal king. Drink the white man's blood. I know all about it. Don't have to tell me. Them Republicans up in

Washington, D.C., been working with 'em hand in glove ever since the day General Lee give it up. They just waiting for us to let our guard down." The sheriff stopped to clear his throat and spit. "Bunch of bush monkeys couldn't run that store of yours, much less a country, but guess it's part our fault. Us, up in Clarkesville, getting so involved in fighting the Kaiser, shouldn't let matters get this far out of hand."

"Judge's nephew Drake, Drake Bailey, stole a fountain pen out of my store," Blaine Fitchum began explaining. "Now the judge has got some men out looking for Drake and the Allsons' nigger Sammy. Ain't no revolt, though. Not that I heard of, Clarke."

"Ain't the message I got. Said revolt was starting up. Said was going to be murder and rape going on everywhere." He looked up and down the empty street. "I got to admit, it do seem quiet, at least 'round here."

"Whoever sent that message got it wrong, Clarke. Ask Albert. He'll tell you. Ain't no uprising. They ain't trying to start no country. Nothing like that."

The sheriff turned back to my uncle, who until now had been pleased to see the sugar biscuit theft finally getting the attention it deserved.

"That's so, Sheriff," the grocer agreed reluctantly. "Ain't no revolt, but Drake stole a fountain pen. The Negro stole some biscuits, and now the judge is tracking them down."

"Tracking 'em? Walker couldn't catch his ass with both hands. That ain't the point of the matter, though. No, sir. I didn't drive ten straight hours 'cause of no fountain pen and biscuits."

"Drake got more than a fountain pen," the pharmacist volunteered. He took some cigars, sodas. Some laxatives, too."

"Christ Almighty, Blaine," the sheriff swore, removing his hat as he did and wiping his forehead on his shirtsleeve. "Some of you people down here are bat-shit crazy. Who's this Drake? Is that the bully? That's him, ain't it? Whipped our boy good last spring?"

"Yeah, that's him."

"And the nigger belongs to the Allsons?"

"Yes," Blaine answered.

"All right. All right." He paused to pull a scrap of paper out of his shirt pocket. "Who's this woman Liza McGill? Was her who wrote to me."

I should've guessed that Liza was behind this.

"Not a woman, Sheriff," Uncle Albert said. "She's just a schoolgirl. Her daddy's the doctor here."

"Dr. McGill." The sheriff nodded his head in recognition. "He's the one that threw old Franklin down the well. They were fighting over the Allson dowry, weren't they?"

"No, Clarke. Nobody ever figured out who got Franklin."

"That so? Well, don't matter. Go get this doctor. Tell him it's a matter of life and death."

"Go on." Uncle Albert turned to me. "Go get the doctor."

I did as I was told, even repeated that it was life and death, and rode back in the steamer to where the sheriff still waited. He was chatting a little more amiably, now, for a small crowd had gathered. The sheriff shook hands with the doctor, and you couldn't help noticing a strange similarity. Both men were small and broad about, and both had neat, trimmed mustaches. Unlike the doctor though, the sheriff was hard-muscled, and he dressed differently. Instead of a boater the sheriff wore a weathered felt hat, and unlike the doctor he carried the shotgun. It turned out the matter of life and death concerned a death that was going to happen in the very near future.

"Hanging or burning?" the sheriff asked.

"To whom are you referring?" the doctor replied.

"The nigger. This Sammy. Since you are the girl's pa, you get the choice. Hanging or burning."

"There'll be no hanging or burning here, sir." The doctor puffed himself up and drew away from the other man. "This is not Clarkesville. This is a law-and-order town."

"A law-and-order town?" The sheriff waved the note that Liza had sent in front of her father's face. "That ain't what it says here."

"Let me see that," the doctor demanded.

The sheriff handed it over with an assured smile. The doctor read it with an increasing frown.

"My daughter exaggerates. There is no uprising of the Negroes in progress, and the only wrong this Sammy has done her is to steal some biscuits that she intended to buy."

"Blaine!" the sheriff shouted, turning back on the pharmacist as if this were somehow his fault. "You hear what this man just told me? What kind of joke is this? You think you can drag us down here for nothing. Taxpaying dollars. Taxpaying dollars, that's what you're looking at right there." He pointed at the three deputies and the six dogs that rested comfortably in the two trucks.

"Sorry, Clarke," Blaine said.

"Don't you people know we're fighting the Hun?"

"Sorry, Clarke," Blaine said.

"Where are they now? Where's Walker?" The sheriff shook his head and spit.

"Up on the river, I heard. I think he and his men were just up from the ferry landing this morning."

"Men? Goddamn baby parade." The sheriff dismissed the pharmacist with an offhand wave. "Good day to you, Albert." The sheriff tipped his hat to the grocer and then nodded, as a good politician would, to the five or six others who were gathered together. Then he got back behind the wheel of the front truck and drove away.

It was late afternoon before the sheriff caught up with Judge Walker. That's what Uncle Jimmy reported back to us that night. The judge was furious and told Colgrove to go back to Clarkesville and stay there. The sheriff pretended concern and said, having come this far, he'd conduct the manhunt himself. There wasn't much the judge could do short of shooting it out, so he'd divided his nine men up between the sheriff's gang. If there was somebody on each side of a Clarkesville deputy, it might decrease the chance of Sammy getting shot. Drake was fairly safe. Colgrove was just taking part to torment the judge, the governor, "the Washington Hotel bunch and all them fancy pants Crowns Bluff lawyers," and he'd expressed an admiration for Drake's fist-cuffing abilities. They'd shoot Sammy in a minute, though, Uncle Jimmy concluded. "I heard 'em laughing and saying one less nigger in this part of the county wasn't likely to be noticed."

Of course, Uncle Jimmy repeated none of this to Maum Anna or my mama. He'd said it to me out on the porch before asking a question that left me truly astonished.

"Where's this Isle of Negroes they keep raving about?"

"Where? Right here," I said. "You standing in it."

"Willie T., what are you talking about?"

Somehow my cousin had existed all this time among us living in a state of blissful ignorance, and now I explained the matter as Grandpa had explained it to me so many times before.

"You know that island, Santo Domingo, down in the Caribbean Ocean? Slaves revolted and set up an independent nation that's still being run by the Negroes today. You know that?"

"I heard of it," he conceded.

"Same thing could happen here. Skull and crossbones will be flying from the flagpole at school. Human flesh, our own human flesh, will be eaten. Won't even be a democracy."

"Won't be a democracy?" This seemed to affect my cousin the most.

"No, sir. Isle of Negroes will be ruled by a cannibal king, a prince of darkness, Jimmy. This man will be a black Satan and the Republicans will welcome him. They'd let him have his kingdom." I lowered my voice for the last part just as Grandpa had always done. "All this around us would be the Isle of Negroes and our own dear little Cedar Point will be the dark and bloody capital of the whole business."

My cousin considered these somber facts for some seconds before waving his hand out at the dark night and speaking with some conviction.

"Do people 'round here truly think the president of these United States or the governor of this state is going to let a corner of Clarke County be broke off and turned into a foreign country run by a bunch of cannibals?"

"Yes, they do. It could very easily happen."

"Everybody think this?"

"No reason they shouldn't."

Shaking his head, my cousin walked off the porch and into the night. Soon I heard Rose thudding off towards the river. He went back carrying a healthy Colt revolver strapped to his side in a fancy hand-tooled holster. He'd brought these back from Savannah and kept them hidden until now.

The next morning, Maum Anna was gone, as well. I could guess where she'd headed, but I kept it to myself and was thankful she hadn't asked for the cross back.

Two nights later, my cousin returned home once more

and reported the news. On the first evening Colgrove and his men settled in not far from the judge's group. They'd brought tents and netting, so despite the mosquitoes being fierce, they'd slept well. On waking, though, they'd discovered the sheriff's truck circled with a broad white strip of chalk powder. A lemon had been quartered and a section set on each fender. A skinned rabbit, with a fishhook embedded in each eye, was hung by its ears from the rearview mirror. Uncle Jimmy saw all this himself, for the sheriff had gone to the judge's camp and invited them over.

"Look at all this hoodoo shit," the sheriff marveled. He took a lemon section and, peeling the rind back, ate it, spitting seeds out as he spoke. "Christ, have you ever seen such?" His three men, all shabby, poorer, and thinner versions of himself, were a little reluctant to follow suit, but they each ate a section, puckering their lips and pretending to enjoy the treat.

"These I got a use for." The sheriff pulled the fishhooks out of the rabbit's eyes, and threw the skinned carcass to his waiting dogs. They lurched away with their legs between their tails, which made a noticeable impression on the deputies and caused the sheriff to curse the animals and kick the one closest to him.

"Goddamn monkey magic, I got a cure for all that right here." He opened the breech of his long-barrelled shotgun, gave both shells a morning inspection, and snapped the gun closed. "I got something here will make one disappear permanent."

It hadn't been a good day for the sheriff. The dogs struck a trail early but then lost it, and the Clarkesville deputies were having other troubles. First, they'd been seized by with terrible cramps, and then the shits hit and they'd spent most of the day squatting in the bushes, swatting mosquitoes. It was impossible to take a breath without inhaling at least two or three bugs, and the men's arms were bloodied from what they'd slapped. Late in the afternoon, the dogs finally picked up a scent that excited them and carried the party to a deserted Negro cabin. Drake and Sammy might have paused there not too long before. At least, the sheriff chose to think that. He'd been growing sullen but now took heart, and the clamoring dogs led everybody off in a wide loop that brought them, at sundown, back to the cabin. The Cedar Point group had already endured two days of this sporting travel but kept all previous knowledge to themselves. At noon, the judge had ridden off, leaving instructions for them to stay close and keep their mouths shut.

The next morning, another chalk circle was waiting for the sheriff, only this time it didn't circle his truck, because his truck was gone. At least, it appeared to be gone to everyone except one of the Clarkesville bunch. The man kept insisting he saw it and even went through the motions of opening a nonexistent truck door and sitting down on the bare ground. The sheriff accused the deputy of being whiskey crazy and kicked him, breaking at least three ribs. Then, they wrapped the wailing offender up and made him come along. The truck could be found afterwards.

Of course by now, my cousin realized these little entertainments might not be helping matters in the long run. The sheriff was boiling mad, and no longer was it just Sammy who was in danger.

"Can't tell me those monkeys ain't hiding 'em. We going to start hanging 'em one by one until we get results."

Up to then the search had been conducted largely in wilderness, but the following morning the hounds had dragged them off towards a more populated area. Trouble seemed unavoidable, but every cabin they came to that day was empty, apparently vacated minutes before they'd arrived. The sheriff's men would bust in, throw things around, and storm out. The mosquitoes were joined that day by an unusually late hatching of deerflies, which caused the dogs particular concern. Yes, the dogs had gotten the worst of it that second day, by far the worst of it. Three were kept on leash and three ran loose ahead, with the men crashing along behind. And, towards four o'clock, enough busy howling and baying was coming from the three free dogs for the sheriff's men to start whooping congratulations to one another.

"I had made up my mind I wasn't going to let them shoot Sammy," my cousin explained, "and then they take off running like it was a gingham sale. That Clarkesville bunch all knotted up together, puffing and blowing, and them dogs howling bloody murder."

It turned out to be a dead end, though. The front animals began to yelp. One passed them running three-legged in the opposite direction. At the end of the trail, the other two hounds waited dead. Both had their skulls crushed in by some kind of animal, and one had even been torn in half.

"Bear," the sheriff said, kicking at the carcasses and swatting the deerflies away. "If this ain't the Goddamn most Godforsaken corner of the earth. Can't even let a dog run free."

"Wasn't a bear," my cousin confided in me. "No bear tracks at all, but nobody was going to contradict the man. Anyway, something done it. Something worse than a bear."

Out on the road, they were met by the judge. His full-blooded mare was lathered and the rider was pleased with himself.

"Here, Colgrove," he said. "This here is a telegram from the governor." The man had left them the afternoon before, ridden the sixty miles to Crowns Bluff, crossed the harbor, telegraphed the governor, waited for a response, and then ridden at full gallop back. The sheriff snatched the paper.

"That's a pardon sent by the governor forgiving Drake Bailey and the Negro Samuel of any and all crimes they may have ever committed in their entire lives," the judge said. "And you'll notice that it orders you to stop this manhunt and return at once to Clarkesville."

Sheriff Colgrove balled the paper up and tossed it back to the judge.

"I done lost my truck and the three best dogs in the county chasing them bastards. You full of shit as a Christmas turkey, you think that piece of paper going to stop me now?"

"I don't know about them dogs," Judge Walker said, "but I passed your truck at the hard turn. It's sitting inside one of them white circles."

"Bear got the dogs," my cousin said at that point. "No fault of ours."

"You James Allson, ain't you?" The sheriff suddenly turned on my cousin.

"That's so."

"You a nigger lover, ain't you? I been watching you these last couple days. Watching close."

"Sammy is my man. That don't make me a nigger lover. I got a right to protect what's mine."

"Nigger lover. Wouldn't surprise me if you was a German spy. I know you're a slacker. Fact you're standing here tells me that much."

"Slacker!" Uncle Jimmy put his hand on the butt of his pistol, but before he could draw it, Judge Walker stepped his mare between the two men.

"This man is doing his part, doing a darn sight more

than any of you Clarkesville people, I suspect." Judge Walker's maternal grandfather had been German and he'd taken a wait-and-see stand on the war.

"This man?" the sheriff repeated and pointed around the front of the mare. "Shit, only one 'round here man enough to run the niggers was old Colonel Allson. Dead now, poor soul.

"That's this man's grandfather, and he ain't dead, Colgrove." The judge said this in a conciliatory tone, and in the same voice added, "How old is the Colonel, Jim?"

"I ain't no slacker," my cousin called angrily back across the mare.

"The Colonel ain't dead? Well, a shame he done lived to see the way you people pamper these monkeys." The sheriff spit. "Sad. Yes, sir, get sadder the day these cannibals set up that kingdom of theirs."

Then the lawman and his deputies headed off towards the truck, kicking and dragging their remaining dogs along. Judge Walker declared the manhunt to be officially ended. Everybody could go home and they did, but not right away. Reaching Main Street well after dark, the judge and his posse discovered the handful of black men who usually hung around in front of Blaine's pharmacy on the weekends had swollen to at least a hundred.

"Nothing but teeth and eyes, that's all you could see," my cousin recounted. "Could be armed. Didn't know what to expect."

The judge announced the hunt for Drake and Sammy was over, and the governor had officially pardoned both men of all crimes. He ordered the Negroes to disperse. They shifted around and spoke among themselves, but none left.

"I'm ordering you men to go back to your homes," the judge repeated.

"What right them fella got to come 'round bust up the people house?" someone in the crowd called.

"They say they going cook Sammy and feed 'em to the dog," another spoke out. "That ain't no way to do. He ain't take nothing but a biscuit!" a second shouted.

"This is a law-and-order town," the judge shouted back. "You men know that. They'll be no lynching, no burning, either. Not while I'm running things."

"Captain Blaine say—" someone else began.

"Blaine?" the judge shouted even more impatiently. "Blaine? You people listening to Blaine Fitchum now? It's me that's the elected magistrate and I'm telling you the sheriff's gone and he won't be back to bother any of us."

"The boys are in God's hands now." This was my pa speaking. He stood to one side of the crowd, his voice barely raised. "Remember the Sabbath and keep it holy."

The Negro men whispered among themselves, and then, unable to deny Captain Tom's commandment, drifted away in small groups. Uncle Jimmy gave my pa the horse and walked home. Before going to sleep he told me and Brother everything and insisted with much feeling that he was no slacker. The next morning, Maum Anna was back in the kitchen cooking breakfast. She was trying to pretend nothing had happened, but she was considerably weaker— smaller and more bent down than ever.

That afternoon Sammy was led into town with a rope about his neck. Half a handcuff dangled from his raw, chafed wrist. His clothes were rags, his feet bare. His head hung forward and he stumbled on occasion, but kept his balance because to fall meant being drug and hung. The other end of the rope was attached to the horn of the saddle, which was cinched onto a small gray-white horse and in the saddle sat The Hard to Catch Mercy.

I watched this peeking through the grocery window. I

watched alone, for Uncle Albert had left the store to lead the small parade that followed the captive. This excited procession I would later be told had ended at our front gate where Mercy had fired his rifle into the air. In a moment, my mama was there and Maum Anna was rushing to Sammy's side to undo the rope.

"Tell the old man I brought back his nigger," Mercy said. "I reckon that's worth a dollar to him." Mama went for the money at the same time Grandpa, wearing only robe and slippers, wandered out onto the porch.

"Young fella!" he shouted at Mercy. "You hear that? Sound like a rifle shot."

"I brought your nigger back, Colonel."

"Obliged, son. You men on patrol do a service to the community, an invaluable service."

"Can run, but they can't hide."

My mama brought the money out to the gate and stood holding up the coin. He leaned forward and stared at her hard for a moment.

"Colonel's money," he said, and then, straightening up, added to no one in particular, "Was my nigger, I'd cut his toes off."

He'd reined the little horse about in a tight circle, and left at a brisk canter, the hog dog trailing along in his wake.

As I said, I would hear of this only later. At that moment I waited alone in the store, standing close by the window so I would have time to hide. Maum Anna's cross might work on a ghost, but I doubted it could persuade a flesh-and-blood version of this demon to depart. No, far from joyous at Sammy's return, I waited in terror and wasn't the least surprised that Mercy wasted no time on pleasantries. By pressing my face against the glass, I could see him coming, a distant rider at first, but so unmistakable in his approach that I abandoned the window and took up my post behind the counter. From there I could hear the too familiar hoofbeats sounding louder and louder as they once had in my haunted dreams and visions. The sound drew closer and slowed. Just beyond the range of my view it stopped altogether. Mercy hadn't ridden by. He'd stopped outside the store. I knew this. Knew I should duck down beneath the counter and did just that when the torso of the man showed through the store window. The face turned my way, his deep-sunk eyes peering from beneath the flopping hat. All that stood between us was the thin glass and the gold lettering that spelled out Albert Allson, Proprietor. He searched between the "n" of Allson and the "p" of proprietor.

I was hidden, crouched down low behind the counter, and felt relatively certain he wasn't going to dismount. If he called, I wouldn't answer, so there was little chance of us meeting unless he rode the horse into the store, which, of course, is what he did. I heard the first tentative thud on the wooden sidewalk and then a scrambling clatter on the steps as the double doors exploded inward and the man and horse were both waiting for service on the far side of the counter.

"Get up, boy," Mercy said in his singsong voice.

I was silent and pressed up tighter against the inside of the counter.

"You want me to send this dog?" I'd forgotten about the dog, but the reminder only caused me to curl into a tighter, silenter ball. "You must want me to ride this pony 'round there and drag you out."

I eased my head about and tried to judge the space in question. There was room enough. Still, I couldn't move. From the far side of the counter came the sound of the horse urged forward, a gentle sound. Looking over my shoulder I could see the neck of the white horse appear, and then the rider, too, gracefully slipping into the narrow aisle that should have been my avenue of escape if I'd had any sense at all, which by now, it was obvious I didn't.

"You do good to hide from me," he said smiling. The black void of missing teeth cut a crude triangle in the tangle of his matted gray beard.

"I wasn't hiding," I whispered, getting slowly to my feet.

"What was you doing?"

"Dropped my pencil. I can't find it."

"Might be sticking out there behind your ear."

I felt for the pencil and had to admit that so it was. Wasn't that a funny joke on me? He seemed to think so because he actually laughed and spit tobacco juice down the front of my store apron.

"You got tobacco?" he asked.

"Yes, sir."

"Gray Valley?"

"Yes, sir," I took the pouch from the rack right behind me and stood there with it.

"How much?"

"A dime," I answered.

Slowly, he searched through his coat pocket and retrieved the coin. Leaning down along the horse's neck he offered it. I was dubious of the exchange, but figured it unavoidable and stepped up close enough to complete the transaction. He took the tobacco and my hand as well, and with amazing strength yanked my feet clear up off the floor. The pouch of Gray Valley disappeared out of his free hand and was replaced by the great knife that he held up close against my throat.

"I could cut your head clean off, couldn't I, boy?"

"Yes, sir," I whispered hoarsely.

"I ain't going to. Know why?"

"No, sir," I managed to gasp.

"Too many witnesses. They find your head sitting on the counter and they done seen me riding out the front doors. Say I done it, now wouldn't they?"

"Yes, sir."

"Even if it weren't me, they say it was, wouldn't they?"

"Yes, sir."

"I ain't forgetting what you and your cousin done to my little sister."

"It wasn't me," I pleaded once more.

"I ain't never forgetting."

"It wasn't me, Mr. Mercy. I didn't have nothing to do with it. As God is my witness, it wasn't me." I should never have called God as my witness, of course, because all the time I was saying this I could only think over and over about the wages of sin being death. God would witness against me, not for. Just as on the Swamp Road, I began to cry. He didn't seem to notice, and jerked me an inch or two higher by the arm and pressed the knife until it had to be breaking flesh. Maybe my throat was already cut and I didn't even know it. I'd heard that could happen.

"I'll be back. Don't you go and forget that. Mr. Mercy will sure enough be back for you."

He dropped me and I went straight down in a pile. My face was resting no more than an inch from the front right hoof of the little gray horse. That little hoof seemed to fill up an entire corner of the store at that instant, and I watched hypnotized as it raised off the floor and took one dainty step backwards and then another. The horse and rider came into full view as they picked their way backwards down the narrow aisle, turned, and without so much as a brush against a single box or can, regained the far side of the counter.

I'd long since given up on the outside world. Once again The Hard to Catch Mercy was departing with me reduced to something far less than upright, courageous, or even human. Only then did I remember my possible weapon, and without rising, pulled Maum Anna's cross out, kissed it hurriedly on both sides, and began to rub the metal hard between my thumb and forefinger. "Ghost ride on," I whispered. "Ghost ride on." All this took no more than ten seconds and from the far side of the counter I could hear almost immediate results—a great crashing sound and a surprised shout from Mercy. An even greater clatter came. I stuck my head up and was amazed to see the horse heading not out of the store, but further in. And it moved not at a cautious step, but a rough buck, leaving behind a great scattering of canned goods, brooms, and biscuit flour.

"Ghost ride on the other way!" I shouted out with hands in the air. "Go the other way."

Mercy, too, continued his shout and reined in without effect.

"Ghost ride on the other way!" In the excitement I'd forgotten to kiss and rub the cross, but as I did so now, the animal half turned about in midair and landed hard against the back side of the vegetable bin. Mercy must have hit his leg a good lick, for he cried out in genuine pain, and I went on rubbing the cross with enough strength to bend the silver of the true nail.

Beyond the middle row of shelving, the horse still rose and fell, only now it was headed out. The ghost was definitely riding on.

"I ain't forgetting you either, Mercy!" I shouted out as loud as I could. He heard me. He looked straight my way with a look that would have killed the uninitiated dead away. Not me though. I was through being scared of that man. "I ain't forgetting you!" I shouted again and in a grand explosion the horse and rider went sailing straight through the glass window on the far side of the store.

Gone. Ghost ride on. Only the ragged edges of the broken glass remained. I came from behind the counter before I realized the hog dog was still inside. Confused, it looked at the hole, then back at me, growled out a final order of retreat, and vanished as its owner had through the newly opened window.

I walked to the hole and looked out. Gone. Down the street and out of my life. It had been some time, months in fact, since I'd considered myself under Mercy's spell. The cross from Maum Anna and the return of my cousin had long since cleared the fog from my mind. Yet, standing before that broken window I could feel myself becoming whole again. One person, mind and body. The gray depression that I had apparently accepted as a normal state was lifting to let in a brilliant afternoon sunshine. Light seemed to almost splash through the broken window and the glass scattered outside across the sidewalk shone like bright winter ice—like diamonds. I could see things, really see their shapes, recognize colors. The objects inside the store seemed solid once more. They could be touched. For the first time since Amy's funeral I realized I had a sense of real life.

"I ain't afraid of you either, Mercy!" I shouted out to no one. The sound of my own voice startled me. I clapped my hands together and was shocked by the hard feel of flesh against flesh and the "pop" as loud as cannon fire. "Hallelujah!" I shouted. "Hallelujah! I'm free of that man."

I shouted all this thinking I was alone, so I was startled to see the puzzled faces of Barnus, Scooter, and Gander peering in at me through what had once been the window. They said nothing at all, looked at one another, and ran off. That was all the rejoicing I had time for because looking out on the street I saw them racing to tell the returning multitudes what they'd seen and heard. Of course, they wouldn't have told Uncle Albert directly, but he'd have to be deafer than my pa not to get an account out of somebody.

I hurried back behind the counter to get the broom and began sweeping up. Only then did I notice that my hand and forearm were bloody. My throat wasn't cut, though. I'd rubbed the cross hard enough to raise a blister. Rubbed through that and drawn blood, a fair amount, which I wiped away with the same apron Mercy had spit upon.

Tactfulness. I told Uncle Albert what would anger him the absolute least. The Hard to Catch Mercy, because he wasn't inclined to walk, had ridden into the store and bought tobacco. Upon leaving, the horse had accidentally spooked and, after tearing up and down the aisles, crashed through the window. He called me a liar, saying he'd already heard the truth coming up the street. I'd picked a fight with the man and intentionally driven the horse through the window. It was a particularly foul deed, considering the service that same man had just done the Allson family. I protested my innocence and pointed out that if he checked, he'd find the source of his information was the three notorious liars and thieves who'd caused all these troubles in the first place. He must have known this already because he huffed and puffed about, and then, pursing his lips, asked me who did I think was going to pay the thousands of dollars in damage to his store. I said I didn't know, but suggested he seek the advice of Judge Walker next door. He suggested it be taken from my wages over the next two or three hundred years. I suggested I wasn't at all happy being a grocery clerk and quit right then, thus escaping most of the cleanup. The next day, he came to the house and made my mama make me go back to work, but there was no more talk of me paying the damages. He even spoke once of signing a warrant against Mercy, but if he did it probably went into the judge's trash can.

I had a slightly different version of the story for Uncle Jimmy, and mentioned as directly as I could that his life might be in danger. He just laughed. There was no way to tell him about the magic worked by Maum Anna's cross, but I did try to thank the old woman herself. She was too excited over Sammy's safe return to really listen and made no attempt to take the cross from me.

Sammy had his own story to tell, and while it went along with my cousin's pretty close, some important details were added. On leaving the school yard, Drake went home and retrieved an old cavalry pistol he kept hidden away in his uncle's stable. They could have taken a horse, too, but Drake felt that wouldn't be fair. He'd drug Sammy off on foot and once out of earshot, used the pistol to blow the cuffs separate. Then Sammy was told that Drake found him to be agreeable company, but he was free to go as long as he didn't object to being shot in the back as he was leaving. Sammy stayed. And together, they played their game with the judge and his men.

No big surprises there, but Sammy added that Drake would take the pistol, cock it, and draw a bead on various members of the posse when they came close. He'd done this to each man at least once, including Uncle Jimmy and his own uncle. Then Sammy, who'd been ordered to hold completely still, would have to beg for the life of that particular target. Whether or not Drake ever intended to actually shoot was left to our imaginations, but none of the targets ever thanked Sammy, as I recall, not even Uncle Jimmy. On the other hand, none ever criticized him for not trying to run away, disarm Drake, or, at least, reveal their presence.

When the sheriff arrived, Drake put discretion far before valor and widened his lead considerably. In fact, the afternoon the sheriff returned to Clarkesville, the fugitives were up the river a good ten miles drinking chicory in the cabin of an old Negro woman who had welcomed Sammy and endured Drake. They'd still been there the next morning. Breakfast was being served when they smelled smoke. A second later flames were coming up between the floorboards, and the old woman went wailing out the front door. But Drake didn't follow because he wasn't certain this was an accidental blaze. There was only one window. Small and high up, it was to the rear, with the woods not far off. After poking his head out for a quick look around, the judge's nephew ordered Sammy through the window first. The Negro went, declared the coast was clear, and Drake followed. One of his legs was in and one was out when The Hard to Catch Mercy had stepped the little horse around the corner of the cabin and nudged the end of his rifle up the crack of Drake's behind. He told Drake he figured Sammy was worth about one dollar delivered alive back in town. He didn't figure Drake was worth much to anybody except dead. All this time Drake was still hanging there and the fire was consuming the little cabin around them. The smoke had the horse prancing around a bit, but they didn't move, not any of them.

Drake started to laugh and agreed only a couple folks would mourn his passing. After this admission, The Hard to Catch pushed hard with the rifle barrel and sent him falling out the window on top of Sammy. That was it. Taking Drake's old pistol satisfied the horseman. The bully declared he'd try Panama for a while. Sammy was brought home. The cabin burned to the ground, and we heard the old woman went to live with her sister.

It was a happy enough ending, all things considered,

but the following week, when we'd lowered our guard, Liza went to visit Grandpa and behind the closed door of his bedroom, gave him her version of Sammy's adventure. Whatever it was, it must have been bad.

"Sam-u-el. Sam-u-el." The next day, the old man called the unsuspecting Negro to his bedside, and then, slipping his straight razor out from under the sheet, he sliced off one of Sammy's ears.

I say "sliced off" but it wasn't completely severed. When I saw it several minutes later, it hung by a thin sliver of skin. Sammy appeared quite calm, taking this all as no worse than any of the old man's many cuffings and, I guess, feeling somehow deserving of the insult. Dr. McGill, brought immediately to the scene, announced the ear a total loss and offered to clip the connecting flesh and free the appendage. Maum Anna intervened, saying she had great respect for the doctor's medicine, but would like to save the ear, if possible. That night, at our kitchen table, she bandaged the ear firmly against the scalp and applied a poultice, the only recognizable ingredient of which was Octagon soap. Two weeks later, when the ear began to protrude cankered and blue about the corners of the bandage, she attached two leeches to its lobe. They hung there growing daily in length until, at five inches, they were replaced by two more, and so on until, at the end of six weeks, the bandage was unrolled to reveal the ear, slightly cockeyed and battered, but firmly attached to the side of Sammy's head.

It was decreed a miracle by all, but the only one truly surprised was Dr. McGill, who questioned the old woman at some length on her methods. The medically impossible had been accomplished, but even more wondrous was the side effect. From the moment the bandage was unraveled, Sammy claimed he could hear a sound that he described as angels singing. We, each of us in turn, put our ears to his and listened. We heard nothing. Even Maum Anna heard nothing. Only Brother, who went last, heard the sound in Sammy's ear, and he said it wasn't singing at all. It was talking. When we asked what was being said, he shrugged. It was foreign talk.

The Prodigal
Daughter

A SCHOOL without a bully was like a ship without a rudder, so naturally the departure of
Drake Bailey left us a trifle disordered. Of the remaining
scholars I was the biggest, the tallest anyway, and all that
fall and winter I'd been putting on weight. Still, I wasn't
a bully by temperament or training and refused from the
outset to even play at it. Nonetheless, a certain amount of
authority had been thrust upon me by my classmates, most
especially by Gander, Barnus, and Scooter, who continued
to consider my handling of The Hard to Catch Mercy as
somehow heroic. They'd arrived in time to see the horse
and rider come crashing out of the grocery window, then
heard me shout that I wasn't afraid. After that, my saying the horse had accidentally spooked wasn't acceptable
and the more I claimed it, the less they believed me. The
less I made of the incident, the grander it loomed. I'd
fought the man. They could only guess why. Maybe The
Hard to Catch had insulted me or my family, my mama in
particular. That he'd been robbing the grocery was their
least-favorite speculation. That I held a grudge because the
man had carried away the body of Amy Mercy was my least
favorite.

Of course, the idea that Mercy would hear of all this and return frightened me, but as time passed and he didn't, I began to take a certain pleasure in my classmates' versions. As for the cross, well, I kept that under my shirt and patted it from time to time. No, I didn't share my knowledge of its secret powers with my new friends or anyone else. What I did share was my wit, charm, and company. I'd misjudged these fellows. True, they weren't the finest of gentlemen. All three drank, smoked, and cursed, but they had good hearts sunk down deep beneath those coarse exteriors, which was why we were getting along.

Surprisingly, Gander was the readiest to seek out my company and counsel. The sudden departure of Drake, no matter what promises Drake had made to kill his brother, left the boy at loose ends. Gander was always around me at recess, and after school he'd slip into the grocery whenever Uncle Albert left. To entertain him, I began to tell stories about my employer's miserly habits. These were a big hit, and once in the swing of it, I managed to improvise some fine pantomimes. Pretending to clean my ears with a candy cane and then returning it to the display case was Gander's favorite. But gradually, I realized it was only necessary to purse my lips and pick at the seat of my pants. My young friend would burst into fits of weeping laughter and run off to get Barnus and Scooter, so that I would repeat the stunt and he could be convulsed again.

If Uncle Albert was an easy target, he was a deserving one. Though I'd mastered a few of the basics of salesmanship and been allowed to run the cash register, I'd never received a raise or a single compliment in all the months I'd been there. Still, I was enjoying the job in a way. I managed to smile and chat with the customers—nothing like my cousin had done, but passable. Certainly it was better to be in the store than at home where so much was not remembered, or heard, or understood, and the boyhood I'd recently abandoned was hardly preferable to the life I now enjoyed.

On Friday and Saturday nights after work I'd slip over to lounge in front of the mercantile. I was trying by example to improve my chums, but the taffy was bound to pull both ways. I'd take a sip to show I was an ordinary fellow. On my few afternoons off, we'd play ball or fish or hunt. That Christmas I went back to the Allson Place to shoot ducks, not with my cousin, but with my new friends. I showed them the well where the disbarred lawyer had floated. I showed them where the bull had chased us and told of how I'd saved Amy Mercy's life in the cabin, but forgot to point out where my cousin had actually shot the animal. The hunt itself was a big success. I shot a little better than either Barnus or Scooter and far better than poor Gander, who only got one duck. When it came time to retrieve I waded right in. I didn't complain and I didn't fall. It was a most satisfactory outing, and when we returned to school after Christmas, I had to admit things weren't going so badly for me. At a get-together for young people, I somehow found myself holding hands with Leala Fitchum's younger sister, Lucy, and it was only a matter of time before I would invite her to a church picnic or maybe even a dance. But my life, which had finally wandered onto something resembling a straight course, was about to take a tack to the windward.

It snowed that day. It rarely snowed in Cedar Point, so when the grayish flakes began to drift against the window-panes of the schoolroom, we naturally assumed they were falling ashes and the roof was on fire.

"Fire!" As fire marshal it was my job to sound the alarm, but others had yelled it first and the room emptied in a great stampede that left Miss Gaye standing lonely at the blackboard. The cause of this exodus, of course, was not panic, for no one was particularly concerned about burning alive. No, we all, even the girls, even Liza, were rushing not away from the fire, but outside and towards it. Even Barnus and Scooter, who under normal circumstances had no use for schooling or the building that housed it, joined in this stampede to form a bucket brigade. Once in the yard we were quick to perceive that the excitement was of an entirely different nature. The flakes fell thicker now. Not fire, but ice. Some, like Brother, stood looking calmly skyward, or contented themselves with the examination of a single quickly melting crystal. Others, myself included, ran wildly about, shouting and attempting in vain to scrape together snowballs.

The schoolbell began to ring, a call to order by Superintendent Baker, who, with heartless bullying, lined us up at attention. By this time the building was lost in a haze of flurries and the man himself was visible only to those in the forward ranks—ranks, which because of my size, I'd moved to the very front of. All behind me would slip quietly away and take their chances on the morrow. I alone would miss the snow. Then, in a rare display of compassion, the superintendent had us say the Lord's Prayer and dismissed school. The world was ours and we expected snowmen and igloos and sleigh rides. The delicate crystals melted too fast, though. We packed our few meager snowballs as hard as icy bullets, threw them, and then, in broad daylight, tipped over the school's privies. By lunchtime only puddles of gray water remained. Still, it had been an exciting day, and I was feeling happy enough when I went that afternoon to meet the *Redbird*—and was greeted with a second surprise.

She stood on the bow of the freight boat, not at the stern with the other passengers, but forward and alone holding a stay wire. As the boat slid beside the wharf, I reached out to catch the line tossed by Black Jimmy Allson. This put my back to the whispering—loud whispering, since it was difficult to be heard above the labored popping of the Lathrop engine. Then came that final explosion when my pa rang for Red Willie Allson to shut the engine down and reverse its stroke. The Lathrop roared, the propeller spun in the opposite direction, and the journey came to a shuddering, silent end. The strange woman stood before us in an ankle-length coat, trimmed about the collar with furry glass-eyed animals. Each of the animals was biting the tail of the one before it, and perched on the woman's head was a small green hat whose brim was pulled far down at the sides and tied in place with a long yellow scarf.

Someone behind me began to snicker, perhaps Gander, and another to laugh outright. She was looking at me, though, and for a moment I stared back. She was old, but the wrinkled skin of her face and neck were covered with a thick layer of powder and caked-on rouge. She wore lipstick, too, which I'd never seen on a woman outside of Crowns Bluff. Not sure what my position on lipstick should be, I was considering joining the growing conspiracy against her. If she hadn't spoken, I probably would have.

"Willie T.," she said. "You don't know who I am, do you?"

I didn't, but at that moment, Captain Tom leaned out of the pilothouse window, and for the first time in ten years, he didn't shout, "Good Friday, ain't it?" Instead he shouted, "That's your cousin Aunt Lydia." Then he offered his only hand to guide her up into the pilothouse and out of sight. At once, the mood on the wharf shifted and the discussion quickly changed to matters of news and freight and, of course, the identity of the woman. She was somehow related to the Allsons and she was traveling with her husband—a man my pa was now escorting ashore. He was a slender, bent figure with thinning white hair and a white linen suit turned up at the pants cuffs and coat sleeves, as well. He wore small, round, black glasses and tapped his way with a white cane. Pa put the man's hand on my arm and told me to guide him up to the house. I did, but the tapping with the cane continued. My new aunt walked the distance describing what she saw to her companion.

"This is our Aunt Lydia and her blind husband." That's how I introduced the guest to my mama, who accepted the strange couple into her home with whispered apologies for my inconsiderateness and further apologies for not being better prepared. But, of course, she couldn't have expected them. Aunt Lydia was equally gracious, apologizing for the inconvenience she was causing after being absent all these years. And how wonderfully kind my pa was to rescue her and her sightless husband, George, from a horrid Crowns Bluff hotel. By this time, luggage had begun to appear on the front porch, and kept coming until trunks and crates cut off the view completely.

"Not my things. They're most all George's," my Aunt Lydia explained to me in particular. "It is an embarrassment to travel with so much, but what can I do, Willie T.? We are lucky, don't you think, to have escaped with so much when others left with nothing or have not escaped at all."

"Was you in prison?"

"No, no, no." Big as I was, she pulled me into a hug. It was like being pitched into a lilac water fountain. George, who was sitting back on the couch with his legs crossed and his cane tucked away, began to chuckle and repeat what I'd said in a soft voice thick with some accent.

"Paris, you silly boy."

"Paris? You come from Paris? Paris, France?"

"That's such a long way to come," my mama seemed to agree with me.

"We had no choice. Not after that Bolshevik treachery. The embassy informed us. They instructed us to return home and we have."

"Put to flight by the Hun," George whispered to himself.

Well, it was no longer possible to ignore the war with Germany. America had been involved for ten months and Uncle Jimmy regretted more than ever not joining up. Still, that wasn't what jolted me.

"Home?" I asked. "You mean Cedar Point is your home?"

"Yes." The old woman smiled at me. "I was born in this house."

As she talked, she'd been peeling off parts of her costume and folding them away. Now, with her scarf unwrapped and hat off, her wrinkles appeared deeper. I saw her aging eyes were finely inked around the edges and when she opened her broad painted mouth, a large gap showed between the two front teeth. The snow white hair was like my mama's, but even less tidy—a loosely piled mountain waiting for a nudge to set it tumbling. She was heavy like my mama, too, which surprised me considering the smallness of her face. But most surprising of all were the woman's hands, hands which she now revealed by a careful removal of gray leather gloves. The fingers were bent and quite yellow, especially towards the ends, and strangest of all, her fingernails were painted to match her lips. The nails were impossible to ignore, because the hands moved to demonstrate what she was saying. And what she was saying then was how she'd like my mama's permission to smoke. When it came, she took out a silver cigarette case, fit a long, prerolled cigarette into an ivory holder, lit it, and began to puff away. From time to time, she'd slip the holder into George's mouth so he could do likewise.

"I was born in this house, too," was all I could think to say.

"I know," Aunt Lydia replied. "Your mama told me all about it."

"I did?" This clearly surprised my mama, but much else did, too.

"Wasn't it you? Well, someone did."

The strange woman would've hugged me again if I hadn't sidestepped.

"It has changed a great deal since you were here last?" Was this a question or was my mama simply stating a fact?

"Not nearly so much as I thought it might. You know how it is when you are away. The image is fixed in your mind—a sacred shrine."

My mama said yes, maybe that was so, and suggested I go for my pa, which I was about to do, when Grandpa wandered into our midst. He seldom left his bedroom these days, but when he did, he dressed in suit and tie for the occasion and he carried his cane. He was shouting, of course, though it was he who'd grown deafer, not us.

"Who are these people?"

"Lydia and George," Mama answered.

"Who? Who are they? Is that woman smoking?" he bellowed.

"Apparently they are our kin people." Mama was at his side.

"What kin people? This woman is smoking a cigarette!"

"Uncle William," Lydia whispered low but quite dramatically. "I'm not surprised you don't recognize me, but I would know you anywhere."

"Who are they?" the old man demanded.

"Lydia!" Mama shouted in his ear.

"Your sister Catherine's daughter!" Lydia herself now coaxed quite loudly.

"Catherine's dead," the old man said and rapped his cane hard against the floor to emphasize the fact. "She was my half-sister."

"Yes, may her blessed soul rest in peace. I am her daughter, Lydia!" our guest shouted at the top of her voice. "We visited here in sixty-six. I was just a child, but I remember you well."

"I don't recall any such visit," the old man shouted back, and went on to repeat that Catherine was dead and he was quite certain that if she had any children, they were dead and buried in our own cemetery. If one was actually named Lydia, which he doubted, then she too was dead and buried out there beside her mother Catherine.

"My mother is buried beside my father in Morristown, New York," Lydia replied. "You of all people should know that, Uncle William."

Before the old man could reply, George spoke out rapidly and at length in what I assumed was French. Aunt Lydia answered him in kind, but only a word or two. She felt compelled, it seemed, to hug Grandpa, which caught the old man completely off guard and caused him to ask again who these people were.

We could have gone in circles all night, but my mama called Maum Anna, who'd probably been spying from the dining room.

"Anna!" Aunt Lydia exclaimed at once. Maum Anna showed no sign of recognition and only bowed and said, "Yes, ma'am."

"Don't you remember me?"

"You Miss Catherine gal?"

"Yes—Lydia."

"I remember Miss Catherine have a gal called that." The old black woman would commit herself no further on the matter.

"Anna," my mama said, "take Grandpa and return him to his bed."

"Yes, ma'am." She turned the reluctant old man about and escorted him from the room.

"I thought surely Anna would remember me. How very disappointing. . . ."

"She's very old. Grandpa is even older," Mama said.

"Yes." Aunt Lydia smiled. "He'll be ninety-eight in April. A half century since I have seen him and he'd lived nearly that long already. A long time, *n'cest pas, mon Willie?*"

I'd have been hugged again if my pa and Uncle Jimmy hadn't arrived. Liza came along to spy. Introductions were passed around once more, and dinner announced. Naturally, Liza accepted an invitation that was made only in politeness. She never ate with us under normal circumstances but now acted like she was one of the family and spoke French. Aunt Lydia complimented her on her accent, but almost always answered back in English so the rest of us would understand they were discussing the theater, opera, ballet, and other things that I was certain Liza knew nothing about.

Uncle Jimmy asked for news of the war. Who was fighting, where and how they were doing, and had America's entering the war made the difference yet? Aunt Lydia spoke gravely on the subject, explaining that the people of her adopted country and their brave English allies had stood alone too long a time. Perhaps the war was lost. She couldn't conclude without chiding my cousin for not being in uniform. A grown man, and an Allson at that, had no business sitting here safe at home while others were giving up their lives to preserve that sacred foreign soil.

"Remember Lafayette? He came to this very shore, did he not?"

"Is that another long-lost relative?" My cousin didn't smile. He was tired of hearing about what he should be doing.

"Do not tease me," the strange woman said. "This is much too serious for you to make jokes about it."

Liza agreed completely with Aunt Lydia, and Uncle Jimmy didn't bother saying it was Liza's own English-hating father who'd kept him out of the war and in the freight boat business instead. He just shook his head and claimed his present duties couldn't be escaped, but he knew he was missing out on a darn good fight.

Finally, my mama brought the discussion back to matters closer to home. Since the two visitors had come to stay for a while, Anna had suggested they might be more comfortable in a small pole cabin that had recently come into Uncle Albert's hands. Not the grandest of palaces, it was still comfortable and close by. And there'd be no rent. The guests thought this a very generous offer, and the decision was made to clean the place first thing in the morning. For that night, they were given my parents' room, and my roommate and I ended up on the parlor floor. Brother had said nothing since their arrival. I was almost asleep before the words came.

"That's the foreign talk I heard in Sammy's ear. That what them two and Liza was saying to each other."

"French?" I asked. "Are you sure?"

"Pretty sure," he said. "I could go listen at Sammy's ear again."

"French?"

"How you reckon that French talk got in Sammy's ear?"

Brother was asking me this—Brother who heard voices coming out of tree trunks and thin air. For some reason, the sound of French truly puzzled him.

"I don't know," I said.

Apparently that answer satisfied him, and he was going to go to sleep without saying more.

"Was they in the dream, Brother?"

"Yep."

"Both of them?"

"Yep. Both of them. Had fangs. Burning eyes."

I'd dozed off considering this, so in the pitch dark it took me a moment to get my bearings and remember where we were. It took even longer to figure out that Grandpa was poking at me with his cane. I lit a lamp. He was fully dressed. In a very loud whisper, he was commanding us to wake Uncle Jimmy because we were all going to take a trip. Always willing to humor the old man, my cousin rose quickly and organized a silent exodus. We even pushed the truck some distance from the house, with Grandpa tottering along and hollering as if we were oxen and not his own flesh and blood.

"That will be satisfactory," the old man declared finally.

I cranked the truck. We all piled in and headed off to our mysterious destination, which turned out to be the cemetery. Despite my newfound courage, I'd been giving the graveyard a wide berth, but the truck was crowded with company and the light of dawn already filtered through the tree branches. We stopped, as I might have guessed, at the the Allson plot, which was a particularly large and beautiful section where the stones were known to be slightly more substantial and the foliage greener. Grandpa was out and leading the way. He shouted as he went.

"Yes, I have brought you here so that you will see for yourself the woman is an imposter. It's true my half-sister Catherine is buried beside her husband in the Congregational cemetery in Morristown, New York. A willful and selfish woman, her burial there was a sad but unavoidable consequence of her having chosen to spend life among an alien peoples." Last night he'd said Catherine was buried here, but he'd apparently been reconsidering. "Her daughter is here, however. You will see that in just a moment."

The old man paused to get his bearings, pushed back the thick growth of flowers and weeds with his cane, and studied several inscriptions. Then, circling a large japonica, he pointed at two small stones set slightly off by themselves.

"Read that, James. Tell me what it says."

"Patricia, Infant Daughter. Born April 8, 1858. Died—"

"Yes, yes. Read the other one."

Uncle Jimmy studied it for a spell, as we all did, because the stone was blank. If it had ever held an inscription, the weather had worn it away.

"Well," the old man demanded. "Read it to these boys who before God are my witnesses."

Uncle Jimmy was trying to think of some way out, maybe pretending a name, but finally he just told the truth. Naturally, the old man didn't believe him. With our assistance, Grandpa crouched low over the stone and even traced its surface with his fingertips. Yes, here was the proof. This was indeed the grave of Catherine's second daughter. The woman in our home was an imposter.

Even Brother nodded in agreement. We weren't convinced. At least, I wasn't. The old man could say whatever pleased him, though. I'd already turned my attention to the other moss-covered monuments, for I'd never realized how many Allsons were already buried in this little cemetery.

Infant deaths. Dozens of these small stones were scattered like seed fallen on fallow ground. And most of the Allsons who'd been lucky enough to grow up had eventually perished, as well. Except for my pa and Uncle Albert, Grandpa had outlived all of his children, and all but the drowned James were right here. They and many of their offspring had passed over into what the old man was referring to at that very moment as "the Great Beyond." "Beyond what?" I couldn't help muttering, since my own hope of a Presbyterian salvation had been replaced with a healthy concern for staying alive.

As Uncle Jimmy eased the old man slowly towards the truck, I stopped before the three stones I knew best. Three of my four sisters were already out here. Long before I was born, Sara had died of smallpox and Martha was taken by typhoid fever. Dorcas had married a man named Smith and moved to California a year before I arrived. My mama had stopped writing to her, but still received notes telling what Dorcas and our three Smith relations were doing in California. Esther was the only one of my sisters I had known. She'd died when I was nine.

"Mama, I am dying." Brother had chosen to kneel before Esther's stone. A strange coincidence even for him. Esther was dead. I heard her baby cry, but there was no stone beside Esther's. Perhaps that was the blank marker the old man was claiming for our visitor. Esther was owed an infant stone.

"Mama, I am dying," Brother repeated, and I kicked at him.

"Quit praying that. Pray something else."

"This lamb is lost."

"Not that."

"The wages of sin is death."

"Shut up. Get off your knees."

"Poor blood. Poor blood."

"Shut up." I kicked at him again.

"Casket is the only cure." I grabbed him by the back of the shirt and yanked him to his feet.

"Where'd you hear that? All that you're saying?"

"From you."

"Me? Maybe I said, 'Mama, I am dying,' that one time. Maybe, just that once."

"You say all them things to yourself."

"Never. No, I don't."

"Most times you talk it in your sleep."

"No. No, sir. You're lying."

"Yep. You wave your hands around and shout them words out. Sometimes you wake Jimmy up and he comes over and listens, too."

"You let him listen?"

"Had to."

"You could have woke me up."

"Bad luck."

"Bad luck? Who says it's bad luck?"

"Jimmy."

"Bad luck, my foot. He's spying. Don't you listen no more. I mean it."

"Can't. You done quit talking."

"Good. If I start again, you wake me up, understand?"

"All right."

"When you pray, pray something else."

"What?"

"Pray to Jesus, if you got to pray."

"All in Glory, boys. Everyone you see here has passed on to Glory," the old man shouted at us suddenly.

"Yes, sir," Uncle Jimmy agreed. "Doubt you'd ever find a more deserving lot."

"The great shepherd has gathered in His lambs."

Amy was to be buried here, but wasn't. If Uncle Jimmy was thinking that, too, he gave no hint, but then he'd listened to me ranting in my sleep for months without giving a hint of that either.

"Died for our sins. That's the beauty of it," my cousin said.

"Yes, came down to earth, was born, crucified, and buried. So that we might enjoy eternal life."

"You got this world here and fireworks in the next," my cousin said.

"What, Jim? What?" the old man asked.

"Yes, sir!" my cousin shouted, coaxing him the final bit.

"You boys are my witnesses!" the old man cried out.

I cranked the truck and we piled in. Once in motion, I leaned forward and asked Uncle Jimmy an important question.

"How come you listened when I was talking in my sleep?"

"Didn't," he whispered. "Not but a couple times, anyways."

"Brother said you did."

"Thadius has the answers!" Grandpa shouted at us, then fell silent and looked at the passing scenery.

"No, Brother's the one who listened," my cousin whispered. "Your raving didn't make a lick of sense to me."

"Thank you very much for not waking me."

"You're entirely welcome."

Grandpa now insisted on stopping at the grocery that Uncle Albert was just opening, and without even a good morning, he began to question his son.

"Do you remember anyone named Lydia who is now claiming to be Catherine's daughter?" he demanded.

"Catherine?"

"My half-sister Catherine, Albert. She felt that her destiny lay with her husband's people. A sad choice that won no approval here, must I remind you."

"Yes," Uncle Albert was able to answer after pursing his lips and giving careful thought.

"Fine, fine. And do you recall if she had a child called Lydia?"

Uncle Albert thought for several moments longer and shook his head no. "I believe the older daughter was named Irene after our grandmother's sister."

"So," the old man exploded in triumph. "There you have it, boys."

"You don't remember anyone at all named Lydia?" Uncle Jimmy asked his former employer.

"No. There were no Lydias in our family."

"None?" I asked. "Maybe a middle name or a nickname?"

But since it was me who asked the question, Uncle Albert didn't respond to it at all. He suggested that Grandpa check the Bible. This was thought to be such a grand suggestion, the old man quickly took credit for it himself. And we raced home leaving the grocer with a half-told tale of a strange woman living in our home with a blind Frenchman.

"Where have you been?" My mama met us at the door, anxious.

"Grandpa took us to the graveyard," I said.

Already, the old man had the family Bible flipped open to the endsheets where each birth and death in the family had been recorded for the last seventy-five years. He was right. Catherine had had two children. Patricia who died in 1858 and Irene who died in 1866. Grandpa was triumphant, but I knew something was amiss. Maum Anna had admitted the night before that there was a Lydia, and I trusted her far more than I did the Bible. I went straight to the kitchen and asked if the daughter in question was named Lydia as she herself had implied, or was it Irene? To my surprise, the Negro woman didn't bother to look away from her stove.

"That a long time ago. Maybe the gal Irene. Maybe the gal Lydia. Been so many of them white Allsons can't keep the name straight."

I asked her again.

"Get way from here unless you come to cook," she replied.

At least my mama remained hospitable. Despite Grandpa's evidence, she quietly insisted that the people were still guests in our house. The matter could be talked over with my pa when he came up from the wharf to get breakfast. Grandpa thought very little of that idea, so little, in fact, that he went to my parents' bedroom door and beat his cane until it opened. Lydia appeared wearing a floor-length dressing gown. Her white hair was undone and it did tumble like an avalanche down her back. Without makeup, the deep crevices in her face seemed like canyons. She smiled wide, showing the gap between her two front teeth. The smile was directed particularly at Grandpa, but she bid us all good morning in turn. She was smoking a cigarette. She was barefoot. Her toes stuck out beyond the hem of the robe when she moved into the dining room.

All this, of course, was more than the old man could handle at one time, but he began by pointing out that no Allson woman had ever appeared in public in her bare feet. They were women of breeding and even in the worst of the war times, they were always shod. He then went on to give a racing account of our morning's activities, concluding with the Bible record showing Catherine's last daughter was not named Lydia and had died in 1866.

"I do not know what you expect to gain by posing as a member of this family. Perhaps, you hope to take ad-vantage of our generous and unsuspecting natures. But, woman, I must tell you that you and your consort have been found out."

The woman being debated calmly asked to see the Bible. Grandpa wouldn't allow her to actually hold the book, but she was shown the entry.

"This, you see, is me." With a yellow finger she traced the name of the elder daughter, Irene Elizabeth Allson, who'd been born in 1845 and marked as dead in 1866.

"But you claim your name is Lydia and you ain't dead at all," I pointed out the obvious discrepancy.

"Yes, Willie T., but that is because Lydia is what my parents named me."

"You are not an Allson!" The old man shouted, not listening to anything that was being said. "You must leave immediately."

"Uncle William did not approve of the name Lydia or of my father either and took it upon himself to name me Irene, which is what the Allson family called me. My parents went along in order to make peace, but once we moved North I was Lydia once and for all."

"Barefoot. This woman has no shoes on and she is smoking a cigarette. She has red paint on her fingernails!" the old man wailed.

"Is that why the Bible says that Irene Elizabeth is dead?" Uncle Jimmy smiled when he asked this because he liked her, too.

"I can't imagine why that is written there," the woman who called herself Lydia continued. "But it does appear to be in the same handwriting as the birth entry. Perhaps Uncle William took it upon himself to put an end to me."

"Why would he do that?" I asked, fairly confident the old man was well distracted.

"We came South at the War's end, and went back after

only a few months. Perhaps he thought I would not survive the northern climate." She chuckled and winked, seeming to suggest the old man had always been hauling a few bricks short of a load. "I was never his favorite, as you might have guessed by now."

"Out! Out! Out!" Grandpa snatched the Bible away.

"Why didn't you say something last night?" Uncle Jimmy asked.

"It slipped my mind, James. In all honesty I couldn't understand why Uncle William didn't remember a Lydia."

She looked at each of us in turn. Of all those confronted, only my mama looked away as if embarrassed. She still had some memory of those early days, and yet throughout this discussion she'd remained silent.

"Leave," the old man commanded.

"Yes," Aunt Lydia said suddenly. "I sense that you doubt my claim. We will impose on you no further."

"Please, no," Mama said with equal suddenness. Uncle Jimmy and I both echoed, "No." There must be some explanation, we insisted, which might have suggested we hadn't believed our new aunt. I didn't care if she was an Allson or not. I only wanted her to stay.

Aunt Lydia thanked us, but said her mind was made up. She retired to her room and couldn't be coaxed out even by my pa, who had a hard time understanding exactly what was happening. At eleven o'clock she appeared with George, dressed once more for travel. Could an automobile be arranged to take them back to Crowns Bluff and the luggage be sent on the *Redbird* the following week? Yes, it could be done, but no one except Grandpa wanted her to leave. Yet she was going. We all stood about in the yard. Uncle Jimmy had borrowed Dr. McGill's steamer. Liza, who'd done her share of pleading, would ride with them. It was settled. The couple were helped into the back-seat of the automobile. Then, to everyone's surprise but mine, Brother had one last request. Would Lydia say something in French so that Sammy could hear the language being spoken? He didn't bother to say why, but she agreed cheerfully. Turning to a puzzled Sammy, she spoke out a long, fast sentence of babble that seemed to please both the Negro and Brother.

"What did you say?" I asked.

"She asked Sammy to get her a bottle of wine," Liza answered.

"Did you?" I asked the woman herself.

"Yes," Aunt Lydia said. "Buried there under the sill of the house. Unless someone has found them. Four bottles of Madeira." She leaned forward on the seat of the steamer and pointed with a gloved finger. "They were lying down. Just a few inches below the surface."

I scrambled under. Though I'd been beneath that house a hundred times and never seen a single wine bottle, I went, certain she was my Aunt Lydia. She was. I scraped away the shallow layer of earth and passed each bottle out carefully. The corks had rotted away and the contents drained, but that was beside the point.

"My lands," Mama whispered.

"Kin are always welcome," Pa remarked.

Uncle Jimmy held up two wine bottles and I held up two. We were laughing, and Brother and Sammy smiled. Liza clapped her hands. Maum Anna didn't join in this celebration, but she was watching over Grandpa who was angrily waving his cane around and demanding to know the meaning of the discovery.

Aunt Lydia calmly explained to him that at the War's end, it had been necessary to hide spirits from the Yankee troops and the newly freed slaves, because once intoxicated, they were much more inclined to loot and burn. Though he seemed to have forgotten, he, Grandpa, had poured out most of his wine and hidden these few bottles of the very best. Then, turning to us, she said, "A wise precaution. One of many that Uncle William made during those trying times." She winked at us and smiled, showing the gap between her teeth.

With gallantry, Pa extended his arm to the woman, and she stepped down from the automobile. Uncle Jimmy and I helped blind George do the same. Grandpa was led away to bed by Maum Anna.

We spent the afternoon scrubbing out the pole cabin, and that same night our newfound relations were settled in. It wasn't a big place, only three rooms—parlor, bedroom, and kitchen. George's belongings filled the parlor and spilled over into the bedroom—leaving only enough room for the serviceable mattress my mama had placed on an abandoned bedstead. Lydia and George assured her it was a wonderful arrangement, and for the time being they'd set up housekeeping in the kitchen. They did. In the center of this room, they placed a low table with six assorted chairs about it. That was it. Most of the many crates would remain nailed shut, but on that first night Aunt Lydia broke open a few to retrieve "the bare necessities of life."

The first held linen, china, and crystal, some of which had miraculously survived the trip through enemy lines. The next crate held nothing but George's own supply of Madeira. By then, only my cousins, Sammy, myself, and Liza remained at the cabin, and my aunt insisted that we drink a toast with her husband's fine wine. Uncle Jimmy popped the cork and poured wine into fine crystal glasses for everyone, including Sammy. Gathering us about the table, Aunt Lydia spoke.

"To our new house in beautiful little Cedar Point. To our wonderful new young friends. To where it all began. To where it will all end. *Vive la France!*"

Of course, I figured wine was meant to be drunk slowly and was surprised to see my aunt toss hers back like a sailor. Uncle Jimmy did likewise. The rest of us copied George's more civilized sipping, and on nights to come I'd nurse a single glass through the evening.

Yes, there were to be other evenings—many, in fact. Once the toast was completed, Aunt Lydia got down to the real business at hand. Taking a key from her purse, she went into the front room and stood before a large, brass-bound, red leather steamer trunk. I went too, thinking she might need help but she sent me back. This trunk contained her most important treasures. All the rest were George's, but this was hers and no one was to look inside until after her death. When she returned to the kitchen, she carried a small, black lacquered box.

"Pandora's box," she said to us very seriously, holding the object up for inspection. "You all know who Pandora was and the troubles she brought into this world."

I spoke right up and said, "No, we don't."

"She was a Greek woman," Liza said.

"That's right," Aunt Lydia proceeded without giving Liza a chance to say more. "She was the first woman. Some say Zeus gave her to man just to cause trouble. Prometheus had given them fire to make their lives easy, so Zeus gave them women to make them miserable. What do you think of that, Willie T.?"

"I don't know no Greek women," I said, thinking that was a tactful answer, but apparently it struck Aunt Lydia and George as funny, for they laughed together.

"Willie T., you are incredibly stupid," Liza volunteered. "It's a myth."

"I knew a few Greek women in Paris. They seemed quite ordinary," Aunt Lydia began again. "But what I was telling you about was Pandora's box. You see, all the gods had contributed to the making of this first woman. One gave beauty, another cunning, but Zeus gave a box filled with all of mankind's troubles—the sickness and wars and famines and worries—because he knew that though Pandora had been told not to open the box, her woman's curiosity would get the better of her." The old woman smiled on each of us in turn. The gap between her teeth seemed wider than before, the inked-in eyes lighted with mischief. "Well, of course she looked in. What else would you expect? And when she did, all of our problems poured out of the box. Pandora could only clamp the lid down in time to save hope. That was a great piece of luck, because that was the only blessing Zeus had put in there. Hope is what Pandora saved in her box."

"You've got 'hope' locked up inside there?" I asked when it was apparent that the story was finished.

"Willie T., you are getting dumber by the minute. Not even Sammy would think that," Liza muttered.

"Willie T. is not dumb at all," Lydia defended. "I wonder, though, what Sammy does think is in the box."

She held the box up to the light of the lantern so we could study the outside carefully. It was made of a blond wood and trimmed out with black lacquer to show some kind of Oriental garden scene—little willow trees growing beside a bridge and a temple. "Make a guess, Sammy," she said. "What is inside here?"

With some reluctance, the Negro bent forward to inspect the box and then shook his head no.

"Take a guess," the old woman coaxed. Uncle Jimmy and I also urged him to guess.

"You ain't been tell the truth about this box," he said at last. "All the troubles in this world ain't going fit in that little box."

"Sammy," I said. "That ain't the question."

"If she say they been in there, they been in there," he corrected himself. "If they in there I ain't see how she do 'em. I can tell you that."

Lydia was quite satisfied with this reply, and it brought a nod of approval from George once it had been translated into regular English.

Brother was told to guess next. He asked to hold the box and studied it from all sides, top and bottom. Then he gave it back.

"Hard to say. Playing cards, maybe." He returned to the shadows and watched.

Uncle Jimmy didn't bother to handle the box himself. He said it contained important papers—deeds and probably some cash.

I hefted the object, studied the garden scene, and announced that it held love letters. This declaration I regretted immediately, because Liza yanked the box from my hands saying I knew absolutely nothing about love or letters or anything else.

"So Liza, if not love letters, then what is in the box?" Aunt Lydia asked. This, of course, brought Liza up short because she realized her own guess might be equally stupid. She shook the box lightly.

"No fair." I said at once. "No fair shaking the box."

"Yes, that's fair," Aunt Lydia said.

"See, Willie T. I can shake it if I want." Liza shook it to show off and then held it up at eye level trying to peek beneath the lid.

"Come on, Liza," I said. She ignored me and shook it again.

"I would have said jewelry but it doesn't sound like jewelry. Can you give me just one clue?"

"No. No clues," I said. "We didn't get no clues."

"Willie T. is right, but I can tell you this. One of the other three has guessed right."

"You can't say love letters," I said with new confidence. "You can't even say letter. I picked letters."

"I don't have to guess at all, Willie T. I could just open this lid and look inside. Isn't that so, Aunt Lydia? There's no rule that says I positively have to guess."

To my horror, Aunt Lydia agreed and instantly Liza popped off the top and looked inside.

I'd like to say all the world's problems suddenly flooded out. That pestilence, famine, and war descended immediately on the little village of Cedar Point. I'd like to say that even hope was allowed to escape so that there'd be no hope for Liza, whose willful curiosity brought our ruin. I'd like to say all that but I can't. The interior was divided into four compartments and each held a deck of cards. Brother had guessed right.

Aunt Lydia took the box gently from Liza's hands and placed it in the center of the table.

"Will you please be seated," she said.

We seated ourselves around the table.

"Do any of you know how to play rummy?" she asked.

Uncle Jimmy could play, but the rest of us, including Sammy, had to learn. If we wanted to be in the company of Aunt Lydia, we had to play rummy. She played continually. From that moment on, she played the card game with us, and when we were gone, she played with blind George, dealing his cards face-up on the table. She claimed she'd played the game with him enough before he lost his sight to know what he'd keep and what he'd discard. He did win a few, but if the truth be told, George wasn't always allowed to win when he should have.

The blind man took the cards as they were dealt and never complained. We learned to do the same in the months that followed. Aunt Lydia always dealt. She shuffled too. The cards flew through her twisted hands with astonishing speed. She was always at the kitchen table, usually wearing her dressing gown, but with her makeup on and her hair pinned. She always had a cigarette burning between her yellowed fingers, and a glass of George's fine Madeira wine at her elbow. She never asked us about ourselves. Somehow, she seemed to know us already. She dealt the cards and told the many adventures of her own life.

It was her great sorrow, she swore repeatedly, not to have borne children. It wasn't George's fault. They'd met far too late in life. It was her own selfish decision, one she did dearly regret. Still, she was a product of her own making and bore full responsibility for her life. Yes, she'd known true love. Not the kind of sheltering love she felt for George, but true, passionate and reckless love. Aunt Lydia claimed she'd known it, as most women do, only once in her life. She was young then, and the end was tragic. She said the balance of her life had been interesting and often amusing, but only that brief romance had real meaning.

Aunt Lydia had been born here, but as we'd already been told, she was brought up in Morristown, New York. The family had a small, neat house—a bungalow. Her father was born in America, but his mother had come from France and she lived with them. This grandmere insisted on speaking French. She made Lydia learn it, and the two of them spoke it to the many cats the old lady kept.

It was her grandmere's claim, one she shared with only Aunt Lydia and the cats, that she'd left behind a wealthy family and exciting life when she was tricked into coming to America. This wasn't true at all. When Aunt Lydia finally got over there, she saw for herself that the French family were just peasants. In fact, they weren't nearly as well off as her father, a good man who ran a bakery and paid the bills with help from his seamstress wife Catherine.

Her parents weren't poor. Only the grandmere's claims made them seem so. Still, Aunt Lydia had decided at an early age that she wanted a better, or at least a more expensive, existence. Yes, her tastes had always run to the extravagant, but she managed to hide this vice from her parents until she'd put the safety of an ocean between them. It was in France, where she went after her unspoken tragic romance, that she lived out the life her grandmere had invented. She met many great men and women over there. She danced with Lafayette's grandson several times, and once with the Emperor's grandson. She knew some of the Impressionists. They were artists. She knew Mary Cassatt. Sadly, Liza had heard of Mary Cassatt. Aunt Lydia herself was a good artist, but not nearly good enough. She claimed even the best sometimes went hungry, and going hungry didn't interest her in the least.

My aunt preferred a night at the opera with friends of the Rothschilds and, at the turn of the century, she'd enjoyed a marriage of sorts with a count of sorts. Then her money ran out and the lovable but shallow man disappeared with her very last franc. Well, by this time she'd seen all of Europe, but if that same week she hadn't met an eccentric woman of the Russian nobility my aunt might never have visited the rest of the world. She was hired by this Russian to be a lady-in-waiting, and her employer wasn't the least demanding. A staff tended to the menial duties, so Aunt Lydia's principal occupation was to play rummy and take in the sights with the noblewoman. Yes, my aunt could tell me from firsthand sightings that lions lived in Africa and tigers in India. She circled the globe, traveling in high fashion, before her patron dropped dead on the streets of Liverpool. Crossing the English Channel, Aunt Lydia arrived in Paris as penniless as she'd started. And this state of affairs more or less continued until she witnessed the accidental death of the famous scientist Pierre Curie. In fact, she'd cradled the dying man's head in her own lap. A sad event, but fortunate in a way, because she met the equally famous Madame Curie. How could we not know of Marie? She'd discovered radium. How could we not know what radium was? Had we been raised as savages? Liza, in particular, should be ashamed of not knowing. Good. I agreed.

Aunt Lydia and Madame Curie hadn't become close friends, for their temperaments were too far apart. It was this wonderful woman, though, who'd introduced her to George. He was already going blind, but they proved right for each other at that time in their lives. Besides—and she said this right in front of the man—George had a modest allowance that allowed them to live a comfortable life in Paris.

The invasion of the Huns brought an end to all that. Didn't we understand the debt America owed to France? This was a favorite topic. Hadn't all the crusades but the fifth been led by the French? Wasn't France the world's arbiter of good taste? And when General Washington confronted the English at Yorktown, hadn't the French Navy saved the day? Now we must return the favor.

The Great War—she spoke of it at length and with a

familiarity that in Cedar Point was reserved only for the battles of the Confederacy. She got out maps and drew for Uncle Jimmy the advance and retreat of foreign armies across distant frontiers. Nations—couldn't we imagine a political body broader than a county? I thought we could but wouldn't risk an answer. "Bleeding Belgium"—that we'd heard of, and we could identify the Lusitania, which seemed to give her some satisfaction. We knew about the submarines because a few had almost made it to our very shores.

Uncle Jimmy should forget his obligations here. Dr. McGill be damned. She said that in front of Liza. My cousin belonged at the front and so did Sammy. She told them both. A soldier's calling was the noblest. "The warrior, by his very nature, is the greatest of God's creations. The Norse understood this. The Greeks. The men of Sparta."

But as time went on, she'd speak less and less about the World War. She claimed that it saddened her to mention it. I noticed, though, that on Friday nights, Uncle Jimmy would bring her the Crowns Bluff papers, and sometime during the weekend, the two of them would read the news to George. Aunt Lydia stopped criticizing my cousin in front of the rest of us and left him to blame himself.

"It's a bloody shame what's going on in them trenches," he confided in me. "Gas. Mustard gas got both of George's sons, right at the start. Them boys didn't know what hit 'em. Buried their heads in the mud. Died sucking mud."

I guess he knew more but didn't volunteer it, and I didn't encourage him. Whether he'd accept the fact or not, my cousin could die right around here, and it could be easily arranged for him to be sucking mud at the time. We had a whole swamp full of mud. "Over there," he said. "That's where I'm needed."

Aunt Lydia would sigh, brush the cigarette ashes from the table to the floor, and begin again about how the great sorrow of her life was not having sons she could send off to defend that sacred foreign soil. Then she'd start in on other things.

I listened to her and played cards every chance I got. The others came back, as well. Absent on the *Miss Liza* during the week, Uncle Jimmy was always in attendance on the weekends, and he dragged Brother away from his clocks on those nights. Only the gravest of illnesses would have kept Liza, Sammy, and me from visiting every night, so we were practically living in the pole cabin. To please Aunt Lydia, Liza was forced to forgive the Negro for stealing the sugar biscuits and accept his presence, and I was forced to do the same with Liza. The card dealer, after listening to us debate Pandora's box, refused to let the bickering go on. Either we called a truce or one would have to leave. Actually, it wasn't so hard to pretend to tolerate Liza for I was growing weary of the battle myself. It was harder to accept the fact that Lydia seemed to prefer Liza's company to my own—probably because Liza had taken French lessons and had a good ear for the language.

French. That was the price of admission to this charmed circle. We had to try and learn French, for how else could we manage in the civilized world? French was the language of the card table, or would have been if the majority of us could have picked it up. Of all involved, I was the worst and Brother was a close second. We could say "thank you" and "good day," and that was it except for a couple of numbers. Though he pretended not to care, Uncle Jimmy picked up a bit more. It was Sammy who amazed everyone by learning quickly a version of the language that George in particular found amusing and completely understandable.

I couldn't judge. What Sammy was saying was gibberish to me, but Lydia assured me that besides naming the face cards, he could count to ten in French. This, I had to declare, was truly amazing, since we'd never gotten around to teaching him to count that high in English. Sammy was also a passable rummy player, as good as the rest of us, except Brother, of course. According to Aunt Lydia, Brother was remembering each card played, so he'd know what remained in the deck and calculate the odds. Sammy wasn't that good, but he won his share.

Aunt Lydia said this didn't surprise her at all. The Negro in the South was much maligned—in France they lived a far better life. Over there the Negro was considered to be the same as everyone else. Sometimes they were even thought to be rare and exotic. She encouraged Sammy to learn the language and made Liza speak to him only in French. The girl hated this, of course, for even before he stole the sugar biscuits, she'd never addressed my playmate directly. Still, it did please her that I couldn't understand what was being said.

"Sammy has many abilities that he will never be able to utilize if he remains in this Godforsaken backwater," Aunt Lydia declared. "Speaking French is only one such talent." Brother had a different view of the matter.

"That foreign talk's been in there since she put his ear back on."

By she, he meant Maum Anna.

I didn't feel qualified to pass judgment. If the surprise visit of Aunt Lydia had done one thing besides teach me rummy, it had shown me how little I knew of the world and its ways, and how much lay beyond even Uncle Jimmy's horizons. I had noticed one thing, though. There was still something unsettled about Aunt Lydia's connection with the Allsons. Except for Pa, no member of the older generation had actually acknowledged her as our kin. They didn't visit the pole cabin, either. In reference to them, Aunt Lydia would give a casual wave of her hand and an accompanying sigh.

No, we'd get no answers from our elders, but they let us visit the woman without much complaint. Maum Anna did become angry at any suggestion her nephew Sammy go to France and fight. Negroes were being drafted, but she was certain he wasn't old enough. "White people," she muttered. "Praise Jesus. Deliver my Sammy." Mama occasionally worried that we might be wearing out our welcome, but she seemed half asleep a lot of the time. Dr. McGill held firm to his anti-English bias but was happy to have Liza picking up so much culture. They let us go, and we were seldom interrupted by other visitors. After Aunt Lydia's run-in with the preacher, the rest of the community tended to shy away.

When Aunt Lydia and George first took up residence in the cabin, Mr. Friendly had come calling to welcome them to the community and invite them to attend his services. The preacher's visit started out well enough, but the conversation turned quickly to the war. In all earnestness, he suggested that no matter how bad it might look for our side, God wouldn't allow the Germans to win.

"*Gott mit uns!*" Aunt Lydia began to scream at him. "*Gott mit uns!* That is what the Hun has stamped on the buckle of his belt. *God with us.* What the hell has God got to do with anything? It takes men to win a war!"

The preacher made his exit and stayed away, commenting that Lydia was a woman of passionate but misguided convictions. He'd pray for her—a generous notion on the poor man's part, since he had tribulations of his own.

Mrs. Friendly had lost forty pounds or more in her guilt-ridden suffering over Amy Mercy's death. Of course, I didn't dare defend him to Aunt Lydia. She didn't "suffer fools or preachers gladly." He was praying for her anyway. Others weren't nearly so generous. Except for my parents, I doubt anyone else was praying for the outsider.

If Aunt Lydia's world was cut off from the older generation, though, it was a whole different universe from the one my mates inhabited. I was still attending school and clerking at the grocery, but I couldn't expect the likes of Gander or Barnus to appreciate my evening's entertainment. Still, whatever jokes they made, they made them well behind my back, almost out of hearing. One day at recess, Lucy Fitchum and a girlfriend came up to me and asked outright what it was that we did every night at the pole cabin. It was the first real exchange we'd had on any subject. I told her we played rummy and spoke French. She and her friend went off giggling. Aunt Lydia was costing me hardwon ground on that front, but I felt compelled to charge forward to wherever it was we were heading.

Every night my strange aunt made us stop and pray for the soldiers fighting to the death to hold that sacred foreign soil. Then with wineglasses raised, we'd repeat the toast even Brother and I had mastered.

"*Vive la France.*"

The Grapes of Wrath

UNCLE Jimmy was the first to make the connection between Aunt Lydia and another
mystery in our lives. By the time he approached me with
his suspicions, it was apparent he'd thought the matter
through.

"Listen," he said. "Don't it strike you as mighty strange
the way this woman is being treated?"

"How so?" I asked.

"Well, Grandpa says she ain't kin and nobody else really
backs her up. All we going on is the wine bottles that she
knew was hidden under the house."

"Yes," I agreed. "It's a peculiar business."

"More than peculiar, I'd say." He rubbed his jaw, which
meant he was waiting for me to ask more.

"How so?"

"If she knew about them wine bottles, then she might
know about something else hidden." He stopped.

"What else?"

"What if she knew where the Allson dowry was buried
and she dug it up and stole it?"

"That ain't possible," I said.

"Where else would she get the money? Living in France

for thirty years and spending a fortune, but she ain't said one word about where it come from. Money don't come out of thin air, Willie T."

"No, but that don't mean it comes from the Allsons."

"She stole the Allson dowry and that's why they act so strange towards her."

I shook my head no and pointed out that Pa had accepted her outright and Mama treated her well enough. He said that my parents were naturally generous, so their actions had no bearing on the matter. Grandpa, Uncle Albert, and Maum Anna had yet to claim her. I pointed out that those three could be contrary for no reason at all, but my main argument was that Aunt Lydia had been hardly more than a girl when the War ended. How could she find the treasure, much less steal it? Uncle Jimmy stuck to his version, though, and added the finishing touches, including a nighttime visit to the Allson Place and a hairbreadth escape North by steamer. I repeated that Aunt Lydia couldn't have done it, but he had the bit between his teeth. It was a Saturday morning, and he went off to try the story out on Liza.

Liza didn't believe him either, but she said if any part of the dowry was left, then it was surely hidden in the mysterious steamer trunk. She came by the grocery to tell me that whatever was in that trunk now belonged to her because the dowry was removed from the Allson Place that now belonged to her daddy.

"Fine and dandy," I said. "Why don't you bust open the trunk and have a look."

"If I were to ask her, she would let me look."

"No, she wouldn't."

"She would, too."

We decided to settle this in a simple, straightforward

manner, and that night I asked Aunt Lydia what was in the trunk at the same time Liza was asking what was in the trunk.

"Ah," she replied. "Pandora's box. Now, haven't I warned each and every one of you about the dangers of sweet curiosity?" She shuffled the cards with those curled yellow fingers, and after cutting to herself, began to flip them skillfully about the table.

"Is there something in there that once belonged to the Allsons?" I asked this confident that the answer was no.

"Why do you ask that?" She didn't stop dealing but did glance briefly in my direction.

Before I could answer, Liza began to speak to Aunt Lydia in rapid French. I got the easy words like "dowry" and "Allson Place" and, from the look on the old woman's face, I could tell that Liza was telling all. Of course, Uncle Jimmy wasn't too happy about this, but he should've known better than to tell Liza. Anyway, we were getting to the heart of the matter, and my cousin's tale would be put to rest. When Liza was through, Aunt Lydia addressed us all in English.

"Yes, Liza has guessed my secret. She is a clever girl, but then we all know that."

"Too smart for me," Uncle Jimmy said in disgust.

"You stole the dowry?" I asked. "You stole it and there's something left." If this was true then it occurred to me we should be angry with the woman.

"Stole? No. I took the dowry. And yes, I suppose you could say something is left. There is a last remnant of what the dowry bought. It's in my trunk. The rest I spent. You could say squandered, but I prefer to say spent in the pursuit of a rather selfish but wholly satisfying enjoyment."

"All the Allsons' wealth?" I wailed. "That was Grandpa's dowry. He made us dig for it!"

"The spoils of war," she said, lighting a cigarette from the one about to burn out.

"We had to dig and dig and all that time you were just going around having a good time. We had nothing. We had to work. All the Allsons had to work."

"It would have been hardly enough to change your lives, even if your grandfather had divided it among all the Allsons, and I can guarantee you he would not have. Better for one of us to have escaped and enjoyed life, than for that crazy old man to have sunk it back into this useless wilderness." She swept a free hand generously about the kitchen to indicate what lay beyond these walls.

"No!" I shouted. "No! No!" Why was I the only one speaking out? Uncle Jimmy stood to the side filling a wine-glass to the brim with George's fine Madeira, and Brother and Sammy sat holding their cards, waiting for the game to begin. "No!" I insisted.

"Yes, Willie T. *Oui.*" She finished the sentence in French, and whatever she said caused Liza to smile.

"Talk English!" I stood up, pushing the table with enough violence to spill wine and even give blind George a jolt.

"I must ask you to behave as a gentleman or leave my home," Lydia said.

"This ain't your home. The Allsons own this house."

"But why?" she asked.

"Why, indeed?" I shouted. "What do you mean why?"

"Why would they provide a residence for someone they claim they do not know?"

"My pa claims you."

"Yes, bless him for that, but he only says it because I told him so. Of them all I would think perhaps he is the only one who honestly doesn't remember me."

"You claiming my mama remembers you and won't say it? Maum Anna knows?"

"Yes, I think your mama does remember something. I'm certain the rest know me very well."

"Not well enough, I would say." I'd begun to suspect she was at least partly right but couldn't let it go. "Not well enough," I shouted, "if they let you sneak away with the dowry!"

"I didn't say they knew of my connection to the dowry. I doubt some of them even knew it was in the well."

"The well?" Uncle Jimmy spoke at last.

"An innocent man died in that well!" I added.

"Who?" she asked.

"Franklin, the disbarred lawyer who was going to help Dr. McGill swindle the Allsons out of their dowry."

"That is a horrible lie, Willie T.!" Liza screamed.

"How could he be innocent if he was a swindler?" Lydia asked.

"Well, he could be. He could be both."

"I'm going to tell my daddy what you said."

"Everybody knows it, Liza!"

"Make him apologize, Jimmy," the girl commanded.

"Make her apologize." I pointed at my Aunt Lydia. "She cheated Grandpa."

"But your grandfather cut Sammy's ear off." The strange old woman held her wineglass to her lips and stared at me with her inked-around eyes.

"Who told you that?" I demanded. "Who? That ain't connected."

"Sammy told me," Aunt Lydia said, and then she addressed the Negro in French, and he answered her in his drawling version of the language, going on at some length. She was nodding in agreement.

"Talk English," I said, through clenched teeth.

"You remember that, Willie. Ain't you remember that? He cut the ear clean off the side of me head." Sammy touched the offended ear gently with his fingertips.

"So," I said, ignoring him altogether. "That is how it is."

"How what is?" Aunt Lydia asked.

"You steal the dowry and then you twist things around to make it right."

"Was I doing that?"

"You know you were."

"Making excuses?"

"Yes, excuses."

"Such a compliment. No one has ever accused me of doing that before. I always just took what I wanted, but in this case I will come right out and say I earned that money."

"Earned it? What do you know about earning? Uncle Jimmy there could tell you about earning."

"What about Sammy?" the woman asked. "Don't you earn money, Sammy?"

"Yes, ma'am. I drive the truck." That was so. Sammy now made the fuel deliveries for my cousin and Dr. McGill, a fact that one person at the table chose to ignore.

"He steals," Liza said. "He steals biscuits."

"That's a lie. He don't steal." I defended. "She's the one that steals." Again I pointed across the table at my beloved Aunt Lydia. "We could have got snakebit rooting around in them bricks, and it would have made no difference to her. She run off and spent the dowry."

"To begin with," the woman said, "it wasn't the well out at the Allson Place. It was the well right here at Cedar Point. It was the house well you are all still drinking from."

"Here?" At last Uncle Jimmy showed proper interest. "Right in our own backyard?"

"I believe it was first hidden on the plantation." Aunt Lydia shrugged and smiled at him. "Perhaps they thought it safer here."

"They was sure wrong, wasn't they?" I snapped. "Either place, it was still Allson property. It was Grandpa's dowry and you stole it!" I pointed my finger across the table a third time.

"Sit down, Willie T. I've heard enough from you," she snapped back. "I am a very old woman and you are a very ill-mannered young man whom I will tolerate only if he is silent. I have something to tell you all. It is a true story and after all, aren't they the best kind?" They were all looking at me—as if only I stood between the listeners and the honest truth. Already I didn't believe her. Or perhaps I did. I sat back in my chair and was silent as a stone.

"Yes, now that is better. Before you are told the truth, though, I have two requests. First, what is said here tonight must never be repeated, and second, you must agree that when I am done, you will do a favor for me in return." Not one of them bothered to ask "what favor?" Even Brother nodded yes. I didn't agree, but Aunt Lydia didn't seem to care. She filled her wineglass once more and lit another cigarette. Then she began to tell us of the great and tragic romance that had altered the course of her life and put an end to the Allson fortune.

"I was a young woman, not so very young as your mother, Willie T., and not nearly so adventurous at that time. We had sat out the War in comparative comfort. In fact, if it were not for the newspapers I'm not sure many of our neighbors would have known there was a war. We knew, though. My mother made us pray every evening for the safety of her brother's family, and my father made several enemies simply because he was married to a Southern woman. Neither of them felt sympathy for your cause. They were only concerned for your safety. It was Grandmere who cared for the poor besieged South, especially when it appeared to be a truly lost cause. Though gravely ill, she rose from her bed on the announcement of Gettysburg with the intent of going to the window and shouting out a praise of General Lee.

"She died before the War's end, leaving me somewhat adrift, as you can imagine. And so it was I, far more than my mother, who insisted that we pay a visit. A letter from the Allson family had arrived and it stated simply that though there was no true hospitality and hardly any food to spare, we would always be welcomed at Cedar Point. My mother and I had written many letters during the War, and after the surrender, I personally had written three times asking permission to come. Do you know who answered my letter, Willie T.?"

"My mama, I suppose." It seemed a matter of course that she would be the one who invited our betrayal.

"So, you are not the blockhead you pretend to be." Aunt Lydia smiled at me, showing the broad gap between those front teeth, which only slightly made up for the fact that she'd told me to sit down and be quiet and the fact that I'd never pretended to be a blockhead. "Yes. It was your mother. A young girl's handwriting. We did not know then who she was or what her connection to the family could be. My mother was dubious about accepting such an invitation, but I insisted. My father would stay behind. He had his bakery and by then had recognized that I was capable of tending to myself and Mother both. As soon as possible we had booked passage and were landing in Crowns Bluff, a town which at that point was reduced to a rather desolate rubble. We were immediately advised by the Union officers at disembarkment against traveling on to Cedar Point. Two women alone would not be safe in such a country. It was occupied territory, you see, lawless and wild, remote—not so remote as today, my children, but remote all the same. I was not to be deterred. No. For two days we stayed in our hotel trying to make arrangements, for even then, it was easier to circle the globe than to make that fifty mile journey.

"The Allson name was well recognized, even honored. Many knew our family, and a few of these knew who my mother was and could forgive her for waiting out the War in New York. Still, even those most sympathetic could not help us make the trip. A Negro was walking the mail that direction once a week. We heard rumors of a boat scheduled to sail there sometime before Christmas but that was months away. I could stand it no longer. I was twenty years old and quite pretty, I'd been told, and, by damn, if I wanted to go to Cedar Point, I would. That is exactly what I told them at army headquarters, but they were not so impressed as I might have hoped. In fact, the sergeant actually laughed at me, which caused me to curse him with words I can not repeat to you. Then I slapped his face with all my strength. He was not injured, but did suggest with equal bluntness that I was about to be arrested. Who knows? I might have been if a young officer had not suddenly taken me by the arm and steered me out of harm's way.

"I was so furious I hardly knew what I was doing, or what he was doing either, and I yanked my arm away before I had even looked into his eyes. Pale blue eyes, almost gray, and blond hair that was combed carefully to one side. He was tall and handsome in his uniform. I was in love even before he disclosed that he had not intended to eavesdrop, but it was unavoidable. If I would allow, he could

be of service, for by coincidence, he was the military direc-
tor of Cedar Point. He would be returning there the very
next morning. He knew the Allsons. They were not friends,
which was understandable, but he considered them to be
an honorable family. If my mother and I would trust ourselves to his care, he would arrange for a carriage to deliver
us to the doorstep of our relatives.

"Of course, I accepted and rushed back to the hotel to
convince my mother that our newfound friend was not
only the most honorable of men, but the most handsome
and intelligent as well. She was far more cautious but I
prevailed. We accepted the escort and the next afternoon
arrived by carriage at that same gate." Aunt Lydia paused
in her story to point off in the direction of our house and
request that Uncle Jimmy pour from the bottle of Madeira.

"He was a Yankee," Liza said. "I don't suppose Grandpa
liked it too well when you arrived with a Yankee."

The old woman set her filled glass aside, for she was
suddenly anxious to get on with her story. The words
tumbled out.

"It was worse than that, Liza. I mean, he was worse
than being a Yankee officer. You see, he was leading Negro
troops. Our escort for the carriage were Negro troops.
They were stationed right here at the wharf. They were
camping practically in the Allsons' front yard. From the
Allson point of view, we did not present a pretty sight, and
were treated accordingly. Uncle William would acknowledge that my mother existed, which is more than he has
done for me, I should remind you. The rest, including your
father, Willie T., and our Uncle Albert, just stood there and
nodded. It was only your mother who made us welcome.
She was not an Allson yet. She would not marry Thomas
until the following year, but she and this same woman Anna
were running the house. Room was found for us and we

were fed, but aside from this young girl five years my junior, I could make no friends or even acquaintances. Perhaps I wanted none. Perhaps I had already made up my mind to walk into the Union camp and renew my friendship with the captain who was only too happy to have my company.

"He, it seemed, was as desperately lonely as myself and felt the isolation far more keenly than his conquered foe would have imagined. He was from a small town in Rhode Island. The son of a minister, he'd joined up when he was eighteen and spent most of the War with the beseiging army at Crowns Bluff. He felt strongly about what he was doing. The freeing of the slaves had been for him a religious conviction, but now that they were freed, he was tired and homesick and ready for a little civilized company. I was only too happy to provide it. I began to share his mess each evening." Aunt Lydia motioned vaguely in the direction of our wharf or, at least, that wall of the room. "We sat beside the cedars where Uncle William had been making his salt. A strange place, for the ground was packed white with the gritty mineral. Still, it suited our mood. We pretended the salt was snow and spoke nothing but French during those repasts. The Negroes under his command took great delight in all of this, but it was less well received by the Cedar Point community, whose members began to pass casually by at suppertime and observe us from a distance.

"This only made me behave more foolishly. I spoke louder and began to sing French tunes at the top of my lungs. I insisted that only one lantern be lit, the fire built brighter, more wine served, and more laughter echo from the enemy camp. The captain objected quietly to each of these demands, for he was a true gentleman. I was headstrong and, as I say, not unaware of my charms. It was fairly easy to have my way under those conditions.

"My mother was outraged, more shocked than outraged,

for to behave like this was, at the least, unseemly, and under present conditions, unpardonable. Even your mother, Willie T., spoke a few words to me about indiscretion and the importance of a chaperone, but I had begun to take more than a little satisfaction in Uncle William's displeasure. No. I would not pass up a chance to flaunt my acquaintance with the enemy, even going so far as to praise the valor of the Union Blue, the justice of their cause, and the obvious preference that God showed in granting them the victory. When I came in at night I would loudly hum the 'Battle Hymn of the Republic' on my way to bed.

"I was young. That is the only excuse I would make if I were to make excuses. To outrage seemed a noble enterprise at the time and, more importantly, I was deeply in love with the captain and he with me. There was nothing between us then, nothing of scandal, a brush of the hand, and then an occasional kiss stolen in a brief moment of privacy. I was his for the taking, and he knew it. That was his undoing I suppose—his honor. He thought it necessary, finally, to call upon my mother and ask for my hand in marriage. He would do this in private, he insisted. I was not to be present. He made an appointment for an evening interview. He dressed in full uniform and carried as a gift a small bouquet of wildflowers. My mother would have had no objections. I had already told her our marriage plans and she approved readily. She wanted only to be out of Cedar Point. It was arranged and their meeting was only a formality, or should have been.

"It was Uncle William, however, who met the captain at the front door. Not my mother, but Colonel Allson, the head of the house himself. I was watching, hidden in the garden, but had promised the captain that under no circumstances would I interfere. I watched quietly as Uncle

William invited him not inside, but around into the back of the yard. I followed at a distance and was there just in time to see my uncle pull out a pistol and shoot my fiancé dead before my very eyes."

Though she paused now in her story to light another cigarette and sip the wine, there was no word of denial or outrage coming from her listeners. Not even Liza tendered a defense of the old man.

"It happened so quickly that I did not think at all, but ran forward, threw myself on the body, and sobbed hysterically. Blood was everywhere—it poured from his chest like a bubbling fountain that could not be contained. It spilled on my hands and dress and in my hair. I screamed things at the murderer. He said nothing. He was not sorry, only surprised to have me present. He was a mute statue that I rose to attack with these bloody stained claws that I now call fingers."

Again, Aunt Lydia stopped her recital; this time to put down her cigarette and present her arthritis-bound, yellowed, card-dealing fingers for our inspection. "I was like a cat, a lioness, and would have killed him or he me if they had not pulled me away." This time the pause was to enable her to look in turn at each of us seated there around the table.

"They," she resumed at last, "all of them—Willie's mother, my mother, the woman Anna, Albert, even Tom—came rushing out of the house when it was much too late, and pulled us apart. They carried me inside. They claimed to be shocked. They claimed to share my sorrow and to view the actions of the murderer with revulsion. They all claimed that. Each of them spoke earnestly to me and I suppose they meant it, but no one suggested that Uncle William be punished or brought to justice in any way. From the beginning, it was taken for granted that the crime would be covered up and it was. My fiancé simply disappeared, and since he had been the sole representative of law and order in this entire end of the district, it was weeks before anyone even showed up to investigate. I told the officer who finally came that the captain had been homesick. It hurt to say it, I claimed, but I suspected that the man had deserted.

"I can't say if I was believed or not and did not care one way or the other. No, I was already plotting my revenge, for you see, I knew that a search for the dowry was going on daily. On my arrival, I'd been taken to see the damage done by my Yankee brethren to the Allson Place. I saw the burned house and I saw the excavation work, as well. The digging struck me as both thorough and futile, and I had returned to Cedar Point that day quite certain something was amiss. This was more than idle suspicion. I felt certain that there was a dowry, but it was not going to be found by Uncle William.

"At that time I had done nothing further, but soon after the murder of my fiancé, I set to work to discover the dowry for myself. The well here was one of the first places I looked. Lowering myself down on the bucket rope, I slipped my arm as deeply as I could into the water and came up with a silver serving tray. A fortune was mine for the taking and I intended to take it. There was no one to stop me but your mother, Willie T., and of course, the woman Anna.

"Them?" I questioned. "Why do you say only them?"

"I knew it had been moved from its original hiding place on the Delta and put where your grandfather would not find it. I was certain your mother had moved it."

"How? How?" My anger rose again. "How can you accuse my mama of this?"

"It was simple—simple, I suppose because I was an outsider. What passed for subversion in this family seemed no more than child's play, and in fact, your mother was a child. Every morning, when the men prepared to leave the house for the search, your mother would try to dissuade your father, Willie. She would tell him he was too weak to be taking part in such a strenuous exercise, and when he refused and went anyway, you could see it in her face. It was written there for any stranger to read. Guilt. Resolve. Of course, Anna had to be her accomplice. I had recognized the guilty parties on first arrival but was content then only to observe."

"I will not believe it," I said firmly, though I was beginning to believe it.

"Who else was capable at that time and place? Even now, today, even with only that jumble of calendar dates and lines and notes, I see no one else here capable of logical action."

"Why? Tell me why my mama would have stolen from the very people who were raising her. Why? Just tell me that."

"Stolen is too strong a word. I assumed at the time that she only wanted to keep your grandfather from buying more and more of those worthless rice fields. We will never know what she would finally have done, for I denied her the privilege." At last the old woman paused to drink down her wine, but she kept her free hand raised, demanding silence. "Now," she began again. "To retrieve the treasure without an accomplice was a possibility, but haste was required and help was close at hand. The overseer's son, a boy named Allson Mercy, was sleeping in the barn. I'd sensed from the beginning that despite the hospitality being extended to him, he was no friend of the Allson family and so it proved when I threw myself on the mercy of this young Mercy."

"Oh, no," I moaned.

"I declare!" spoke Uncle Jimmy.

"What did you expect?" Liza demanded.

"You're acquainted with that family, aren't you?" It was more taunt than question. Aunt Lydia continued. "That very night, I tied a rope about his waist and lowered the boy into the depths. Again and again I brought him sputtering to the top with another treasure—all of it, every single plate and spoon, even the diamond tiara, which came last. When the sun rose on that deep, dark night of intrigue, the Allson dowry was safely packed away in three steamer trunks. The Mercy boy would take nothing for himself. I tried to force coins upon him but he laughed and would only accept the Dutch painting, for which he could have no use. Obviously, Uncle William had dealt him some injury that money could not heal. I, on the other hand, felt the opposite and happily thanked the boy as he slipped away into the night's remaining shadows. That same morning I left Cedar Point under the escort of the officer who had been sent to investigate the disappearance of my fiancé."

Aunt Lydia was finished. What shocked me more, her betrayal or the participation of Allson Mercy? I doubted Amy Mercy knew her father's part, but The Hard to Catch did, for he'd told me on the River Road that we'd never find the dowry. The Mercys wanted a revenge, but it was Aunt Lydia who'd exacted it. In fact, she'd had a second reckoning. We of the next generation had pried the story from her and thus been disinherited a second time.

"That ain't nothing to be proud of," I commented at last.

"Yes, it is," Liza said. "You had a right to that dowry."

"It wasn't your money, Liza," I said. "You got no right to an opinion."

"What about you, Jim? Do you feel I acted fairly?" Lydia asked.

"Can't put drunk wine back in the bottle," my cousin said.

"Is that a yes or a no?"

"What I think ain't going to bring home one red Indian penny. Glad you enjoyed spending it." He raised his wine-glass to her in a mock toast.

"Spoken with all the evasion of a true Southern gentle-man. Tactfully put. The essence of tact.

"What about you Sammy? Was I right or wrong?"

"I ain't know 'bout all that right and wrong thing. That happen 'fore my time."

"Do you think you would have received a share of the Allson dowry?"

"Shush, ma'am. That white people money."

"You are glad I had a good time spending it then, aren't you?"

"That's not fair!" I shouted, because I finally realized that she was going about the room gathering up forgive-ness for what she had done. "Sammy ain't entitled to an opinion."

"What about you, Brother?" she asked next. He was allowed an answer. I didn't object, but he had none to give. He shrugged and held his cards out in front still waiting for the game to begin.

"George?" she asked. "Do you think I acted honorably?"

"I simply cannot imagine you acting otherwise," he said, smiling.

I wanted to set him straight and tell him that she took ad-vantage of his blindness to occasionally cheat him at cards, but I held my tongue. I was angry, but not that angry.

"There we have it. The votes are in."

"Not mine," I repeated.

"Remember that you promised never to repeat a single word of this."

They all agreed, even Brother.

"What about the favor?" Uncle Jimmy said. "You said you was expecting a favor from us in return for the story."

"Not from me," I said. "I didn't agree."

"We don't need your help," Liza said.

"Hush, both of you. I want you to help, Willie T. This is something that I ask mainly of you and Jim. Though the others may assist, the responsibility is in your hands."

Liza said something in French that was answered in English.

"No, Liza. This is for the Allson men. Reparation you could call it—my due."

"Your due?" I cried. "It's us that's owed."

"What is it?" my cousin asked.

"I want you to dig up my fiancé's body and rebury it in the cemetery. I want it buried in the Allson plot."

"Where it is now?" my cousin asked.

"They buried him beneath the grape arbor. At the end furthest from the house."

"The grape arbor?" I asked in true astonishment.

"The Grapes of Wrath." Aunt Lydia smiled her broad gap-toothed smile and puffed her cigarette.

"How do you know that?" Uncle Jimmy continued.

"They kept me inside for two days, but as soon as I was free, I searched about until I found a place where the earth was soft. There was no question as to where it was. They had barely moved the body."

"All right," Uncle Jimmy said.

"Not me," I said.

"I'll help," Liza said.

"I'll do it alone," Uncle Jimmy said.

"When?" Lydia asked.

"How 'bout tonight?"

"Tonight would be fine."

My cousin didn't do it alone. I don't think he ever expected to. Liza couldn't be there for she had to be home, but the rest of us were. Even though he knew it was a grave, Sammy couldn't say no to either Lydia or Jimmy. It fell to him to do the bulk of the digging, but I relieved him occasionally. The business wasn't as gloomy as I'd expected. It might be more than a coincidence that the ghost of The Hard to Catch had trampled this particular ground on countless nights, but the Mercy connection to this mystery hadn't been mentioned again by my cousin and I wasn't about to bring it up. I had the cross about my neck and plenty of company to help me deal with whatever we'd find—which wouldn't be much after all these years. Only some bits of bones, and only that if this was the right place to look. After an hour's digging for nothing, I started to have my doubts. Uncle Jimmy had brought along a bottle of the good Madeira and was, as the evening wore on, taking a more detached view of the proceedings.

"There ain't nothing here," I said. "Maybe she told us the wrong end of the arbor. Maybe they buried him somewhere else."

"Good enough story," he mused.

"What you mean?"

"Maybe it was all a lie. Whole story about the captain and the dowry, too."

"Maybe? Why didn't you say something before this?"

"Why? It's a lot simpler to come out here and just dig a hole, ain't it?"

"It ain't you digging," I pointed out the obvious.

"Something down there all right," Brother said with quiet conviction. He was holding the lantern while Sammy shoveled.

"Brother? First you got no opinion and now you say you

believe her?" I was disgusted with my other cousin as well and ready to go to bed.

"See here?" Brother nudged at the pile of fresh dirt with his shoe tip and a small round object rolled free.

I picked it up and held it to the lantern.

"A button," I whispered. "Brass button. Could be from a uniform, all right."

Just then the shovel hit an object that rang out with a sharp clang, and we all peered immediately into the dark hole where Sammy now stood knee-deep.

"What you got there, Sam-u-el?" Uncle Jimmy asked.

A very reluctant shoveler to begin with, Sammy had reached the limits of his grave-digging depths. He was getting out with haste.

"I ain't know what it be. Thing is hard. I tell you that."

Uncle Jimmy thanked him for this information and climbed down into the hole himself. After scratching around with his hands for a minute, he pulled out a rusted but still recognizable remnant of a long saber.

"So," my cousin said, climbing out of the hole and retrieving his wine bottle. "What do you say now, Willie? Still doubting your Aunt Lydia?"

"Me? It was you that doubted her."

"Looks like a Union blade to me," he said, making a few swishing passes through the winter dead branches of the grapevines. "The grapes of wrath, indeed. Wonder how many noble Southern boys he ran through with this pig-sticker before Grandpa put an end to his bloody work?"

"She said the War was over. It had been over for months."

"Dig, Sam-u-el," my cousin commanded.

But Sammy was not to be commanded further, so Brother and I dug out another foot without result and were headed on to the center of the earth.

"Do Jesus. What you boys do out here?"

We'd been discovered by Maum Anna, which didn't surprise me all that much. The more Madeira Uncle Jimmy had drunk, the louder his directions had become, and during the last half hour, he'd made several cavalry sweeps with his new saber in close proximity to Maum Anna's house.

"Fulfilling an obligation," Uncle Jimmy answered for us all. "A promise to a lady."

"Do boy. Get out of here with that talk. You been drinking too much of that poison."

"Poison, Miss Anna? This is just the fruits of the vine. Ain't we all that, now?"

"Don't talk that trash to me. Mind your mouth. You tell me, Willie. What you doing out here?"

The woman was truly angry. She took hold of my arm and straightened her bent body to full height. Still, she was so shrunk down she had to crane her neck to look me in the eye. I figured it best to tell her the truth.

"We're digging up the bones of Miss Lydia's fiancé. She asked us to bury them for her in the cemetery."

"Ain't no bones in that hole," she said, releasing me.

"No," my cousin questioned. "And I suppose this ain't a Union sword I got here in my hand?"

"Sword don't put no bone in the hole."

"Then the Union captain wasn't buried here?" I asked.

"He bury here, but he gone now."

"Where to?" I asked.

"Maybe he climb up out that hole and walk away. Dead will do that if they don't rest easy."

"That so," Sammy joined in.

"What Aunt Lydia told us is true?" I pointed at the empty hole. "This man came to ask permission to marry her and Grandpa brought him around here and shot him?"

"That may be," the old woman said, beginning to open her mouth in a familiar wide smile. "That may be, but he come calling mighty perculiar. When the old man shoot him, the gentleman caller running through the backyard buck naked. He got he sword in one hand and he clothes in the other. I ain't know if he stop to ask 'bout marrying the gal. I ain't hear him say nothing 'bout that. Pow!" She clapped her hands together. "He dead. Ain't no way for bring him back so we bury him right here where he fall."

Well, that part didn't match, but I knew we were getting close. Uncle Jimmy was down on his hands and knees laughing so hard that he couldn't talk. The rest of this questioning was up to me.

"Did she get the dowry? Did Lydia find the dowry in the well and carry it away?"

"That child full of surprises. Ain't never seen so many surprises in a child. Come all at once. That the worst part."

"You knew all along. My mama and you put that treasure in this same well here?" I pointed off to the well hidden by the shadow of the kitchen house.

"I forgets. Maum Anna too old to remember all them kind of thing."

"You put it there, and all these years you've known it was gone, but you let us keep digging."

"I forgets."

"You ain't forgot. You lied."

The old woman tapped her temple with a fingertip, and then spoke with a pretended hesitancy. "Old Sister tell Anna she must come get dowry. If Anna done give her promise to look after Miss Gin, she must come 'cause the Allson too fool to trust with the valuable. Coachman got 'em in the attic. Miss Gin and me bring 'em here." She pointed to the well. "Then ride the train to Virginia."

"And you went right on lying. You said Old Sister told

you on her deathbed the dowry was still buried out there."

"Anna must be mix up. That the overseer, Tyler Mercy, they bury out there. Ain't nobody asking how he get the bump on he head. He just dead and that old man putting him in the ground. 'Cept it ain't a true burial 'cause your grandpa throw away the body and hide the dowry in the poor man coffin." The confession ended and she turned towards her little building.

"What are you talking about?" I shouted.

She paused and only turned half about.

"Ain't I tell you that the deed that set the coachman crying? He a Christian man and he know it ain't right to treat the dead that way. He dig up the coffin and bury that dowry in the cellar. Then he dig the thing up again and put 'em in the attic."

"You ain't told us nothing 'bout this. You knew . . ."

"Ain't I tell you Old Sister hiding in the bush? She see the buckra hang that damn coachman. Hang 'em, then steal some chicken. Overseer boy, Allson, he help 'em tote them wardrobe." Maum Anna chuckled. "Old Sister so disgust she follow 'em right down to the Yankee boat, beg 'em to come back and burn the Allson house. Beg 'em. Sailor laugh at Old Sister. Say that against the law. She go up the hill and light that house herself and that little Allson Mercy laughing when she do it."

"That's it? That's what you forgot to tell us?" I screamed.

"Old Sister proud. Say that the one thing she do right since she grab that calico 'em slave catcher been waving round she face."

"Burned our house? Her and that boy, both. I ain't believing this. You hear what she's saying, Jimmy?"

He must have. Once more he was bent over double laughing.

"Fine," I said to Maum Anna. "Now you remember all

that and you still forget what happened to his body?" Again I pointed a finger at the empty hole.

"That body ain't walk away. I remembers now where it go."

"Where?" I demanded.

"The old man dig him up and sell 'em to the Masons' Lodge. They looking for a skeleton to use in their services. Them secret celebration ain't nobody know 'bout."

"Grandpa sold the skeleton?" Uncle Jimmy, half on his feet, began to laugh anew.

"They give him five dollars."

"Nobody stopped him?"

"How they going to stop him? He done have it dug up and sold."

"They still got it?"

"Must be so. Ain't here. That the fact." It was her turn to point beneath the vine.

I shook my head and Uncle Jimmy laughed.

"Sad thing when a body ain't get that Christian burial. Allson Mercy know his daddy body ain't treated right. When him time come, he disappear." The old woman shuffled off towards her house. Enough secrets for one night. Too many, maybe.

As for our present night's work, we quickly refilled the hole and restored the leaf cover pretty much as we'd found it. Already I was planning a raid on the Masonic Lodge for the following night. If at first I'd been reluctant to help Aunt Lydia, I now felt it was a point of honor that the skeleton of her loved one be liberated. Not only for her sake, but maybe for Amy Mercy's, too. I was determined to see at least one body reach a normal resting place. If necessary, I would have gone alone, but it turned out my cousin was committed to the search, as well.

The incidents involving the Mercys and Old Sister, though, were to remain a secret. Even in his relaxed condition, Uncle Jimmy demanded this and I was quick to agree. I did object to him telling Liza about the fate of the fiancé's skeleton, but he insisted she had a right to know and would demand to know, anyway. The next morning after church he told her, and it was fortunate that he did. Liza contributed a valuable bit of information. The Masons no longer had the skeleton. For the past ten years they had been using an empty coffin because, upon Dr. McGill's arrival in town, they'd secretly sold the ceremonial relics to him for a substantial ten dollars. With his own hands, the doctor had wired the bones together, and the skeleton hung in his office for several weeks before he discovered that it didn't have the desired calming effect on his patients. Rather than store it away for good, the doctor contributed it to the school, where it had been used to teach me and hundreds of others about the inner mysteries of the human body. "Femur. Cranium. Pelvis." Each had been pointed to, and we had sat in class and sung out the names until, at least as a group, we knew all the bones in the body.

For almost a decade, this practice had been an essential part of a Cedar Point education, and Calvin, as the skeleton was affectionately called, was an unwilling participant in many a prank. Done up in dress and bonnet, he had once made a Halloween tour of the entire town. His excursions had been sharply curtailed with the arrival of Superintendent Baker, though. A strongbox had been built to house the skeleton, and this was bolted to the floor and locked. "You was there when the school burned down," my cousin reminded. "You know the ending."

"They didn't find a trace. Just the bolts that was used to hold the box in place."

"What'll we tell Aunt Lydia?"

"Could tell her the truth."

"I don't think she would want to hear that."

In the end we did, we told her the truth. In a way, Maum Anna made it easier for us. That same afternoon, she turned over a knotted man's handkerchief, which held all the Union captain's valuables, at least all the ones he'd had on him when he came calling that last night. Before dinner, Uncle Jimmy and I went to the pole cabin so we could talk to Lydia and George alone. Not surprisingly, we found them playing rummy.

"We brought you news about the body," my cousin said.

"I can see from your expression it is not good."

"Well, it ain't good and it ain't bad."

"Tell me," she said lighting a new cigarette off an old. "Just go on and say it."

"The Masons got the body."

"They did?" Suddenly she was smiling. "They knew he was a Mason. He told me that."

"Yes, ma'am," Uncle Jimmy nodded.

"The men he was leading had taken heavy casualties, and there'd been some hangings here. They were ready to burn this town to the ground and some freed slaves were ready to join in. He was so tired and angry himself, he told me he didn't care. It was a Matthews. A Major Matthews met him on the road and gave the Masons' sign. He knew then that the property of the citizens had to be protected. He marched his troops straight through and bivouacked at that wharf. He gave orders that he would personally shoot the first man who set fire to a house or so much as stole an egg. He was a Mason. He was a gentleman, you know."

"Yes, ma'am," my cousin said. "Here's his watch. The chain is with it and the fob has got the Masons' symbol."

My cousin slipped the watch Maum Anna had given us into the old woman's hands, and for the first time since she'd arrived, Aunt Lydia began to cry—not much—just a few tears but they cut deep messy traces through all the ink, powder, and rouge they crossed.

"Where did they bury him?" she asked through shining eyes.

"Didn't," my cousin said. "He was cremated. His ashes is blowing to the four winds."

"Good. That's as it should be. I wish I could join him in just such a state at this very moment." She had a short coughing spell, which was halted by a generous taste of wine. Then she turned her attention back to the card game.

"There's more," my cousin said. "These was saved, too." Out of his pocket he pulled four military medals and laid them on the table. Maum Anna had given us these as well. I wasn't quite sure what they meant. The ribbons were faded, but they looked impressive. Two might have been made out of real silver.

"Oh. Oh." Aunt Lydia let out a wail of strange emotion. Recognition? Grief? Joy? It was hard to say. All were mixed up in there together. Gathering up the medals one by one, she hugged them to her ample bosom, and began to weep again, and spoke to us between sobs.

"He was so brave. I didn't tell any of you that part. I know it was selfish, but I kept that part of him to myself. I didn't even tell you, George. Please forgive me. I kept that part of him a secret even from you." George, too, seemed greatly moved, for tears were forming beneath his clouded glasses and trickling down his cheeks. He reached out and patted his wife on the shoulder as she continued to speak. "He hardly ever talked about it, even to me. He had led his men time after time into a merciless hail of bullets. Twice he was wounded but he had survived. He was convinced that God was protecting him for some reason. God was saving him for something, and once he left Cedar Point, it was his duty to discover what that something was. He was going to find out."

"Yes, ma'am," my cousin said. "He was an honest-to-God hero."

I, too, told Aunt Lydia the captain was a hero, and we left her clutching the medals, with George comforting her softly in French. Brother and Sammy were both told to keep their mouths shut about exactly what had happened and to stay away from the pole cabin at least for the night. They nodded. Then we walked over to Liza's house and requested she do the same thing. She agreed, said goodnight, and closed the door. I guess only Uncle Jimmy was truly disturbed by this last turn of events. Walking home from Liza's, he had a lot of questions for me. Not really questions, more like statements.

"Christ, how do you figure it, Willie T.? Man fights the whole four years. He's a hero. It's a miracle he's alive. The War ends and he's just trying to have a little fun. Bang. He's dead. He doesn't even get a decent burial. His skeleton ends up hanging in a schoolroom. Doesn't make sense. He thinks God is saving him for something, and schoolchildren end up singing out the names of his bones and toting him around on Halloween."

Only the day before, my cousin had found most of this to be pretty hilarious. Now he seemed to think it the matter of utmost concern. I could have mentioned that the wages of sin are death—that the Union captain's carnal desire for the powdered, rouged, weeping old woman we'd left that evening had brought him a well-deserved end—but I hardly believed that myself anymore. It would certainly be no comfort to my cousin.

"They was Negro troops he was leading," I pointed out.

"Sammy's a Negro." I guess that was his defense, but I didn't see how Sammy being a Negro was relevant at all.

"He was on the other side," I said finally. "A Union officer."

"Shouldn't matter. Shouldn't matter whose side you're on. A man has a right to a better end than that."

"I guess so." I was hoping that my cousin wouldn't launch into further morbid speculations and was thankful when the conversation took a new tack.

"Lydia is right. I shouldn't be here running this boat. I should be in France fighting the Huns. It's crazy, me staying here."

"Why don't you go?" I wasn't sure I wanted him to go, but after all our time together, I knew this was the question he expected from me.

"I gave my word to the doctor. We shook hands when he put up the money for the *Miss Liza*."

"You could sell her."

"Afraid it's too late for that. I should have gone last spring. I just wasn't thinking clear. You remember?"

"Yes."

"I ought to be doing my part. I ain't a slacker."

I'd heard him out, and now turned to the subject that concerned me. What did he make of Tyler Mercy being buried outside of his coffin and the damage Allson Mercy had done to our family? Wasn't it possible that The Hard to Catch might bear us some ill will, as well? My cousin said he didn't want to discuss any member of the Mercy family.

"Especially not her," is what Uncle Jimmy said.

Then he made me promise again not to repeat the part of Maum Anna's tale that concerned the plantation or the dowry. It would change nothing and we already had our hands full putting away the Union captain. I couldn't argue. The ground was shaky, but all things considered, the story we told Aunt Lydia about the Masons and the cremation held up surprisingly well. There were a few close calls, mostly involving something Liza said or failed to say, but we got by. Eventually though, Aunt Lydia would have discovered the truth, so it was fortunate in a way that she died soon after. I say that now, but at the time, I didn't see it as fortunate. Just the opposite. We had all come to depend on her presence, and her death came as a shock, especially to me, who found her.

I'd gone over on a Sunday afternoon right after dinner, knocked, and, when no one came, let myself in. I called a greeting but got no response. This was odd, and as I walked between the crates towards the kitchen, I heard a low moaning. That was my only warning before stumbling upon the tragic scene. The card table had been knocked over, spilling cards and wine across the floor, and Aunt Lydia lay as she'd fallen. Her eyes were open. A cigarette had burnt to a stub between her yellowed fingers so you could smell the faint odor of charred flesh. George was on his knees, hugging the body. His glasses were off and tears poured from those sightless eyes as he gently stroked her shoulder.

Well, she was dead. That was obvious from the start, but before I could say a word to George or do anything else, Liza was standing at my shoulder.

"Go for my father," she whispered.

"She's dead," I whispered back.

"Go for my father. He'll be the judge of that."

"What about George?"

"I'll watch over him. You go. Hurry, Willie T. Go."

Glad to be free of the room where death was, I ran breathless the three blocks to the McGill house and hurried back to the cabin as fast as the doctor was able to travel. From my description, he figured her to be dead but said you never could tell. There was always hope.

Well, there wasn't any hope. There wasn't any Liza, either. George was bent over the body just as I'd left him. At once suspicious, I checked the bedroom. Liza wasn't there and neither was the steamer trunk that held all that was left of the Allson dowry. Without bothering her father, I ran from the cabin. It took no great tracker to follow the girl because the backside of the trunk had left a deep impression in the lawn grass and bushes where she passed from backyard to backyard. She was dragging it, using the strap on one end. This wasn't a guess. I saw her bouncing it up the last step at the rear of her house.

"Liza!" I screamed from the street. "That's the Allson dowry. You drop that trunk right now. I mean it." She didn't slow down and I raced on only to have the door slammed in my face at the very last second.

"Liza! You ain't getting away with this." I rattled the doorknob in vain.

"Go away, Willie T.," she called from the other side.

"I ain't going nowhere 'til I got what is mine."

"She gave this trunk to me."

"When? When did she ever give you that trunk?"

"Right after you left. She gave it to me with her dying breath. She said, 'Liza, take the trunk.' She said, 'All that remains of the Allson dowry is yours.' Then she died."

"That is a damnable lie. She was dead when I got there!" I hollered this last into the keyhole.

"No, she was not, but I don't intend to stand here and discuss it with you."

"I'm telling your father."

"You do and you'll never get your share."

"My share?"

"The day I marry Jimmy you will get half."

"Liza, you ain't ever going to marry Jimmy."

"Yes, I am."

I could hear her telling the maid to help carry the trunk up to her room and under no circumstances was Willie Allson to be let into the house. I knew I was beaten, or more exactly, I no longer cared to argue with Liza about this or anything else. Aunt Lydia had said that little of value remained, anyway, and even the entire dowry wouldn't have brought me the kind of happiness my aunt had enjoyed. I can't say I exactly mourned her, but walking home I began to consider life without the woman. This consideration, in turn, brought on a numbing presence I'd almost forgotten. The bleak fog banked itself in the corners of my mind and threatened to roll in. I shook my head to clear it out and tried to think other thoughts. I thought of George crying tears through sightless eyes. I reached inside my shirt and touched the cross. Instead of comfort, this brought forth the image of The Hard to Catch's grinning devil face. After that, I counted to one hundred twice and recited the alphabet to myself. By then I'd reached home.

Mr. Friendly and my mama were in the parlor quietly making arrangements for the funeral. I spoke to them and then went upstairs. Brother wasn't there, but when I returned to the parlor I found Uncle Jimmy alone with the preacher. My cousin was suggesting that Aunt Lydia be cremated. I nodded in agreement, but the idea wasn't taken seriously. This woman who called herself an Allson would be buried among the Allsons. Grandpa wasn't consulted on the matter and wasn't urged to attend. It was a quiet occasion, for only Mr. Friendly and those of us who'd known her came. George was led through the ceremony by his temporary caretaker, Maum Anna. The old black woman sang a solo at the graveside and seemed smaller than ever—dwarfed beneath the limbs of those majestic oaks. Somewhat forlornly, Mr. Friendly admitted he didn't really know Lydia, but judging by the many fine young friends she'd made, he felt her heart was in the right place. If it was God's will, then she was surely with Him now.

It was time for George to depart. He and all his crates were packed up and shipped off to relatives living in Connecticut. Apparently there was some question as to whether the two had actually been married, by at this point it wasn't a question worth asking. He left and we began to retreat—turn back to that normal time before we'd learned to play rummy, speak French, drink wine, plot the course of the war, circle the world, and all the rest.

Liza kept the contents of the trunk a secret, but upon his request, she did give Uncle Jimmy the medals and the Union captain's pocket watch—a watch that refused to tick. Maum Anna claimed it had stopped the exact second the man was sent back to his maker. She said, "Stop dead. Watch like that one ain't never going fix." Uncle Jimmy ignored her and gave it to Brother to repair. Though not a Mason, my cousin attached the chain and Masonic fob to his own timepiece. The medals were laid out in a neat row on top of his bureau and, passing by once, I saw him studying them. He'd gotten another present, as well, for George had generously left him the remaining cases of Madeira. The wine was hidden in the barn, and he and Sammy could sometimes be found there lying in the straw, speaking a few words of butchered French to each other and drinking numerous toasts. Even while Aunt Lydia had been with us, Brother had never deserted his clock experiments and repairs, his prayers, or his voices, but now I would sometimes catch him with the worktable cleared and the cards dealt out for solitaire.

The older generations were the least affected, and I suppose that was natural. They knew what they knew, and what they didn't know they weren't going to learn from us. By now it could make no difference to them that Aunt Lydia had squandered the dowry or that the Old Sister had burned the Allson house or that Amy Mercy's father had aided in this to avenge some wrong still unknown. As my mama had once said, such memories would be of little use to her. At school, I gradually slipped back into my role of guiding Gander and the others. My cousin showed me in the newspaper where preparations were being made for Americans to man sections of the front lines. Cool and intrepid, American men would soon be waging war on sacred foreign soil.

The Red Dragon

THE tide rose. The creek had spilled over its banks, crossed the street, and lapped at the front steps of our house. Spring tides. We were used to these watery advances, but this one was early in the season and particularly high. A great full moon, fuller than natural, it seemed, lit the night sky and brought from the ocean a solid sheet of risen water.

"Planets lining up," Uncle Jimmy explained. "Lucky stars, Willie T. Lucky stars."

Maybe.

I was no stranger to flood, for the Great Storm of 1911 that left so many dead and homeless along our coast had struck hard at Cedar Point. It had come without warning, just a steady worsening of the weather and a climbing tide until the realization that a hurricane had arrived sent my mama and Maum Anna rushing out to the barn. Grandpa, who'd been told to stay, followed them there, and Sammy and I were left alone to endure the tempest in the comfort of the kitchen. The house trembled, the darkness howled, but we were content to feast on emergency rations, at least until the water rose, flowing suddenly through a thousand cracks to gather high about the chairs we sat in. Then the kitchen door pushed open. Outside the furies raged, and then the door was shut. The adults had entered—wet through a hundred times over, their clothes pressed hard into their flesh, their faces bleak in the meager light of the kitchen lantern. Grandpa appeared dazed, his snow white hair plastered down about his ears and forehead, his goatee soaked to a fine point. Mama clung to his arm, pushing him forward with silent determination. Maum Anna issued the orders, her long arms snaking out to snatch us from our perches.

"You boys fool. Get out of them chair. Get up them stair. Go on."

To my surprise, the front door was off its hinges and the parlor was awash—a foaming chaos of floating chairs and tables battering the walls. With Maum Anna on one side of Grandpa and Mama on the other, we waded through the knee-deep water and climbed the stairs to my bedroom. The storm's eye passed over soon after, a mysterious calm that sent Sammy and me rushing to the window in expectation of God knows what. Only a black nothing met our gaze, and in no more than five minutes, the cyclone came blasting in from the opposite direction. The room responded with a whole different set of groans and whistles, and we raced once more to find shelter in the skirts of the giant black woman.

Above this bedlam, Maum Anna had kept up a steady stream of songs, prayers, and invocations that my mama would occasionally join in. Grandpa, as I recall, slept most of the time and I must have dozed, as well. I remember crawling into the black woman's lap and the next thing I knew, I was waking to the sight of her huge smile. "Thank Jesus," she said as I flew to the window. And there it was—

if not a sunny day, at least a battered version of this world and not the next.

Since that great one of 1911, we'd had two lesser storms: One in October of 1915 and another in August of 1916, but neither had pushed the water beyond our front steps. It was that high now. A strange sight on an even stranger night. Abandoning the porch, I waded towards the wharf to observe Uncle Jimmy.

Liza had made him take her rowing in the moonlight and was forcing him to sing to her—two tasks he'd perform only after a generous fortification. The chilly water reached my calves and I stopped in the Cedars of Lebanon. The couple floated before me on that pale bulging creek. Only one short year since Amy Mercy had lived and died. Another Christmas had come and gone. Another Easter. My cousin never spoke of her. I certainly didn't. What was worse, I realized I didn't think about her all that often. It was as if she were someone I'd heard of. Perhaps, someone who'd been pointed out to me in the store or on the playground. Not someone I had known.

Maybe my cousin felt the same. He rowed in the moonlight singing:

> *When I went to town*
> *I learned to rob and steal,*
> *And when I robbed a cowboy*
> *How happy I would feel.*

It wasn't right to be singing a song Amy Mercy had taught him, a song she'd sung to me.

> *I wore a broad-brimmed strawhat,*
> *My horse and saddle was fine,*
> *When I courted a pretty girl*
> *You bet I called her mine.*

I guess it made no difference to my cousin. Amy had sung it better but Uncle Jimmy had the tune. He was enjoying himself. Why shouldn't he? He and Liza were unofficially engaged. The freight boat enterprise, after a shaky start, was doing handsomely. A capable black captain, Arthur Allson, had been found to run the *Miss Liza*, leaving Uncle Jimmy free to conduct business. On Wednesdays, my cousin was driven down to supervise the unloading and loading of the freight boat in Crowns Bluff, and on Thursday mornings he was driven back. The rest of his life was his own.

Yes, the *Miss Liza* had turned out to be a lucky boat, after all. She hadn't missed a single appointed round, either with my cousin or the new captain at the wheel. Dozens of fifty-gallon drums of kerosene and gasoline were stored in our front yard, and the new boat owners were making more money than they'd imagined possible. Suddenly Cedar Point was prosperous, for the great World War was causing shortages everywhere but here. Beef, turpentine, lumber, and even firewood were all in great demand, and cotton and corn could bring a king's ransom.

The doctor was buying a tractor, my cousin confided. Such a machine could pull a twenty-four disc plow and do the work of a dozen mules. On a visit to Atlanta, his partner had seen one demonstrated and swore it would change the face of the earth around Cedar Point. The time had come. Not that it mattered to Dr. McGill. The doctor didn't actually need a tractor to grow cotton because he'd made a small fortune that winter on cotton he'd never seen. Foreign cotton had been cut off from the market, and then with America gearing up for war, the price had soared in New York. Dr. McGill had bought this cotton even before the seed was in the ground, and after Christmas, he'd sold it all. A couple weeks later, the price dropped, but he had his money and was gone.

"Never even seen it. Jesus, ain't that something?"

Naturally, my cousin was getting more interested in the "cotton he'd never seen" end of the business, and less interested in the actual sale and delivery of fuel. Still, he planned to get a bigger truck with a tank built on the body. The market warranted such an investment, for these were boom times, and once the war ended, we would go on booming. Cedar Point was on its way. In fact, Uncle Jimmy and the doctor felt it wouldn't be unfair to the citizens of the town to increase the freight boat rates, especially since such an increase could be passed on to the desperate buyers in Crowns Bluff. They suggested my pa do the same and even told Mr. Britt he could get four dollars more a barrel for his turpentine if he'd only demand it. Neither man took their suggestions.

"Too old to change!" Mr. Britt shouted in my pa's good ear. "Time to give it up. Give it to them young pups."

"Dogs?" my pa shouted back, not quite understanding.

"Yes, sir, Captain Tom. Every dog has his day."

By this, I assume Mr. Britt was referring to my cousin and Dr. McGill, who he seemed to view with more curiosity than respect.

"Dogs?" my pa shouted back.

"Yes, sir, Captain Tom. Dogs."

The two old friends still spent their Saturday mornings on the bench beneath the Cedars of Lebanon, conducting their business in the open air.

That night the rising tide covered the wharf and lapped up around the turpentine barrels waiting to go out on the *Redbird* and the fuel drums waiting to be hauled away in the truck. A few of the empties had even begun to drift and before leaving the serenading couple I secured them. Both Pa and Uncle Jimmy's boats were due in the next afternoon and, of course, I already knew my cousin's plans for the following morning. Sammy was to push him through the tide-covered marsh in that same rowboat of Dr. McGill's, and standing in the bow with his shotgun, my cousin would shoot down whatever marsh hens they came across. He never missed the awkward birds, not once. It was more public service than sport, and when he'd shot enough to feed not only us but the entire town, he'd come in. The remainder of the day would be spent up at the mercantile, where he claimed to be "reading the law" with Judge Walker. He smoked Havana cigars and bought his clothes from a respectable haberdashery in Crowns Bluff.

Most thought it an enviable life, despite the presence of Liza, and I numbered myself among that majority. I wasn't having all that bad a time, though, for I'd gotten back my pals and had chatted with Lucy Fitchum on several occasions. My life was interesting enough, but on a curious full moon night like this it seemed only my cousin could turn life into an honest-to-God adventure. Perhaps, that's why I considered myself lucky the next day. It was good fortune for me, at least, that the *Miss Liza* was broken-down at Camel's Landing. Since the *Redbird* was cruising well ahead and my pa had no knowledge of the mishap, it would be necessary for someone to either fix the stranded boat or make arrangements for towing her home.

By the time Uncle Jimmy explained this, he'd already received Superintendent Baker's permission for me to leave school. Sammy was waiting to drive us in the truck. Yes, Arthur Allson was a good boatman, but only a passable mechanic, and the engineer knew nothing about engines. It didn't matter. With me standing by holding the wrenches, the boat owner figured he could fix anything. Of course, I thoroughly appreciated this excuse to escape the school-house and the grocery. Still, I said we should get Brother, too, since he was the one with the real fixing ability. Uncle Jimmy said he would get in the way.

Those were hard words, but I couldn't deny them. Brother was acting stranger and stranger, and many complaints were now heard about the repaired timepieces. They'd tick. They'd tell time, but it was an erratic time, fast, then slow, then correct, and just when confidence was restored, they'd slip once more. Brother swore he was doing nothing different, but I'd seen him removing more and more of the gears and balances until a fixed watch was more than half emptied—the leftover mechanisms were dumped into a small box under the table. True, the least number of moving parts required the least exertion to put in motion. A quarter of a turn on the winding stem could set a watch running for weeks, but unfortunately its accuracy was fatally affected. Brother saw it differently. He claimed people were forgetting how to tell time, and when he returned a clock or watch, he now delivered a lecture on the uses of the big hand and the little hand. Needless to say, his adult customers didn't appreciate this, and needless to say, fewer and fewer timepieces waited in our bedroom to be repaired. Brother didn't mind. His voices, prayers, and games of solitaire kept him more than busy.

Uncle Jimmy had given up and begun to laugh at the complaints. But he stopped laughing after Brother repaired the watch of the ill-fated Union captain. Sadly, Aunt Lydia's fine heirloom now ran backwards, and even sadder, the little clock-mender insisted the correct time could be read in the reflective surface of the hinged cover, or better yet, in a mirror. He couldn't be convinced otherwise, even when proven wrong by an exasperated older brother who stood with mirror and watch in hand. Yes, Uncle Jimmy had lost all patience at that point, so I didn't argue when he said Brother was staying behind. I got in the back of the truck, we drove off the school grounds, and I considered myself lucky.

It was a good twenty-mile drive down to the landing, and Uncle Jimmy sipped along from a pint he kept between his feet on the floorboard. Though packaged as such, I don't think it was true store-bought liquor. Each time he passed the bottle my way, the fumes made my eyes water.

"More for me," he said each time I declined.

A taste on Saturday night lasted me a week. Sammy wasn't sipping either, but it was his job not to. Besides delivering fuel, he was now our chauffeur. Uncle Jimmy had begun to take too many detours with the truck, bouncing out of the ruts of the road clear up into the woods before beating back through the brush to the normal roadway. Erratic—that was putting it kindly. Enjoying a drink was a natural part of life, but some were suggesting that, enviable as my cousin's life was, he'd "fallen into the bottle." I was inclined to agree. Much of his conversation during the last stages of this particular trip made no sense, and when we got to Camel's Landing, he lurched out of the truck before it stopped rolling. Arthur Allson was waiting to greet him, but Uncle Jimmy staggered by and stepped off the side of the dock. When we pulled him out, he wasn't mad, just spitting and laughing. "Over the top, boys," he kept shouting. "Over the top." Maybe the cool dip helped him some, but I didn't see how he was going to be much good to anybody. He went below with Arthur Allson, though, and after banging around for about an hour, they got the engine going. It started with a sudden roar but quickly idled down to a miss-every-third-stroke, sputtering run.

"Purrs like a calico tiger," my cousin declared, coming topside again and wiping his greasy hands on my shirttail.

"Fine," I said. "Let's get back 'fore dark catches us."

"Not so fast, young man. Not so darn-fool fast. I'm thinking we'd better escort this beauty into port ourselves. Arthur Allson can take the boys on home in the truck, and you and me and Sam-u-el will carry this little lady the rest of the way."

Now, only a drunk would have thought that was a good idea, but he couldn't be talked out of it. Arthur Allson stepped ashore. My cousin eased the *Miss Liza* away from the dock, got her midstream, and handed me the wheel.

"There now," he said, pointing off across some twenty miles of winding creeks and oyster bars. "Steady as she goes." He crawled into the bunk behind me and passed out.

Well, I'd made this trip a number of times in my youth, and Sammy had traveled it even more often. We weren't total strangers to the way, and it was a good feeling to be at the helm with the Lathrop pounding away in a slightly broken but satisfying rhythm. I called Sammy to stand beside me and together we started off steady as she goes.

Like Pa's boat, the *Miss Liza* had the pilothouse to the stern above the engine room, and you steered by looking over the cargo—the cargo, in this case, being potash fertilizer, eleven fifty-gallon barrels of gasoline and eight more barrels of kerosene. She was deck loaded, plus some, and because the barrels were metal and because it was warm enough during the day for the fuel to expand, a wooden plug was loosely placed in the top of each. Around these bungs, a steady stream of vaporous liquid bubbled up and formed shallow pools on the drum tops. And above all this rose a haze of distorting fumes that I was forced to peer through. Worse yet, the fumes drifted back into the pilot-house and soon made Sammy and me dizzy. The *Redbird* had never carried such a cargo, but we were going to make it. In fact, I was beginning to consider how proud Pa would be when Sammy stuck his head out the door and reported that we were on fire.

"No!" I shouted, as if this single word would somehow make it not so. "No, I don't believe it."

"Willie, ain't meant for you to pass judgment."

"It ain't, huh?" I looked out the door myself. Small flames were beginning to lick out of the engine room port-holes below us. Looking back across the bow, I caught the first wisps of smoke as they rose from beneath the deck and mingled with the fumes of the gasoline and kerosene.

"Jimmy!" I shouted. "Jimmy!" And when he didn't stir, I put Sammy's hand to the wheel and shook my cousin violently. He flopped over, opened one eye, and then closed it tight. Fine. Fine and dandy. Actual flames were now licking around the top of the nearest gasoline drum and threatening to blow us all to sweet kingdom come. The engine, of course, could only be stopped from down below, and it showed no sign of quitting on its own. If anything, the old Lathrop was running better than before. Commanding Sammy to hold the course, I picked up the single fire extinguisher on board and descended. I can't say why. I could have drug Uncle Jimmy from the bunk and jumped overboard, but instead I descended with my fire extinguisher into much thicker smoke. At the far end of the engine I could make out the bright orange fire, and with pin pulled and handle pumped, the device spewed a steady stream of foam in that direction. Holding my breath, I watched through watering eyes as the flames diminished to the size of a small campfire. Then, of course, the fire extinguisher gave out. Like something alive, the fire crept rapidly out of the bilge and back up the sides of the hold.

Gasping for air, I stumbled back on deck and into the pilothouse. Our one chance lay on the bunk—not my drunken cousin, but the two old blankets on which he lay. These I unceremoniously snatched up, and soaking them quickly over the stern, I waded once more into the fray. Breath held again, I smothered the fire with my two open blankets, and finally slapped it with my bare hands.

Victory. I crawled above and lay coughing on the stern until it was necessary to reach the rail and retch. Then, propped beside the engine-room door, I examined the extent of the damage, not to the boat, but to myself. My clothes had burnt through badly in several places, but only my hands had actually been scorched. I was black all over with soot and grease, but alive and suddenly elated, realizing for the first time in my life that I'd done something truly brave. Not like the run-in with The Hard to Catch. This time, I was a real hero and had a witness, a witness calling to me from the pilothouse. I took a quick look into the engine room. The fire was out. The engine pounded along, not missing a beat.

"Willie," my witness called again.

"I'll take her." Easing him aside, I reached for the wheel as casually as possible.

"Do Jesus, look at you!" he exclaimed. "You done walk through Hell and come back home."

"You could say that." If he forgot to say it when we reached Cedar Point, then I'd remind him. "Walked through Hell and come back home." Maybe, "strolled through Hell" had a truer ring.

That decision could wait. Merely steering this final portion would be something of a feat, for the spring tide was again flooding above the creek banks, and we had only an occasional tilted pole or scrub cedar to keep us in the channel. An hour later, the sun set in an orange blaze on our left, but on our right that grand familiar moon was lighting the sky as bright as day. By then the rising tide had submerged most of the outer islands, and the marsh around us was far below the surface. Indeed, it was as if every fountain of the great deep had broken open and water prevailed on the earth. An almost shoreless sea, with gentle slowmoving swells, rose and fell beneath the heavily laden *Miss Liza*. At that point, we quit worrying about the twisting path altogether and set the course straight for Cedar Point.

Naturally, I was feeling pretty good when we rounded the final bend, especially since I'd watched my pa's arrivals practically all my life. There, in the glow of the silver moon lay my own hometown with water spread like a great white sheet tucked taut across the creek bed. Water had long since overlapped the banks and run across the streets and about the houses.

Despite the flooding, a crowd had gathered. I could see several lanterns, and as I drew closer, could easily make out the numerous well-wishers. Though the wharf itself was underwater, a true boatload of citizens stood on the tied up *Redbird*, and onshore, dozens more perched on the half-submerged drums and barrels.

I still had a hundred yards to go, but I was taking no chances.

"Get below, Sammy," I said in my quiet voice of newly assumed command.

This was an intricate maneuver, one I'd refused to attempt, even with Pa standing at my side. But on this special day, it could be accomplished. I'd swing the slowed boat in beside the *Redbird*. One bell and Sammy would shut down the Lathrop. Two bells, he'd crank it in reverse, and the *Miss Liza* would settle in her cradle. Then, I would lean out the cabin window and nod to the crowd. Perhaps I would even mention it was a good Friday. Yes. And somewhere out there my parents waited.

"All right, Sammy, get ready now. If we mess up, it'll be your fault, not mine." I was whispering this to myself, of course, because Sammy was in the engine room waiting for me to sound the bell.

"Yes, sir, Captain Willie," the Negro said. He was just outside the pilothouse door.

"What are you doing up here?" I demanded. Ahead I could see the landing clearly and the crowd that waved and cheered. If the so-called engineer didn't get below immediately, I'd have to come about and make a second approach —something my pa never had to do.

"Fire!" Sammy shouted at me. The whites of his eyes had grown as big as two full moons. "She on fire. All down there. Willie, she on fire."

"No!" I shouted for the second time that day and, leaving the wheel unattended, scrambled past him and back to the engine room hatch. And there I was met by a solid doorway of flames, flames that were beginning to spread out on the stern itself and lick up into the surrounding night.

The wheel had been abandoned no more than ten seconds, but when I climbed over Sammy again and grabbed the helm to spin down hard, there was no response. The hemp line connecting the wheel to the quadrant of the rudder had burnt through, and the spokes spun freely beneath my rapidly fumbling hands.

"Stop!" I screamed at the unstoppable engine. "Stop. Goddamnit, stop." But the only answer I got was the relentless pop, pop, pop that turned the propeller through the water and drove us steadily, straight towards the *Redbird*.

I could see the crowd on board her much more clearly. A few still waved and shouted, but now I understood that they'd been shouting, "Fire!" all along. And now they understood that I meant to run them down and incinerate them in the process, the retreat was on. Some stumbled to reach the flooded wharf, while others already swam for shore. I saw Gander. He appeared frozen, his mouth opened in a permanent holler. Then I saw my pa and mama seated in an old bateau. They watched, floating beneath the Cedars of Lebanon. They showed no sign of excitement, at least none exaggerated enough for me to make out. They simply watched as the blazing *Miss Liza* closed in on the helpless *Redbird*.

Pa's boat now appeared to be empty of well-wishers, but I couldn't be certain because at that moment, the top of one of the kerosene drums stacked on my bow rippled alive with a clear blue flame. The fire burned a bright ring for a split second and then leapt to the top of a second drum and so on until the entire left half of our cargo was ablaze with these bright blue circular flames.

I stared hypnotized, my hands still anchored to the useless spokes of the wheel, and wondered why I hadn't already been blown clean off the planet. I was certainly ready. Then the bow of *Miss Liza* struck the *Redbird* midship with a splintering crunch, and I was thrown hard over the wheel. Of course, the engine kept popping away, pressing on as the blue flames sprung higher and higher into the night.

"Jesus Christ! Jump, Willie! Jump!"

As I recall, that was the extent of Uncle Jimmy's conversation, and I felt myself being thrown through the pilothouse door—felt myself hitting the water hard and sinking forever. Surfacing, at last, I discovered my cousin struggling to keep Sammy afloat and shouting further orders.

"Swim away! Swim."

The first of the gasoline drums exploded in a great fireball that hurled flaming debris hundreds of feet in every direction.

"Dive!" my cousin commanded, and I dove. He and Sammy did the same, and we surfaced together downriver.

The other drums were going off as well, and the fire was spreading rapidly, flames everywhere, leaping one upon another. Of course, you couldn't recognize what was burning. You would have had to have spent your entire remembered life playing on that wharf, spent all those Friday afternoons waiting for the arrival of the *Redbird*. Gone, disappeared and replaced with only a great wall of fire. Blue, bright blue at their base, these flames turned bright yellow, then orange, and finally, red, deep red, as they licked about like the branches of a mighty oak. It wasn't a tree, though. I recognized that crackling roar. The arms swung out through the blackness to gather in the whole world. The claws ripped pieces out of the very sky. Seven redheads turned quickly from side to side to search me out, and when one spied me, its fiery mouth opened to the universe and let out a howl of recognition. I'd been expecting the arrival of this creature. In the back of my mind, I'd been expecting it for over a year.

"Woman-manchild!" I cried out to my cousin. "The great Red Dragon!" There it was. The great Red Dragon was lashing out with ever grander consuming force, eating up the earth, growing higher and wilder before our eyes. "Fornication and idolatry!" I screamed. "Oh, Babylon! Fornication and idolatry!"

"Willie? You gone fool?" My cousin had me by the shoulders and was shaking hard. We were still chest deep in the water.

"The Red Dragon!" I screamed on, pointing out to him the creature that was so very obvious. "Promise of the Revelation. Woman-manchild, the great Red Dragon!"

"You talking about the Bible?" my cousin shouted.

"Talking 'bout the end of the world!" I wailed.

"It's a fire." He was laughing at me. He'd gone crazy, but that was to be expected because he was certainly not among the elect—and neither was I.

"A lake of fire! Fire and brimstone!"

"Fire and gasoline." He stopped laughing and began to drag me along by the arm. "Don't you remember, the boat was burning?"

"The Red Dragon!" I tried to pull free. There was no use resisting. "You can't run! Can't hide!" I shouted.

"Listen to me!" My cousin yanked me around until our faces were only inches apart. "Listen. You got to straighten up. We got to find your ma and pa."

"Mama!" I screamed. "Pa!" I did remember then. Jerking free of him, I swam and stumbled onto the street. The water was still knee-deep, but I splashed off in the direction of where my parents had last been seen. The fact that this spot was now a sea of flame didn't bother me in the least. From behind, I heard Uncle Jimmy and Sammy calling for me to stop, but I couldn't imagine why. "Mama!" I wailed. "Pa! I'm coming!"

The heat was intense. My clothes had dried already, and even at a distance the air itself was hotter than the engine-room fire. Ahead of me, the Cedars of Lebanon began to ignite, each with a crackling explosion that left the trunks burning like a candelabra. Silhouetted against the flames, I saw figures moving, but they turned out to be wading towards me. Several unidentified hands flew out in vain to halt my progress.

"Willie, stop!" My cousin shouted once more. Then he tackled me. I went under and swallowed bitter water by the screaming mouthful until I was yanked to my feet.

"Let me go!" Against my will, I was being carried away from the fire.

"Shut up!" Uncle Jimmy tightened his hold.

"Mama! Pa!"

"They there." Sammy pointed and for a brief second I did see them. They were still floating along in the old bateau, an elderly couple, drifting in the orange glow of cataclysmic events.

"Mama! Pa!" I called out, and then we were all knocked from our feet by a great white blast. This, I would learn later, was the explosion of one of the gasoline drums stored at the wharf's edge. The earth rocked as the other drums ignited in close order. The gasoline, the kerosene, and then the barrels of turpentine—they all blew like a great cannonade and sent an even grander fireball raging up into the night air and brought a rain of white-hot ash upon our heads. And in its aftermath the sheet of flame spread across the entire width of the creek, and of course, up over its banks on both sides. The tide was still rising and the fire moved on the water's surface.

Here was the world's true end. All about us the boiling heat sucked in the air, causing a wind like a great cyclone. High above the top of the flames, a shower of burning sparks now burst out like a spouting volcano and whirled off to settle elsewhere.

"Mama!" I screamed once more. "Pa!"

"See them, Willie?" Sammy pointed again. "They done reach the house."

And so they had. Though our house seemed to float in

a flaming pool of water, that was only an illusion created by the glare, and my parents were docking at our own front porch.

"Oh, Jesus," I swore. "Thank you. Thank you. Thank you, Jesus."

"Yes," Uncle Jimmy laughed. "Thank you very much, Jesus. We couldn't of done it without you."

"Shut up!" I yanked free and waded to the house, clambering onto the porch just as my parents came struggling out the front door. They guided Grandpa between them. Weak or not, he had to be moved, but my mother, seeing me, left the burden to my pa and hugged me with wordless sobs.

"It wasn't my fault!" I shouted at her. "It wasn't me. I swear. It was Jimmy. Drunk. He passed out. It wasn't my fault."

"That's so." My cousin was right behind me. "Wasn't Willie's fault. I should have been at the wheel."

"It doesn't matter," my mama cried. She held me tight.

"Where's Brother?" Uncle Jimmy shouted.

"Who?" Mama asked.

"My brother!" Uncle Jimmy demanded. For several weeks now Mama had had great difficulty remembering any of our names. She'd been referring to me simply as "son."

"The one sharing my room," I reminded her.

"The little clockmender, Gin!" my pa prompted. "They want to know where the little clockmender is!"

"Thadius!" Grandpa shouted. "Thadius has the answers."

"Him? That child? We thought he was on the boat with you." My mama brought her hands up to her face and began to sob anew.

Uncle Jimmy pushed past us and disappeared inside.

"It wasn't my fault," I shouted in my pa's good ear. "Jimmy did it."

"Take him." Gently, Pa delivered a bewildered Grandpa into my care. "Get Anna. Get them both away from here."

"I'm sorry," I shouted.

"What?" he shouted back.

"I'm sorry I blew up your boat!"

"Go on," my mama said. "Take the Negro with you."

Brother, being propelled by the none-too-gentle hand of Uncle Jimmy, came through the front door. "Can you believe that? He was up there playing solitaire, playing cards by himself."

"Go on, son!" my mama commanded. "Get the Negro woman who lives in the kitchen building. Take the Negro boy. Your cousins will stay here with us."

I did as I was told, not bothering to ask what they, even with the help of my cousins, could possibly do to halt the great storm of flame now drifting towards the house—a storm igniting shrubbery as it came and only fueled further by the pickets of the fence. The white house shone blood red like a mirror reflecting the inevitable destruction that approached.

Sammy and I had looked back at first but soon had other concerns. The old man said nothing, but naturally, he wasn't content to be propped up in the stern of the bateau, and it took firm hands and considerable pleas to keep him aboard. Once in the backyard, though, he fretted less. The water was shallower, too, no more than a foot deep when we reached the kitchen building—still deep enough to float the bateau and flames, as well. We entered and found the old woman lying quietly in bed. Eyes wide open and alert, she smiled her broad smile.

"You come for see your Anna. I know you boys ain't forget your Anna."

She thought we'd come to visit. She'd been sick in bed, not moving for over a month, and I'd only been to see her once.

"We have to take you out of your house, Maum Anna," I said quietly. "There's a fire coming. Pa wants you moved." I pointed out the window at the glowing night.

"That fine. I been study on that light. I been study on 'em. You do what your pa tell you." She closed her eyes as if going to sleep.

"Yes, ma'am," I said. Together, Sammy and I lifted her from the cot.

Maum Anna had grown tiny. No other word could describe her. She'd shrunk to the size of a child, and probably weighed seventy pounds or less. Even her great arms and legs had somehow contracted so that the cuffs of her nightgown and its hem extended far beyond her limbs. It didn't take two of us, so I let Sammy carry her through the doorway and lower her gently into the bow of the bateau. He propped her up facing the old man.

Now what? I wasn't sure where to float them. Where would be safe on such a night? We must choose, and quickly, because in another few minutes our house, the old kitchen, the grapevines, and all this yard would be only a memory.

"What is that woman doing here?" For the first time since he'd come into our care, Grandpa spoke.

"Pa told me to get her," I said. "He wants me to take you both away from here."

"Why?"

" 'Cause we can't stay here."

"And why not?" the old man demanded.

" 'Cause the creek is on fire."

"That cannot be."

"Well, it is. See?" I pointed in the direction of the glow.

"I will not go in the same boat with that woman." He waved his cane.

"I know that old man," Maum Anna began. "I know that gentleman. I know 'em better than you children ever going know 'em. Ain't nobody know that old man like Anna know 'em."

Sammy took the initiative and began to pull the boat with the bowline. I waded along pushing from the stern. Though we were trying to stay at a safe distance, we soon had a clear view of the great fire storm. It growled and snapped as before.

"The world dying," Maum Anna whispered when the extent of the destruction was evident.

"Put that woman off. Set her ashore!" the old man bellowed.

"I feels the cool breeze of death fanning over me." Maum Anna spoke louder. She smiled. A hot wind whipped about us, the outermost edge of the fiery hurricane drifting closer and closer to our home.

"Remove this woman!" Grandpa raised his cane and slapped it down hard on the seat between them.

"I know that old gentleman!" Maum Anna cried out. "Ask Red Willie Allson who he pa is. You ask 'em." She raised a small finger and pointed it straight at the old man, taunting him, accusing him of a crime of which she herself had declared him innocent.

"That woman is not an Allson!" the old man shouted. "She took that name only to cause me discomfort."

"Chain Anna. Chain 'em . . . Red Willie, who your pa?"

"I will not share this bateau with that woman."

"I know that gentleman very well. Ask Red Willie who he pa is."

The two old people continued their exchange, and I nodded to each in turn until they finally fell silent. I didn't bother to ask Sammy where he was leading—he just splashed along as we crossed below the edge of the blaze and floated the bateau up the street almost to the McGills' house. By then the water was only ankle deep.

"That should do," I called, panting for breath. The fire was at least a quarter of a mile behind, and we were a good fifty yards from the creek edge. "Tie them off and let's get back."

Sammy did as he was told, looping the bowline over the branch of dogwood.

"Stay in the boat," I said to Grandpa. "Will you do that, please? Stay in the boat and wait." Since she was too weak to move, there was no need to tell Maum Anna, and though he wouldn't answer, the old man appeared calmer.

In silence, we waded back in the direction of the house. I knew it would be gone by now. My parents could stay out of the way of the flames, but would they? For the first time, I considered genuine prayer on their behalf, and for the first time, remembered that I was wearing Maum Anna's cross. Carefully, I pulled it out of my shirtfront, kissed both sides, rubbed it, and tried to say something other than, "Ghost ride on." I wanted to say, "Protect my mama and my pa," but instead, the only word that came to mind was idolatry. Idolatry and adultery. I rubbed the cross, determined to say my prayer, and still no decent words came.

"There the house, Willie."

"What?"

"The house still there. See 'em." My companion's black

finger aimed at the spot where our house stood. It hadn't burned down, and the fire that threatened was now much lower to the water's surface. The tide had turned at last and was carrying the diminished flames out to sea. Small patches of floating fire drifted by. We began to run. Off to one side, the gray shadows of other survivors moved quickly past us on errands of their own. Ahead, standing on our front porch, my family waited. My parents. My cousins. They leaned exhausted against the porch rail and looked out on the blackened yard. The beast had come within arm's length of the step and then retreated.

"Turned on the tide," Uncle Jimmy said. "Wasn't a thing that we could have done. It's a miracle."

I brushed by him and tried to embrace my mama, but her arms held a tremendous collection of papers. Thinking the house was lost, she'd pulled her calendar from the kitchen wall and now clutched it to her bosom. My pa had been entrusted with a small portion, but about her feet were scattered dozens of paper scraps. Through the open door I saw where others had been dropped.

"I'm sorry," I sobbed.

"Merciful heavens," she whispered. "This is nothing." My attempt to hug her was causing more papers to dislodge.

"It was me who did it. I tried to blame Jimmy, but it was me—"

"No, it was me," my cousin interrupted. "You was right the first time."

"Hush, both of you. Was God's will. Not for us to take credit nor to question."

"No!" I shouted, angry to be denied. "It was me. Not God. It was me that did it all."

"What?" my father shouted at me.

"He's sorry!" Uncle Jimmy shouted in the man's good ear.

"Act of God!" my pa shouted back. "Nothing to be sorry for. God's will."

"We're safe," my mama said. "That's all that matters, son."

"The boat? The *Redbird*? What else the Allsons got beside that boat?"

"He'll provide," my mama said.

"I'll provide," Uncle Jimmy said. "Now listen to your mother. Be thankful we're still living. Some others might not be so lucky."

That was reassuring. I might be responsible for murder as well as arson. I remembered the startled look on Gander's face in those final moments and wondered if he'd made it to shore. What would I say to the Widow Bailey? What would I say to others I might have widowed or orphaned? I couldn't go on living here. A son who turns his parents into paupers, a lad who murders his well-wishers. Maybe I had been right the first time. Maybe it was my cousin's fault. I began to recall all the reasons why he was guilty. In fact, I'd have started to name them if Pa hadn't sent Sammy and me off to retrieve Grandpa and Maum Anna.

Of course, Sammy had been with me all along, but I made him listen to my version of the day's events. He said nothing but would occasionally nod in agreement when I insisted. Our pace quickened for the street was almost drained, but then he stopped to point out more disaster. A block over, the great rain of ash and flaming debris had set two roofs ablaze, and I could see the frantic trafficking of the bucket brigades about the houses. Thankfully, these fires seemed close to being put out. Still, other homes might have burned to the ground already. I fell silent and studied the horizon. Would my neighbors be as willing as my parents to accept this as God's will? I didn't think so and began again to lay the blame at Uncle Jimmy's feet. And it was in this ungenerous state of mind that I approached the corner where we expected to see the bateau ebbed high and dry and to find the two old people propped up as we'd left them. Sammy was running ahead. There was no boat. No passengers. Nothing.

"Maum Anna!" I wailed.

"Maum Anna!" Sammy echoed.

Reaching the corner, we ran off in separate directions and then joined back up in mindless confusion.

"Where would they go?" I asked him.

"Willie, I ain't know. I ain't know where they going."

"Did you tie the boat?"

"Yes, I tie 'em."

"Good? Did you tie 'em good?"

"You see me tie 'em. I loop the rope round three times. I knot 'em."

Well, he'd done something, but I didn't remember it being so elaborate.

"It's gone. I don't know if you tied it or not, but I know it's gone."

"I tie 'em. You think I ain't going to tie up my auntie boat?"

I didn't bother to answer. We followed the path the receding tide would have taken, which was down the short lane to the creek's edge. There we found Grandpa. He stood on the doctor's dock looking out towards the sea. The tide rushed by beneath his feet, carrying on its back the dying embers of the great fire storm.

"Where is she?" I yelled at the old man.

"Who?" he asked.

"Maum Anna."

"There." He pointed into the distant night.

"Is she in the bateau?"

"I presume so. She refused to give it up and I was determined not to share it with her."

Sammy and I looked with stunned horror in the direction he indicated. What explanation could there be for this tragic turn of events? The bateau floated half a block and then the old man got out? He stood before us high and dry and Anna had gone to sea.

"I tie that bateau," Sammy moaned.

"You looped the line," I corrected.

"I loop 'em two time and then I flip a knot in 'em."

"It don't matter what you did if it didn't hold."

"I tie 'em. That my auntie."

Before I could get Grandpa turned around and off the dock, the Negro was pulling off in the McGill's rowboat, entering the moonlit expanse of open creeks and marsh. Tide was ebbing fast, but it seemed possible, even likely, he'd catch up with the bateau and set things right.

He didn't. Many of us searched through the night, but it was midmorning before Sammy himself came upon the missing boat. It had drifted over halfway to the ocean and sunk. It was empty. They were only guessing, but most figured the old bateau had taken on water shortly after Grandpa got out and settled to the gunnels. Otherwise, Sammy would have quickly spotted it. Whatever the case, Maum Anna was gone. Gone without a Christian burial, too. I knew that would upset Sammy even more, and while still in the creek, I made up my mind to agree with him. I would say he had tied the bateau, and Grandpa had become confused and untied it. Such a statement would relieve some of the guilt my playmate was surely feeling and cost the old man nothing. But I never got around to saying it.

Sammy rowed in that morning towing the sunken bateau. Uncle Jimmy rowed the next boat. I sat in its stern. Other searchers filed in behind us, like a funeral procession. Anna's mourners were legion. They lined the banks waiting for our return. A thousand people, I suppose. All black faces, they stood shoulder to shoulder, young and old, man, woman, child. Her entire community turned out. And when the realization of what had happened came to them, the news rippled along the bank like a breaking wave, and a sound of great lamentation rose from the multitude. A wail, it began at our approach and ended in a distant echo far down at the remains of my pa's wharf.

It was Sammy they carried away in place of a body. The thousand Negroes departed and none would return soon to Cedar Point. The houses of the white families would go uncleaned and the meals uncooked. The spring gardens would go unplanted. The Negroes would stay to themselves, carrying on an extended wake to which not even the Allson family was invited. We couldn't know that then, though. Uncle Jimmy leaned on the oars and let us drift as we watched Sammy's exodus.

"What now?" he asked finally.

I didn't answer and he rowed us on to what remained of the wharf. The pilings that still stood were canted at odd angles, burned or sheared off at the previous water level. The pilothouse roof of the *Redbird* was the only visible evidence of either boat. Miraculously, it had escaped and someone had thoughtfully tethered it to the bank. The shoreline was pocked with great desolate craters, and the forest that had been the Cedars of Lebanon was reduced now to a collection of charcoaled stumps. Over all this hung the thick smell of burnt fuel, an oily, relentless odor.

"It wasn't my fault," I complained to my cousin's back as we trudged towards the house.

"I said it was mine." He didn't even bother to look over his shoulder at me.

"Well, it is."

"Quit your Goddamn whining." He turned on me in sudden anger. "Last night you thought the world was ending. You were a Goddamn lot of help then, and I expect you'll be even less help now. I'm going to take care of these old people. So quit worrying about it."

"Yeah!" I shouted back. "Well, Anna's dead. How you going to take care of her?"

"I didn't kill her, so leave me alone."

No one's house had burned down, and Gander had been among the first to reach safety. Only Maum Anna had died. It was a death that my cousin and I would somehow have come to terms with, and quickly. Three days later, my mama insisted on peace and we apologized to each other immediately. During that time we'd both been witnessing the sad spectacle of the ample woman in the soot-smeared, flower-print dress—kneeling on the kitchen floor with the salvaged bits of her calendar spread out in every direction. Each of us, even enfeebled Grandpa, made some attempt to help, volunteering what we could remember about the organization and trying in vain to match up items, dates, lines, and inscriptions that had only made sense to her. Now, hopelessly jumbled, they made sense to no one at all. Finally, on the third afternoon, she looked up with tears in her eyes and asked me to get the Negro woman who lived in the old kitchen. Surely, the Negro woman could fix the calendar. Uncle Jimmy wasn't there, so I had no choice but to go to the parlor and shout in my pa's good ear that Mama was asking for Maum Anna.

"Anna's gone!" he shouted at the kneeling woman.

"Gone where?" she shouted back.

"Gone to Heaven!"

"No," she said. I helped her to her feet, and whispering, "No, no, no," she went and looked inside the empty kitchen building. She held my arm. Pa hadn't kept up.

"Anna?" she screamed. Then, releasing me, she rushed past my pa and back into the house, wailing and calling out for Anna as she went. Through all the rooms, including Grandpa's, she conducted this search and ended back in her own kitchen sobbing quietly. Pa caught hold of her at last.

"Gin," he said.

Of course, we'd all been to church by then, and Mr. Friendly had come to see us. In fact, he'd discussed the death of Maum Anna with my mama during his visit. He was summoned back, though, and spoke at length of God's mysterious will. By then, Mama was quite composed and offered refreshments, which the poor man greatly appreciated. Even before our apocalypse, Mrs. Friendly had been accusing herself of murdering Amy Mercy, and on the two nights since the fire, those passing the manse had heard her howling of poison. Of course, the preacher mentioned none of this, but the visit seemed to perk him up. After he left Mama ordered me to take all the pieces of the calendar outside and burn them. She went along to make sure I did, and when the pencil-marked papers began to blacken and curl into crisp ash, she called me Willie. By nightfall she was able to recall the names of the rest in the household. It was not a complete return of memory—far from it—but it was a start, and when she said, "Jim, Willie, I will not have you living as enemies beneath this roof," we apologized immediately.

I'd stated my case often enough, anyway, and my cousin readily allowed that his habits had gotten a bit dissolute.

In the future he'd keep his drinking under control. Of course, the main problem he faced now was money. All along he'd been wanting to join up and fight in France. This was his golden opportunity. The *Miss Liza* had vanished and Dr. McGill could survive without him. Unfortunately, a private's pay, even if he spent nothing on himself, wasn't sufficient to keep our family going. Much to his regret, Uncle Jimmy would accept the doctor's generous offer to purchase another freight boat and start over.

With me as a witness, my cousin made his resolutions— barely in time, I should add. The next day, Drake Bailey showed up and he came in uniform. It wasn't a convict's either. Drake was an army officer. He'd gotten in on the ground floor, and by a mysterious process not even he could explain, the bully ended up a lieutenant. Perhaps Judge Walker could have shed some light, but he remained silent—proud but silent. Drake hung around the mercantile showing off the uniform and drinking his usual share, but managing to maintain the dignity of an officer and a gentleman. Soon he'd be fighting the Hun to the death on sacred foreign soil. Maybe he'd even die a hero's death after he'd shot a couple thousand of the Teuton bastards and bedded all the mademoiselles in Paris.

Uncle Jimmy hung close by, and they conversed like long-lost buddies. Drake couldn't begin to understand the nature of my cousin's dilemma. He said I should quit school and take care of my parents. This war could be over quicker than anybody dreamed, and if my cousin fooled around much longer, he'd miss the whole turkey shoot. Uncle Jimmy shook his head no, but you could see he was sorely tempted. He didn't do quite as well on his pledge of moderation. On Drake's last night home they went on a rip that left my cousin groggy for several days.

I was back in school and back at the grocery. My pa spent

his days rocking in the parlor or on the porch, chatting with his old friend Mr. Britt. Apparently Captain Tom had no intention of going back on the water, and the turpentiner thought this a wise choice. He, too, claimed to be considering retirement. Brother was rousted out of our bedroom and put to work raking the charred stubble that had once been our front yard. No clocks remained to be fixed, and Mama, once again capable of needlepointing roses, felt any activity was better than none. Her reasoning was sound, but as Brother labored I would often see his head tilt. Sometimes he'd stop altogether and lean on the rake handle, staring heavenward. Apparently, the voices were demanding even more attention. I mentioned none of this to my mama, though. She had her hands full with the cooking and housework and the care of Grandpa. I don't think she could have managed without Liza. Yes, Liza.

The day after Mama burned the calendar, she put on her Sunday dress, walked down the street to the McGill house, and asked Liza to come to her aid. And Liza, who'd done nothing of a domestic nature in her entire life, now came every afternoon to do housework for the Allsons. I gave her a wide berth. I had problems of my own.

Gander and a few of the others teased me once or twice about burning down the town, but even they realized a disaster of this proportion wasn't a laughing matter. Anyway, they didn't truly blame me. Uncle Jimmy was accepting the responsibility, and they wouldn't have dared blame him. Some in the community did, but a surprising majority wrote the incident off as an act of God.

I should have been free and clear, but when I considered my actions following the ramming, I had difficulty settling on the exact nature of my relationship to this God. First, I'd mistaken that night of terror for the promises made in the Book of Revelations, assuming them to be the natural outcome of my carnal desires for Amy Mercy. Once corrected, I'd immediately thanked Jesus for preserving my parents, and then minutes later been unable to pray for them using my cross. Maum Anna, my protector, was gone. Perhaps this was a sign I'd been mistaken to put such faith in a somewhat heathen cross, especially now that the heathen was no longer around.

Perhaps my fear of The Hard to Catch Mercy had driven me away from the true Word of God. My parents seemed content with their Presbyterian faith, and in the end I made up my mind to visit Mr. Friendly and give him a censored version of my concern. I began to form a picture of Jesus, a Jesus something like Mr. Friendly—a lanky man with a crooked jaw, an ex-baseball player, only with the usual beard and long white robe. On the following Sunday afternoon, I went to the manse and knocked. But the door was opened by a shadow of the man I'd imagined. He wasn't even recognizable as the man I'd seen in church a few hours before.

"I come to see Mrs. Friendly," was all I could think to say.

"Follow me. Follow me, Willie T." Eager with pleasure, the preacher led the way to the bedroom where the woman lay propped up by two large pillows. Her face, thinned down to the bone, turned towards me, and at the moment of recognition, she brought her curled fingers to her blistered red lips.

"I did not poison the girl," she whispered. "It is not my fault."

"No, ma'am," I said. "It's nobody's fault."

"I wished for it!" she wailed.

"Was God's will," I assured her. "God's will." I was backing out the door, but before I fled the house completely, I stopped and told the preacher, "It ain't her fault."

The Sin of David

WE WERE finishing breakfast when Sammy appeared at the back door. Since he wouldn't enter, my mama went out at once to welcome him back. My cousin followed in her footsteps, and echoed her sentiments of regret at Anna's passing and joy at his return. Sammy seemed embarrassed by the attention. He chewed on his lip and looked at the ground. He let Uncle Jimmy shake his hand, but said nothing. Standing further off in the yard was a man I'd never seen.

He was large, barrel-chested, larger than my playmate, much larger in fact. And blacker, too. His skin was like soot, like stove polish, I should say, for it shone as if oiled. His hair was snow white and his eyes were sad and yellowed with age. An old man, soft-spoken, slow, David entered our lives with surprising ease.

"Miss Allson," he said, when the greeting of Sammy had ended. "I sure you ain't remember me. I David Allson. Some call me King David."

On coming outside my mama had nodded at the man. We'd all done that, but now she studied him in earnest, and after a moment's hesitation, replied.

"You're Anna's husband, aren't you? I remember you, David. Certainly, I remember you."

"Yes, ma'am, that so." He bowed to her, happy to be recalled. "Yes, ma'am, that me. I the one."

"Anna is sorely missed here. Our sorrow . . . Your sorrow . . ." Whatever the thought, my mama couldn't complete it and she turned away.

"Yes, ma'am," David called to her. "I come for ask you a favor. I ask it 'cause I know you an understanding woman."

My mama nodded but didn't speak.

"You know that me and Anna ain't live together for a long time, but I got it in my mind to stay in her house now that she gone." He pointed off at the old kitchen building. "Ain't for worry 'bout me. I take care myself. David got a trade." He paused to smile at my nervous playmate. "Maybe I teach this boy Sammy. Give him little something make he way in this world."

"You know you're welcome here, David. You'll always have a place with the Allsons."

"Thank you, ma'am. Thank you very much."

My mama smiled at him and nodded again. To my amazement she was inviting this stranger to live in our yard. I followed her back into the house to protest, but she assured me that despite considerable evidence to the contrary King David was a gentle person and would be good company for Sammy. Besides that, he was Anna's husband, and as such had a claim on the old kitchen. There was no use arguing with her. That was clear enough and I was already late for school.

When I got home from the grocery that evening, Sammy was helping David unload his possessions from the Texas cart. Actually, he didn't own many things. The two pairs of pants and the wool sweater could be carried under one arm, but they'd needed the cart in order to transport the grinding horse. Here was how David made his living, bent over a great gray grindstone set into a wooden frame and turned by the pumping of a foot treadle. He was a sharpener by trade. A keen sharpener.

"I a fine man with a blade," he boasted that evening as he straddled the horse and gave the wheel a quick spin. "Yes, sir, King David a fine man with a blade."

It wasn't a hollow boast. By then, I'd learned of David's reputation. The facts were well-known—he'd killed several men with knives and razors, and in the course of these encounters it was obvious he'd received substantial nicks himself. Four broad pale scars crisscrossed down his left forearm, and both sides of his neck showed two similar marks. They didn't quite meet, these last two. One was slightly higher than the other, but the pale slashes appeared so nearly fatal, I couldn't help but wonder why his head hadn't fallen off.

These scars hadn't concerned my mama, though. She'd seen them that morning, and when I mentioned them again that night, she assured me whatever David's past sins were, they were long in the past. She felt sure God had forgiven him, and it wasn't her place to pass judgment. She sent me out to the kitchen building with supper for our new tenant. I set the plate down on the step, knocked on the door, and backed away. I wasn't waiting around, especially not after dark, but he called me by name so I had to stop.

"This been sew up in the mattress," he said. "I know Anna want your ma to have 'em." He held the present out, insisting.

"What is it?" I asked.

"It for your ma. That what I know."

And so I received the gift, a narrow, long package

wrapped about several times in aging homespun. It was heavy, surprisingly so, and rose and fell disjointed in my hands like a snake, which for a second I feared it was. I even considered dropping it.

"Take 'em," David commanded. "Ain't nothing be 'fraid of."

Thus assured, I held fast to the package and discovered he was probably right. Whatever it was had no life of its own. It was only a gift from Maum Anna, a gift that I carried inside the house to where my mama sat rocking. I laid it in her lap, explaining as I did the source and what little else I knew. It wasn't alive or dangerous.

"Land's sake. It's heavy. What do you suppose is in there, Willie T.?"

"Money, I suppose. Gold dollars probably." I don't know why I guessed that, but it proved to be right.

My mama unrolled the cotton shroud from around the object and with patient and deliberate attention began her examination. It was a money belt of heavy stitched canvas, a belt made to fit tight against the wearer's middle and remain unseen. Midway on its length were the elaborately embroidered initials, J.C.

"Who can that be?" My mama was apparently more interested in the needlework than in what the belt might contain.

"Ain't Jesus Christ," I said.

"Willie T.!" She looked upon me as a true blasphemer.

"It's your pa, Captain Jack Cage," I said.

"Yes. I suppose it is."

"Couldn't be nobody else." When Maum Anna gave me the cross, she'd promised a second gift, a gift sent by the blockade-runner a half century before.

Mama emptied the belt of its contents, removing one by

one the twenty dollar gold pieces, which I then stacked in small piles at her feet. There were one hundred altogether.

"Two thousand dollars," I told her when the belt had been emptied. "And not one of them coins is dated after 1859."

"Merciful heavens! How could she have got them?" My mama asked this as if it were I who had been there and not her.

"She must have been wearing them when the captain sent her to be your nurse. I guess the five gold pieces were just a decoy to throw people off."

"What five pieces?"

"Maum Anna also carried five gold pieces in a little leather bag around her neck."

"I don't recall that."

"Grandpa took those five and you stole them back."

"I did?"

"Yes, ma'am."

"And Anna kept these other coins all this time? Why would she do that?"

"I don't know." I had to confess that at last Mama had exhausted my knowledge of her own life. "You want me to go out and ask David Allson if he knows?"

"Yes," she said. "Ask David."

David replied that he wasn't exactly sure what was in the package, but it had always looked like a money belt to him. Whatever it was, Maum Anna had promised Captain Cage that the Colonel wouldn't ever get the use of a single penny. By the Colonel, he meant Grandpa, because he pointed straight at our house.

"She promised your pa that Grandpa was never to benefit from them dollars," I told my mama. "I guess that promise is over 'cause Grandpa has outlived her."

"How sad," my mama reflected without saying exactly what was sad. "You know my father won her in a poker game."

"Yes," I said. "In Nassau Town."

"Savannah, I believe."

"No, ma'am. Maum Anna came out of Jamaica. She was in the salt works, nearby Nassau."

"She told me she was born and raised in Brunswick County, Georgia. She said she was her mistress's favorite, and had begged to be taken along on that trip to Savannah. Two pair won her. Threes and tens."

"Are you certain?"

My mama only smiled and shrugged.

"What'll we do with them dollars?"

"I have no earthly idea."

While we talked, Pa slept in his chair right beside us, so we had him there to study on as we plotted the future.

"He could get another boat. He could get five boats if he wanted them."

"He appears happy just so."

"You won't tell Grandpa, will you?"

"No, I won't tell him either. Put the money back in the belt. We'll hide it."

"In the well?"

"Not in the well. Land's sake, no. Never again in the well." She laughed a young girl's laugh, and for that one instant it's possible I glimpsed a person who by the accident of birth I could never truly know.

I suggested we keep the money belt a secret between us, but Mama knew how concerned Uncle Jimmy was for our well-being and told him that same night. All he said was, "Thank God." I could see it was as if the doors of a prison had swung wide open. He'd be enlisting.

The next evening Dr. McGill came around, because my cousin had gone immediately and told him about the windfall. The doctor wanted my mama to know that he loved all the Allsons dearly and would do nothing to jeopardize our financial stability. Gold shouldn't be kept hidden around a house, though, and if my mama would entrust him with her affairs, he'd see that our wealth was deposited into a Crowns Bluff bank account. He'd even arrange for her to receive a monthly allowance. I didn't voice my fear that he'd spend our fortune on invisible cotton, and she agreed to his proposal. He carried away the gold dollars and the money belt, and true to his word, looked after my parents from then on. Under those circumstances, we couldn't keep the money a secret, but my mama referred to it simply as an inheritance. I don't think either Grandpa or my pa ever bothered to ask more. It was manna from Heaven. The Allson due.

"Write me down to go to France," Uncle Jimmy whispered when the doctor walked out with the money belt, and a couple days later, he set out in his truck with Sammy at the wheel. I knew he was off to enlist, and though frightened at the prospect, I considered joining up myself. I was big enough, but still too young, and there was no denying that my parents needed me. It didn't really bother me until they returned late the next night and I discovered Sammy had joined up, too. This didn't seem fair, not at all.

I wasn't the only one who felt that way. When Liza found out what my cousin had done, she threw a tantrum and then a screaming fit, and wouldn't calm down until he agreed to marry her before setting out to chastise the Hun. Uncle Jimmy seemed to think this a trifle to pay for a little peace and independence, a shortsighted logic that I found hard to follow. Dr. McGill wasn't all that happy with the enlistment either, but he was delighted to be getting this new son-in-law. The marriage would take place when training camp was finished, in the two week period before my cousin would be sailing "over there." It was a tight schedule, but all of them agreed to make the best of it. Three mornings later Sammy and Uncle Jimmy were leaving in the truck for Crowns Bluff. From there, they'd take the train to camp. All the good-byes had been said, except mine, for I walked alongside the departing vehicle refusing to give up.

"This ain't fair," I said. "If Sammy gets to go, so should I." Sammy grinned at me. I don't think he understood why it wasn't fair.

"Guard the homefront, lad," Uncle Jimmy said. "I want you to look after Liza while I'm gone."

"Liza don't need no guarding."

"Take care of your ma."

"Liza's doing that." Much to my surprise Liza still came to the house every afternoon to help out.

"Watch David, then. Learn yourself a trade."

"I don't want no trade. This ain't fair."

"Nobody claimed it was going to be fair. They just said it'd be fun." He waved to me and told Sammy to speed up.

I ran a few hopeless steps and stopped. It wasn't fair or fun, not for me. But things were working out all right for my cousin. They always did.

Returning from the pasture that same morning I stopped to watch David Allson as he bent over his grinding horse. His leg was busy pumping and his hands, steady like an iron vice, moved the edge of an axe along the perimeter of the spinning stone. Sparks flew, tiny stars flying away from the honed steel edge. They sprung into our backyard where they burned out as quickly as they were struck.

At first, it was only the sparks that interested me. David didn't offer to teach me the sharpening trade, and I didn't ask to learn it. There was little need, for he'd quickly sharpened everything on our place—axes, adzes, scythes, a lot of old tools that were never used. He did all the kitchen knives and even my mama's scissors, and when nothing was left to sharpen for us, he started to work for everyone about. White people began to come to our backyard to have their implements sharpened, but Negroes came, too. Many Negroes came, and all during the day they could be seen bringing in their dull axes, hatchets, knives, and machetes, and carrying away glistening, finely honed weapons. That was how Grandpa saw it anyway. He'd been told of David Allson's presence and that the man worked a grinding horse, but it made no impression. From his bedroom window the old man could see the Negroes leaving our yard, and he soon began to mutter and raise up from his bed on his elbows.

"The Allsons are arming the Negroes," Grandpa declared to anyone who'd listen. "The Allsons are arming the Negroes. Cannibals. Savages. I have warned you all. The Isle of Negroes. The Isle of Negroes . . ."

My mama just smiled at the old man, and for several days assured him nothing was wrong. But, finally, she decided to let him see for himself. She helped him dress and with me as a guide, he was sent out into the backyard to meet the grinder. Frailer than ever, he tottered with every step, but he understood the purpose of the trip. He knew where we were going and why, and David had been warned he was coming.

"Grandpa, this is David Allson." I made the introductions. David stood to one side of the wheel, his head slightly bowed.

"Afternoon, Colonel, sir." David nodded his head a notch lower.

"Where is he?" Grandpa bellowed.

"I right here." David spoke louder and looked up to search out Grandpa's face.

"Where is he? I see no one. Where is this grinder? Where is this man who is sharpening the weapons for the other Negroes?"

"Ain't weapons, Captain. Just axe, tool, thing like that."

"This is him." I held Grandpa by the forearm and pointed my finger straight at David Allson. The two men were only three feet apart, and I was absolutely certain that the old man wasn't blind.

"Take me inside. I see the grinding wheel is still here. The man has fled. When he returns for the wheel you must be ready to spring the trap. Do you understand me?"

"Yes, sir," I said and leading the old man back inside, I helped my mama put him back to bed.

Soon after, David Allson came tapping at the back door and had to be assured that Grandpa wasn't blind, only confused. Then he had to be assured it wasn't necessary for him to leave. I did suggest, for the sake of harmony, that in the future his Negro customers approach and leave the backyard from behind the barn. He didn't ask why, but agreed readily. He bowed to my mama and retired for the night.

The next morning as I passed on my way to do the chores, he called me over to his doorstep. This was the time of morning when he sat, meditated, and smoked his pipe before getting down to the day's work. A nod and "morning" had been our usual exchange.

"She coming back," he said. "Anna coming back."

"Most think she's drowned." I assumed he knew that. I assumed he was talking about her ghost, but I didn't want to hear him say it and wished he'd only nodded.

"They say she coming back 'cause she ain't got a decent

burial. No Christian burying. That ain't so, boy. She ain't expecting none. Got no burial orders. Got no apron. Anna know she ain't for bury. She done made that deal with Jesus, though. She done gone straight up to Heaven like she knew she would and now she coming back."

"Glad to hear that." Could this be true? Somehow, the confrontation with the Red Dragon and my visit to the Friendly's house had left me surer of myself. I'd even begun to wonder if ghosts truly existed.

"She ain't expecting to bury, but she ain't expecting to leave so sudden-like. Anna got business to tend to. I going wait here for that visit. Your ma ain't mind. She a good, patient woman. Always been that way."

If the unfinished business was protecting me from The Hard to Catch, that didn't sound bad, but I still had my doubts about the spirit world. In fact, I was so busy considering the matter that it took a while for the comment "always been that way" to sink in.

"How long you known my ma?" I asked.

He didn't answer.

"How long you say you known my ma?" I asked again.

David Allson tapped the ashes out of his pipe, slipped it inside the doorway, and picking up a heavily rusted scythe, took his place on the grinding horse and went to work. That was the end of that day's conversation, but in the mornings to come there'd be others. As I walked away he'd begun to sing to himself in a very low voice, a spiritual of undetermined length. I say undetermined because I realized he was still singing the same song when I passed that way a good forty minutes later. The sparks flew from the edge of the grinding stone and the scythe looked shiny new.

The next morning we spoke again.

"Jesus been a powerful man." That was one of the first

things David Allson had to tell me. He wasn't talking about powerful in spirit, though. He meant Jesus was a strong man.

"Big arms. Arms big 'round as another man's thigh and a chest wide as a wagon wheel." David sat on his stoop and clenched his pipe between his teeth so that he was free to show me with both hands spread just how much bigger Jesus was than he. The blue smoke rose out of the bowl, past his yellowed eyes, shiny forehead, and snow white hair, and was lost in the pale blue mist of morning. "I a big man." That was true. When he removed the pipe from his mouth it disappeared inside his fist. "You see that. I big, but Jesus twice as big as David. Jesus hit a man, that man stay down." The old Negro clenched the pipe in his teeth once more, leaving him free to drive a fist into his open palm with considerable force. "That ain't all. No, sir. Jesus got a head like a rock. They tell you Peter been the rock. Jesus been the rock. Yes, sir. Rock hard." David tapped his own forehead. "When He butt head, He always win. Ain't no fair contest. Can't be, 'cause He the Son of God. He ain't tell the folks that right off, though. He butt head and knock the other fellow cold every time. Then He take the money and go off laughing. That the kind of man He been. He don't mind trick a few. He trick 'em for they own good. You know 'bout the fight with Samson and Hercules, ain't you, boy?"

I had to admit I didn't.

"Anna ain't tell you that story?"

"No, sir."

"What kind of instruction she give you, boy?"

"She might a told me and I forgot."

"That seem most likely. You remember Jesus been double-jointed? You ain't forgot that?"

"No, sir," I lied.

"Well, that how He do it. Samson and Hercules, they both claiming they the strongest man in the world, but they done made a pact, agreement between gentlemen, that they won't fight with each other. That how they work it out, and then Jesus come along and they start hearing the story about Him being the true Son of God and the strongest living man. They jealous. That natural. They can't stand to hear this kind of talk so they come together and they arrange to catch up with Jesus in a dark place when He all alone. Then the two of them together going to settle the question.

"Two against one. That just how it turn out. They start out talking peaceable, just joking 'bout different thing and then when Jesus turn He back, Samson throw he arm 'round Jesus neck and squeeze down hard. That enough to break an ordinary man—squish 'em flat, crack 'em like a pecan—but Jesus just laugh and flip 'em over He head. Whump." David got to his feet to show me this maneuver and worked it out slow so I'd understand exactly. He ended with a healthy slap to his own thigh before sitting down again. "Hercules on 'em now, though. He step in from behind the same way, coming from behind and he grab Jesus 'round the chest and he squeeze hard. Enough to cut the wind from an ordinary man, but Jesus, He just hold He breath and puff up." David halted his tale long enough to puff his cheeks as Jesus had done and expelled the air with a loud puff. "Pop Hercules off 'em like a tick off a dog back. Pop." The old Negro snapped the fingers of one large fist in my face. "Pop. Hercules done flip off.

"They ain't through, though. No, sir. They getting mad now. These two gentlemen getting mad. They ain't planning on killing Jesus at first. First they just going to teach 'em a lesson, but now they seeing blood. They come on Him both together, and that when they discover the truth 'bout Jesus being double-jointed. One got a arm pulling one way and the other pulling the other way. They pulling so high up them two arm of Jesus should be breaking off. Then Jesus arm just twist 'round and 'round like a windmill, and He spin 'em both off and throw 'em against the side of the house. He bloody 'em good that time, and they mad. Yes, they mad as can be. Hercules pick up a bottle. That be bad, but Samson pull a razor. He pull out a razor and start flipping it about, laughing at Jesus. Except he don't know that Jesus have a razor in He shoe. He carry a razor for just such occasion as this and when he see what coming, Jesus slip it out and now it He turn to laugh." David showed me how Jesus laughed by laughing himself, and then began to draw imaginary slashes through the air with the stem of his pipe. "He bring that razor 'round this way and 'round that way, and He slice them two up and down, and when they leave that alley they ain't never mess with Jesus no more 'cause they agree He is the strongest man and the Son of God."

I couldn't help noticing that David took his own story to heart, and when it was done, he'd absently run the pipe stem along one of the broad scars circling his throat. This gesture gave me the courage to ask him about his marks.

"How'd you get your scars?" I tried to make the question seem everyday and casual. "Oh, by the way, how'd you get your own throat cut?"—something like that.

"I ain't know for sure," he said after a brief hesitation. "I ain't remember how I get 'em all. Must be fight. I figure I must be fight with some fellow."

"You ever kill anybody?" I tried to make this an everyday question as well. I already knew he'd killed several.

"Killed six fellow," he said. "David done kill six head."

"What was you fighting about?"

"Shu boy, I ain't remember for certain. I kill one 'cause it a Tuesday. I kill one 'cause I ain't like the way he crack he teeth. I ain't know 'bout the rest. The women probably. Must be the women."

I nodded as if to say those seemed like reasonable enough reasons. "Nobody ever arrested you?"

"Twice," he answered with a note of pride. "Twice they lock David up, but the captain come for get 'em. Ain't going to sail without David. He too good a man to leave behind."

"You never been to trial then?"

"Trial? Shu boy, I ain't studying on no trial. Ain't but one judge David going stand before and that Jesus Christ. Yes, sir, David done talk with that judge already. He done pray to be forgiven. David done want that washing in the blood of the lamb. He want to be innocent as the newborn. He want to take his place inside them pearly gate. He done beg to sit at the feet of the Master. Yes, sir, boy. He done try but David guilty. David going to Hell. The devil got he soul. Done had he soul for a long time and now David studying on Eternity."

Our morning interview had come to an end. Without saying more he went to his grinding horse and began to arrange himself for the morning's work. Already he'd begun to hum. It was useless to ask more questions and besides, I'd have to run through my chores to get to school on time. Tardiness was the one sin Superintendent Baker wouldn't forgive.

"Jesus loved the women." That's what David told me the next morning. "Do boy, that man love the women. They don't tell you 'bout that in the Bible, but that man love the women. He a natural man. They tell you that much. They tell you that God done put 'em in the womb of Mary so He come birthing out a natural man. You know He have all the desires of a man and since He the Son of God, He got some extra desire thrown in. He love the women and they love him right back. I don't expect Maum Anna told you this, now did she?"

I admitted she hadn't.

"Don't make sense she would. Ain't something a woman going to admit to, 'specially not that woman. No, sir, she ain't going to tell you the whole truth 'bout Jesus. She always going to hold a little bit of the truth back. That the nature of a woman, ain't it, boy?"

I admitted that it probably was.

"That what the fight all about. When he fight with Samson and Hercules, that what they fighting about. They say it who the strongest, but everybody know it just women they fighting over. They know about Jesus. Jesus getting 'round. He can't stop Heself. Even if He want, He can't stop, and after that fight ain't nobody else to stop 'em. He go right on and love the women. Mary Magdalene the one he love the most, though. She the one He acknowledge. Them children the ones that call Him Pa, but He have plenty more children 'cause He always stepping up the road. It tell you that in the Bible. He a traveling man. Galilee to Jerusalem. He always traveling." The old Negro had finished and was starting to knock the bowl of his pipe clean. I knew this was a bad sign, so I asked my question.

"You traveled around a lot yourself, ain't you?"

I'd heard rumors, so I wasn't surprised when he nodded his head yes. I was surprised, though, at the extent of his travels. "They talking 'bout this World War. I seen 'em. Seen the whole world 'fore the war start up." Yes, David had been a great traveler. He'd been to seven countries. He couldn't remember all their names but England was one and Cuba was another. He'd been a rough-and-ready fellow in his early days, but in old age he'd settled down and been working most of the last dozen years on a paddle-wheel steamer around Mobile, Alabama.

"Yes, sir, boy. Just like Jesus. David been a traveling man. Ever since he been a free man, he been traveling. He been on all kind of vehicle. All kind of vehicle. Anything that float, David been on 'em. Been on automobile, too. Every kind of locomotive they ever was. Bicycle, roller skates, wagon and cart, merry-go-round. Ain't never been in no airplane. That the one I ain't travel on. David ain't never going up in the air. No." The old man paused and for a moment I thought he'd rise, but then he turned to face me and asked a solemn question. "You know what, boy?"

"No, sir," I said. He appeared so grave I was almost afraid to ask. "What?"

"They all got wheels. All them vehicle. Even the boat got wheel. Propeller ain't nothing but a wheel. Paddle wheel. That a wheel, sure enough. All them vehicle got wheel for take you place, so I always going. Then one day, ain't so long ago, Jesus come to me and He say, 'David, I ain't got but one more wheel for you and that the grindstone.'" David's solemn countenance gave way to a grin and then an outright laugh, and he pointed at his grinding contraption with particular pleasure. "Jesus say, 'Go back where you start, David. I want you to finish your traveling with this here grinding wheel.' So I do 'em. I got me a vehicle here. I got this grinding horse. Just stay where you put 'em. The wheel turn 'round and 'round but David ain't go no place. No place at all."

I laughed along with him as he rose up from the stoop and steadied himself in the doorway. I could see he was truly happy to be stationary at last. He had a home. He had a sunny spot where he could sit and work. I'd turned away, certain he was through for the day, but he wasn't.

"That the curse Anna put on me." He sounded grave once more. "Always moving. 'David,' she say to me. 'You a young man now, but you going grow old and you ain't never going to have no peace from this day forward. You always going to be moving. Turning like a wheel. Just traveling.' She know I love her and she do that to me."

"Why so?" It was an amazing declaration to begin with, but I was doubly surprised to hear Anna had known David when he was young.

"Shu. I ain't know that. Don't ask me what on a woman mind. Ask me anything but that, boy." This time I knew our conversation was ending for he was easing a leg over the grinding horse and settling in to go to work.

There was a mystery here all right. I was more and more certain of it. Here was a missing part. Something Uncle Jimmy didn't know or maybe anybody else, and I was bound and determined to get to the bottom of it. For solving mysteries, though, you needed clues, and I stumbled on one first thing the next morning.

"When did Maum Anna tell you about the money belt?" He had already said he suspected the packaged gift was a belt, and now he answered the question without hesitation.

"That money belt? Well, I can't say she ever did tell me about 'em. Not exactly. I kind of discover 'em on my wedding night." That was all he said. This was obviously an intimate occasion that he wasn't interested in discussing further. I had to guess, and I guessed right.

"She was wearing it?"

"That so." He chuckled and nodded congratulations in my direction. "I pull the dress up over her head, and that all she have on underneath. Nothing but that belt strapped round her waist and 'em chain between her ankle."

"Chain?" I was truly surprised by this. "You talking about slavery days?"

" 'Course I is."

"I thought you was Anna's last husband."

"No, boy. Who tell you that? I ain't her last husband. I her first husband. She have two more after me. Look like, now, I going to be first and last." This thought got him chuckling again and so I took the liberty of asking more. How did he come to marry Anna?

"I been the boss man favorite. I the Colonel's favorite man." David motioned to the house where Grandpa was lying in the bed. "I ain't but twenty years old, maybe. I big as full grown, but I a young man. I a young man and that when the old driver run off. The Colonel come to me and give me the whip. He say, 'David, I trusting you to do right by me. These is terrible times when you can't trust your own not to run off!' Well, sir, I take the whip, but I know I ain't need 'em. Ain't nobody on my crew but ten women and three men, and two of them men was so old can't work or run neither. It a easy task for me, I tell you that. I had 'em cutting firewood for the salt making. Keep a fire going night and day right down there on the creek bank. All the time we keep the fire going, boiling water down to nothing but salt. That why it ain't hard for the old driver to run off. Most done gone already. The boat men, all 'em fellow gone. Then the old driver walk off and leave the fire heself. He make a little raft and paddle off to the blockade ship."

"They was that close?"

"Stand on the point you can see the ship light. Ain't far. Them the ship Abraham Lincoln done sent to set the people free. Lot of the men done go. Boatmen go. The old driver go, but I ain't see no reason for run off. I getting fed. I ain't working myself, and I got the women. Out the ten I got six young gal and they mine anytime I want. What for I run? I hear 'em talking 'bout freedom. I just laugh. I 'bout as free as a man going get. That what I telling myself anyway. That when Anna come. She come on the wagon chain up and the Colonel there, he want to give her to me. That fine. That just fine, but it don't work that way. This new gal tell your grandpa to he face that she ain't having nothing else to do with salt, even if it's just cutting the wood to boil the water. She say she gone beyond that. Your ma agree with her." David pointed off in the direction of our house and smiled. "Anna stay in the house. I ain't see her 'cept that one time, but that all it take. Boy, I in love. You know 'bout love, don't you? You know how that make a man do fool things."

I nodded yes. For once I did know.

"When I see I ain't going to get her no other way, I propose to the gal. She just laugh at me, but I know what I want and I keep coming and proposing every evening and finally she say yes, and we been married by a true preacher, a white preacher. I promise then to forsake all others for this one gal. I figure she worth it. She were. Yes, she were. How many husband pull up they wife dress on the wedding night and find a girdle with a hundred twenty-dollar gold pieces in 'em?"

"Not many, I reckon." He knew exactly what the belt held, but he'd given it to us anyway.

"That surprise me. Yes, sir. That a surprise. Already I starting to figure I getting gal and money, and maybe I take a boat after all and row us on out to the other side. Go up North somewhere and spend that money. Cut the chain off the gal's feet. Maybe I try some of this freedom they all talking 'bout. That just what I tell her afterwards. I tell her then, 'cause I quite satisfied with my new wife. I more than satisfy." This reflection brought a short pause. He relit his pipe and then, without prompting from me, went on. "You know what she say, boy? You ain't even going guess. That gal just laugh at me. She say that ain't our money. That money for Captain Cage daughter and Anna ain't worry about no chain. She tell me she can step out them chain anytime she want. She say she know how to grow wing. When she feel like it she can grow them wing right out her back and fly to Africa. She ain't need me. She ain't need no paddleboat.

"She scare me. Right then on my wedding night she scare me good, 'cause I see for the first time that she do have them powers. Some of the other one already suspect it, but I ain't listen to 'em. Now I got to believe 'cause I married to her and I can see they telling the truth. That gal know all the roots. She come here, she know 'em. She get off the boat, she know 'em. That same night she make water boil in the pot without fire. She do that just so I know. She know all. She handle the serpent, put spell on people, make 'em disappear and come back. She see the future and the past. She talk every tongue that be. Every man and animal. She talk with alligator and cat, don't matter. She converse with the seen and the unseen, the supernatural in all its form. Haint, ghost, haig, witch, apparition of every kind. The dead and living. Make no difference. She make 'em come and go when she please.

"'Course, the people start to seek her now. They come at night, you know. Come to our cabin to get the conjure and the turn back root. She a good woman. I can see that. Everybody all 'round here can see that. She ain't hurt nobody less absolutely necessary, but I still scared. Can't help be scared of a woman like that. She satisfy. Lord, she satisfy, but she scare me still with all that talking about Africa, 'specially when she say she going to grow them wing and go flying back just for visit. Take a short home visit and put me on her back. Fly across the ocean, see Africa."

"Maum Anna?" I couldn't help but interrupt. "She was from Africa? She truly was?"

"Boy, where else she going come from? She talk all about Africa. Not the jungle part. The grassy wilderness, the pasture where all them different animals is running free. She call that home, and she speak the funny words with the Old Sister. They talk about Africa all the time. She call the Old Sister 'countrywoman.' That all I know for certain about Anna. She from Africa."

Apparently our interview for the day was over, for he'd tapped the pipe empty once more and was rising. I had to ask my last question quickly.

"You said she cursed you? Why would she do that?"

"I ain't know why," he said in an offhand manner. "I ain't know why a woman do anything. I tell you this, though. I know the curse wearing off last year. I in Mobile and I could feel it losing the grip. That why I come back. I came back here three week before the woman go. I come at night to this same little house where she been sleeping.

"Lord, I ain't recognize the woman. She shrunk down so. Folk 'round here tell me she grow some more after I leave. They say she shrunk down more than I know. She low. I see that. I see them powers 'most gone. I ask her where they go and she say she give up them powers for Jesus Christ. I agree that the sensible thing to do. Only way to get to Glory. That what she tell me. Still it sad to see her shrunk down. It sad. Then she go and take that same boat ride she won't take with me. I ain't think she expecting that ride. That why I come back here to stay. I ain't think she quite satisfy with how this world turn out."

David had had his say, and now he seated himself at the grinding horse and began a low song. Still, I knew that if I was patient I'd learn the whole story. Actually, it only took about a day's worth of patience, because the next morning, he was waiting. He called me by name, though he must have known I was headed his way.

"She back," he said at once. "Last night she come. I know she coming. I know she ain't been satisfy. She ain't satisfy with this world and she ain't satisfy with the next. Ain't no woman ever is. Lord knows that, and if He ain't know it before, He know it now."

"How does she look?" I was half inclined to believe him and really wondered how she would look.

"She look good. She look fine. She still little. Shrunk up, but she ain't so weak as she been, and she got them wing. Great wing with silver feathers that go sweeping down 'cross the floor. That her main complaint. Them wing." The old black man stood up long enough to demonstrate the wings. Then he sat back on the stoop. "They so sure she going to Heaven they take her measurement when she still a tall woman, and now she done shrunk up, the wing too big. She have trouble flapping 'em, and she always bumping into them things in Heaven. She claim there a lot of furniture up there. She figures it be more open field. She counting on them open savannah like she remember from Africa. Pasture with all them different animal running free. She figure it going to be more open, but she say most parts is very closed in and they is all kind of sofa and chair and piano to go bumping into. She been graceful person down here. You remember that. She been a easy-moving person, so she ain't happy 'bout bumping 'round things. She done talk to St. Peter 'bout it. She done carry her complaint right on up to Jesus Christ, and she said He a fair and reasonable man, but He sitting on the right hand of God, and if they starts to move the furniture around, His chair could get shifted. She say she could see the man's point of view, but she tell Him, as respectful as she capable, that God's throne weren't nailed down and that if they shift it back up into the clouds 'bout a hundred miles, might give folks a chance to breathe.

"Jesus say, 'No, daughter. That ain't possible.' But He agreed that an argumenting woman could make a place seem more crowded than it truly is." David laughed out and slapped his knee. "Now my Anna can see she ain't going change things, and she ain't going be happy there. She done shook off the water of the grave and walk up that golden ladder and through them pearly gate. She done said her hellos to St. Peter and got them wings that been too big. She done talk with all the saints and touch the remnant of her Savior. She done look on the radiant face of God Hisself, and most important she done got to talk with her own dead mama. She did glory in that, but it weren't just right. You know her ma still a young woman and Anna 'bout a hundred and something. Can't be like a daughter talking to her mama. Was the other way 'round. Still, they enjoy it. They say all them things they both been saving up to say, but afterwards, Anna still know she ain't going to be happy there. Too much furniture. Too many white people, too. She expecting some. She always a generous woman. She figure plenty going to get in but not this multitude. White people and furniture. Her whole life ain't been nothing but that. She told Jesus Himself, and He said if she weren't happy, she welcome to fly back to Africa.

"Anna ain't know if the man mocking her. She ain't know,

but she tell Him right to He face that she would surely go if God give His blessing. Jesus get up out of He chair. He step over to He left, and He converse with God for a long time. Then He come back and He say, "Yes, daughter." He tell Anna God done look her up in He ledger. God been well pleased with her conduct down here, and she done earned His blessing. If it please Anna, she can fly back to Africa, and God going arrange it so that when she get there, the place be exactly the way she remember 'em.

"Weren't but one problem, then. Them wing. They is too big and heavy for such a long trip. She ain't got the strength to make it, not yet, she ain't. She able to fly straight back up to Heaven, but that all she can manage for now. There ain't no room in Heaven for practice, so she going keep flying up and down 'til she certain she have the power built up to make the long crossing."

"She'll be coming again?" I asked.

"Every night. She be coming every night 'til she ready."

"Could I see her?" Did I believe him? If there was even the slightest chance to see her, I wasn't going to pass it up.

"No. She say you musn't look. Ain't for you to see. And she say you must promise not to tell your mama. Anna ain't want her to know that she disappointed in Heaven."

"I promise," I said. "I got to go now, but I promise I won't say nothing about this." For once it was me who was going to have to end the conversation. If I didn't get Ruth milked and out to pasture right then, I'd be late for school.

"Wait!" David shouted after me.

"I'll be late."

"You wait, boy. Anna say I must tell you about my sin. She done listen every morning. She hear everything I tell you. She say it ain't right I should leave out my sin."

I returned to squat down beside the stoop. The chores

could wait, for I had to know what sin could possibly separate itself out of David's hellraising life to the point it could be called "my sin."

"I kill them six men. I done told you that, but I pay the price for every one." He ran a finger down the broadest of the scars on his forearm. "Ain't a one of them fellow been a saint. I tell you that. Yes, sir. I done kill 'em and I done mess with a lot of women, but that just been my nature. Ain't nothing there Jesus Christ Hisself can't look past. I know that and Anna done told me so herself last night. I got one sin though, boy, one I ain't told you 'bout at all. You see they call me King David back then before I marry Anna. They call me King David 'cause I got the whip and I got all the women. It meant to be a mean tease, but I ain't care. I like the sound of it 'til Anna come. After that, they call me David again. And I satisfied with that 'cause I satisfied with my life with this new gal. Then she gone. One night she done slip off with your mama. She ain't say where she going. She ain't even say good-bye. She just gone.

"I mix up at first. I mope 'round for a week and then I start to get mad, and when I get very mad I get crazy. I tell you there be six women work under me. I can have them six anytime. I could go see 'em right then. I ain't need Anna. There be six women but I want seven. I got one woman name Hattie married to the man Louis. Louis the only man I got worth anything and the only reason that he ain't run off is 'cause of Hattie. I been looking on Hattie long time. Long time before Anna come. She a good-looking woman. Good looking, but I don't want trouble with Louis so I let her be 'til that time Anna run off. Then I gets so mad I got to have Hattie too, and I tell her so. 'Course she say no. She Louis's woman. I tell her I can fix that quick. That same night I whip Louis. Ain't no reason. I whip Louis twenty lashes with the rawhide. I open he back up some, but not so serious. He don't cry out and he ain't faint. When I go to cut him down I whisper in he ear that he better run, 'cause they worse coming the next night and worse than that if he still 'round."

"Well, that all it take. He know something up, and he figure it have to do with Hattie. He know it have to do with Hattie when I lock him and the gal up separate. He know I got the devil in me then, but he don't say nothing at all. He just run. That night he paddle off to join Mr. Lincoln's navy. I sitting by the fire when he leave. I watch him go." David paused to indicate the scorched area beyond our house, the spot that had once been my pa's landing. "I watch him go. He take a couple log and make a little raft. He weak from the beating, but I ain't care if he drown. He getting a chance. He going to be a free man and I getting Hattie.

"Ain't work out that way. No. Ain't work that way at all. Hattie, she ain't have me that night or the next. I ain't going to force her, 'cause I figure there weren't no need. A week time, she forget about Louis. Most them women ain't too dependable. I going to wait. I ain't count on Louis, though. I ain't figure him to be such a tricky fellow. He come back three nights later and sneak her out. They both caught right on that creek there." He pointed again. "Right out yonder. The Provost row 'em down. They drag 'em up to the shore and hang 'em both right there on the bank. Provost leave 'em hanging as a warning to the others.

"The Colonel furious mad. That old man, he claim the Provost steal he property. Claim the government of them Confederates owe him a thousand dollars. Ain't matter. Two more days, the war over. Everybody free then. Everybody free to do what they want. I cut 'em down myself. I free to cut down Louis and Hattie. They know 'bout me, though. All my people call me King David to my face. All the gal turn they back on me. The men been coming home. They say they going to get me. They just waiting. They say I done commit the sin of David. I done like King David, the true King David. He want Bathsheba for heself so he send the husband into battle to be smite by the enemy and die. Only difference I ain't get the wife. I done cause the death of a good man. I done got the husband and the wife smite and ain't get nothing out of it. Ain't no adultery. It the sin of David, but I done turn 'em inside out.

"I ain't know what to expect then, but I hoping Anna coming back. I thinking she going forgive me. She going to protect me. It ain't that way, no, sir. Ain't that way at all. She come home, all right. She learn what I done, and she spit on me and curse me. She say, 'King David, you always going be traveling. I going fix you up with them wheels of Zekiel. Them fiery wheels going be spinning you along all your life. You ain't ever going know peace in this world.'" David stopped speaking and for a moment I thought he was going to rise and go to the wheel.

"You understand me, boy?"

"Yes, sir," I said.

"Good. Anna say you a smart boy. She say she raise you up to understand. She say I must tell you so you understand."

"I do." I nodded, though I wasn't sure that I did understand it all.

"She done talk me a deal with Jesus. She know I a changed man, but she know I bound for Hell. Ain't no natural way to be saved from the sin I done. She tell me that last night." He nodded his head back through the open doorway. "She standing in there at the fire, warming her front. All I see them great silver wings turned to me, and that little bit of head with the white kerchief on 'em.

"She say, 'Brother Allson.' She call me that even though I

her legal husband David. Everybody up there Brother and Sister, you see. She say, 'Brother Allson, I done make a deal with Jesus. 'Fore I go flying off, I done make arrangement to keep you out of Hell.' You see, she done gone to Jesus and she ask His pardon for me. 'Cause it is her who is asking He give it careful consideration and after some more coaxing He agree. Jesus say it seem like the only thing I good for is killing men. I done kill six. I kill one more for him then He let me in Heaven. I taking that offer, Willie. I ain't so particular as Anna 'bout what Heaven like. I kill that one just to stay out of Hell." David did rise now. He was finished for the day.

"What one?" I asked. "Who?"

"I ain't know. Jesus say it the devil hisself. He tell Anna that David know when the time come. He say the spirit going move me."

The grinding had begun. A double-headed axe was laid firm against the wheel and the sparks began to fly. I couldn't think of what to say, so I got up and stood there.

"Them sparks like shooting stars, ain't they boy?" He hadn't begun to sing this time.

"Yes, sir," I agreed.

"Them shooting stars is the tears of God. That's what Anna tell me and the Old Sister say that, too. That what they say in Africa. That just an old people saying. God ain't got no tear. Jesus do all the work. God ain't even look down here. He sitting on that throne with He hand in He pocket. Yes, sir, I know that gentleman. Ain't in His nature to shed no tear."

I took Ruth out to pasture, and even though I ran the whole way back, I was still late for school. Superintendent Baker asked me why, and I lied and said I was running an errand for my mama. That afternoon and the next morning and for several more mornings, I asked David to elaborate on this last discussion, but he shook his head no. From the beginnings of our talks, I guess, I'd felt safer with him around. He was there not only to solve riddles, but to protect, and one way or another Maum Anna had brought him there. Yes, after careful consideration, I knew I wanted Maum Anna to still be looking after me. I'd depended on her for sixteen years. She'd been my guardian angel, and she'd done the best she could. Life had been pretty rough on the Allsons, but still she'd been the angel for us all. And now she was truly in a position to carry out her duties. Finally, I came out and asked David point blank what I'd been figuring all along.

"It's The Hard to Catch Mercy? It's James Mercy that you're supposed to kill, ain't it?"

"I hear 'bout that one," he admitted.

"Did Maum Anna tell you?"

"I hear 'bout 'em."

"It's him, ain't it?"

"I done tell you, boy. I ain't got no idea who this devil going be. Jesus say when the time come the spirit going move me. That all I know. Don't ask me 'bout what on Jesus mind. Ain't for David to know."

By this time, the old black man had lost all patience with me on that subject. He admitted Anna was still flying down each night but said I absolutely could not peek in.

"Here, boy," he said at last. "Take this."

It was a small silver feather, a tiny piece of work, more like down than a true feather. Delicate. Every rib was clearly marked, and all so light that it threatened to float out of the palm of my hand. In the days to come, I'd need it to remind me—"Silver for things of silver, and stone for things of stone."

Liza's Wedding

MRS. Friendly hung herself. Most people figured this to be about the worst that could happen in our little village. "She'd been quite despondent" is what they said. They also said she and Amy Mercy appeared amazingly similar in death. I didn't look, and when Gander suggested the preacher's wife had really poisoned the girl, I struck him hard. Gander survived. I apologized and heard no more about Amy Mercy being poisoned by anyone. We buried Mrs. Friendly in a well-attended ceremony. I was a pallbearer. A preacher from Mumford said the words. Mr. Friendly wept.

Some felt this to be the beginning—the beginning of the unraveling—but David Allson claimed the tragedy started up about ten days later. Uncle Jimmy and Sammy had returned from training camp, both sporting new uniforms and just waiting for a boat trip to France. David said seeing Sammy grown up had done something to Maum Anna. She'd been unusually quiet that night, and he thought she was feeling poorly, especially when the sun rose and she still sat warming by the fire. She wasn't sick, though. She'd been waiting on the sun. "I going today. I going home."

She bid him farewell, flopped about the barnyard for a few discouraging minutes, and then with strong steady flaps of those great wings, she rose above the trees and began to circle.

"Oh, she shine so. She shining with the radiance of the pure in heart. Yes, it blind the sinner to see the sun bouncing off them multitude of silver feathers, and her drifting 'round and 'round with them slow easy strokes. 'Bout dozen times she go 'round like that, and then she take one last look down at me, and she strike off to the southeast straight for Africa."

It was a wonderful sight, but one that put spots dancing in his eyes and left him weak. When Mama brought his lunch plate, she found David in the bed. She summoned Dr. McGill. The old Negro smiled and refused the doctor's remedies. The next day he returned to the grindstone. The dizzy spells hadn't left him, though. Now, he rose later and some days wouldn't begin work until midmorning. He didn't complain because his deal with Jesus was made, and once that business was complete, Heaven would be waiting. David would be fine. It was Grandpa who had suffered as a result of the grinder's illness. If David hadn't been lingering in the cabin that particular morning, he would have spotted Grandpa. He apologized for this over and over, and over and over I assured him it wasn't his fault or Maum Anna's either. Even if our angel had truly gone off to visit Africa, I figured she'd left us in David's hands and he'd done the best he could. It wasn't his fault. I told him it was an act of God. Of course, I didn't believe that either. I knew whose fault it was and exactly when the curtain had gone up on this villainous happening.

It didn't start with Mrs. Friendly's hanging or Maum Anna's departure, nor as some said, with Grandpa's decision to let the hogs in his corn. Perhaps it is a mistake even to search out first causes. How can we be certain that first cause is the culprit? Perhaps it is the second or third cause, or a cause as immediate as the moment preceding catastrophe.

With Grandpa I knew the cause was almost immediate, for our trouble began the moment the boar was returned. True, Grandpa had hogged his corn the fall before. Once the last of the good ears were picked, he'd opened the field to Mr. Britt's hogs and in exchange got both a sow and the loan of Mr. Britt's boar, Ajax. Grandpa was more than satisfied. After all, Ajax was a prized breeder—a stringy animal with narrow haunches and a broad chest. "A thinking animal." Uncle Jimmy said that because the hog was half head. It was a joke. Extending up on each side of the great snout were curving tusks that suggested no thought beyond wanton destruction. The wide pointed ears had been ripped to shreds in countless encounters with dogs and God knew what else. A thick mane of coarse black bristles began at the head, ran uninterrupted down the back, and petered out at the tail.

"Meanness," Uncle Jimmy observed.

"Spirit," Grandpa commended.

Anyway, they weren't looking to show, and an animal capable of living on pine roots and killing a few dogs on the side was about perfect. In fact, Grandpa thought Mr. Britt's offer foolishly generous, at least until Ajax arrived and refused the sow. Uncle Jimmy had called out encouragement, and the old man had muttered complaints. But Ajax ignored both them and the sow—right up to the night he chewed through a plank two inches thick and disappeared from the pen.

Good riddance. I was the one tending the animal and

felt only one emotion for it—fear. When I threw in the slops the boar had always ignored the meal and come crashing into the lumber that barely separated us. I tossed the water into the trough from a distance of several yards. My cousin could laugh all he wanted, but that hog wanted to cripple me for life. I silently cheered the disappearance. Two days later the hog was back. Trussed fore feet to hind and laid in the back of an ox cart that forded the passage from Brittle Branch, Ajax came as a present. The cart driver was unknown to us, but he addressed Grandpa with great respect. "Mr. Mercy" had caught the hog, the man explained, and was sending the animal back free of charge to make up for the damage done to Uncle Albert's store.

Grandpa was delighted and insisted on witnessing the brute's return to captivity. He was doubly delighted when Ajax immediately mounted the squealing sow and did his duty with grunting enthusiasm.

"Good," Grandpa remarked. "That Mercy boy has done well by the Allsons. Always has."

Then Uncle Jimmy and I helped the old man back to the house. The outing had exhausted him. Yes, few doubted Grandpa's days were numbered. Even leaning on us, he tottered, and though David Allson stood up when the old man both came and went, the sharpener was still unseen. Grandpa appeared to look right through him.

"What do you make of that hog?" I asked my cousin when we returned to the pen.

"Ham," he answered. "Bacon. Butts."

"Very funny," I said. "You know what I mean."

"No, I don't, Willie. Less and less do I know what you mean."

"That ain't Ajax."

"You saying the hog's got a twin brother?"

"Mercy sent back another hog."

"Cousin, I don't know anymore who's the looniest, you or Brother."

"That ain't the same hog."

"Jesus Christ, look at it. It's got the exact same broke tusk and the split ears."

"They all got split ears. But this boar's got a busted tusk on the right. Ajax had his good tusk on the right."

"Willie, this is the same hog."

Uncle Jimmy wandered off to the mercantile, leaving me to study the imposter, who now backed into a far corner. When I took a step up to the rails, he lowered his head, eyeing me with a purely evil intent. Sammy leaned over the fence. He still wore his uniform. So did my cousin. Both swore the brown wool outfits would shield them from the Kaiser's bullets.

"That ain't the same hog," I said.

"How that?"

"That ain't Ajax. Mercy has sent us another hog."

"Sure that Ajax. Ain't be but one Ajax." He pointed.

"No," I insisted. "It looks most the same, but the broke tusk is on the wrong side. This animal has never been in a pen. Not once."

Without warning, the boar charged the fence that I'd dared to lay a hand on. The strike was hard, far harder than Ajax ever delivered. The boards buckled and the top pole actually snapped. I stumbled backwards and fell. Though Sammy hadn't exactly stood his ground, he was in a position to laugh and he did.

"Ain't matter if you call 'em Ajax. He mama ain't call 'em Ajax."

"That ain't Britt's hog," I muttered getting to my feet, and with a final look at the black snout and tusks that were trying in vain to pry a hole between two bottom planks, I went inside. I knew I was right but didn't have my proof until late that night when I heard the sound of horses hooves down below in the barnyard. Quietly easing myself from bed, I peered out the window. There was the horse and rider and the dog, too. They waited, silent and still. Ghost or not I couldn't say, but I pulled out the cross, kissed it, and began to rub the silver hard. I whispered, "Ghost ride on." The rider took off his great flopping hat and appeared to run a hand through his hair. He was looking up at my window. So was the expectant dog. "Ride on, God-damn you," I whispered, drawing away from the window. I rubbed the cross harder and pleaded. "Maum Anna, make him go away." When I looked again the yard was empty.

The next morning I couldn't make out the little horse's hoofprints from the hundreds that were usually there. David Allson wasn't up yet so I couldn't ask him what he'd seen or heard. I was quick to notice one thing, though. The hog was in a much better disposition. He lay in the mud, just as the sow did, and only rose with a normal swine's interest to root out his slops. Maybe I'd been wrong or maybe the prayer I'd made to the angel Anna had an effect on the boar, as well. Anyway, I went off to school reassured, so it came as a shock when I was called from my second class and told an emergency awaited me at home.

Somehow, Grandpa had risen and dressed himself in his Sunday best. Then, slipping past my mama, the old man had by some unimaginable exertion and for reasons equally unknowable climbed into the hog pen. Ajax, the imposter Ajax, made short work of him. Short ugly work. Not only was the old man dead, but about a third of him had been eaten by the boar and sow. They'd have devoured all of him if David Allson hadn't stepped outside for his morning smoke and realized what was going on. The Negro didn't hesitate to leap bravely into the pen and lift the old man's body out, but by then it was far too late. The catastrophe was over. By the time I was summoned home, it was long over. Dr. McGill was seeing to the body, and Mr. Friendly was seated in the parlor with my parents.

I can't say exactly what my emotions were at that point. The old man had been around a long time, all my life and another fourscore besides, but to die this way was both horrible and unexpected. And yet I should have expected it for I'd recognized the substituted hog and warned everyone except Grandpa.

"Well? You believe me now?"

Uncle Jimmy sat at the kitchen table drinking a cup of coffee. Brother watched him.

"What you talking about?" my cousin snapped.

"That weren't the same hog."

"What difference does it make?"

"I'd say it made plenty."

"Say it somewhere else."

"I'm going to shoot that hog."

"I done shot 'em both," he said.

"If you'd listened to me, we'd have shot him yesterday and Grandpa'd still be alive."

"Mr. Britt would've loved that, all right. Grandpa would have pinned a medal on us."

"That hog was evil."

"Jesus Christ," my cousin whispered. "Shut up before you get Brother praying."

But it was too late. Brother knelt on the kitchen floor, hands clasped, eyes turned heavenward. His lips moved in silent prayer.

"See what you done?" My cousin studied the coffee in his cup and ignored his brother.

I went out back and discovered Sammy and several of

the field hands rolling the boar's carcass into the back of the wagon. The sow already rested there. She was large, a round hill of animal that could have been merely sleeping. The boar appeared less at peace. His teeth and tusks, bloodied now, were as bared and lethal as before, and the eyes, though lifeless, still held a diabolical spark. With a thud the coarse, bristled carcass was settled into place by Sammy.

"What you going to do with them?" I asked him.

"Eat 'em, Willie." He was climbing out of the wagon.

"You can't do that!"

"That a pretty good mess, for true." To amuse me, Sammy rubbed his belly and rolled his eyes about. He grinned.

"A mess?"

"Ain't for waste. Better to bust belly than for good vittle to waste. Yes, sir, I going to take my share. Plenty for all, though."

This time when he rubbed his belly, he looked for approval at the hands who were helping. Several nodded, but at least none smiled.

"No!" I shouted. "I mean, you can not eat a pig that's eaten a human being! You know that, Sammy."

"I know that if you say I know that." He said this rather sheepishly and only after a pause.

"Well, then, you know it. The hogs ate on Grandpa. Would be the same as eating the old man himself, now wouldn't it?"

"That so, Captain Willie. I'm glad you catch up with these fellow before they make that kind of mistake." The voice came from behind me. It was David Allson. I shook my head in a show of disgust, glad at last to have a reasonable ally. "You fella, take them pig and bury 'em in the deep wood. You hear me?"

"That's right," I echoed. "Bury 'em."

"I do that," Sammy nodded to both me and David. "I do that. I bury 'em in the deep woods."

"You fella go with him," David Allson ordered the other hands. "Make sure he do the right thing with all this pig meat."

Bowing and muttering their apologies the men boarded the wagon and drove away. David Allson walked back with me as far as his house, and that's when he apologized for not saving the old man and suggested the tragedy resulted because he'd gotten dizzy spells from watching Anna circle. And that's when I told him it wasn't his fault and thanked him for taking Grandpa's body out of the pen. Once more he expressed his sorrow and once more I thanked him, and then we parted.

The time had come for me to go inside and do what I could to ease the burden of my parents' pain. Not much it seemed, for they sat calmly in the parlor. Mama's tears had dried and whatever grief my pa was feeling was apparently being absorbed by the Bible that lay open on his lap. Mr. Friendly was on his way out and beckoned me to follow.

"The saddest of times," he remarked once we'd reached the porch.

"He was old," I said. "He shouldn't have been out there."

"Rest easy, son. It's not your fault."

"I didn't claim it was," I snapped back.

"You've forgotten that Jesus died for you, Willie," he said quietly. "You have forgotten that your sins can be forgiven. Jesus is the Redeemer."

"I ain't got no sins."

"We all have sins."

"What do you know?" I shouted this, forgetting in my anger that we'd buried his wife only a few weeks before.

"Plenty, I know plenty." He paused. "When I said this was the saddest of times I wasn't referring just to your grandfather, God rest his soul." He paused. "Or my wife." I looked down at my feet and he continued. "I was considering all those dying of the fever, as well. Pray to God that it doesn't reach us, Willie T." The preacher rubbed the deep black circles beneath his eyes, and nodding his sad long-chinned face, went down the steps.

The fever. Mr. Friendly was talking about the strange plague sweeping the countryside south of Crowns Bluff. For the past week, this illness had been a favorite topic at the mercantile. It started with some stomach discomfort, followed by chills, and then a sudden raging fever that brought on delirium. Several reports had even been made of victims sweating blood, tiny drops appearing on the forehead. Miraculously, the majority survived, but the rest didn't. The preacher was right. If I'd had a prayer left in me, I'd have prayed one.

Two days later we buried Grandpa. Not surprisingly, the church was full and at least another fifty mourners waited at the cemetery. Worn down as he was, Mr. Friendly didn't shortchange the old man. He delivered a lengthy sermon and then for his graveside text chose the flight of the Israelite children out of Egypt—with Grandpa as our Moses and the years since the War as our time in the wilderness. Standing erect beside that fresh-dug hole and waving his arms about, the preacher made the connection straightforward enough, and it sounded possible. The old man hadn't been perfect, but he'd started making Cedar Point into a city. Now, it was up to those who cared about such things to complete the business. We were to do this not for our own glory, but as he had done it, for the glory of God. According to Mr. Friendly, Grandpa was up in Heaven looking down on each and every one of us. Amen.

That's what I remember, anyway, but towards the end a good bit slipped by me. On arriving at the cemetery, I'd been surprised to find no Negroes present. I'd expected at least Sammy and David Allson to put in an appearance, and it seemed odd that Pa's old boat crew and our field hands hadn't shown up either. Once the service resumed, though, I'd forgotten about their absence and wasn't reminded until the black faces began to emerge out from the surrounding woods. Late arrivals, I thought at first, but as their numbers grew and the sun began to sink below the tree line, I became more anxious. I still didn't see a familiar face, not even a customer from the grocery, but the number of Negroes mourning was triple the number of whites, and by the time the sun set the number had tripled again. Close to a thousand encircled the hundred white citizens who'd come to see Colonel William Thomas Allson committed to the earth.

What else could I think? No sign of sadness showed on their unrepentant savage faces. Under their coats most assuredly they'd hidden the weapons newly sharpened in our own backyard. In the darkness I began to make out the clear shine of scythes and knives. There was an axe and there another, and nowhere in this crowd of black strangers did I see either Sammy or David Allson. Had they been murdered by their own people? Had they escaped? On every side lightwood knot torches began to light up the night, giving an even more sinister mood to the ceremony. Grandpa's hour had come. The revolt was starting. Mama sat on one side of me, Uncle Jimmy on the other. It was my cousin I leaned to in order to suggest some desperate plan that would save my parents' lives and perhaps our own, as well.

"The Isle of Negroes," I whispered. "The old man was right. They going to get us all."

"Shut up," he whispered back. I could smell alcohol on his breath. Not a reassuring sign.

"I'm telling you this here is it. When I give the signal I'm going grab Mama and run. I want you to take care of Pa and Brother."

"Run where? Jesus Christ, you crazy bastard. What are you talking about?"

At that moment the lowering of the coffin began, and on every side the Negroes started to clap their hands and sing, "I live the life, going to die the death." It was just that single line repeated like a chant over and over for several minutes. As they sang, though, they bobbed and weaved and clapped louder and louder. If they were using their hands to clap I realized they couldn't be holding onto weapons. For no reason at all, I had almost grabbed up my mama and drug her away from the funeral of her husband's father.

On our left, two of the Negro women suddenly broke from the encircling crowd and drawing near the grave, began a dance. I'd witnessed short demonstrations at other funerals, but this was unlike any seen before. Spreading their feet wide apart, the mourners bent over at the hips and began to swing their arms so that they crossed back and forth just at the knees. Then with a shout they stood straight, extending their arms up to the sky fingers spread wide. Bending once more, they proceeded to repeat the gesture again and again and again. As I watched three more women came out to join them, and then from the far side of the grave a whistle blew high and shrill. A bugle answered long and loud from somewhere in the distant woods behind us. I looked around, once more on guard, but no one else showed concern. Mr. Friendly took no notice at all. He was bending over to shake my pa's hand. Next he kissed my mama's cheek. When he shook my hand I whispered it was getting late and we should be heading home, but he just nodded to me soberly and quoted some scrap of Scripture that couldn't be heard because of the wild commotion surrounding us. When he got to my cousin, the preacher winked. His eye could have twitched, but I would have sworn at the time it was a wink. Uncle Jimmy shook his hand for an extra long time and even laughed.

Once the clergyman had passed, it was the custom for family members to rise from their chairs, so others could approach and offer their condolences. Sammy came first. I suppose some thought this a presumption, but I was relieved to see him at last. Dressed in his army uniform and carrying a torch that lit the area in a ten foot radius, he took off his cap to Uncle Albert and bowed. Then he spoke a few words and moved on to my parents. After him came Dr. McGill, and then Liza. A short line was forming behind her.

"This here a terrible sad day, Captain Willie," Sammy said when we finally faced. The army cap was held over his heart. His head nodded forward. I noticed that he chewed on the corner of his lip. A habit from his boyhood had, under the stress of the circumstances, come back to haunt him.

"Thank you, Sammy," I said.

He looked up at me sad-faced, ready to move on, and I noticed a thin circle of grease about his lips. There was another streak across his chin. It glistened in the light of the torch he carried. As if hit by a bolt of lightning, I was struck by revelation. And before he could step away, I grabbed his arm.

"You ate those hogs, didn't you?" I whispered. "You ate those same hogs that ate Grandpa. After I told you not to, you ate them anyway."

"No, Captain Willie. No, sir." He looked down at his feet.

"You're lying."

"We ain't ate no hog."

"You're lying. You ate those two hogs, hogs that had eaten human flesh." I whispered still, but it was difficult to hold back what I was feeling. I wanted to shout it at the top of my lungs.

"No, sir, Willie. We eat different hog. We eat two different hog. We buy them hog we eat. We done bury your hog in the deep wood. These here different hog."

"You're lying, you leather-headed beast."

"Others is waiting," Uncle Jimmy said, and prying my fingers loose, he yanked Sammy away.

Dr. McGill was shaking my hand and saying something, but I could only nod. Liza passed before me as if in a dream. My mind raced on to other matters. Sammy had lied to me. He'd disobeyed me. He'd disobeyed David Allson, as well. David had said, "Do the right thing with all that hog meat." That's what he'd said, or something to that effect. But what did that mean? "Do the right thing." Harder than a bolt of lightning, the answer struck. David Allson mocked me. Behind my back he'd been telling them to eat the hogs.

With tears in his eyes, Mr. Britt wrapped me in an embrace. I didn't respond in any way. David. King David. That man had never told me the truth. Had he watched Grandpa fall into the hog pen? No! He had thrown the victim in. Here was the Prince of Darkness! David Allson was surely the long-awaited Cannibal King! And Grandpa, poor Grandpa had been sacrificed to gain this murderer's entry into Heaven. But how could I have listened to his stories in the first place? How could I not recognize David Allson as an outrageous liar and the grandest of villains?

Blaine Fitchum was pumping my hand and expressing his unlimited admiration for the fine old gentleman who had passed on. What proof did I have Maum Anna was even dead? One tiny silver feather. Right before my very eyes a black giantess, with twining arms, was throwing herself full-length alongside the open grave. Though her back was to me, the meager gray dress and white kerchief were unmistakable. It was Maum Anna. Anna was alive.

The Isle of Negroes was upon us.

The Widow Bailey stood before me, but Judge Walker was next. He was speaking to my mama.

"Your friendship has meant a great deal to my son Gander," the Widow Bailey said. "I wanted you to know that, Willie T."

Pushing the woman aside, I grabbed up my mama's arm. Surely, our only hope for salvation lay with the judge. Free hand raised to the sky, I screamed out: "Save us! Jesus Christ! Save us!"

The response was immediate and gratifying—in a way, I suppose. Mama threw her arms around me and burst into tears. The Widow Bailey hugged me from the other side.

"He will, son. He will. You can rest assured, Christ is with us at this very moment!" the widow shouted in my ear.

"Christ is here. He hears your prayer, Willie. We will be saved. Through His sacrifice we are redeemed. We are redeemed, believe me." That was Mr. Friendly. He appeared out of nowhere at my back.

"Your grandfather was a fine old gentleman. We won't see his like again, I'm afraid." That was from Judge Walker. He was nervous about entering into the eye of this theological storm, but he held a torch high above the rest of us.

"Jesus going save us all, Willie. All we got to do is ask 'em. Just got to ask 'em." These instructions came from Sammy, whose face appeared on my right. The grease was gone from his lips. Perhaps he'd wiped his mouth on his sleeve.

"I done tell you that, boy. It Jesus got to do all the Lord's work. Yes, sir, that Man got He hand in He pockets." There at last, peering high over the Widow Bailey's head, was the reassuring, soot black face of David Allson. "Jesus going to do the Lord's work," he sang out to me at the top of his voice, and the cry was picked up by the other thousand black mourners.

"Jesus going to do the Lord's work." They began to sing one after another, and then all together, clapping out a complicated rhythm that was accompanied by an earth-shaking stomping of the ground. At this, all the faces around me, both black and white, broke into smiles. The Widow Bailey still hugged me on one side. My mama on the other. The judge's torch shone in my eyes, but I was able to make out the giant black woman being pulled from the edge of the grave. She wasn't nearly so tall as I thought. She was a normal-size woman, not even a woman really. She was no more than eighteen. A girl. She'd fainted and was being carried away by two women. They, too, sang the all-pervasive refrain, "Jesus going do the Lord's work."

"Can we go home now?" I asked, and was granted permission.

Sammy gave me his torch and we departed that place. I held Mama's arm and helped her step among the tombstones of so many Allson dead. She insisted on stopping at each of my sisters' graves and identifying them to my pa.

"Sarah! Esther! Martha!" she called out to him. In a much softer voice she said, "All my babies are sleeping."

"Yes, ma'am," I said.

"I have not told Dorcas of your grandfather's death. Remind me, Willie. I must send a letter to California."

"Yes, ma'am."

"Do you remember Esther?"

"Yes, ma'am." Esther poured blood.

Then together as a family, we walked the half mile back to town, leaving behind that mass of clapping Negro strangers. Our torch led the way and the torches of the other white mourners were stretched out behind us, bobbing along in the black darkness. Finally reaching the church, I loaded my elderly parents into the Texas cart for the last leg of the journey home.

"They are such a joyous people," my mama remarked. "Anna would have so loved to have been there."

"What?" my pa shouted.

"It's sad that Anna wasn't there to sing him across," Mama repeated for his benefit.

"Yes. Joyous," he agreed.

Grandpa had taken great pride in my pa's war record and saw, as most did, his wounds as badges of courage. Yes, his son had been crippled, but to the old man's way of thinking the real damage had been done on the inside of Tom's head. The boy came back from the War with the curious notion that the Negroes had souls and nothing could be done to dissuade him. When it was hot, my pa sat the field hands in the shade, gave them cool water, and read them endless passages from the Bible. When it was cold, he took them into a shed or barn, gave them hot chicory, and read them endless passages from the Bible. Was it any wonder that we'd lost the Allson Place? How was a crop to be made under those conditions? Still, the colonel could not bring himself to blame his son. "It's not Tom's fault!" Grandpa wailed.

Actually, Pa had held out longer than practically anyone else on the Delta. When the hurricane of '98 ended the rice-planting once and for all, he'd struggled on with cotton and corn and finally the Irish potatoes that no one would buy at any price. It wasn't his fault that he gave the potatoes away or that the Allson Place was now the McGill Place. If there were souls to be had and the Negroes had them, then my pa had done the right thing.

Lying in my room that night, I heard a distant thudding sound. Not hoofbeats. Drums. I drifted off to sleep. The new day broke overcast, with a rumble of early morning thunder. Strange weather. I did the chores as I had since the beginning of time. David Allson was working at his grindstone when I returned from the pasture. He sang to himself, but nodded as I passed. I was ashamed to look him in the eye, and more than thankful I hadn't made a complete fool of myself at the funeral. School went along as usual, but at lunch word reached us that the Negroes were leaving. Packing their few belongings, our black citizens were setting out in every direction.

I refused to believe such a thing, but believed it enough to slip out of school and drag Brother with me. We didn't get close, barely entered Slabtown, but it was clear the news was at least partly true. A few wagons were already loaded with crude furnishings and bales of ragged clothing, and as we watched handcarts were being piled high with satchels, bags, and even livestock. Next stop was the mercantile, where I was sure to find Uncle Jimmy sipping on something "stronger and wetter" than coffee.

"What's happening out there?"

"Turpentine recruiters," he said. "They're offering two dollars a day."

"Wives and families, too?" This was highly unusual.

"Yep. Whole families going. 'Bout a hundred head altogether. Going get rich in Florida. Maybe you ought to join 'em."

"Can't miss your wedding. Hear it's going to be the social event of our lifetimes."

Liza, of course, had claimed that, but she'd have her hands full pulling off a wedding, plain and simple. To begin with, one of the major parties concerned was less than enthusiastic. Uncle Jimmy said he'd marry her, but he didn't want the affair to inconvenience him. He promised to say, "I do" or at least, "I'll try." A worse obstacle was Liza's own mother. Everyone knew Mrs. McGill had withheld her blessing and even refused Liza the use of her house. And everyone knew Dr. McGill would bring the woman around, or simply hold the wedding reception there without her permission. But to the community's amazement, that hadn't happened. The plague of fever had now spread north of Crowns Bluff, and the doctor, perhaps worried by the threat of an approaching epidemic, was unusually subdued. He spoke quietly in short sentences. That left only Liza's friends. Margarite couldn't come. She was now a genuine Red Cross nurse waiting in reserve. In fact, if Uncle Jimmy didn't hurry, she might beat him to France. Liza's other friend, Leala Fitchum, wanted to help, but she was nearly hysterical with happiness for the bride. Liza had no one. If the wedding was to be the "social event of our lifetimes" then a miracle was needed, and Uncle Jimmy, rocked back in his chair at the mercantile, didn't look ready to provide one.

But at that very moment my confused mama was putting on her hat and walking down the street to the McGill house. When she returned from her mysterious interview with Mrs. McGill, it had been decided that Liza's reception would be held in our yard. By the time I got home from the grocery, plans were well under way. Over the last months, Brother had managed to rake most of what remained of Mama's garden into hundreds of small cone-shaped piles.

The piles still remained, though, as did the thick smell of burnt fuel. It was no place for a party or habitation of any sort, so the backyard would have to be cleaned up and made as presentable as possible. When I entered the house, questions of wedding dress and bridesmaids and shower and trousseau were being discussed with great vigor and determination by my mama. Liza was calling her "Auntie" and acting for all the world as if this were her mama and not my own. I had brought news of the Negro exodus, but there was no one to give it to.

"Willie, will you help me?" Liza asked.

"Yes," I answered.

That was on a Tuesday. The following Friday Mr. Friendly united my cousin and Liza as man and wife. They pledged to love, honor, and obey in a ceremony that was remarked on as being quite lovely, perhaps the loveliest ever held in our town. The day was perfect. Sunlight burst through the limbs of the giant oaks and bounced from each leaf with a gleaming radiance. The magnolias in the churchyard bloomed as never before. Inside the church, more magnolia blossoms had been placed in profusion about each window and upon the altar, and garlands of smilax and ivy were strung above the doors and all along the cornice. The outside was carried in. I had done it. Brother and Sammy helped. Mama directed us.

Six bridesmaids, girls almost too young to know Liza, were recruited for the day, and they, too, were loaded down with magnolia blossoms. I had picked them. Before getting down to business, Mr. Friendly complimented the bride on the magnolia blossoms she carried. I had picked them. He complimented her on the wedding dress she wore. It was Mama's. He complimented Uncle Jimmy on the uniform he wore. Technically, it belonged to the army. Then the preacher went through the ceremony of marriage. Pa was best man and stood up for Uncle Jimmy with amazing gallantry. Attending without his wife, a happy Dr. McGill gave away his only daughter. He beamed and then wept. Mr. Friendly pronounced the couple man and wife, and my mama cried from her seat in the front pew all the way out the door. Going back to our house she cried. It made me sad.

The reception was more of the same, only worse because I was expected to show some enthusiasm for what had just transpired. I smiled. I was proud, at least, that we'd been able to disguise the backyard by stripping the town of practically every hydrangea bloom. These, along with more ivy and smilax, were intertwined even through the branches of the grapevines. And the vines were serving as a backdrop for two long trestle tables covered with white embroidered spreads. Here, piled high were all the simple delicacies familiar to such occasions. An ample spread, a variety certain to impress all. Not showy. Ample, as was God's pleasure.

I was happy about that part. Yes, I was happy for my mama, and even happy for Liza, especially when I began to hear the arriving women whispering about how well it all looked, and how decent Virginia was to take Liza under her wing. The Allson family had lost so much in the last year, and yet this Christian woman could find it in her heart and soul to give to others. Yes, it pleased me to hear such remarks, but then they began to comment on the piano. For this special day the piano had been taken from the parlor and placed here in the yard. The same had been done at Esther's wedding. Most thought it a beautiful gesture, but some sensed a hint of decadence. Our church pianist couldn't make up her mind and was glad when the

Episcopals' organist offered to play. A widow of one of the Fitchums, this pleasant woman was being escorted to the piano bench.

I suppose I should have expected some comparison with Esther's wedding. She'd married in the late Spring. No doubt the decorations were similar. Also, that was the last time a piano had been carried out-of-doors by anybody. Despite dire prophecy, the piano had survived. Esther had not. After hearing her name mentioned a few more times, I wandered around to the front yard where my mama's garden had once been. New growth was pushing pale green through the blackened stubble. I kicked at one of the small conelike piles. The ash and dust exploded with surprising ease and scattered the debris once more.

"Mama, I am dying." I'd heard her from my own room. The doors were open, but I was too frightened to go and see. Instead, I'd waited three days. By then Dr. McGill was in attendance. Maum Anna was there. When my mama saw me standing in the hall, she told me to go downstairs and wait with Pa and Esther's husband. Then she closed the door. I could still hear Esther's screams, and after a few moments in the dark hall, I knelt at the keyhole. The room glowed yellow in the pale lantern light. I saw the keyhole-shaped section of the floor and the window centered in the far wall. My mama's flower-print dress moved across this space. By pressing my cheek flat against the lock plate, I could follow her as she returned to the bedside.

I'd already seen the blood-soaked mattress and the red pool on the floor—seen that much before the door was closed, but now I heard Esther's gasping. Now I heard the baby cry. I didn't see it, though. The view afforded by the keyhole was only of the doctor and Maum Anna bending over the bed, and my mama with the wash pan in her hands would sometimes block even this. Still there was that keyhole-shaped vision of frantic attendance, and the single cry of the dying infant.

"Jesus, take me." At the very end Esther whispered that, and those other three, who'd been speaking in anxious hushed voices, fell silent. "Jesus, take me." I heard that again and saw through the keyhole between the arms, legs, backs of adults, the small face of my sister turned straight towards the door. She brought a hand up as if to wave good-bye to me, and it was red with blood.

Off in the distance, the organist began to play, but I didn't recognize the tune. Muted discordant notes reached me as if crossing some vast ocean. A foreign language but not a spoken language. Thoughts. Quickly, I walked out towards the creek in the direction of the wharf and the music followed, louder even, note piled upon note. Perhaps Mama had played this one before she'd forgotten where to put her fingers on the keyboard. Liza played. So had Esther, my sister, who wore the same wedding dress and ended pouring blood. I wouldn't want that for Liza, especially not now. She was family.

Brother was standing at the water's edge. Tide was low. The rows of piling which had once been the Allson wharf formed a double column—two lines of blackened splintered stubs extending uselessly into the channel. As I watched, Brother stepped between the two closest to the water's edge and out into the creek itself.

"Brother!" I shouted. "You done ruined your shoes."

He looked back at me with those dark Gypsy eyes. The water was halfway up his shins.

"Come out of there. We suppose to be up there in the yard."

He turned around and walked up the bank, his shoes squishing water and caked with mud.

"Wipe your shoes off," I said. "You can't stand around

like that." He stood on one leg and wiped his shoe on the back of his pants leg. My old suit. It was still far too large for him, but the coat sleeves had been shortened and the pants brought up high and cinched with his belt. He stood on the opposite leg and cleaned the other shoe in the same manner. Now he was completely streaked with mud and water from the knees down.

"Fine," I said. "Fine and dandy."

I walked with him up to the reception and he disappeared behind the grape arbor. I put myself well off from the center of activity, leaned against a hickory, and began once more to watch. Sammy, as a favor to Uncle Jimmy and no one else, had taken off his army uniform and was wearing a tuxedo the doctor had worn in college. Like Brother's attire, it wasn't custom fit. The coat would pass, though, and the pants, which stopped a good foot short of his ankles, were hidden by the tablecloths. He needed this livery to serve in or, at least, pretend to serve. A half dozen Negro women in white aprons were standing beside him to offer up refreshments, ladle out the punch, and pour the tea.

The crowd was large and growing larger still. Surprisingly so. I counted one hundred and three. The adults drifted about the backyard, balancing their food and drink, chatting and waiting for Liza to make her grand entrance. The children fidgeted and a few even broke into quickly halted romps of true happiness. My parents beamed and only Dr. McGill could have been happier. Even Mr. Friendly was once more upright and courteous. It was hardly the end of the world to be a part of such an occasion, and I decided that if anyone approached me, I would do my best to smile.

Liza's Honeymoon

Liza was changing into her trousseau traveling dress, but there'd be no honeymoon trip. She and Uncle Jimmy would only spend two nights as man and wife, and they'd spend them in the pole cottage last occupied by Aunt Lydia and George. Then my cousin and Sammy would be heading "over there," and Liza would be heading home for the duration. Still, it was permissible for the bride to go through the motions of travel and let the groom drive her the two blocks in the steamer.

Knowing this, I wasn't caught off guard when the girl appeared wearing an elaborately pleated skirt and cloak of pale gray. My uniformed cousin paraded her on his arm. Someone in the crowd began to clap, perhaps her father, and then everyone, myself included, joined in. After that, Mr. Friendly gave his blessing, which took the inevitable form of a prayer. Speeches by Judge Walker and several others followed, and Dr. McGill came last. With great emotion, he told how once upon a time he had slowed down in front of this very house to let Uncle Jimmy jump off the steamer. A year and a half had passed, but he'd known then that his daughter had made the right choice. He thanked

Grandpa and my mama and pa and every Allson who'd ever lived.

Actually, Dr. McGill wanted to say more, but began to sob, and Liza left my cousin's side to comfort the man. Still wearing the muddy suit, Brother returned from behind the grape arbor and stood beside me. Uncle Jimmy had a few hands left to shake, something he'd been doing with a fair imitation of enthusiasm. I didn't figure he had time for us, but he did. The groom appeared out of nowhere to pump Brother's small hand vigorously. He'd been drinking, but that seemed natural enough, considering.

"Ain't you going to congratulate your brother on his good fortune?" he asked Brother.

"No," Brother said.

"You ain't? Well that's a fine kettle of fish. You mean you ain't going to start calling Liza 'Sis'?"

"No, I ain't." You couldn't tell if Brother knew he was being teased or even if Uncle Jimmy was teasing.

"She'll be mighty disappointed," my cousin said letting go of the other's hand.

I figured I'd be the next to shake hands. I wasn't going to call her "Sis" either, but I'd wish them both happiness. I held my hand out. It stuck out there in midair, but Uncle Jimmy just looked at it.

"I thought we was friends," he said to me, not smiling at all as he'd done for Brother. "All this time I thought you and me was friends." He did smile then, a kind of crooked smile, and he walked away.

I couldn't think of what was happening. Even far drunker, he'd never treated me that way. We were joking together ten minutes before the wedding. We were friends at that point, and all that had happened since was he'd married Liza. I couldn't think what to do and stood there dumbstruck as Liza approached.

"Go away, Brother," she said. "I got something to discuss with Willie T."

Brother didn't object to this curt dismissal but he did say something so peculiar, I wondered if it wasn't a joke.

"Sure, Sis," he said. Then he walked away.

Liza slipped her arm around my own as if to enter into some sort of newly formed family conspiracy, and began to walk me even further from the others.

"Willie, I know we haven't gotten along like we should have in the past, but I want us to be friends, real friends."

"Did you tell Uncle Jimmy something about me? Did you tell him some kind of lie to make him hate me?"

She ignored my question and went on with her proposition.

"Your mama has been so kind to me. Your pa, too. It made me realize how truly selfish I've been about the dowry. Lydia's trunk . . . she had a set of those Encyclopedia Britannicas. I know I promised you half on the day I married Jimmy, but I want you to take them all."

"Is this what you talked to Jimmy about? You giving me encyclopedias?"

"I did discuss it with him. He thought it was a wonderful idea." She didn't smile, but she did stop walking. Apparently we'd come far enough.

"There's something going on here. You tell me what it is."

"I burned the letters," she remarked with the same casualness. "Your mama had written that woman one hundred and ninety-two letters. The first was mailed in 1865 and the last just over a year ago."

"I don't believe you." I whispered, hoarse with rage. "I will not believe you."

"They were thick letters telling her all that was going on. All the gossip, everything that had ever happened. Did you know Uncle Albert risked his life on that battlefield to save your father? Uncle Albert sent the message telling your mother to come to Virginia. I was amazed to learn so much, but the last, those involving my courtship with Jim, were short. Her memory was beginning to fail. Sad, your mama is such a good woman."

"I do not believe you, Liza." My fists were tightly clenched.

"Why would I care if you believe me?"

"Why would you burn such letters?"

"They were harmless for the most part, but there were details in them that could have proved embarrassing to our family."

"Our family?"

"Yes, the Allsons."

"You ain't no Allson!" I shouted this loud enough to turn the heads of some in the crowd. "No ma'am. No way."

"Yes, I am. I will always be an Allson."

"No, you ain't!"

"Shh, Willie." She put a finger to her lips. "People will think we're fighting."

"I could kill you, Liza." She smiled happily, waved to someone, and taking me once more by the arm, paraded us even further away.

"I had to tell him, you understand," she said next.

"You had no right to burn letters written by my mama."

"I didn't realize how angry it would make him."

"We ain't ever going to be friends. You can forget that. I mean it."

"He said he'd kill you, but he didn't mean it."

"Who said that?"

"Jimmy."

"Why would he say that? Why would he want to kill me?" I shouted. She brought a finger to her lips once more.

"There can be no secrets between husband and wife, Willie. Inside, after I changed from the gown . . ." She paused to touch the collar of her new outfit. "I told him."

"What did you tell him?"

"The truth."

"What Liza? What truth?"

"I told him I'd seen you rutting on the floor of the Friendlys' attic. I told him I had seen the two of you like animals—rutting."

"No," I whispered. "No."

"Yes," she said in a quite normal voice. "Yes, indeed."

"You couldn't have seen that."

"I would have been blind not to have seen it."

"Amy Mercy was sitting at the table. She was operating the wireless telephone when you came up."

"Amy Mercy was a white-trash whore. I had to tell him. A man and wife can't have such a thing between them."

Through all this Liza still held me by the arm, but now I wrenched free and stepped away. I looked her squarely in the eye.

"You're lying. Mrs. Friendly called us, and you was behind her, Liza."

"I had already come up the ladder and gone back down. Mrs. Friendly did not realize that when she caught up with me on the top landing." Again Liza smiled and waved at someone over my shoulder.

"You told Jimmy that? You told him all that?" I looked down at my feet. There was nothing more to say.

"Fornication is a sin, Willie. Did you know that?"

"What?" I looked up. Her cold blue eyes were set like smoked glass in that cameo ivory face. "What?"

She smiled and I turned my back to her. I was beaten. Even if I were to deny that anything final had occurred between Amy Mercy and myself, and even if my cousin believed me, it wasn't going to change what had actually happened.

"Congratulations," I said, my back still turned to her. "You win, Liza."

She screamed. The cry was loud and piercing, and I spun around to find her elevated, rising up into heaven with her special traveling boots at my eye level. She kicked frantically at the sides of the gray-white horse. An arm circled about her waist, the arm of The Hard to Catch Mercy. He was grinning down at me, that half-toothed, dark-eyed devil's grin.

"Reckon I'll be kissing the bride, if you got no objections," he said in the singsong voice.

I shook my head no. I was terrified, and in truth I had no objections, anyway.

"Willie T.!" wailed Liza. "Stop him."

My immediate interest was in locating the hog dog, which turned out to be ranging in the direction of the wedding party. The other guests were now aware of the intruder's presence and reacted in varied forms of alarm. Avoiding the dog, the quickest of the men were running in our direction. When I looked back at Liza, her face was lost in a filthy mat of furlike beard. Mercy was kissing her firmly on the lips.

Mr. Friendly arrived first. That was probably for the best, since he might be able to talk this thing to an ending, one that wouldn't involve me further. The preacher stopped a pace short of the horse. Those behind him, of which Uncle Jimmy was not one, came to a halt almost as close and fanned out in a semicircle. Liza, who'd been squirming during her kiss, was now held tight. One of Mercy's hands circled her waist. The other was clamped over her mouth.

"Put her down, Mercy," Mr. Friendly said. "You've had your fun."

"My fun ain't started yet, preacher."

"You best let her go and be on your way."

"I'm a widow man. Need me a wife." He spit my way but I stepped aside. "This one'll do."

"I think not. She's another man's wife."

"Where is he? Don't see but one man 'round here and that's me." Mercy made certain to take me into this sweeping appraisal. In fact, half of the statement was made to me alone since I was the only one on his right side.

"Where's Jimmy?" someone in the crowd yelled. "Get Jimmy," several more joined in.

Liza was looking at me. Only her pleading eyes showed above the large hand muzzling her mouth, but I could read in them a degree of terror that matched my own at that moment. Perhaps, it had always matched my own.

"All right," I whispered.

She closed her eyes. On the other side, Judge Walker had pushed Mr. Friendly aside and begun his own warning.

"Don't take this no further," he said. "The law can find you. Even you, Mercy. Let her down and be on your way 'fore her husband gets here."

Then my pa began to shout from somewhere unseen. "What is this man doing with our Liza? Tell him to put her down." After that, I had to speak out.

"Put her down." I smiled and tried using the voice of a person who appreciates a good joke.

"I ain't forgot about you neither," Mercy said, whipping around to face me.

Further argument was unnecessary. Liza bit his hand as hard as she could, triggering a chain of events that were primed, cocked, and ready to go.

Mercy cursed her and brought away his hand.

"Shoot him!" Liza screamed.

Judge Walker grabbed the reins of the little horse, while

Mr. Friendly reached with his long arms to pull Liza down. And acting on the promise just made, I reached to pull her from the other side. Of course, she couldn't go both ways and so went neither, and Mercy didn't need but this moment to regain control. At a word from him, the little horse reared up on its hind legs, disengaging both the preacher and me. It pirouetted, came down beside me, and loped off, not away from, but towards the house. And then David Allson came out from behind the grape arbor to meet the uninvited guest. He came running, with a bright double-headed axe held firmly in his great hands. Nothing separated them but a patch of barnyard, and Mercy did not see his attacker. Mercy was looking back over his shoulder. He was laughing at us. The hog dog saw, though. It left the ground with a single bound and launched high towards the Negro's throat. The axe caught the animal with a clean lick between the eyes, the blade driving down and through the white steel teeth of those coal black jaws. For the briefest of seconds the weapon was embedded and before it could be withdrawn, David Allson had been run down by the little horse and had his throat cut ear to ear by the great knife of the rider.

The sight of this stopped us in our tracks. The black man sank to his knees with the blood pouring from between his fingers. Beyond him the little horse trotted wide in that exact same spot where I'd seen it either in vision or for real on so many occasions before. Only Liza was different. Never in these previous visits had there been a Liza pinned across the saddle horn and screaming.

"Shoot him! Jimmy, shoot him!"

"Where's Jim Allson?" the Mercy called out. No one knew but at last I saw Sammy. He'd run forward to kneel helplessly beside David's reclining form. "You tell Allson I can't wait no longer. Tell him thank you for me."

Then Mercy rode straight into our barn and out the far end. Crossing the house pasture and leaping the fence, he disappeared behind the hedgerow.

Where was Jimmy? He'd been in our parlor, sitting alone with my mama. He'd taken her in there to thank her for everything she done for him and for Liza, and it took quite a while. He was still at it, in fact, when he was given the news his bride had been carried away.

"This can't be happening," is all he said.

Dr. McGill wasn't believing it either. The bride's father had slipped home to get a special wedding present, one he'd at first planned to give later and in private. It was the deed to the Allson Place. He'd signed it over to my cousin and his daughter Liza. He waved the piece of paper before us thinking somehow the promise of property would bring the girl back.

"My baby!" he screamed. "My baby!"

Uncle Jimmy was more purposeful in his actions. When I caught up with him he was cinching up the saddle on Rose. Sammy was riding Gal bareback. He held my pa's shotgun in one hand and had a rifle I'd never seen in the other.

"I'm going, too," I said.

"Don't need you," my cousin muttered through clenched teeth.

"Yes, you do."

"Nope." He pulled himself into the saddle, and reaching over, took the rifle from Sammy. How strange the Negro looked in the tuxedo much too small for him, covered with blood, and mounted on a saddleless mule.

"It ain't her he's after," I said. "It's you."

"He'll be getting more of me than he bargained on then." My cousin reined about hard.

"It's me and you both!" I shouted but he was gone.

"Take me with you, Sammy!" I shouted, but he'd followed my cousin out the far end of the barn and they were galloping away. How strange it all was. I didn't want to go. In secret, I didn't mind that my cousin hated me enough to leave me behind. I had no wish at all to catch up with The Hard to Catch. For the first time, the very first time, it occurred to me to finger the silver cross still hanging about my neck. I didn't touch the metal itself, only rubbed it through the starched white cotton of my dress shirt and mumbled the sacred incantation, "Ghost ride on." I'd ride with the posse. It was the manly thing to do, and no posse would get within miles of Mercy. At the far end of the pasture, Uncle Jimmy and Sammy leapt their mounts across the fence, and they too disappeared from view.

"Here," Brother said. "I brung you these." He'd entered the barn leading Judge Walker's mare with one hand and holding my shotgun and four shells in his other. He'd strapped on Uncle Jimmy's Colt pistol. It hung from his side almost to the knee.

"Stay here, Brother," I said. "I'll go with the others." Outside I could hear the judge shouting orders, and it occurred to me that he'd never have lent Brother his thoroughbred. "Give me the horse," I ordered. But the boy had pulled himself up in the saddle and both reins were firmly in hand.

"You coming?" he asked.

"Ride double?"

"Only one horse. All I could get."

I climbed up behind him, and we galloped off across the pasture. I heard the angry calls of the Judge demanding the return of his horse.

"Turn around!" I hollered. "This is crazy!"

He didn't listen. The big mare rose with the grace bred to her and cleared the back rail by a good foot and a half.

"Stop!" I kept insisting, but Brother didn't stop until we were far down the hedgerow and the trail petered out.

"Where you reckon they turned off?" he asked.

"I ain't no pathfinder." It was a relief not to be hanging on for dear life, and now I had an opportunity to reason with the boy.

"Where you think they would be headed?"

"The Branch, I suppose. Eventually Mercy will show up there."

"What about Jimmy?"

"Him, too."

"How do we get there?"

"That'll take us to the Swamp Road." I pointed diagonally across a freshly plowed field. "But, that'll catch us up with the posse." I pointed in the opposite direction. Brother shook his head no.

"You seen what Mercy done to David Allson?" he asked. "Yes. I seen it."

"You scared, ain't you?"

"No," I said. "I just ain't foolhardy. There's a difference."

"I seen you praying the other night with your cross. Telling Mercy to ride on. Been a long time since you had to do that."

"I say we join up with the posse."

"You can get off and walk over there."

"You know I can't do that."

"Why not?"

"I'd look pretty stupid walking back, 'specially if you went on alone and got killed."

The time for discussion had apparently ended, for he kicked the big mare forward. We entered the field and were soon thundering down the Swamp Road towards Brittle Branch. The way was empty. We saw no one. On either side, the giant cypresses rose and beneath them the black water stood unmoving. I passed with a silent shudder the place where The Hard to Catch had stopped the wagon to unload the coffin. We'd had a wet spring, and the water was higher than before. It rose beneath the mare's belly. It rose up on my calves, chilling them to the bone's marrow. The cypresses loomed higher, far grander, and more menacing than I remembered. The sunlight seemed dimmer, the track narrower. The uncommon silence was broken only by the splashing and snorting of the animal we rode. But gradually the water grew shallower, and we reached firm ground once more. Only then did I decide this adventure had reached its conclusion. Seizing the reins, I brought the mare to a halt.

"Look," I said, pointing to the roadbed. "Not a one of them tracks looks near as fresh as ours."

"We're ahead of them."

"Yes, we're ahead of them."

"Let's wait here and join up."

"With Jimmy?" I asked.

"We ain't going to join up with Mercy, is we?"

"I meant the posse."

"I'm looking for my brother."

"It'll be dark in a few hours," I coaxed. "Best we head back."

"We're orphans," he said. "Me and Jimmy is orphans."

"I know." It would not be difficult to retreat in the face of such an argument.

"Dying ain't so bad," he added. "I been dead."

"I know."

"The hard part is getting there. They keep calling you back, making you do the same things over and over again."

"I know," I said for the third time. "You told me."

I was going no further, and Brother was in no condition to argue otherwise. Slowly, I began to turn the big mare about.

"Dying's like rocking in a boat. Starry night. All them stars and I can hear Pap calling."

"Hush," I whispered. "Somebody is coming."

I raised the shotgun needlessly. Already Uncle Jimmy and Sammy had splashed out of the swamp and halted beside us. By the looks of their ripped and muddied apparel, they'd had a far harder ride than we.

"Lost him," my cousin said to me. "We figure he'll show up here before long, though." He seemed neither angry nor even disappointed. Hard-eyed, I guess. Determined. It was difficult to say exactly what his feelings for me were at that moment. I nodded.

"Where's the rest of them?" he asked.

"We came first," I said. Since I had the reins, it did look like I was the leader of this "we" who had stolen the judge's horse and charged forward.

"You shouldn't have done that," he said. "I appreciate it, though. I reckon saving Liza is something we can all agree on."

"Yes," I agreed.

"Yes, sir," Sammy seconded.

"What we going to do?" Brother asked.

"If I had good sense, I'd send you home. Willie was crazy to bring you out here."

"I ain't going back," Brother said.

"I could take him if you think it best," I volunteered.

"No, he's come this far. Let him see this through."

"You sure?" I asked.

"Yeah, the others will be along shortly. When they show, we'll put him with them."

"Fine," I said. Yes, fine and dandy.

Uncle Jimmy dug his heels into Rose's side and with a surprising leap, she started down the path towards the swamp community of Brittle Branch. The rest of us fell in behind.

"Did you see what he did to David Allson?" Brother asked Sammy.

"Yes, I see that. I going to kill 'em."

"We'll take turns," Uncle Jimmy corrected.

Deeper and deeper we rode into that world where Maum Anna had promised us nothing human would live. We took one fork and then another, passed by the few rough cabins, but saw no one around them or on the road either.

Our first stop was the Mercy house, the one marked with the sign promising to catch hard-to-catch animals for a price. Here, my cousin had patched up both a domestic quarrel and a falling out over the axle tree, and come away with a dozen eggs. The place was quiet now. Permanently quiet. The corrals were empty and to one side of the cabin were three fresh graves.

"He said he was a widower. When he first took Liza he said that," I told Uncle Jimmy.

"He cut 'em up," Sammy volunteered. "Cut 'em up and bury 'em."

"Stay here," my cousin said. "All of you." He rode up to the house, got off, and, without knocking, kicked the door off its hinges. His visit was brief and his report grim. "The fever," he said. "Looks like it took 'em all."

The next stop was the log store where my cousin and I had passed the time of day with the helpful proprietor, the man who'd accused me of being a midget revenuer on a trick mule. Apparently he too had passed away, because the door was locked with a padlock and a small scrap of black ribbon was nailed to its center.

"You reckon they all dead?" Already I was terrified, but this was a strangeness of a deeper nature. We'd stumbled into a graveyard where there was supposed to be a living community. "I don't like this."

"This a haint place," Sammy reassured me. "Always been a place for the devil do his work."

"Shut up. I don't want neither of you saying another word. Do you hear me?" Uncle Jimmy was pointing his rifle straight at me, so I turned the horse away and gave him a wide berth to lead us on to the Widow Mercy's house.

The house was pretty much as I remembered. A small cabin built of poles and weathered slabs. There was the door where my cousin had knocked and Amy Mercy had opened. Fateful day? Godforsaken? We didn't approach the front this time, but skirting the edge of the woods, rode around back. This, too, seemed unchanged. In fact, the wash still hung out to dry on the same winding spider-web of clothesline. I saw the same few pieces of gray, worn clothing and the same two patchwork quilts—complicated patterns of colored scraps fitted together and brought outside to brighten a forlorn wilderness. Perhaps the black iron wash pot had sat here since the beginning of settlement, but now no fire burned beneath it. No old woman tended the flame. Only one sign of life was back here. A squabbling flock of buzzards jumped about like anxious chickens come to feed on too little grain.

"Stay here," my cousin said.

He crossed the open space, riding into the flock. The birds scattered reluctantly, hopping and skipping across the yard. Then, realizing he'd come to stay, they flapped off to the far tree line. As we watched, he dismounted, took down one of the patchwork quilts from the line, and wrapped it around whatever had been the buzzards' meal. This done, he took a quick look inside the cabin, and signaled us to come.

"It's the widow," he said. "You, Willie and Brother, I want you to bury her. Then go in the cabin and wait." He'd pulled out his watch and was studying it like a compass. "You got a couple hours of light. Should be plenty."

"All right," I said after a slight hesitation. Being left with just Brother wasn't much safer than riding on with them, and I doubted the posse would reach here by dark, if ever.

"Don't look inside that blanket. Them birds done ate most of her." He mounted Rose. "You understand me?"

"Yes." I eyed the bloodstained quilt. "Where you heading?"

"The cow dips. Then up to the bottomless pool. That's where he buried her. Maybe he'll take her there."

"Maybe." There were two "hers" involved here—apparently my cousin had realized there was a connection between Amy Mercy and his new bride. "It's you he wants," I repeated. "I don't think he means to hurt Liza at all."

"Maybe. You just do what I say. Bury the old woman and lock yourself in that house."

"You'll be back 'fore dark?" I asked, assuming he would be.

"I can't promise." My cousin nudged the horse forward and then reined up to give one final instruction. "Do what Willie tells you, Brother."

Brother nodded, and we watched them ride out of sight before hunting up a shovel and a broken-handled hoe in the shed. That didn't take long, but the buzzards had returned when we came out and were pecking at the quilt. We ran at them with the utensils, but they weren't as frightened of us as they'd been of Uncle Jimmy. Four of the bravest flopped off to the side and sat on the ground waiting. I could have killed one with the shotgun, but a shot would have brought my cousin riding back or even worse, brought Mercy in our direction. The birds could stay. I patted the cross that hung beneath my shirt and began to dig. Brother was to stand guard, but the ground about the wash pot was like cement on top and soupy below, so it took us both scraping and shoveling to get a decent hole. Anyway, we'd be in the cabin before dark, and I could see this adventure ending soon.

"That'll do," I panted. "Let's put her in." I threw the shovel aside and grabbed up one end of the colorful shroud. A more leisurely Brother took up the other end, and together we lowered it down and stuffed in the extra corners of the bloodied material.

"Ravenous birds and beasts of the field will eat them up," Brother said, looking down at our handiwork.

"Where'd you hear that?" I placed the hoe in his hands.

"Sunday school."

"Oh." In all our time together, I'd never heard him mention the Bible directly.

"Don't pay to get old, do it?" he asked.

"Guess not." I was shoveling dirt on the widow. I was working fast. The filling in would be much easier than the taking out.

"Hogs ate Grandpa. Buzzards ate the Widow Mercy. You remember that other old woman fell on top of her card table? Cigarette burnt her fingers after she was dead. You remember that?"

"Come on, Brother. Help me fill this up."

"Maum Anna floated off. Most think she's dead, too."

"We got to have this done by dark. Jimmy will be mad if we ain't finished." I didn't look up, just kept shoveling.

"Ma got the fever. Pap drowned. He didn't get no proper burial. Preacher came to the house, but Jimmy wouldn't let him say the words." I nodded and worked. Brother wasn't helping at all. He leaned on the broken hoe handle looking down into the grave. "Wouldn't be surprised if your ma and pa died too, Willie. Then you'd be an orphan."

"Yes," I panted in complete exasperation. "I suspect I will be if I'm lucky enough to live that long."

"You going to live." He shifted his gaze from the hole to the shoveler.

"Don't be so sure," I gasped. "Come on now. Help me."

"It's me they want."

"Who?" I stopped and took a quick frightened look around the clearing. "Where? Who wants you?"

"Liars and murderers. Most of 'em. You was one. Had fangs." He opened his own mouth, pointed inside.

"Listen! I don't want to hear no more about your dream!" I had him by the shoulder, shaking hard. "You understand me!" I shouted loud enough to send two of the remaining buzzards off to the trees.

He did as instructed but wasn't satisfied to fill the hole level. A true grave was mounded up and then patted down. He did this with his bare hands, smoothing out the dirt as a child at play until the time came for him to pray. Towards the end, I held the shotgun and stood to one side. I'd even considered watching him from the cabin, but didn't. His lips moved silently. His hands were clasped together and held high above his head.

"Jesus, take me," he whispered.

The judge's mare whinnied and paced about restlessly, and the last pair of buzzards sidestepped and took flight. I looked about and saw a movement at the tree line. There, at the same spot we'd ridden in from, there half hidden in the deep shadows of late afternoon was the unmistakable—a pale horse outlined against the dark forest. Shining in the gloom was the silver glint of a rifle barrel.

I brought the shotgun up and fired both barrels.

"Brother!" I shouted. "Brother, run!"

But Brother remained before me in his trancelike state of reverence, and in another instant a bullet caught him high in the chest. The boy was knocked over backwards and lay on the lye-soaked dirt where the Widow Mercy had stood a lifetime washing out her laundry.

He didn't die, not right away. No, once down, he started to flip about and clutch at his shirt buttons. Pressing flat behind the slight mound of the grave, I crawled to him. His eyes were wide open. The blood bubbled, foaming from the neat round hole in his front. I grabbed him beneath his armpits and dragged him behind the black iron wash pot. Brother was quiet now. His dark Gypsy eyes followed me.

"Did you get him?" he whispered.

"Not yet." I had no reasonable expectation of even staying alive. To start with, I'd left the shotgun behind. At this range it was useless, particularly useless since my two remaining shells were in the suit coat draped across the distant woodpile. The judge's mare was farther still, and the cabin where we should have long since sought refuge was way beyond our reach. I pulled Uncle Jimmy's pistol from the holster Brother had strapped on an eternity before, and steadying my arm on the edge of the pot, drew a bead on the motionless shadow of horse and man. I fired twice. There was movement. A retreat, perhaps. I didn't study long in that direction, though, for when I fired, Brother began to flip about even more violently. I had one other course of action. One hope not tried yet. Frantically, I dug out Maum Anna's cross, kissed it three times, and began to rub. I didn't think this would help. I had only the faith of the truly desperate. "Ghost ride on," I whispered. "Ghost ride on." I crouched low over my little cousin, and suddenly he reached up and grabbed hold of the cross himself—snatching it from my fingers and locking it in his own.

"Brother, let go," I whispered. Then I leaned away hoping to pull the charm free and separate the two of us.

"I can't," he whispered. "I can't let go."

I tried to pry his fingers loose, but this caused him to twitch harder.

"Brother, hold still."

"I can't. There's a hole in me."

I clapped my hand over the hole in his bloodied shirt front and pressed down hard. This seemed to still him some, but turning my head sideways, I saw The Hard to Catch Mercy separating from the trees. Liza was walking out in front of him. They were heading towards us.

"Let go of the cross," I said. I held the pistol in one hand and tried to plug the bullet hole with the other. Brother's blood eased between my fingers. I wanted to be free of him.

"It don't hurt," he whispered.

"I'm glad," I whispered back.

"Say the words now, Willie." He'd fastened those shining dark eyes on my own.

"What words?"

"Say them burying words over me."

"No."

"I'm going beyond."

"Hush, Jimmy will be here soon. Lay still."

"Willie T. Allson." The singsong voice was closer than it should have been. It seemed right beside me. Yanking away, I snapped the leather cord and the cross stayed with Brother. I aimed the pistol over the top of the iron wash pot.

Mercy had ridden across half of the clearing. Liza trailed behind him now, just as Sammy had once done. Her hands were tied behind her back and a rope collar about her neck led up to the saddle horn. She looked at the ground, not at me. It was hard to say if he'd done anything to her. I didn't care. I was far more concerned with what he was about to do to me.

The rider didn't seem particularly concerned with either of us. As he rode forward, he brought a liquor jug to his lips and took a long swallow. The jug rested over his shoulder in a careless manner as if he were out there for some other purpose than to kill people. I held the pistol with both trembling hands, fixed the front sight on his heart, and pulled the trigger twice in quick succession. The little horse reared up, tightening the lead on Liza, and she stumbled forward.

"Whoa there, partner," Mercy called out to me. He reined up the horse. For the moment, they were coming no closer. "Stop all this here shooting. Unprovoked. What I ever done to you?"

"You shot Brother!" I shouted back. "That's one thing you done."

"Was a mistake." He took another pull from the jug. The rifle lay across his lap.

"You did it on purpose!" I wailed. The horse, skittish now, danced a step in place.

"Who you planting there?" he asked.

"Your grandma. Me and Brother was burying your own grandma and you snuck up and shot him. What kind of man are you?" My voice was cracking. I was starting to cry. I guess Mercy had been waiting on this. He tossed the jug to one side. It bounced without breaking, and liquid poured from its mouth.

"That's mighty neighborly," he sang, "considering I was fixing to shoot your pecker off. Reckon I should let you go free." Brother gave a convulsive shudder and I glanced back. He lay in a pool of blood. His black eyes were open wide and sightless. The boy was dead. "You done shot me, though," Mercy sang on. I looked back and was astonished to see the rider's free hand emerge from beneath his jacket. The hand was red with blood. "Getting shot's a hard thing to forgive, even if the boy that done it is burying your grandma." I'd hit him. I'd actually shot this man. There was no time for celebration. The rider raised his carbine and fired off a quick shot that rang the iron pot like a bell. I crouched low behind it, not daring to peek. "Hold still, boy. Hold still, now," he called out. "You and me got to get this over." From the sound of his voice I could tell he was walking the horse in a semicircle to get a clear shot, and I inched about in the opposite direction to keep my protection.

"If that's how you want it, boy. If you really and truly do want your pecker shot off, that's how it gotta be."

I had to look then. I peered over the iron rim and watched as he took the line holding Liza and flipped it loosely about one of the clothesline poles. He was coming for me. I figured that, but not the suddenness of the attack. Mercy screamed a single command to the little horse, and together, as one creature not bound by any mortal rules of gravity and time, they sailed in my direction. I shot twice. I pulled the trigger again and again, but there were no more cartridges to be fired, and I stood there with the gun at my side wondering why I wasn't dead. Mercy clearly wasn't. He'd jumped clean over me and the pot and passed on. Now he was wheeling the little horse in a tight turn.

"Willie!" Liza screamed. "Save me! Do something. Save me!" Her first words. None of sympathy.

No. That request wasn't worthy of a response, but it did

strike Mercy as funny, and when he came riding back he was laughing. The reins were dropped so both hands would be free to aim and fire the rifle.

I ran. I didn't stand there and wait to die as he had asked. I ran away from him and towards the cabin. As I ducked beneath the hanging laundry, a sad homespun dress and tired petticoat reached out to seize me. I pushed clear and ran. I didn't expect to make it. I expected to be shot dead a hundred times over, and Mercy tried. He fired at least three times, but only the last shot connected, clipping my shoe heel and rolling me over into the welcome doorway of the widow's kitchen.

I didn't stop, and wisely not. Slamming the door shut, I threw myself flat on the floor as more shots came into the cabin wall. A bright rain of glass, wood splinters, dust, and scraps of cardboard Jesuses sprinkled down. Somewhere in this house would be a gun. I crawled into the parlor and rose to my feet. No shots were fired. Racing recklessly on, I ransacked the two bedrooms before retracing my steps. Hung in plain sight above the mantel was an ancient muzzle loader. I didn't doubt it was loaded, and with eager hands, I pulled it from the pegs and cocked the hammer back. The mechanism halted in place with a healthy click, and then slipped from beneath my fingers and set off an explosion that punched a hole through the ceiling and roof shingles above. Gray-black smoke filled the low-ceilinged room. A thin stream of fading daylight poked like the accusing finger of God straight down on my bewildered face. No more powder or shot was in sight, and even with them I couldn't have loaded the miserable old weapon. Tossing it aside, I ducked low and returned to the kitchen.

Calendars. Pictures of all recorded Christian time were waiting there pinned to that eternal wall. Jesus here, Jesus there, up the cross and down. Jesus blown into scraps of cardboard by the old woman's own grandson. I stumbled across her chair and made my way to the far end of the room where the stove waited with dead coals beneath an uncooked meal. I wasn't having much luck with guns. I'd be satisfied with a sturdy knife, a knife like the one on the table beside the stove. The widow had probably set it there herself and then taken sick and wandered outside to die alone. What had she planned to cut? I couldn't help wondering this as I turned the handle over in my hand. Broad and long for serious butchering, and honed razor sharp. David Allson would have appreciated such an instrument. If Mercy came through that kitchen door, I'd be waiting. I didn't think he'd come, not really, but if he did, I'd be ready. For the first time since Brother had been shot, I began to consider the possibility that I might live.

"Willie T.," Liza was calling to me. "Willie T., come out. He's gone. He rode off."

Easing to the glassless window, I looked out on the battlefield. The sun was well below the trees but there was still light aplenty. Liza stood as I'd left her, rope lead looped about a clothesline pole. She'd pulled off in my direction until the noose tightened. There was no sign of Mercy. The woodpile was much too low to hide him. The sheds were open for the most part. The patchwork quilt and bits of hanging laundry couldn't have concealed both horse and rider. They might be on the other side of the house or off in the woods, though.

"He's gone, Willie T. Please come and get me."

"He ain't gone, Liza!" I shouted back.

"Yes, he is. He said he was going after Jimmy. He said he would be back for us later."

"If he's gone, it ain't far."

"You hate me don't you? That's why you won't come out and let me loose."

This took some consideration.

"No. But I'm staying here anyway."

"You're a coward then. I'm going to tell Jimmy you acted like a yellow-bellied coward."

"I am a coward," I shouted back.

She screamed and turning away, began to butt the clothesline pole futilely with her head and shoulders.

"That man ain't leaving here with me still alive."

"You!" She screamed anew. "That's all you ever think about is yourself. It's always Willie T. you're worrying about. You don't ever consider the suffering of others."

I could smell it now. Not the explosion of the old blunderbuss. The smell of burning was quite clear, and looking close, I spied a trace of smoke drifting into the kitchen. He'd gone all right. He'd gone around to the front and lit his own grandma's house on fire. What would he expect of me? Whatever it was, I must do the opposite. I must set the least likely course. Ducking low, I slipped up to the door and cracked it open. The view of Brother's dead body was better from here. I realized my shotgun was gone. The judge's mare was gone. And exactly where was The Hard to Catch Mercy? If he was waiting on the side where Liza could see, I figured she'd be watching him instead of screaming at the window I'd just vacated. It didn't matter. Like Brother said, dying was probably the easy part. I broke from the door running straight for Liza who greeted me with surprised delight and thanked me with profusion. I slipped the rope noose free from around her neck and yanked her along.

I hadn't known what to expect next—except that The Mercy would be galloping around the corner. He was. At that very moment he was upon us, reins free, rifle at his shoulder. The shrieking Liza was my shield. I held her towards the enemy, retreated backwards beside the clothesline, and slipped behind the remaining patchwork quilt. Hung doubled over, it provided a small and none too substantial wall of padded cotton.

"Willie T.? What are you doing? Stop him!" Liza wailed.

The Hard to Catch hadn't even slowed down. He rode the little horse at full tilt beneath the highest portion of the line and swung back on me to fire. I'd have none of that. No, with the screaming bride of Uncle Jimmy still between us, I slipped around to the other side of the quilt and peeked over the top at the rider.

"Where are you going now, boy?" Mercy called. He'd slowed the gray-white horse to a walk and approached us with a broad half-toothed smile. "You ain't going to hide there all day, is you?"

I said nothing and ducked from sight. Through the foot-wide slit between fabric and dirt, I could see the four hooves of the horse close up and assumed Mercy was looking down over the barrier at my back. It didn't matter. I shoved Liza aside and rolled beneath the quilt. Once under the horse, I drove the butchering knife up into the animal's belly just in from the girth and ripped backwards as far as the blade would go.

The horse rose above me. All the hooves seemed to leave the ground at once and descend the same, down about my chest and shoulders. I was struck often and knocked breathless, but not so breathless that I couldn't stumble to my feet. The horse was moving away. I watched the rider hang low across the animal's withers and with a few whispered words bring it into a quiet circling lope. To my surprise, opportunities for escape were no better than before. Less so, I realized, for the roof of the cabin was well ablaze.

The quilt and the ragged garments lay in the dirt. All that constrained the little horse was a section of clothesline—somehow attached and dragging behind. As I watched, Mercy untangled this from his stirrup and let it drop. I yanked Liza to her feet.

"Is that it?" I screamed, pointing the bloody blade in the direction of the loping pair. "Is that all?"

"Untie me!" Liza screamed.

"Look!" I shouted. "Look at that!" There was nothing to see. Nothing had happened.

All at once, though, the bowels of the little horse began to tumble out. Stomach, liver, and other innards came spattering into the dirt, and finally an amazing length of intestines—which didn't break off but trailed behind the still moving animal.

"Cut me loose!" Liza was backed up to me offering her bound wrist.

I gave her no more than a passing glance and ran. Still tied, she ran screaming after me—right up to the door of the burning cabin. I threw myself onto the kitchen floor, and she stood on the single step and wailed at me.

"This house is on fire! Can't you see that?"

"Move, Liza!" I screamed back. "Get out of the way."

The doorframe at her side splintered as if by some invisible and silent force.

"Move!" I screamed again. "He's shooting."

This time she did move. She ran straight past The Hard to Catch. She passed by him unmolested, perhaps even unnoticed, and headed towards the woods. The sun had set. Even Liza could hide. The intent of the loping horse and rider were clear.

"You going to burn up in there!" he shouted at me. "You stay there, boy, you going be cooked meat!"

Behind me I heard the crackling of the blaze, and the

smoke boiled thickly above my head. Lying flat and peering around the corner of the doorway, I continued to watch. Though it was dusk dark, the flaming cabin I occupied lit up the pale horse and rider as if they too were burning. They glowed like ash-tinged embers. They passed from sight and when they trotted by again they were much closer. Now, only a short portion of the intestine hung out of the horse. This gray string flipped and bounced along the dirt. The cut I had made had widened into a hollow blood red cavity. I was looking up into this vacuum as horse and rider turned away from the door.

I suppose the heart and lungs were still in place, but how could it be moving? A gutted animal commanded not by the laws of physical nature but by the commands that The Hard to Catch was again and again bending forward to whisper in its ear. Once more they circled before me only this time further out, and for the first time I noticed a falter as the horse passed from view. When they came again the horse walked. They came straight up to the blazing cabin and stopped, holding that pose for the eternity it took Mercy to eye my smoke-filled doorway. Finally, the horse settled on its forelegs and with a plaintive whinny rolled onto the ground.

The rider's feet were free of the stirrups when the horse went down. He didn't go down under it, but stepped off as best he could and fell forward with carbine at the ready.

He couldn't walk. At least I'd been right about that. As I'd long suspected The Hard to Catch Mercy was half horse. That half, if nothing else, I'd managed to kill. Only the man half remained, and it was crawling towards me. It slithered like a snake, pulling on the elbows, the hands firmly gripping the carbine. The man part wouldn't allow me to burn alive—though that would have been simple enough. At my back, the kitchen wall was well ablaze, and on the floor, the air was now a searing fog. The man part would begrudge me even this fate, for he could see my eyes peering out from behind the doorframe. Mercy could see the terror in them and would not let that pass.

He had lost his hat. The last thing I noticed was not the grinning satan mask of his face. No, the last thing seen was the thinning hair on the crown of his head. He looked down while pulling himself onto the step, and I plunged the butchering knife into his back again and again and again. There seemed no end to this jabbing, but finally the knife froze, the wood of the handle buried in blood-soaked pulp.

Satisfied, I staggered away from the collapsing building and vomited until there was nothing left to bring up. Then wiping my mouth on the bloody arm of my own shirt, I rose trembling, walked by the dead horse, and knelt beside Brother's body. I wasn't certain I could remember all the words but knew it was necessary to begin.

"Blessed are they that mourn, for their's is the kingdom of God.

"Blessed are the meek, for they shall inherit the earth.

"Blessed are . . ."

Finis

UNCLE Jimmy wrote me two letters before he died. The first was sent the end of June from Calais. He didn't have too much to say except that they were in France at last and would soon be fighting the Hun. A lot of good Southern boys were in his division. Drake was an officer with another bunch, but he thought they might meet up on a furlough. Maybe he'd get to Paris. Sammy was doing all right in this man's army. My cousin reported our friend was serving in an all-Negro outfit and had gained a pretty soft berth since he could speak a little bit of French and a lot of Southern Negro dialect, two languages foreign to most of the white officers.

What Jimmy really wanted to say, though, was he'd forever be in my debt for saving Liza's life, and he was sorry his grief on losing Brother had kept him from expressing this clearly. What he said about us not being friends, he didn't mean and asked for my forgiveness.

I'm not sure he ever received my reply, but I wrote back immediately, claiming there was nothing to forgive, and as for saving Liza, any other patriotic American would have done the same. I said I was hoping the war would last long enough for me to join up, but if it appeared to be winding down too soon, I'd lie about my age and come give him a hand.

I got no direct answer to that, but Liza told me he'd been in some fighting and gotten to Paris for a weekend. The beginning of September, I received a second letter, one much different from the first. Sad. Melancholy in a way I'd never have expected from Uncle Jimmy. There was only a brief hello to me and then a rambling account of a Belgian village he'd wandered into one afternoon several weeks before. Much of the place had been reduced to rubble, but the church still stood, and one side of the main street was as if unnoticed by the war. In these houses tables were set. The food on the plates was still warm to the touch. Wine poured in glasses waited to be drunk. Beds were made up with clean sheets, and clothes lay folded in the dresser drawers. Fresh flowers were in the vases. It was a life just waiting to be lived, he wrote, and all the people had disappeared. The village was empty, and no matter how often he called out going from house to house, opening each unlocked door, no matter how much he called, no one answered. There was no life there, not a cat or dog even. Nothing. He had sat down at the kitchen table in the final house and waited until far after dark, but no one returned. He asked me to pray for him, so I asked God to protect Uncle Jimmy.

This letter was the last I would know of my cousin, for he died the end of that month in a successful attempt on the Hindenburg line. He was smote by his foe. God was with them. Liza took the news well enough, far better than my parents certainly. It was Dr. McGill, though, who came apart. He blamed the English. He still does. The doctor went to France to visit the grave and brought back photographs. They show wide ribbons of crosses rolling endlessly over a well-ordered countryside. I told him I'd like to see that myself someday.

Sammy survived. I read in the paper his division went through some fierce fighting around Verdun, but I know he lived for I received a short typed letter at the war's end. It was mailed from New York and said only that he was well and would soon be sailing back to France. He'd been offered a job as a waiter in Paris. I knew from the wording my childhood companion hadn't written this or even dictated it directly to the typist. But in large, childlike print, he'd signed SAMMY ALLSON at the bottom. He was alive.

Drake came home. Occasionally, I'd join him at the mercantile. We'd split a pint of something, and he'd tell me tales of battles and of Red Cross nurses. After he married Margarite, he stopped drinking altogether.

I buried Mama in January of 1922. I buried Pa four months later. Since then, I have married and started a family of my own. I wrote this down so I wouldn't forget.